Phantoms and Fantasies

Phantoms and Fantasies

20 tales by RUDYARD KIPLING

Illustrated by Burt Silverman

Doubleday & Company, Inc.   Garden City, New York

Library of Congress Catalog Card Number 65-17269

Printed in the United States of America

CONTENTS

INTRODUCTION

When I was a child, one of my favorite books was a collection of American Indian folk tales. I can no longer recall the plot of a single story in that book, but it contained one particular illustration that is still fresh in my mind. This was a woodcut of a grotesque, bearlike monster, jaws agape, eyes narrowed in rage. The creature terrified me. I imagined it lay in wait behind every piece of furniture, in every dark hallway. And yet I could never pick up that book without being drawn to the page on which it was portrayed—to be newly fascinated and appalled.

Many people have probably had some similar experience, for the unknown—the alien territory at the outer limits of human perception—exerts a peculiarly powerful attraction. Rudyard Kipling must have felt something of this attraction. In a considerable number of his short stories, he explored the region inhabited by phantoms and monsters, by animals that behave like people and people who behave like animals. He found there not only terror, but beauty and humor as well. Out of the bizarre and the fantastic he created tales as tender and moving as "They," as boisterously comic as "The Bull that Thought," and as nightmarish as "The Strange Ride of Morrowbie Jukes."

I think these stories are among the best of their kind, and I hope that they will give you some very pleasant shudders.

the editor

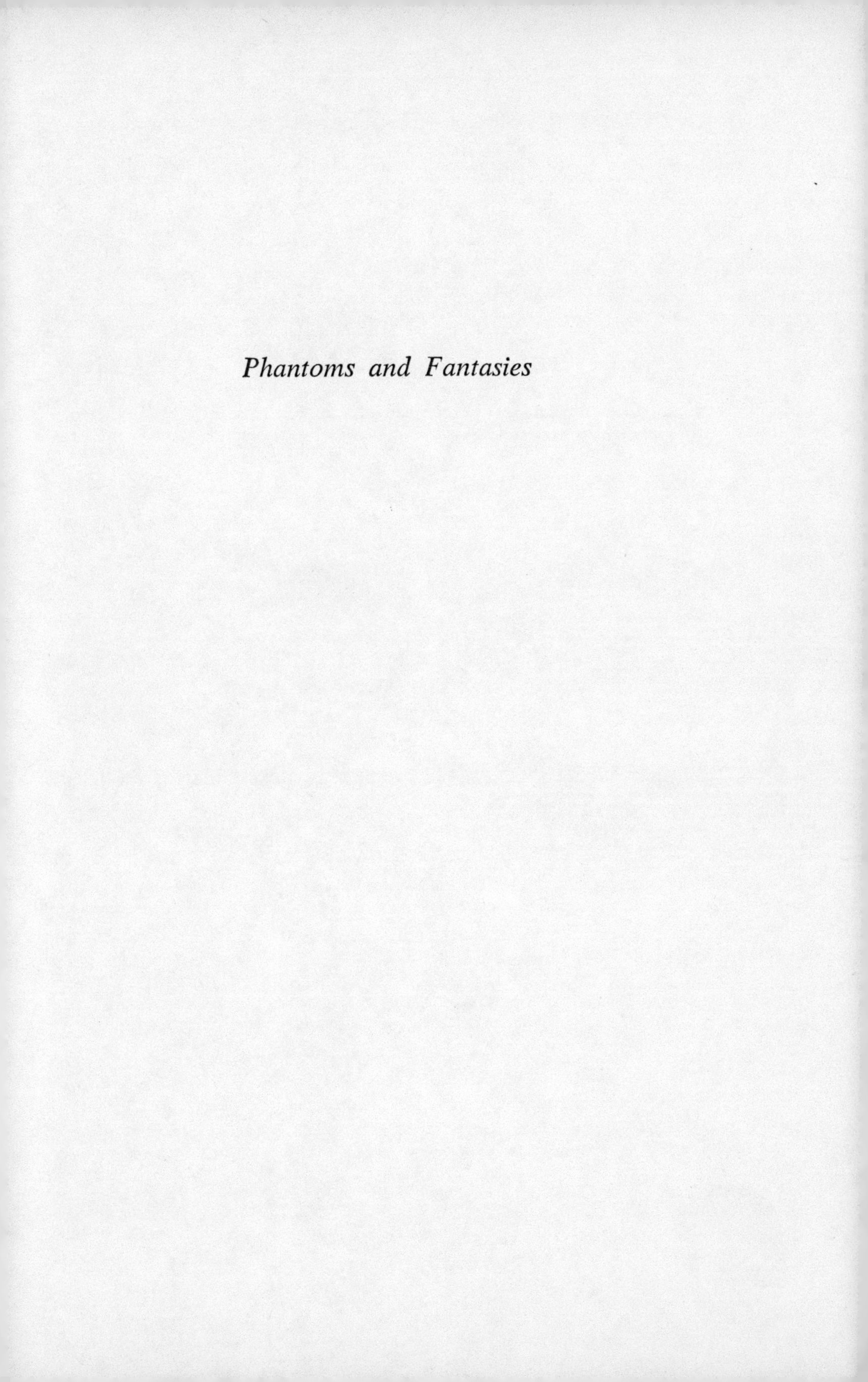

Phantoms and Fantasies

THE HOUSE SURGEON

On an evening after Easter Day, I sat at a table in a homeward bound steamer's smoking-room, where half a dozen of us told ghost stories. As our party broke up a man, playing Patience in the next alcove, said to me: "I didn't quite catch the end of that last story about the Curse on the family's first-born."

"It turned out to be drains," I explained. "As soon as new ones were put into the house the Curse was lifted, I believe. I never knew the people myself."

"Ah! I've had *my* drains up twice; I'm on gravel too."

"You don't mean to say you've a ghost in your house? Why didn't you join our party?"

"Any more orders, gentlemen, before the bar closes?" the steward interrupted.

"Sit down again, and have one with me," said the Patience player. "No, it isn't a ghost. Our trouble is more depression than anything else."

"How interesting! Then it's nothing any one can see?"

"It's—it's nothing worse than a little depression. And the odd part is that there hasn't been a death in the house since it was built—in 1863. The lawyer said so. That decided me—my good lady, rather—and he made me pay an extra thousand for it."

"How curious. Unusual, too!" I said.

"Yes; ain't it? It was built for three sisters—Moultrie was the name—three old maids. They all lived together; the eldest owned it. I bought it from her lawyer a few years ago, and if I've spent a pound on the place first and last, I must have spent five thousand. Electric light, new servants' wing, garden—all that sort of thing. A man and his family ought to be happy after so much expense, ain't it?" He looked at me through the bottom of his glass.

"Does it affect your family much?"

"My good lady—she's a Greek, by the way—and myself are middle-aged. We can bear up against depression; but it's hard on my little girl. I say little; but she's twenty. We send her visiting to escape it. She almost lived at hotels and hydros last year, but that isn't pleasant for her. She used to be a canary—a perfect canary—always singing. You ought to hear her. She doesn't sing now. That sort of thing's unwholesome for the young, ain't it?"

"Can't you get rid of the place?" I suggested.

"Not except at a sacrifice, and we are fond of it. Just suits us three. We'd love it if we were allowed."

"What do you mean by not being allowed?"

"I mean because of the depression. It spoils everything."

"What's it like exactly?"

"I couldn't very well explain. It must be seen to be appreciated, as the auctioneers say. Now, I was much impressed by the story you were telling just now."

"It wasn't true," I said.

"My tale is true. If you would do me the pleasure to come down and spend a night at my little place, you'd learn more than you would if I talked till morning. Very likely 'twouldn't touch your good self at all. You might be—immune, ain't it? On the other hand, if this influenza—influence *does* happen to affect you, why, I think it will be an experience."

While he talked he gave me his card, and I read his name was L. Maxwell M'Leod, Esq., of Holmescroft. A City address was tucked away in a corner.

"My business," he added, "used to be furs. If you are interested in furs—I've given thirty years of my life to 'em."

"You're very kind," I murmured.

"Far from it, I assure you. I can meet you next Saturday afternoon anywhere in London you choose to name, and I'll be only too happy to motor you down. It ought to be a delightful run at this time of year—the rhododendrons will be out. I mean it. You don't know how truly I mean it. Very probably—it won't affect you at all. And—I think I may say I have the finest collection of narwhal tusks in the world. All the best skins and horns have to go through London, and L. Maxwell M'Leod, he knows where they come from, and where they go to. That's his business."

For the rest of the voyage up-channel Mr. M'Leod talked

to me of the assembling, preparation, and sale of the rare furs; and told me things about the manufacture of fur-lined coats which quite shocked me. Somehow or other, when we landed on Wednesday, I found myself pledged to spend that week-end with him at Holmescroft.

On Saturday he met me with a well-groomed motor, and ran me out, in an hour and a half, to an exclusive residential district of dustless roads and elegantly designed country villas, each standing in from three to five acres of perfectly appointed land. He told me land was selling at eight hundred pounds the acre, and the new golf links, whose Queen Anne pavilion we passed, had cost nearly twenty-four thousand pounds to create.

Holmescroft was a large, two-storied, low creeper-covered residence. A veranda at the south side gave onto a garden and two tennis courts, separated by a tasteful iron fence from a most park-like meadow of five or six acres, where two Jersey cows grazed. Tea was ready in the shade of a promising copper beech, and I could see groups on the lawn of young men and maidens appropriately clothed, playing lawn tennis in the sunshine.

"A pretty scene, ain't it?" said Mr. M'Leod. "My good lady's sitting under the tree, and that's my little girl in pink on the far court. But I'll take you to your room, and you can see 'em all later."

He led me through a wide parquet-floored hall furnished in pale lemon, with huge Cloisonnée vases, an ebonized and gold grand piano, and banks of pot flowers in Benares brass bowls, up a pale oak staircase to a spacious landing, where there was a green velvet settee trimmed with silver. The blinds were down, and the light lay in parallel lines on the floors.

He showed me my room, saying cheerfully: "You may be a little tired. One often is without knowing it after a run through traffic. Don't come down till you feel quite restored. We shall all be in the garden."

My room was rather warm, and smelled of perfumed soap. I threw up the window at once, but it opened so close to the floor and worked so clumsily that I came within an ace of pitching out, where I should certainly have ruined a rather lopsided laburnum below. As I set about washing off the journey's dust, I began to feel a little tired. But, I reflected, I had not come down here in this weather and among these new surroundings to be depressed; so I began to whistle.

And it was just then that I was aware of a little gray shadow, as it might have been a snowflake seen against the light, floating at an immense distance in the background of my brain. It annoyed me, and I shook my head to get rid of it. Then my brain telegraphed that it was the forerunner of a swift-striding gloom which there was yet time to escape if I would force my thoughts away from it, as a man leaping for life forces his body forward and away from the fall of a wall. But the gloom overtook me before I could take in the meaning of the message. I moved toward the bed, every nerve already aching with the foreknowledge of the pain that was to be dealt it, and sat down, while my amazed and angry soul dropped, gulf by gulf, into that horror of great darkness which is spoken of in the Bible, and which, as auctioneers say, must be experienced to be appreciated.

Despair upon despair, misery upon misery, fear after fear, each causing their distinct and separate woe, packed in upon me for an unrecorded length of time, until at last they blurred together, and I heard a click in my brain like the click in the ear when one descends in a diving bell, and I knew that the pressures were equalized within and without, and that, for the moment, the worst was at an end. But I knew also that at any moment the darkness might come down anew; and while I dwelt on this speculation precisely as a man torments a raging tooth with his tongue, it ebbed away into the little gray shadow on the brain of its first coming, and once more I heard my brain, which knew what would recur, telegraph to every quarter for help, release or diversion.

The door opened, and M'Leod reappeared. I thanked him politely, saying I was charmed with my room, anxious to meet Mrs. M'Leod, much refreshed with my wash, and so on and so forth. Beyond a little stickiness at the corners of my mouth, it seemed to me that I was managing my words admirably, the while that I myself cowered at the bottom of unclimbable

—"Despair upon despair, misery upon misery, fear after fear, each causing their distinct and separate woe, packed in upon me . . ."

pits. M'Leod laid his hand on my shoulder, and said: "You've got it now already, ain't it?"

"Yes," I answered. "It's making me sick!"

"It will pass off when you come outside. I give you my word it will then pass off. Come!"

I shambled out behind him, and wiped my forehead in the hall.

"You mustn't mind," he said. "I expect the run tired you. My good lady is sitting there under the copper beech."

She was a fat woman in an apricot-colored gown, with a heavily powdered face, against which her black long-lashed eyes showed like currants in dough. I was introduced to many fine ladies and gentlemen of those parts. Magnificently appointed landaus and covered motors swept in and out of the drive, and the air was gay with the merry outcries of the tennis players.

As twilight drew on they all went away, and I was left alone with Mr. and Mrs. M'Leod, while tall menservants and maidservants took away the tennis and tea things. Miss M'Leod had walked a little down the drive with a light-haired young man, who apparently knew everything about every South American railway stock. He had told me at tea that these were the days of financial specialization.

"I think it went off beautifully, my dear," said Mr. M'Leod to his wife; and to me: "You feel all right now, ain't it? Of course you do."

Mrs. M'Leod surged across the gravel. Her husband skipped nimbly before her into the south veranda, turned a switch, and all Holmescroft was flooded with light.

"You can do that from your room also," he said as they went in. "There is something in money, ain't it?"

Miss M'Leod came up behind me in the dusk. "We have not yet been introduced," she said, "but I suppose you are staying the night?"

"Your father was kind enough to ask me," I replied.

She nodded. "Yes, *I* know; and you know too, don't you. I saw your face when you came to shake hands with mamma. You felt the depression very soon. It is simply frightful in that bedroom sometimes. What do you think it is—bewitchment? In

Greece, where I was a little girl, it might have been; but not in England, do you think? Or *do* you?"

"I don't know what to think," I replied. "I never felt anything like it. Does it happen often?"

"Yes, sometimes. It comes and goes."

"Pleasant!" I said, as we walked up and down the gravel at the lawn edge. "What has been your experience of it?"

"That is difficult to say, but—sometimes that—that depression is like as it were"—she gesticulated in most un-English fashion—"a light. Yes, like a light turned into a room—only a light of blackness, do you understand?—into a happy room. For sometimes we are so happy, all we three—so very happy. Then this blackness, it is turned on us just like—ah, I know what I mean now—like the head-lamp of a motor, and we are eclipsed. And there is another thing——"

The dressing-gong roared, and we entered the overlighted hall. My dressing was a brisk athletic performance, varied with outbursts of song—careful attention paid to articulation and expression. But nothing happened. As I hurried downstairs, I thanked Heaven that nothing had happened.

Dinner was served breakfast fashion; the dishes were placed on the sideboard over heaters, and we helped ourselves.

"We always do this when we are alone, so we talk better," said Mr. M'Leod.

"And we are always alone," said the daughter.

"Cheer up, Thea. It will all come right," he insisted.

"No, papa." She shook her dark head. "Nothing is right while *it* comes."

"It is nothing that we ourselves have ever done in our lives—that I will swear to you," said Mrs. M'Leod suddenly. "And we have changed our servants several times. So we know it is not *them*."

"Never mind. Let us enjoy ourselves while we can," said Mr. M'Leod, opening the champagne.

But we did not enjoy ourselves. The talk failed. There were long silences.

"I beg your pardon," I said, for I thought someone at my elbow was about to speak.

"Ah! That is the other thing!" said Miss M'Leod. Her mother groaned.

We were silent again, and, in a few seconds it must have been, a live grief beyond words—not ghostly dread or horror, but aching, helpless grief—overwhelmed us, each, I felt, according to his or her nature, and held steady like the beam of a burning glass. Behind that pain I was conscious there was a desire on somebody's part to explain something on which some tremendously important issue hung.

Meantime I rolled bread pills and remembered my sins; M'Leod considered his own reflection in a spoon; his wife seemed to be praying, and the girl fidgeted desperately with hands and feet, till the darkness passed on—as though the malignant rays of a burning glass had been shifted from us.

"There," said Miss M'Leod, half rising. "Now you see what makes a happy home. Oh, sell it—sell it, father mine, and let us go away!"

"But I've spent thousands on it. You shall go to Harrogate next week, Thea dear."

"I'm only just back from hotels. I am *so* tired of packing."

"Cheer up, Thea. It is over. You know it does not often come here twice in the same night. I think we shall dare now to be comfortable."

He lifted a dish cover, and helped his wife and daughter. His face was lined and fallen like an old man's after debauch, but his hand did not shake, and his voice was clear. As he worked to restore us by speech and action, he reminded me of a gray-muzzled collie herding demoralized sheep.

After dinner we sat around the dining-room fire—the drawing room might have been under the Shadow for aught we knew—talking with the intimacy of gypsies by the wayside, or of wounded comparing notes after a skirmish. By eleven o'clock the three between them had given me every name and detail they could recall that in any way bore on the house, and what they knew of its history.

We went to bed in a fortifying blaze of electric light. My one fear was that the blasting gust of depression would return—the surest way, of course, to bring it. I lay awake till dawn, breathing quickly and sweating lightly, beneath what De

Quincey inadequately describes as "the oppression of inexpiable guilt." Now as soon as the lovely day was broken, I fell into the most terrible of all dreams—that joyous one in which all past evil has not only been wiped out of our lives, but has never been committed; and in the very bliss of our assured innocence, before our loves shriek and change countenance, we wake to the day we have earned.

It was a coolish morning, but we preferred to breakfast in the south veranda. The forenoon we spent in the garden, pretending to play games that come out of boxes, such as croquet and clock golf. But most of the time we drew together and talked. The young man who knew all about South American railways took Miss M'Leod for a walk in the afternoon, and at five M'Leod thoughtfully whirled us all up to dine in town.

"Now, don't say you will tell the Psychological Society, and that you will come again," said Miss M'Leod, as we parted. "Because I know you will not."

"You should not say that," said her mother. "You should say, 'Good-bye, Mr. Perseus. Come again.' "

"Not him!" the girl cried. "He has seen the Medusa's head!"

Looking at myself in the restaurant's mirrors, it seemed to me that I had not much benefited by my weekend. Next morning I wrote out all my Holmescroft notes at fullest length, in the hope that by so doing I could put it all behind me. But the experience worked on my mind, as they say certain imperfectly understood rays work on the body.

I am less calculated to make a Sherlock Holmes than any man I know, for I lack both method and patience, yet the idea of following up the trouble to its source fascinated me. I had no theory to go on, except a vague idea that I had come between two poles of a discharge, and had taken a shock meant for someone else. This was followed by a feeling of intense irritation. I waited cautiously on myself, expecting to be overtaken by horror of the supernatural, but my self persisted in being humanly indignant, exactly as though it had been the victim of a practical joke. It was in great pains and upheavals —that I felt in every fiber—but its dominant idea, to put it coarsely, was to get back a bit of its own. By this I knew that I might go forward if I could find the way.

After a few days it occurred to me to go to the office of Mr. J. M. M. Baxter—the solicitor who had sold Holmescroft to M'Leod. I explained I had some notion of buying the place. Would he act for me in the matter?

Mr. Baxter, a large, grayish, throaty-voiced man, showed no enthusiasm. "I sold it to Mr. M'Leod," he said. "It 'ud scarcely do for me to start on the running-down tack now. But I can recommend——"

"I know he's asking an awful price," I interrupted, "and atop of it he wants an extra thousand for what he calls your clean bill of health."

Mr. Baxter sat up in his chair. I had all his attention.

"Your guarantee with the house. Don't you remember it?"

"Yes, yes. That no death had taken place in the house since it was built. I remember perfectly."

He did not gulp as untrained men do when they lie, but his jaws moved stickily, and his eyes, turning toward the deed boxes on the wall, dulled. I counted seconds, one, two, three—one, two, three—up to ten. A man, I knew, can live through ages of mental depression in that time.

"I remember perfectly." His mouth opened a little as though it had tasted old bitterness.

"Of course *that* sort of thing doesn't appeal to me." I went on. "*I* don't expect to buy a house free from death."

"Certainly not. No one does. But it was Mr. M'Leod's fancy—his wife's rather, I believe; and since we could meet it—it was my duty to my clients—at whatever cost to my own feelings—to make him pay."

"That's really why I came to you. I understood from him you knew the place well."

"Oh, yes. Always did. It originally belonged to some connections of mine."

"The Misses Moultrie, I suppose. How interesting! They must have loved the place before the country round about was built up."

"They were very fond of it indeed."

"I don't wonder. So restful and sunny. I don't see how they could have brought themselves to part with it."

Now it is one of the most constant peculiarities of the English that in polite conversation—and I had striven to be polite—no one ever does or sells anything for mere money's sake.

"Miss Agnes—the youngest—fell ill" (he spaced his words a little), "and, as they were very much attached to each other, that broke up the home."

"Naturally. I fancied it must have been something of that kind. One doesn't associate the Staffordshire Moultries" (my Demon of Irresponsibility at that instant created 'em), "with—with being hard up."

"I don't know whether we're related to them," he answered importantly. "We may be, for our branch of the family comes from the Midlands."

I give this talk at length, because I am so proud of my first attempt at detective work. When I left him, twenty minutes later, with instructions to move against the owner of Holmescroft, with a view to purchase, I was more bewildered than any Doctor Watson at the opening of a story.

Why should a middle-aged solicitor turn plovers' egg color and drop his jaw when reminded of so innocent and festal a matter as that no death had ever occurred in a house that he had sold? If I knew my English vocabulary at all, the tone in which he said the youngest sister "fell ill" meant that she had gone out of her mind. That might explain his change of countenance, and it was just possible that her demented influence still hung about Holmescroft; but the rest was beyond me.

I was relieved when I reached M'Leod's City office, and could tell him what I had done—not what I thought.

M'Leod was quite willing to enter into the game of the pretended purchase, but did not see how it would help if I knew Baxter.

"He's the only living soul I can get at who was connected with Holmescroft," I said.

"Ah! Living soul is good," said M'Leod. "At any rate our little girl will be pleased that you are still interested in us. Won't you come down some day this week?"

"How is it there now?" I asked.

He screwed up his face. "Simply frightful!" he said. "Thea is at Droitwich."

"I should like it immensely, but I must cultivate Baxter for the present. You'll be sure and keep him busy your end, won't you?"

He looked at me with quiet contempt. "Do not be afraid. I shall be a good Jew. I shall be my own solicitor."

Before a fortnight was over, Baxter admitted ruefully that M'Leod was better than most firms in the business. We buyers were coy, argumentative, shocked at the price of Holmescroft, inquisitive, and cold by turns, but Mr. M'Leod the seller easily met and surpassed us; and Mr. Baxter entered every letter, telegram, and consultation at the proper rates in a cinematograph-film of a bill. At the end of the month he said it looked as though M'Leod, thanks to him, were really going to listen to reason. I was many pounds out of pocket, but I had learned something of Mr. Baxter on the human side. I deserved it. Never in my life have I worked to conciliate, amuse, and flatter a human being as I worked over my solicitor.

It appeared that he golfed. Therefore, I was an enthusiastic beginner, anxious to learn. Twice I invaded his office with a bag (M'Leod lent it) full of the spelicans needed in this detestable game, and a vocabulary to match. The third time the ice broke, and Mr. Baxter took me to his links, quite ten miles off, where in a maze of tramway lines, railroads, and nurserymaids, we skelped our divotted way around nine holes like barges plunging through head seas. He played vilely and had never expected to meet anyone worse; but as he realized my form, I think he began to like me, for he took me in hand by the two hours together. After a fortnight he could give me no more than a stroke a hole, and when, with this allowance, I once managed to beat him by one, he was honestly glad, and assured me that I should be a golfer if I stuck to it. I was sticking to it for my own ends, but now and again my conscience pricked me; for the man was a nice man. Between games he supplied me with odd pieces of evidence, such as that he had known the Moultries all his life, being their cousin, and that Miss Mary, the eldest, was an unforgiving woman who would never let bygones be. I naturally wondered what she might have against him; and somehow connected him unfavorably with mad Agnes.

"People ought to forgive and forget," he volunteered one

day between rounds. "Specially where, in the nature of things, they can't be sure of their deductions. Don't you think so?"

"It all depends on the nature of the evidence on which one forms one's judgment," I answered.

"Nonsense!" he cried. "I'm lawyer enough to know that there's nothing in the world so misleading as circumstantial evidence. Never was."

"Why? Have you ever seen men hanged on it?"

"Hanged? People have been supposed to be eternally lost on it," his face turned gray again. "I don't know how it is with you, but my consolation is that God must know. He *must!* Things that seem on the face of 'em like murder, or say suicide, may appear different to God. Heh?"

"That's what the murderer and the suicide can always hope—I suppose."

"I have expressed myself clumsily as usual. The facts as God knows 'em—may *be* different—even after the most clinching evidence. I've always said that—both as a lawyer and a man, but some people won't—I don't want to judge 'em—we'll say they can't—believe it; whereas *I* say there's always a working chance—a certainty—that the worst hasn't happened." He stopped and cleared his throat. "Now, let's come on! This time next week I shall be taking my holiday."

"What links?" I asked carelessly, while twins in a perambulator got out of our line of fire.

"A potty little nine-hole affair at a hydro in the Midlands. My cousins stay there. Always will. Not but what the fourth and the seventh holes take some doing. You could manage it, though," he said encouragingly. "You're doing much better. It's only your approach shots that are weak."

"You're right. I can't approach for nuts! I shall go to pieces while you're away—with no one to coach me," I said mournfully.

"I haven't taught you anything," he said, delighted with the compliment.

"I owe all I've learned to you, anyhow. When will you come back?"

"Look here," he began. "I don't know your engagements, but I've no one to play with at Burry Mills. Never have. Why couldn't you take a few days off and join me there? I warn you it will be rather dull. It's a throat and gout place—baths, massage, electricity, and so forth. But the fourth and the seventh holes really take some doing."

"I'm for the game," I answered valiantly; Heaven well knowing that I hated every stroke and word of it.

"That's the proper spirit. As their lawyer I must ask you not to say anything to my cousins about Holmescroft. It upsets 'em. Always did. But speaking as man to man, it would be very pleasant for me if you could see your way to——"

I saw it as soon as decency permitted, and thanked him sincerely. According to my now well-developed theory he had certainly misappropriated his aged cousins' monies under power of attorney, and had probably driven poor Agnes Moultrie out of her wits, but I wished that he was not so gentle, and good-tempered, and innocent-eyed.

Before I joined him at Burry Mills Hydro, I spent a night at Holmescroft. Miss M'Leod had returned from her Hydro, and first we made very merry on the open lawn in the sunshine over the manners and customs of the English resorting to such places. She knew dozens of hydros, and warned me how to behave in them, while Mr. and Mrs. M'Leod stood aside and adored her.

"Ah! That's the way she always comes back to us," he said. "Pity it wears off so soon, ain't it? You ought to hear her sing 'With mirth thou pretty bird.'"

We had the house to face through the evening, and there we neither laughed nor sung. The gloom fell on us as we entered, and did not shift till ten o'clock, when we crawled out, as it were, from beneath it.

"It has been bad this summer," said Mrs. M'Leod in a whisper after we realized that we were freed. "Sometimes I think the house will get up and cry out—it is so bad."

"How?"

"Have you forgotten what comes after the depression?"

So then we waited about the small fire, and the dead air in the room presently filled and pressed down upon us with the sensation (but words are useless here) as though some dumb and bound power were striving against gag and bond to deliver its soul of an articulate word. It passed in a few minutes, and I fell to thinking about Mr. Baxter's conscience and Agnes Moultrie, gone mad in the well-lit bedroom that waited me. These reflections secured me a night during which I rediscovered how, from purely mental causes, a man can be physically sick; but the sickness was bliss compared to my dreams when the birds waked. On my departure, M'Leod gave me a beautiful narwhal's horn, much as a nurse gives a child sweets for being brave at a dentist's.

"There's no duplicate of it in the world," he said, "else it would have come to old Max M'Leod," and he tucked it into the motor. Miss M'Leod on the far side of the car whispered, "Have you found out anything, Mr. Perseus?"

I shook my head.

"Then I shall be chained to my rock all my life," she went on. "Only don't tell papa."

I supposed she was thinking of the young gentleman who specialized in South American rails, for I noticed a ring on the third finger of her left hand.

I went straight from that house to Burry Mills Hydro, keen for the first time in my life on playing golf, which is guaranteed to occupy the mind. Baxter had taken me a room communicating with his own, and after lunch introduced me to a tall, horse-headed elderly lady of decided manners, whom a white-haired maid pushed along in a bath chair through the park-like grounds of the Hydro. She was Miss Mary Moultrie, and she coughed and cleared her throat just like Baxter. She suffered—she told me it was a Moultrie caste mark—from some obscure form of chronic bronchitis, complicated with spasm of the glottis; and, in a dead, flat voice, with a sunken eye that looked and saw not, told me what washes, gargles, pastilles, and inhalations she had proved most beneficial. From her I was passed on to her younger sister, Miss Elizabeth, a small and withered thing with twitching lips, victim, she told me, to very much the same sort of throat, but secretly devoted to another set of medicines. When she went away with Baxter and the bath chair, I fell across a major of the Indian army with gout in his glassy eyes, and a stomach which he had taken all around the Continent. He laid everything before me; and him I escaped only to be confided in by a matron with a tendency to follicular tonsilitis and eczema. Baxter waited hand and foot on his cousins till five o'clock, trying, as I saw, to atone for his treatment of the dead sister. Miss Mary ordered him about like a dog.

"I warned you it would be dull," he said when we met in the smoking-room.

"It's tremendously interesting," I said. "But how about a look around the links?"

"Unluckily damp always affects my eldest cousin. I've got to buy her a new bronchitis-kettle. Arthurs broke her old one yesterday."

We slipped out to the chemist's shop in the town, and he bought a large glittering tin thing whose workings he explained.

"I'm used to this sort of work. I come up here pretty often," he said. "I've the family throat too."

"You're a good man," I said. "A very good man."

He turned toward me in the evening light among the beeches, and his face was changed to what it might have been a generation before.

"You see," he said huskily, "there was the youngest—Agnes. Before she fell ill, you know. But she didn't like leaving her sisters. Never would." He hurried on with his odd-shaped load and left me among the ruins of my black theories. The man with that face had done Agnes Moultrie no wrong.

We never played our game. I was waked between two and three in the morning from my hygienic bed by Baxter in an ulster over orange and white pajamas, which I should never have suspected from his character.

"My cousin has had some sort of a seizure," he said. "Will you come? I don't want to wake the doctor. Don't want to make a scandal. Quick!"

So I came quickly, and led by the white-haired Arthurs in a jacket and petticoat, entered a double-bedded room reeking with steam and Friar's Balsam. The electrics were all on. Miss Mary—I knew her by her height—was at the open window, wrestling with Miss Elizabeth, who gripped her around the knees. Miss Mary's hand was at her own throat, which was streaked with blood.

"She's done it. She's done it too!" Miss Elizabeth panted. "Hold her! Help me!"

"Oh, I say! Women don't cut their throats," Baxter whispered.

"My God! Has she cut her throat?" the maid cried out, and with no warning rolled over in a faint. Baxter pushed her under the washbasins, and leaped to hold the gaunt woman who crowed and whistled as she struggled toward the window. He took her by the shoulder, and she struck out wildly.

"All right! She's only cut her hand," he said. "Wet towel—quick!"

While I got that he pushed her backward. Her strength seemed almost as great as his. I swabbed at her throat when I could, and found no mark; then helped him to control her a little. Miss Elizabeth leaped back to bed, wailing like a child.

"Tie up her hand somehow," said Baxter. "Don't let it drip about the place. She"—he stepped on broken glass in his slippers, "she must have smashed a pane."

Miss Mary lurched toward the open window again, dropped on her knees, her head on the sill, and lay quiet, surrendering the cut hand to me.

"What did she do?" Baxter turned toward Miss Elizabeth in the far bed.

"She was going to throw herself out of the window," was the answer. "I stopped her, and sent Arthurs for you. Oh, we can never hold up our heads again!"

Miss Mary writhed and fought for breath. Baxter found a shawl which he threw over her shoulders.

"Nonsense!" said he. "That isn't like Mary"; but his face worked when he said it.

"You wouldn't believe about Aggie, John. Perhaps you will now!" said Miss Elizabeth. "I saw her do it, and she's cut her throat too!"

"She hasn't," I said. "It's only her hand."

Miss Mary suddenly broke from us with an indescribable grunt, flew, rather than ran, to her sister's bed, and there shook her as one furious schoolgirl would shake another.

"No such thing," she croaked. "How dare you think so, you wicked little fool?"

"Get into bed, Mary," said Baxter. "You'll catch a chill."

She obeyed, but sat up with the gray shawl around her lean shoulders, glaring at her sister. "I'm better now," she panted. "Arthurs let me sit out too long. Where's Arthurs? The kettle."

"Never mind Arthurs," said Baxter. "*You* get the kettle." I hastened to bring it from the side table. "Now, Mary, as God sees you, tell me what you've done."

His lips were dry, and he could not moisten them with his tongue.

Miss Mary applied herself to the mouth of the kettle, and between indraws of steam said: "The spasm came on just now, while I was asleep. I was nearly choking to death. So I went to the window. I've done it often before, without waking anyone. Bessie's such an old maid about drafts. I tell you I was choking to death. I couldn't manage the catch, and I nearly fell out. That window opens too low. I cut my hand trying to save myself. Who has tied it up in this filthy handkerchief? I wish you had had my throat, Bessie. I never was nearer dying!" She scowled on us all impartially, while her sister sobbed.

From the bottom of the bed we heard a quivering voice: "Is she dead? Have they took her away? Oh, I never could bear the sight o' blood!"

"Arthurs," said Miss Mary, "you are an hireling. Go away!"

It is my belief that Arthurs crawled out on all fours, but I was busy picking up broken glass from the carpet.

Then Baxter, seated by the side of the bed, began to cross-examine in a voice I scarcely recognized. No one could for an instant have doubted the genuine rage of Miss Mary against her sister, her cousin, or her maid; and that a doctor should have been called in—for she did me the honor of calling me doctor—was the last drop. She was choking with her throat; had rushed to the window for air; had near pitched out, and in catching at the window bars had cut her hand. Over and over she made this clear to the intent Baxter. Then she turned on her sister and tongue-lashed her savagely.

"You mustn't blame me," Miss Bessie faltered at last. "You know what we think of night and day."

"I'm coming to that," said Baxter. "Listen to me. What *you* did, Mary, misled four people into thinking you—you meant to do away with yourself."

"Isn't one suicide in the family enough? Oh God, help and pity us! You *couldn't* have believed that!" she cried.

"The evidence was complete. Now, don't you think," Baxter's finger wagged under her nose—"*can't* you think that poor Aggie did the same thing at Holmescroft when she fell out of the window?"

"She had the same throat," said Miss Elizabeth. "Exactly the same symptoms. Don't you remember, Mary?"

"Which was her bedroom?" I asked of Baxter in an undertone.

"Over the south veranda, looking onto the tennis lawn."

"I nearly fell out of that very window when I was at Holmescroft—opening it to get some air. The sill doesn't come much above your knees," I said.

"You hear that, Mary? Mary, do you hear what this gentleman says? Won't you believe that what nearly happened to you must have happened to poor Aggie that night? For God's sake —for her sake—Mary, *won't* you believe?"

There was a long silence while the steam kettle puffed.

"If I could have proof—if I could have proof," said she, and broke into most horrible tears.

Baxter motioned to me, and I crept away to my room, and lay awake till morning, thinking more specially of the dumb Thing at Holmescroft which wished to explain itself. I hated Miss Mary as perfectly as though I had known her for twenty years, but I felt that, alive or dead, I should not like her to condemn me.

Yet at midday, when I saw Miss Mary in her bath chair, Arthurs behind and Baxter and Miss Elizabeth on either side, in the park-like grounds of the Hydro, I found it difficult to arrange my words.

"Now that you know all about it," said Baxter aside, after the first strangeness of our meeting was over, "it's only fair to tell you that my poor cousin did not die in Holmescroft at all. She was dead when they found her under the window in the morning. Just dead."

"Under that laburnum outside the window?" I asked, for I suddenly remembered the crooked evil thing.

"Exactly. She broke the tree in falling. But no death has ever taken place *in* the house, so far as we were concerned. You can make yourself quite easy on that point. Mr. M'Leod's extra thousand for what you call the 'clean bill of health' was something toward my cousin's estate when we sold. It was my duty as their lawyer to get it for them—at any cost to my own feelings."

I know better than to argue when the English talk about their duty. So I agreed with my solicitor.

"Their sister's death must have been a great blow to your cousins," I went on. The bath chair was behind me.

"Unspeakable," Baxter whispered. "They brooded on it day and night. No wonder. If their theory of poor Aggie making away with herself was correct, she was eternally lost!"

"Do you believe that she made away with herself?"

"No, thank God! Never have! And after what happened to Mary last night, I see perfectly what happened to poor Aggie. She had the family throat too. By the way, Mary thinks you are a doctor. Otherwise she wouldn't like your having been in her room."

"Very good. Is she convinced now about her sister's death?"

"She'd give anything to be able to believe it, but she's a hard woman, and brooding along certain lines makes one groovy. I have sometimes been afraid of her reason—on the religious side, don't you know. Elizabeth doesn't matter. Brain of a hen. Always had."

Here Arthurs summoned me to the bath chair, and the ravaged face, beneath its knitted Shetland wool hood, of Miss Mary Moultrie.

"I need not remind you, I hope, of the seal of secrecy—absolute secrecy—in your profession," she began. "Thanks to my cousin's and my sister's stupidity, you have found out——" she blew her nose.

"Please don't excite her, sir," said Arthurs at the back.

"But, my dear Miss Moultrie, I only know what I've seen, of course, but it seems to me that what you thought was a tragedy in your sister's case, turns out, on your own evidence, so to speak, to have been an accident—a dreadfully sad one—but absolutely an accident."

"Do you believe that too?" she cried. "Or are you only saying it to comfort me?"

"I believe it from the bottom of my heart. Come down to Holmescroft for an hour—for half an hour—and satisfy yourself."

"Of what? You don't understand. I see the house every day —every night. I am always there in spirit—waking or sleeping. I couldn't face it in reality."

"But you must," I said. "If you go there in the spirit the greater need for you to go there in the flesh. Go to your sister's room once more, and see the window—I nearly fell out of it myself. It's—it's awfully low and dangerous. That would convince you," I pleaded.

"Yet Aggie had slept in that room for years," she interrupted.

"You've slept in your room here for a long time, haven't you? But you nearly fell out of the window when you were choking."

"That is true. That is one thing true," she nodded. "And I might have been killed as—perhaps—Aggie was killed."

"In that case your own sister and cousin and maid would have said you had committed suicide, Miss Moultrie. Come down to Holmescroft, and go over the place just once."

"You are lying," she said quite quietly. "You don't want me to come down to see a window. It is something else. I warn you we are Evangelicals. We don't believe in prayers for the dead. 'As the tree falls——' "

"Yes. I daresay. But you persist in thinking that your sister committed suicide——"

"No! No! I have always prayed that I might have misjudged her."

Arthurs at the bath chair spoke up: "Oh, Miss Mary! you *would* 'ave it from the first that poor Miss Aggie 'ad made away with herself; an', of course, Miss Bessie took the notion from you. Only Master—Mister John stood out, and—and I'd 'ave taken my Bible oath *you* was making away with yourself last night."

Miss Mary leaned toward me, one finger on my sleeve.

"If going to Holmescroft kills me," she said, "you will have the murder of a fellow-creature on your conscience for all eternity."

"I'll risk it," I answered. Remembering what torment the mere reflection of her torments had cast on Holmescroft, and remembering, above all, the dumb Thing that filled the house with its desire to speak, I felt that there might be worse things.

Baxter was amazed at the proposed visit, but at a nod from that terrible woman went off to make arrangements. Then I sent a telegram to M'Leod bidding him and his vacate Holmescroft for that afternoon. Miss Mary should be alone with her dead, as I had been alone.

I expected untold trouble in transporting her, but to do her justice, the promise given for the journey, she underwent it without murmur, spasm, or unnecessary word. Miss Bessie, pressed in a corner by the window, wept behind her veil, and from time to time tried to take hold of her sister's hand. Baxter wrapped himself in his newly found happiness as selfishly as a bridegroom, for he sat still and smiled.

"So long as I know that Aggie didn't make away with herself," he explained, "I tell you frankly I don't care what happened. She's as hard as a rock—Mary. Always was. *She* won't die."

We led her out onto the platform like a blind woman, and so got her into the fly. The half-hour crawl to Holmescroft was the most racking experience of the day. M'Leod had obeyed my instructions. There was no one visible in the house or the gardens; and the front door stood open.

Miss Mary rose from beside her sister, stepped forth first, and entered the hall.

"Come, Bessie," she cried.

"I daren't. Oh, I daren't."

"Come!" Her voice had altered. I felt Baxter start. "There's nothing to be afraid of."

"Good heavens!" said Baxter. "She's running up the stairs. We'd better follow."

"Let's wait below. She's going to the room."

We heard the door of the bedroom I knew open and shut, and we waited in the lemon-colored hall, heavy with the scent of flowers.

"I've never been into it since it was sold," Baxter sighed. "What a lovely, restful place it is! Poor Aggie used to arrange the flowers."

"Restful?" I began, but stopped of a sudden, for I felt all over my bruised soul that Baxter was speaking truth. It was a light, spacious, airy house, full of the sense of well-being and peace—above all things, of peace. I ventured into the dining room where the thoughtful M'Leods had left a small fire. There was no terror there, present or lurking, and in the drawing room, which for good reasons we had never cared to enter, the sun and the peace and the scent of the flowers worked together as is fit in an inhabited house. When I returned to the hall, Baxter was sweetly asleep on a couch, looking most unlike a middle-aged solicitor who had spent a broken night with an exacting cousin.

There was ample time for me to review it all—to felicitate myself upon my magnificent acumen (barring some errors about Baxter as a thief and possibly a murderer), before the door above opened, and Baxter, evidently a light sleeper, sprang awake.

"I've had a heavenly little nap," he said, rubbing his eyes with the backs of his hands like a child. "Good Lord! That's not *their* step!"

But it was. I had never before been privileged to see the Shadow turned backward on the dial—the years ripped bodily off poor human shoulders—old sunken eyes filled and alight—harsh lips moistened and human.

"John," Miss Mary called, "I know now. Aggie didn't do it!" and "She didn't do it!" echoed Miss Bessie, and giggled.

"I did not think it wrong to say a prayer," Miss Mary continued. "Not for her soul, but for our peace. Then I was convinced."

"Then we got conviction," the younger sister piped.

"We've misjudged poor Aggie, John. But I feel she knows now. Wherever she is, she knows that we know she is guiltless."

"Yes, she knows. I felt it too," said Miss Elizabeth.

"I never doubted," said John Baxter, whose face was beautiful at that hour. "Not from the first. Never have!"

"You never offered me proof, John. Now, thank God, it will

not be the same any more. I can think henceforward of Aggie without sorrow." She tripped, absolutely tripped, across the hall. "What ideas these Jews have of arranging furniture!" She spied me behind a big Cloisonnée vase.

"I've seen the window," she said remotely. "You took a great risk in advising me to undertake such a journey. However, as it turns out . . . I forgive you, and I pray you may never know what mental anguish means! Bessie! Look at this peculiar piano! Do you suppose, Doctor, these people would offer one tea? I miss mine."

"I will go and see," I said, and explored M'Leod's new-built servants' wing. It was in the servants' hall that I unearthed the M'Leod family, bursting with anxiety.

"Tea for three, quick," I said. "If you ask me any questions now, I shall have a fit!" So Mrs. M'Leod got it, and I was butler, amid murmured apologies from Baxter, still smiling and self-absorbed, and the cold disapproval of Miss Mary, who thought the pattern of the china vulgar. However, she ate well, and even asked me whether I would not like a cup of tea for myself.

They went away in the twilight—the twilight that I had once feared. They were going to an hotel in London to rest after the fatigues of the day, and as their fly turned down the drive, I capered on the door step, with the all-darkened house behind me.

Then I heard the uncertain feet of the M'Leods and bade them not to turn on the lights, but to feel—to feel what I had done; for the Shadow was gone, with the dumb desire in the air. They drew short, but afterward deeper, breaths, like bathers entering chill water, separated one from the other, moved about the hall, tiptoed upstairs, raced down, and then Miss M'Leod, and I believe her mother, though she denies this, embraced me. I know M'Leod did.

It was a disgraceful evening. To say we rioted through the house is to put it mildly. We played a sort of Blind Man's Buff along the darkest passages, in the unlighted drawing room, and little dining room, calling cheerily to each other after each exploration that here, and here, and here, the trouble had removed itself. We came up to *the* bedroom—mine for the night again—and sat, the women on the bed, and we men on chairs, drinking in blessed drafts of peace and comfort and cleanliness of soul, while I told them my tale in full, and received fresh praise, thanks, and blessings.

When the servants, returned from their day's outing, gave us a supper of cold fried fish, M'Leod had sense enough to open no wine. We had been practically drunk since nightfall, and grew incoherent on water and milk.

"I like that Baxter," said M'Leod. "He's a sharp man. The death wasn't in the house, but he ran it pretty close, ain't it?"

"And the joke of it is that he supposes I want to buy the place from you," I said. "Are you selling?"

"Not for twice what I paid for it—now," said M'Leod. "I'll keep you in furs all your life, but not our Holmescroft."

"No—never our Holmescroft," said Miss M'Leod. "We'll ask *him* here on Tuesday, mamma." They squeezed each other's hands.

"Now tell me," said Mrs. M'Leod—"that tall one I saw out of the scullery window—did *she* tell you she was always here in the spirit? I hate her. She made all this trouble. It was not her house after she had sold it. What do you think?"

"I suppose," I answered, "she brooded over what she believed was her sister's suicide night and day—she confessed she did—and her thoughts being concentrated on this place, they felt like a—like a burning glass."

"Burning glass is good," said M'Leod.

"I said it was like a light of blackness turned on us," cried the girl, twiddling her ring. "That must have been when the tall one thought worst about her sister and the house."

"Ah, the poor Aggie!" said Mrs. M'Leod. "The poor Aggie, trying to tell every one it was not so! No wonder we felt Something wished to say Something. Thea, Max, do you remember that night——"

"We need not remember any more," M'Leod interrupted. "It is not our trouble. They have told each other now."

"Do you think, then," said Miss M'Leod, "that those two, the living ones, were actually told something—upstairs—in your—in the room?"

"I can't say. At any rate they were made happy, and they ate a big tea afterward. As your father says, it is not our trouble any longer—thank God!"

"Amen!" said M'Leod. "Now, Thea, let us have some music after all these months. 'With mirth, thou pretty bird,' ain't it? You ought to hear that."

And in the half-lighted hall, Thea sang an old English song that I had never heard before.

With mirth, thou pretty bird, rejoice
  Thy Maker's praise enhanced;
Lift up thy shrill and pleasant voice,
  Thy God is high advanced!
Thy food before He did provide,
And gives it in a fitting side,
  Wherewith be thou sufficed!
Why shouldst thou now unpleasant be,
  Thy wrath against God venting,
That He a little bird made thee,
  Thy silly head tormenting,
Because He made thee not a man?
Oh, Peace! He hath well thought thereon,
  Therewith be thou sufficed!

AT THE PIT'S MOUTH

Men say it was a stolen tide—
  The Lord that sent it he knows all,
But in mine ear will aye abide
  The message that the bells let fall,
And awesome bells they were to me,
That in the dark rang, 'Enderby.'

—JEAN INGELOW

ONCE upon a time there was a Man and his Wife and a Tertium Quid.

All three were unwise, but the Wife was the unwisest. The Man should have looked after his Wife, who should have avoided the Tertium Quid, who, again, should have married a wife of his own, after clean and open flirtations, to which nobody can possibly object, around Jakko or Observatory Hill. When you see a young man with his pony in a white lather, and his hat on the back of his head flying downhill at fifteen miles an hour to meet a girl who will be properly surprised to meet him, you naturally approve of that young man, and wish him Staff appointments, and take an interest in his welfare, and, as the proper time comes, give them sugar tongs or sidesaddles according to your means and generosity.

The Tertium Quid flew downhill on horseback, but it was to meet the Man's Wife; and when he flew uphill it was for the same end. The Man was in the Plains, earning money for his Wife to spend on dresses and four-hundred-rupee bracelets, and inexpensive luxuries of that kind. He worked very hard, and sent her a letter or a postcard daily. She also wrote to him daily, and said that she was longing for him to come up to Simla. The Tertium Quid used to lean over her shoulder and laugh as she wrote the notes. Then the two would ride to the Post Office together.

Now, Simla is a strange place and its customs are peculiar; nor is any man who has not spent at least ten seasons there qualified to pass judgment on circumstantial evidence, which is the most untrustworthy in the Courts. For these reasons, and for others which need not appear, I decline to state positively whether there was anything irretrievably wrong in the relations between the man's Wife and the Tertium Quid. If there was, and hereon you must form your own opinion, it was the Man's Wife's fault. She was kittenish in her manners, wearing generally an air of soft and fluffy innocence. But she was deadlily learned and evil-instructed; and, now and again, when the mask dropped, men saw this, shuddered and—almost drew back. Men are occasionally particular, and the least particular men are always the most exacting.

Simla is eccentric in its fashion of treating friendships. Certain attachments which have set and crystallized through half a dozen seasons acquire almost the sanctity of the marriage bond, and are revered as such. Again, certain attachments equally old, and, to all appearance, equally venerable, never seem to win any recognized official status; while a chance-sprung acquaintance, not two months born, steps into the place which by right belongs to the senior. There is no law reducible to print which regulates these affairs.

Some people have a gift which secures them infinite toleration, and others have not. The Man's Wife had not. If she looked over the garden wall, for instance, women taxed her with stealing their husbands. She complained pathetically that she was not allowed to choose her own friends. When she put up her big white muff to her lips, and gazed over it and under her eyebrows at you as she said this thing, you felt that she had been infamously misjudged, and that all the other women's instincts were all wrong; which was absurd. She was not allowed to own the Tertium Quid in peace; and was so strangely constructed that she would not have enjoyed peace had she been so permitted. She preferred some semblance of intrigue to cloak even her most commonplace actions.

After two months of riding, first around Jakko, then Elysium, then Summer Hill, then Observatory Hill, then under Jutogh, and lastly up and down the Cart Road as far as the Tara Devi gap in the dusk, she said to the Tertium Quid, "Frank, people say we are too much together, and people are so horrid."

The Tertium Quid pulled his mustache, and replied that horrid people were unworthy of the consideration of nice people.

"But they have done more than talk—they have written—written to my hubby—I'm sure of it," said the Man's Wife, and she pulled a letter from her husband out of her saddle pocket and gave it to the Tertium Quid.

It was an honest letter, written by an honest man, then stewing in the Plains on two hundred rupees a month (for he allowed his wife eight hundred and fifty), and in a silk banian and cotton trousers. It is said that, perhaps, she had not thought of the unwisdom of allowing her name to be so generally coupled with the Tertium Quid's; that she was too much of a child to understand the dangers of that sort of thing; that he, her husband, was the last man in the world to interfere jealously with her little amusements and interests, but that it would be better were she to drop the Tertium Quid quietly and for her husband's sake. The letter was sweetened with many pretty little pet names, and it amused the Tertium Quid considerably. He and She laughed over it, so that you, fifty yards away, could see their shoulders shaking while the horses slouched along side by side.

Their conversation was not worth reporting. The upshot of it was that, next day, no one saw the Man's Wife and the Tertium Quid together. They had both gone down to the Cemetery, which, as a rule, is only visited officially by the inhabitants of Simla.

A Simla funeral with the clergyman riding, the mourners riding, and the coffin creaking as it swings between the bearers, is one of the most depressing things on this earth, particularly when the procession passes under the wet, dank dip beneath the Rockcliffe Hotel, where the sun is shut out, and all the hill streams are wailing and weeping together as they go down the valleys.

Occasionally, folk tend the graves, but we in India shift and are transferred so often that, at the end of the second year, the Dead have no friends—only acquaintances who are far too busy amusing themselves up the hill to attend to old partners. The idea of using a Cemetery as a rendezvous is distinctly a feminine one. A man would have said simply, "Let people talk. We'll go down the Mall." A woman is made differently, especially if she be such a woman as the Man's Wife. She and the Tertium Quid enjoyed each other's society among the graves of men and women whom they had known and danced with aforetime.

They used to take a big horse blanket and sit on the grass a little to the left of the lower end, where there is a dip in the ground, and where the occupied graves stop short and the ready-made ones are not ready. Each well-regulated Indian Cemetery keeps half a dozen graves permanently open for contingencies and incidental wear and tear. In the Hills these are more usually baby's size, because children who come up weakened and sick from the Plains often succumb to the effects of the Rains in the Hills or get pneumonia from their *ayahs* taking them through damp pinewoods after the sun has set. In Cantonments, of course, the man's size is more in request; these arrangements varying with the climate and population.

One day when the Man's Wife and the Tertium Quid had just arrived in the Cemetery, they saw some coolies breaking ground. They had marked out a full-size grave, and the Tertium Quid asked them whether any *Sahib* was sick. They said that they did not know; but it was an order that they should dig a *Sahib's* grave.

"Work away," said the Tertium Quid, "and let's see how it's done."

The coolies worked away, and the Man's Wife and the Tertium Quid watched and talked for a couple of hours while the grave was being deepened. Then a coolie, taking the earth in baskets as it was thrown up, jumped over the grave.

"That's queer," said the Tertium Quid. "Where's my ulster?"

"What's queer?" said the Man's Wife.

"I have got a chill down my back—just as if a goose had walked over my grave."

"Why do you look at the thing, then?" said the Man's Wife. "Let us go."

The Tertium Quid stood at the head of the grave, and stared without answering for a space. Then he said, dropping a pebble down, "It is nasty—and cold: horribly cold. I don't think I shall come to the Cemetery any more. I don't think grave digging is cheerful."

The two talked and agreed that the Cemetery was depressing.

They also arranged for a ride next day out from the Cemetery through the Mashobra Tunnel up to Fagoo and back, because all the world was going to a garden party at Viceregal Lodge, and all the people of Mashobra would go too.

Coming up the Cemetery road, the Tertium Quid's horse tried to bolt uphill, being tired with standing so long, and managed to strain a back sinew.

"I shall have to take the mare tomorrow," said the Tertium Quid, "and she will stand nothing heavier than a snaffle."

They made their arrangements to meet in the Cemetery, after allowing all the Mashobra people time to pass into Simla. That night it rained heavily, and, next day, when the Tertium Quid came to the trysting-place, he saw that the new grave had a foot of water in it, the ground being a tough and sour clay.

"'Jove! That looks beastly," said the Tertium Quid. "Fancy being boarded up and dropped into that well!"

They then started off to Fagoo, the mare playing with the snaffle and picking her way as though she were shod with satin, and the sun shining divinely. The road below Mashobra to Fagoo is officially styled the Himalayan-Thibet Road; but in spite of its name it is not much more than six feet wide in most places, and the drop into the valley below may be anything between one and two thousand feet.

"Now we're going to Thibet," said the Man's Wife merrily, as the horses drew near to Fagoo. She was riding on the cliff-side.

"Into Thibet," said the Tertium Quid, "ever so far from people who say horrid things, and hubbies who write stupid letters. With you—to the end of the world!"

A coolie carrying a log of wood came around a corner, and the mare went wide to avoid him—forefeet in and haunches out, as a sensible mare should go.

"To the world's end," said the Man's Wife, and looked unspeakable things over her near shoulder at the Tertium Quid.

He was smiling, but, while she looked, the smile froze stiff as it were on his face, and changed to a nervous grin—the sort of grin men wear when they are not quite easy in their saddles. The mare seemed to be sinking by the stern, and her nostrils cracked while she was trying to realize what was happening.

The rain of the night before had rotted the drop-side of the Himalayan-Thibet Road, and it was giving way under her. "What are you doing?" said the Man's Wife. The Tertium Quid gave no answer. He grinned nervously and set his spurs into the mare, who rapped with her forefeet on the road, and the struggle began. The Man's Wife screamed, "Oh, Frank, get off!"

But the Tertium Quid was glued to the saddle—his face blue and white—and he looked into the Man's Wife's eyes. Then the Man's Wife clutched at the mare's head and caught her by the nose instead of the bridle. The brute threw up her head and went down with a scream, the Tertium Quid upon her, and the nervous grin still set on his face.

The Man's Wife heard the tinkle-tinkle of little stones and loose earth falling off the roadway, and the sliding roar of the man and horse going down. Then everything was quiet, and she called on Frank to leave his mare and walk up. But Frank did not answer. He was underneath the mare, nine hundred feet below, spoiling a patch of Indian corn.

As the revelers came back from Viceregal Lodge in the mists of the evening, they met a temporarily insane woman, on a temporarily mad horse, swinging around the corners, with her eyes and her mouth open, and her head like the head of a Medusa. She was stopped by a man at the risk of his life, and taken out of the saddle, a limp heap, and put on the bank to explain herself. This wasted twenty minutes, and then she was sent home in a lady's *'rickshaw,* still with her mouth open and her hands picking at her riding gloves.

She was in bed through the following three days, which were rainy; so she missed attending the funeral of the Tertium Quid, who was lowered into eighteen inches of water, instead of the twelve to which he had first objected.

BERTRAN AND BIMI

THE orangutan in the big iron cage lashed to the sheep-pen began the discussion. The night was stiflingly hot, and as Hans Breitmann and I passed him, dragging our bedding to the forepeak of the steamer, he roused himself and chattered obscenely. He had been caught somewhere in the Malayan Archipelago, and was going to England to be exhibited at a shilling a head. For four days he had struggled, yelled and wrenched at the heavy iron bars of his prison without ceasing, and had nearly slain a Lascar incautious enough to come within reach of the great hairy paw.

"It would be well for, mine friend, if you was a liddle sea-sick," said Hans Breitmann, pausing by the cage. "You haf too much Ego in your Cosmos."

The orangutan's arm slid out negligently from between the bars. No one would have believed that it would make a sudden snake-like rush at the German's breast. The thin silk of the sleep-suit tore out: Hans stepped back unconcernedly, to pluck a banana from a bunch hanging close to one of the boats.

"Too much Ego," said he, peeling the fruit and offering it to the caged devil, who was rending the silk to tatters.

Then we laid out our bedding in the bows, among the sleeping Lascars, to catch any breeze that the pace of the ship might give us. The sea was like smoky oil, except where it turned to fire under our forefoot and whirled back into the dark in smears of dull flame. There was a thunderstorm some miles away; we could see the glimmer of the lightning. The ship's cow, distressed by the heat and the smell of the ape-beast in the cage, lowed unhappily from time to time in exactly the same key as the lookout man at the bows answered the hourly call from the bridge. The trampling tune of the engines was very distinct, and the jarring of the ash-lift, as it was tipped into the sea, hurt the procession of hushed noise. Hans lay down by my side and lighted a good-night cigar. This was naturally the beginning of conversation. He owned a voice as soothing as the wash of the sea, and stores of experiences as vast as the sea itself; for his business in life was to wander up and down the world, collecting orchids and wild beasts and ethnological specimens for German and American dealers. I watched the glowing end of his cigar wax and wane in the gloom, as the sentences rose and fell, till I was nearly asleep. The orangutan, troubled by some dream of the forests of his freedom, began to yell like a soul in purgatory, and to wrench madly at the bars of the cage.

"If he was out now dere would not be much of us left hereabouts," said Hans, lazily. "He screams good. See, now, how I shall tame him when he stops himself."

There was a pause in the outcry, and from Hans's mouth came an imitation of a snake's hiss, so perfect that I almost sprung to my feet. The sustained murderous sound rang along the deck, and the wrenching at the bars ceased. The orangutan was quaking in an ecstasy of pure terror.

"Dot stop him," said Hans. "I learned dot trick in Mogoung Tanjong when I was collecting liddle monkeys for some peoples in Berlin. Efery one in der world is afraid of der monkeys—except der snake. So I blay snake against monkey, and he keep quite still. Dere was too much Ego in his Cosmos. Dot is der soul-custom of monkeys. Are you asleep, or will you listen, and I will tell a dale dot you shall not pelief?"

"There's no tale in the wide world that I can't believe," I said.

"If you have learned pelief you haf learned somedings. Now I shall try your pelief. Good! When I was collecting does liddle monkeys—it was in '79 or '80, und I was in der islands of der Archipelago—over dere in der dark"—he pointed southward to New Guinea generally—"Mein Gott! I would sooner collect life red devils than liddle monkeys. When dey do not bite off your thumbs dey are always dying from nostalgia—homesick—for dey haf der imperfect soul, which is midway arrested in defelopment—und too much Ego. I was dere for nearly a year, und dere I found a man dot was called Bertran. He was a Frenchman, und he was a goot man—naturalist to the bone. Dey said he was an escaped convict, but he was a naturalist, und dot was enough for me. He would call all der life beasts from der forest, und dey would come. I said he was St. Francis of Assisi in a new dransmigration produced, und he laughed und said he haf never preach to der fishes. He sold dem for tripang—*beche-de-mer*.

"Und dot man, who was king of beasts-tamer men, he had in der house shush such anoder as dot devil-animal in der cage—a great orangutan dot thought he was a man. He haf found him when he was a child—der orangutan—und he was child and brother and opera comique all round to Bertran. He had his room in dot house—not a cage, but a room—mit a bed and sheets, and he would go to bed and get up in der morning and smoke his cigar und eat his dinner mit Bertran, und walk mit him hand-in-hand, which was most horrible. Herr Gott! I haf seen dot beast throw himself back in his chair und laugh when Bertran haf made fun of me. He was *not* a beast; he was a man, und he talked to Bertran, und Bertran comprehended, for I have seen dem. Und he was always politeful to me except when I talk too long to Bertran and say nodings at all to him. Den he would pull me away—dis great, dark devil, mit his enormous paws—shush as if I was a child. He was not a beast, he was a man. Dis I saw pefore I know him three months, und Bertran he haf saw the same; and Bimi, der orangutan, haf understood us both, mit his cigar between his big-dog teeth und der blue gum.

"I was dere a year, dere und at dere oder islands—somedimes for monkeys and somedimes for butterflies und orchits. One time Bertran says to me dot he will be married, pecause he haf found a girl dot was goot, and he inquire if this marrying idea was right. I would not say, pecause it was not me dot was going to be married. Den he go off courting der girl—she was a half-caste French girl—very pretty. Haf you got a new light for my cigar? Oof! Very pretty. Only I say: 'Haf you thought of Bimi? If he pulls me away when I talk to you, what will he do to your wife? He will pull her in pieces. If I was you, Bertran, I would gif my wife for wedding present der stuff figure of Bimi.' By dot time I had learned somedings about der monkey peoples. 'Shoot him?' says Bertran. 'He is your beast,' I said; 'if he was mine he would be shot now.'

"Den I felt at der back of my neck der fingers of Bimi. Mein Gott! I tell you dot he talked through dose fingers. It was der deaf-and-dumb alphabet all gomplete. He slide his hairy arm

—". . . and Bimi, der orangutan, haf understood us both, mit his cigar between his big-dog teeth und der blue gum."

round my neck, and he tilt up my chin und look into my face, shust to see if I understood his talk so well as he understood mine.

"'See now dere!' says Bertran, 'und you would shoot him while he is cuddling you? Dot is der Teuton ingrate!'

"But I knew dot I had made Bimi a life's enemy, pecause his fingers haf talk murder through the back of my neck. Next dime I see Bimi dere was a pistol in my belt, und he touch it once, and I open der breech to show him it was loaded. He haf seen der liddle monkeys killed in der woods and he understood.

"So Bertran he was married, und he forgot clean about Bimi dot was skippin' alone on der beach mit der half of a human soul in his belly. I was see him skip, und he took a big bough und thrash der sand till he half made a great hole like a grave. So I says to Bertran: 'For any sakes, kill Bimi. He is mad mit der jealousy.'

"Bertran haf said: 'He is not mad at all. He haf obey and love my wife, und if she speaks he will get her slippers,' und he looked at his wife across der room. She was a very pretty girl.

"Den I said to him: 'Dost thou pretend to know monkeys

und dis beast dot is lashing himself mad upon der sands, pecause you do not talk to him? Shoot him when he comes to der house, for he haf der light in his eyes dot means killing—und killing.' Bimi come to der house, but dere was no light in his eyes. It was all put away, cunning—so cunning—und he fetch der girl her slippers, und Bertran turn to me und say: 'Dost thou know him in nine months more than I haf known him in twelve years? Shall a child stab his fader? I have fed him, und he was my child. Do not speak this nonsense to my wife or to me any more.'

"Dot next day Bertran came to my house to help me make some wood cases for der specimens, und he tell me dot he haf left his wife a liddle while mit Bimi in der garden. Den I finish my cases quick, und I say: 'Let us go to your house und get a trink.' He laugh und say: 'Come along, dry mans.'

"His wife was not in der garden, und Bimi did not come when Bertran called. Und his wife did not come when he called, und he knocked at her bedroom door und dot was shut tight—locked. Den he look at me, und his face was white. I broke down der door mit my shoulder, und der thatch of der roof was torn into a great hole, und der sun came in upon der floor. Haf you ever seen paper in der wastebasket, or cards at whist on der table scattered? Dere was no wife dot could be seen. I tell you dere was noddings in dot room dot might be a woman. Dere was stuff on der floor, und dot was all. I looked at dese things und I was very sick; but Bertran looked a liddle longer at what was upon the floor und der walls, und der hole in der thatch. Den he pegan to laugh, soft and low, und I knew und thank Got dot he was mad. He nefer cried, he nefer prayed. He stood still in der doorway und laugh to himself. Den he said: 'She haf locked herself in dis room, und he haf torn up der thatch. *Fi donc*. Dot is so. We will mend der thatch und wait for Bimi. He will surely come.'

"I tell you we waited ten days in dot house, after der room was made into a room again, and once or twice we saw Bimi comin' a liddle way from der woods. He was afraid pecause he haf done wrong. Bertran called him when he was come to look on the tenth day, und Bimi come skipping along der beach und making noises, mit a long piece of black hair in his hands.

Den Bertran laugh and say, *'Fi donc!'* shust as if it was a glass broken upon der table; und Bimi come nearer, und Bertran was honey-sweet in his voice and laughed to himself. For three days he made love to Bimi, pecause Bimi would not let himself be touched. Den Bimi come to dinner at der same table mit us, und her hair on his hands was all black und thick mit—mit what had dried on his hands. Bertran gave him sangaree till Bimi was drunk and stupid, und den"—

Hans paused to puff at his cigar.

"And then?" said I.

"Und den Bertran kill him with his hands, und I go for a walk upon der beach. It was Bertran's own piziness. When I come back der ape he was dead, und Bertran he was dying abofe him; but still he laughed a liddle und low, and he was quite content. Now you know der formula of der strength of der orangutan—it is more as seven to one in relation to man. But Bertran, he haf killed Bimi mit sooch dings as Gott gif him. Dot was der miracle."

The infernal clamor in the cage recommenced. "Aha! Dot friend of ours haf still too much Ego in his Cosmos. Be quiet, thou!"

Hans hissed long and venomously. We could hear the great beast quaking in his cage.

"But why in the world didn't you help Bertran instead of letting him be killed?" I asked.

"My friend," said Hans, composedly stretching himself to slumber, "it was not nice even to mineself dot I should lif after I had seen dot room wit der hole in der thatch. Und Bertran, he was her husband. Goot-night, und sleep well."

"THE FINEST STORY IN THE WORLD"

"Or ever the knightly years were gone
With the old world to the grave,
I was a king in Babylon
And you were a Christian slave."
—W. E. HENLEY

HIS name was Charlie Mears; he was the only son of his mother who was a widow, and he lived in the north of London, coming into the City every day to work in a bank. He was twenty years old and suffered from aspirations. I met him in a public billiard-saloon where the marker called him by his first name, and he called the marker "Bullseyes." Charlie explained, a little nervously, that he had only come to the place to look on, and since looking on at games of skill is not a cheap amusement for the young, I suggested that Charlie should go back to his mother.

That was our first step toward better acquaintance. He would call on me sometimes in the evenings instead of running about London with his fellow clerks; and before long, speaking of himself as a young man must, he told me of his aspirations, which were all literary. He desired to make himself an undying name chiefly through verse, though he was not above sending stories of love and death to the penny-in-the-slot journals. It was my fate to sit still while Charlie read me poems of many hundred lines, and bulky fragments of plays that would surely shake the world. My reward was his unreserved confidence, and the self-revelations and troubles of a young man are almost as holy as those of a maiden. Charlie had never fallen in love, but was anxious to do so at the first opportunity; he believed in all things good and all things honorable, but at the same time, was curiously careful to let me see that he knew his way about the world as befitted a bank clerk on twenty-five shillings a week. He rhymed "dove" with "love" and "moon" with "June," and devoutly believed that they had never so been rhymed before. The long lame gaps in his plays he filled up with hasty words of apology and description and swept on, seeing all that he intended to do so clearly that he esteemed it already done, and turned to me for applause.

I fancy that his mother did not encourage his aspirations, and I know that his writing table at home was the edge of his washstand. This he told me almost at the outset of our acquaintance; when he was ravaging my bookshelves, and a little before I was implored to speak the truth as to his chances of "writing something really great, you know." Maybe I encouraged him too much, for, one night, he called on me, his eyes flaming with excitement, and said breathlessly:—

"Do you mind—can you let me stay here and write all this evening? I won't interrupt you, I won't really. There's no place for me to write in at my mother's."

"What's the trouble?" I said, knowing well what that trouble was.

"I've a notion in my head that would make the most splendid story that was ever written. Do let me write it out here. It's *such* a notion!"

There was no resisting the appeal. I set him a table; he hardly thanked me, but plunged into the work at once. For half an hour the pen scratched without stopping. Then Charlie sighed and tugged his hair. The scratching grew slower; there were more erasures; and at last ceased. The finest story in the world would not come forth.

"It looks such awful rot now," he said mournfully. "And yet it seemed so good when I was thinking about it. What's wrong?"

I could not dishearten him by saying the truth. So I answered: "Perhaps you don't feel in the mood for writing."

"Yes, I do—except when I look at this stuff. Ugh!"

"Read me what you've done," I said.

He read, and it was wondrous bad, and he paused at all the specially turgid sentences, expecting a little approval; for he was proud of those sentences, as I knew he would be.

"It needs compression," I suggested cautiously.

"I hate cutting my things down. I don't think you could alter a word here without spoiling the sense. It reads better aloud than when I was writing it."

"Charlie, you're suffering from an alarming disease afflicting a numerous class. Put the thing by, and tackle it again in a week."

"I want to do it at once. What do you think of it?"

"How can I judge from a half-written tale? Tell me the story as it lies in your head."

Charlie told, and in the telling there was everything that his ignorance had so carefully prevented from escaping into the written word. I looked at him, wondering whether it were possible that he did not know the originality, the power of the notion that had come in his way? It was distinctly a Notion among notions. Men had been puffed up with pride by ideas not a tithe as excellent and practicable. But Charlie babbled on serenely, interrupting the current of pure fancy with samples of horrible sentences that he purposed to use. I heard him out to the end. It would be folly to allow his thought to remain in his own inept hands, when I could do so much with it. Not all that could be done indeed; but, oh so much!

"What do you think?" he said at last. "I fancy I shall call it 'The Story of a Ship.'"

"I think the idea is pretty good; but you won't be able to handle it for ever so long. Now I——"

"Would it be of any use to you? Would you care to take it? I should be proud," said Charlie promptly.

There are few things sweeter in this world than the guileless, hot-headed, intemperate, open admiration of a junior. Even a woman in her blindest devotion does not fall into the gait of the man she adores, tilt her bonnet to the angle at which he wears his hat, or interlard her speech with his pet oaths. And Charlie did all these things. Still it was necessary to salve my conscience before I possessed myself of Charlie's thought.

"Let's make a bargain. I'll give you a fiver for the notion," I said.

Charlie became a bank clerk at once.

"Oh, that's impossible. Between two pals, you know, if I may call you so, and speaking as a man of the world, I couldn't. Take the notion if it's any use to you. I've heaps more."

He had—none knew this better than I—but they were the notions of other men.

"Look at it as a matter of business—between men of the

world," I returned. "Five pounds will buy you any number of poetry books. Business is business, and you may be sure I shouldn't give that price unless——"

"Oh, if you put it *that* way," said Charlie, visibly moved by the thought of the books. The bargain was clinched with an agreement that he should at unstated intervals come to me with all the notions that he possessed, should have a table of his own to write at, and unquestioned right to inflict upon me all his poems and fragments of poems. Then I said, "Now tell me how you came by this idea."

"It came by itself." Charlie's eyes opened a little.

"Yes, but you told me a great deal about the hero that you must have read before somewhere."

"I haven't any time for reading, except when you let me sit here, and on Sundays I'm on my bicycle or down the river all day. There's nothing wrong about the hero, is there?"

"Tell me again and I shall understand clearly. You say that your hero went pirating. How did he live?"

"He was on the lower deck of this ship-thing that I was telling you about."

"What sort of ship?"

"It was the kind rowed with oars, and the sea spurts through the oar-holes and the men row sitting up to their knees in water. Then there's a bench running down between the two lines of oars and an overseer with a whip walks up and down the bench to make the men work."

"How do you know that?"

"It's in the tale. There's a rope running overhead, looped to the upper deck, for the overseer to catch hold of when the ship rolls. When the overseer misses the rope once and falls among the rowers, remember the hero laughs at him and gets licked for it. He's chained to his oar of course—the hero."

"How is he chained?"

"With an iron band around his waist fixed to the bench he sits on, and a sort of handcuff on his left wrist chaining him to the oar. He's on the lower deck where the worst men are sent, and the only light comes from the hatchways and through the oar-holes. Can't you imagine the sunlight just squeezing through between the handle and the hole and wobbling about as the ship rolls?"

"I can, but I can't imagine your imagining it."

"How could it be any other way? Now you listen to me. The long oars on the upper deck are managed by four men to each bench, the lower ones by three, and the lowest of all by two. Remember it's quite dark on the lowest deck and all the men there go mad. When a man dies at his oar on that deck he isn't thrown overboard, but cut up in his chains and stuffed through the oar-hole in little pieces."

"Why?" I demanded amazed, not so much at the information as the tone of command in which it was flung out.

"To save trouble and to frighten the others. It needs two overseers to drag a man's body up to the top deck; and if the men at the lower-deck oars were left alone, of course they'd stop rowing and try to pull up the benches by all standing up together in their chains."

"You've a most provident imagination. Where have you been reading about galleys and galley slaves?"

"Nowhere that I remember. I row a little when I get the chance. But, perhaps, if you say so, I may have read something."

He went away shortly afterward to deal with booksellers, and I wondered how a bank clerk aged twenty could put into my hands with a profligate abundance of detail, all given with absolute assurance, the story of extravagant and bloodthirsty adventure, riot, piracy, and death in unnamed seas. He had led his hero a desperate dance through revolt against the overseers, to command of a ship of his own, and the ultimate establishment of a kingdom on an island "somewhere in the sea, you know"; and, delighted with my paltry five pounds, had gone out to buy the notions of other men, that these might teach him how to write. I had the consolation of knowing that this notion was mine by right of purchase; and I thought that I could make something of it.

When next he came to me he was drunk—royally drunk—on many poets for the first time revealed to him. His pupils were dilated, his words tumbled over each other, and he wrapped himself in quotations—as a beggar would enfold himself in the purple of Emperors. Most of all was he drunk with Longfellow.

"Isn't it splendid? Isn't it superb?" he cried, after hasty greetings. "Listen to this—

"'Wouldst thou,'—so the helmsman answered,
'Learn the secret of the sea?
Only those who brave its dangers
Comprehend its mystery.'

By gum!

"'Only those who brave its dangers
Comprehend its mystery.'"

he repeated twenty times, walking up and down the room and forgetting me. "But *I* can understand it too," he said to himself. "I don't know how to thank you for that fiver. And this; listen—

"'I remember the black wharves and the slips
And the sea-tides tossing free;
And the Spanish sailors with bearded lips,
And the beauty and mystery of the ships,
And the magic of the sea.'

I haven't braved any dangers, but I feel as if I knew all about it."

"You certainly seem to have a grip of the sea. Have you ever seen it?"

"When I was a little chap I went to Brighton once; we used to live in Coventry, though, before we came to London. I never saw it,

"'When descends on the Atlantic
The gigantic
Storm-wind of the Equinox.'"

He shook me by the shoulder to make me understand the passion that was shaking himself.

"When that storm comes," he continued, "I think that all the oars in the ship that I was talking about get broken, and the rowers have their chests smashed in by the oar-heads bucking. By the way, have you done anything with that notion of mine, yet?"

"No. I was waiting to hear more of it from you. Tell me how in the world you're so certain about the fittings of the ship. You know nothing of ships."

"I don't know. It's as real as anything to me until I try to write it down. I was thinking about it only last night in bed, after you had lent me *Treasure Island;* and I made up a whole lot of new things to go into the story."

"What sort of things?"

"About the food the man ate; rotten figs and black beans and wine in a skin-bag, passed from bench to bench."

"Was the ship built so long ago as *that?"*

"As what? I don't know whether it was long ago or not. It's only a notion, but sometimes it seems just as real as if it was true. Do I bother you with talking about it?"

"Not in the least. Did you make up anything else?"

"Yes, but it's nonsense." Charlie flushed a little.

"Never mind; let's hear about it."

"Well, I was thinking over the story, and after awhile I got out of bed and wrote down on a piece of paper the sort of stuff the men might be supposed to scratch on their oars with the edges of their handcuffs. It seemed to make the thing more life-like. It *is* so real to me, y'know."

"Have you the paper on you?"

"Ye—es, but what's the use of showing it? It's only a lot of scratches. All the same, we might have 'em reproduced in the book on the front page."

"I'll attend to those details. Show me what your men wrote."

He pulled out of his pocket a sheet of notepaper, with a single line of scratches upon it, and I put this carefully away.

"What is it supposed to mean in English?" I said.

"Oh, I don't know. I mean it to mean 'I'm beastly tired.' It's great nonsense," he repeated, "but all those men in the ship seem as real as real people to me. Do do something to the notion soon; I should like to see it written and printed."

"But all you've told me would make a long book."

"Make it then. You've only to sit down and write it out."

"Give me a little time. Have you any more notions?"

"Not just now. I'm reading all the books I've bought. They're splendid."

When he had left I looked at the sheet of notepaper with the inscription upon it. Then I took my head tenderly between both hands, to make certain that it was not coming off or turning around. Then . . . but there seemed to be no interval between leaving my rooms and finding myself arguing with a policeman outside a door marked *Private* in a corridor of the British Museum. All I demanded, as politely as possible, was "the Greek antiquity man." The policeman knew nothing except the rules of the Museum, and it became necessary to forage through all the houses and offices inside the gates. An elderly gentleman called away from his lunch put an end to my search by holding the notepaper between finger and thumb and sniffing at it scornfully.

"What does this mean? H'mm," said he. "So far as I can ascertain it is an attempt to write extremely corrupt Greek on the part"—here he glared at me with intention—"of an extremely illiterate—ah—person." He read slowly from the paper, *"Pollock, Erckmann, Tauchnitz, Henniker"*—four names familiar to me.

"Can you tell me what the corruption is supposed to mean—the gist of the thing?" I asked.

"I have been—many times—overcome with weariness in this particular employment. That is the meaning." He returned me the paper, and I fled without a word of thanks, explanation, or apology.

I might have been excused for forgetting much. To me of all men had been given the chance to write the most marvelous tale in the world, nothing less than the story of a Greek galley slave, as told by himself. Small wonder that his dreaming had seemed real to Charlie. The Fates that are so careful to shut the doors of each successive life behind us had, in this case, been neglectful, and Charlie was looking, though that he did not know, where never man had been permitted to look with full knowledge since Time began. Above all, he was absolutely ignorant of the knowledge sold to me for five pounds; and he would retain that ignorance; for bank clerks do not understand metempsychosis, and a sound commercial education does not include Greek. He would supply me—here I capered among the dumb gods of Egypt and laughed in their battered faces—

with material to make my tale sure—so sure that the world would hail it as an impudent and vamped fiction. And I—I alone would know that it was absolutely and literally true. I—I alone held this jewel to my hand for the cutting and polishing. Therefore I danced again among the gods of the Egyptian court, till a policeman saw me and took steps in my direction.

It remained now only to encourage Charlie to talk, and here there was no difficulty. But I had forgotten those accursed books of poetry. He came to me time after time, as useless as a surcharged phonograph—drunk on Byron, Shelley, or Keats. Knowing now what the boy had been in his past lives, and desperately anxious not to lose one word of his babble, I could not hide from him my respect and interest. He misconstrued both into respect for the present soul of Charlie Mears, to whom life was as new as it was to Adam, and interest in his readings: he stretched my patience to breaking point by reciting poetry—not his own now, but that of others. I wished every English poet blotted out of the memory of mankind. I blasphemed the mightiest names of song because they had drawn Charlie from the path of direct narrative, and would, later, spur him to imitate them; but I choked down my impatience until the first flood of enthusiasm should have spent itself and the boy returned to his dreams.

"What's the use of my telling you what *I* think, when these chaps wrote things for the angels to read?" he growled, one evening. "Why don't you write something like theirs?"

"I don't think you're treating me quite fairly," I said, speaking under strong restraint.

"I've given you the story," he said shortly, replunging into "Lara."

"But I want the details."

"The things I make up about that damned ship that you call a galley? They're quite easy. You can just make 'em up for yourself. Turn up the gas a little, I want to go on reading."

I could have broken the gas-globe over his head for his amazing stupidity. I could indeed make up things for myself did I only know what Charlie did not know that he knew. But since the doors were shut behind me I could only wait his youthful pleasure and strive to keep him in good temper. One minute's want of guard might spoil a priceless revelation: now and again he would toss his books aside—he kept them in my rooms, for his mother would have been shocked at the waste of good money had she seen them—and launched into his sea dreams. Again I cursed all the poets of England. The plastic mind of the bank clerk had been overlaid, colored, and distorted by that which he had read, and the result as delivered was a confused tangle of other voices most like the mutter and hum through a City telephone in the busiest part of the day.

He talked of the galley—his own galley had he but known it—with illustrations borrowed from the "Bride of Abydos." He pointed the experiences of his hero with quotations from "The Corsair," and threw in deep and desperate moral reflections from "Cain" and "Manfred," expecting me to use them all. Only when the talk turned on Longfellow were the jarring cross-currents dumb, and I knew that Charlie was speaking the truth as he remembered it.

"What do you think of this?" I said one evening, as soon as I understood the medium in which his memory worked best, and, before he could expostulate, read him nearly the whole of "The Saga of King Olaf."

He listened openmouthed, flushed, his hands drumming on the back of the sofa where he lay, till I came to the Song of Einar Tamberskelver and the verse:—

"Einar then, the arrow taking
From the loosened string,
Answered, 'That was Norway breaking
'Neath thy hand, O King.' "

He gasped with pure delight of sound.

"That's better than Byron, a little?" I ventured.

"Better! Why it's *true!* How could he have known?"

I went back and repeated:—

" 'What was that?' said Olaf, standing
On the quarter-deck,
'Something heard I like the stranding
Of a shattered wreck.' "

"How could he have known how the ships crash and the oars rip out and go *z-zzp* all along the line? Why only the other night . . . But go back please and read 'The Skerry of Shrieks' again."

"No, I'm tired. Let's talk. What happened the other night?"

"I had an awful dream about that galley of ours. I dreamed I was drowned in a fight. You see we ran alongside another ship in harbor. The water was dead still except where our oars whipped it up. You know where I always sit in the galley?" He spoke haltingly at first, under the fine English fear of being laughed at.

"No. That's news to me," I answered meekly, my heart beginning to beat.

"On the fourth oar from the bow on the right side on the upper deck. There were four of us at that oar, all chained. I remember watching the water and trying to get my handcuffs off before the row began. Then we closed up on the other ship, and all their fighting men jumped over our bulwarks, and my bench broke and I was pinned down with the three other fellows on top of me, and the big oar jammed across our backs."

"Well?" Charlie's eyes were alive and alight. He was looking at the wall behind my chair.

"I don't know how we fought. The men were trampling all over my back, and I lay low. Then our rowers on the left side —tied to their oars, you know—began to yell and back water. I could hear the water sizzle, and we spun around like a cockchafer and I knew, lying where I was, that there was a galley coming up bow-on, to ram us on the left side. I could just lift my head and see her sail over the bulwarks. We wanted to meet her bow to bow, but it was too late. We could only turn a little bit because the galley on our right had hooked herself onto us and stopped our moving. Then, by gum! there was a crash! Our left oars began to break as the other galley, the moving one y'know, stuck her nose into them. Then the lower-deck oars shot up through the deck planking, butt first, and one of them jumped clear up into the air and came down again close at my head."

"How was that managed?"

"The moving galley's bow was plunking them back through

their own oar-holes, and I could hear no end of a shindy in the decks below. Then her nose caught us nearly in the middle, and we tilted sideways, and the fellows in the right-hand galley unhitched their hooks and ropes, and threw things onto our upper deck—arrows, and hot pitch or something that stung, and we went up and up on the left side, and the right side dipped, and I twisted my head around and saw the water stand still as it topped the right bulwarks; and then it curled over and crashed down on the whole lot of us on the right side, and I felt it hit my back, and I woke."

"One minute, Charlie. When the sea topped the bulwarks, what did it look like?" I had my reasons for asking. A man of my acquaintance had once gone down with a leaking ship in a still sea, and had seen the water level pause for an instant ere it fell on the deck.

"It looked just like a banjo string drawn tight, and it seemed to stay there for years," said Charlie.

Exactly! The other man had said: "It looked like a silver wire laid down along the bulwarks, and I thought it was never going to break." He had paid everything except the bare life for this little valueless piece of knowledge, and I had traveled ten thousand weary miles to meet him and take his knowledge at second hand. But Charlie, the bank clerk on twenty-five shillings a week, who had never been out of sight of a made road, knew it all. It was no consolation to me that once in his lives he had been forced to die for his gains. I also must have died scores of times, but behind me, because I could have used my knowledge, the doors were shut!

"And then?" I said, trying to put away the devil of envy.

"The funny thing was, though, in all the row I didn't feel a bit astonished or frightened. It seemed as if I'd been in a good many fights, because I told my next man so when the row began. But that cad of an overseer on my deck wouldn't unloose our chains and give us a chance. He always said that we'd all be set free after a battle, but we never were; we never were." Charlie shook his head mournfully.

"What a soundrel!"

"I should say he was. He never gave us enough to eat, and

sometimes we were so thirsty that we used to drink salt water. I can taste that salt water still."

"Now tell me something about the harbor where the fight was fought."

"I didn't dream about that. I know it was a harbor though; because we were tied up to a ring on a white wall and all the face of the stone under water was covered with wood to prevent our ram getting chipped when the tide made us rock."

"That's curious. Our hero commanded the galley, didn't he?"

"Didn't he just! He stood by the bows and shouted like a good 'un. He was the man who killed the overseer."

"But you were all drowned together, Charlie, weren't you?"

"I can't make that fit quite," he said, with a puzzled look. "The galley must have gone down with all hands, and yet I fancy that the hero went on living afterward. Perhaps he climbed into the attacking ship. I wouldn't see that, of course. I was dead, you know."

He shivered slightly and protested that he could remember no more.

I did not press him further, but to satisfy myself that he lay in ignorance of the workings of his own mind, deliberately introduced him to Mortimer Collins' *Transmigration,* and gave him a sketch of the plot before he opened the pages.

"What rot it all is!" he said frankly, at the end of an hour. "I don't understand his nonsense about the Red Planet Mars and the King, and the rest of it. Chuck me the Longfellow again."

I handed him the book and wrote out as much as I could remember of his description of the sea fight, appealing to him from time to time for confirmation of fact or detail. He would answer without raising his eyes from the book, as assuredly as though all his knowledge lay before him on the printed page. I spoke under the normal key of my voice that the current might not be broken, and I know that he was not aware of what he was saying, for his thoughts were out on the sea with Longfellow.

"Charlie," I asked, "when the rowers on the galleys mutinied how did they kill their overseers?"

"Tore up the benches and brained 'em. That happened when a heavy sea was running. An overseer on the lower deck slipped from the center plank and fell among the rowers. They choked him to death against the side of the ship with their chained hands quite quietly, and it was too dark for the other overseer to see what had happened. When he asked he was pulled down too and choked, and the lower deck fought their way up deck by deck, with the pieces of the broken benches banging behind 'em. How they howled!"

"And what happened after that?"

"I don't know. The hero went away—red hair and red beard and all. That was after he had captured our galley, I think."

The sound of my voice irritated him, and he motioned slightly with his left hand as a man does when interruption jars.

"You never told me he was red-headed before, or that he captured your galley," I said, after a discreet interval.

Charlie did not raise his eyes.

"He was as red as a red bear," said he abstractedly. "He came from the north; they said so in the galley when he looked for rowers—not for slaves, but free men. Afterward—years and years afterward—news came from another ship, or else he came back——"

His lips moved in silence. He was rapturously retasting some poem before him.

"Where had he been, then?" I was almost whispering that the sentence might come gently to whichever section of Charlie's brain that was working on my behalf.

"To the Beaches—the Long and Wonderful Beaches!" was the reply after a minute of silence.

"To Furdurstrandi?" I asked, tingling from head to foot.

"Yes, to Furdurstrandi," he pronounced the word in a new fashion. "And I too saw——" The voice failed.

"Do you know what you have said?" I shouted incautiously.

He lifted his eyes, fully roused now. "No!" he snapped. "I wish you'd let a chap go on reading. Hark to this:—

"'But Othere, the old sea-captain,
He neither paused nor stirred
Till the king listened, and then
Once more took up his pen
And wrote down every word.

"'And to the King of the Saxons
In witness of the truth,
Raising his noble head,
He stretched his brown hand and said,
'Behold this walrus tooth.'"

By Jove, what chaps those must have been, to go sailing all over the shop never knowing where they'd fetch the land! Hah!"

"Charlie," I pleaded, "if you'll only be sensible for a minute or two I'll make our hero in our tale every inch as good as Othere."

"Umph! Longfellow wrote that poem. I don't care about writing things any more. I want to read." He was thoroughly out of tune now, and raging over my own ill-luck, I left him.

Conceive yourself at the door of the world's treasure house guarded by a child—an idle irresponsible child playing knucklebones—on whose favor depends the gift of the key, and you will imagine one-half my torment. Till that evening Charlie had spoken nothing that might not lie within the experiences of a Greek galley slave. But now, or there was no virtue in books, he had talked of some desperate adventure of the Vikings, of Thorfin Karlsefne's sailing to Wineland, which is America, in the ninth or tenth century. The battle in the harbor he had seen; and his own death he had described. But this was a much more startling plunge into the past. Was it possible that he had skipped half a dozen lives and was then dimly remembering some episode of a thousand years later? It was a maddening jumble, and the worst of it was that Charlie Mears in his normal condition was the last person in the world to clear it up. I could only wait and watch, but I went to bed that night full of the wildest imaginings. There was nothing that was not possible if Charlie's detestable memory only held good.

I might rewrite the Saga of Thorfin Karlsefne as it had never been written before, might tell the story of the first discovery of America, myself the discoverer. But I was entirely at Charlie's mercy, and so long as there was a three-and-sixpenny Bohn volume within his reach Charlie would not tell. I dared not curse him openly; I hardly dared jog his memory, for I was dealing with the experiences of a thousand years ago, told through the mouth of a boy of today; and a boy of today is affected by every change of tone and gust of opinion, so that he must lie even when he most desires to speak the truth.

I saw no more of Charlie for nearly a week. When next I met him it was in Gracechurch Street with a bill-book chained to his waist. Business took him over London Bridge, and I accompanied him. He was very full of the importance of that book and magnified it. As we passed over the Thames we paused to look at a steamer unloading great slabs of white and brown marble. A barge drifted under the steamer's stern and a lonely ship's cow in that barge bellowed. Charlie's face changed from the face of the bank clerk to that of an unknown and—though he would not have believed this—a much shrewder man. He flung out his arm across the parapet of the bridge and laughing very loudly, said:—

"When they heard *our* bulls bellow the Skroelings ran away!"

I waited only for an instant, but the barge and the cow had disappeared under the bows of the steamer before I answered.

"Charlie, what do you suppose are Skroelings?"

"Never heard of 'em before. They sound like a new kind of sea gull. What a chap you are for asking questions!" he replied. "I have to go to the cashier of the Omnibus Company yonder. Will you wait for me and we can lunch somewhere together? I've a notion for a poem."

"No, thanks. I'm off. You're sure you know nothing about Skroelings?"

"Not unless he's been entered for the Liverpool Handicap." He nodded and disappeared in the crowd.

Now it is written in the Saga of Eric the Red or that of Thorfin Karlsefne, that nine hundred years ago when Karlsefne's galleys came to Leif's booths, which Leif had erected in the unknown land called Markland, which may or may not have been Rhode Island, the Skroelings—and the Lord He knows who these may or may not have been—came to trade with the Vikings, and ran away because they were frightened at the bellowing of the cattle which Thorfin had brought with him in the ships. But what in the world could a Greek slave know of that affair? I wandered up and down among the streets trying to unravel the mystery, and the more I considered it, the more baffling it grew. One thing only seemed certain, and that certainty took away my breath for the moment. If I came to full knowledge of anything at all, it would not be one life of the soul in Charlie Mears's body; but half a dozen—half a dozen several and separate existences spent on blue water in the morning of the world!

Then I walked around the situation.

Obviously if I used my knowledge I should stand alone and unapproachable until all men were as wise as myself. That would be something, but manlike I was ungrateful. It seemed bitterly unfair that Charlie's memory should fail me when I needed it most. Great Powers above—I looked up at them through the fog smoke—did the Lords of Life and Death know what this meant to me? Nothing less than eternal fame of the best kind, that comes from One, and is shared by one alone. I would be content—remembering Clive, I stood astounded at my own moderation—with the mere right to tell one story, to work out one little contribution to the light literature of the day. If Charlie were permitted full recollection for one hour—for sixty short minutes—of existences that had extended over a thousand years—I would forego all profit and honor from all that I should make of his speech. I would take no share in the commotion that would follow throughout the particular corner of the earth that calls itself "the world." The thing should be put forth anonymously. Nay, I would make other men believe that they had written it. They would hire bull-hided self-advertising Englishmen to bellow it abroad. Preachers would found a fresh conduct of life upon it, swearing that it was new and that they had lifted the fear of death from all mankind. Every Orientalist in Europe would patronize it discursively with Sanskrit and Pali texts. Terrible women would invent unclean variants of the men's belief for the elevation of their sisters. Churches and religions would war over it. Between the hailing and re-starting of an omnibus I foresaw the scuffles that would arise among half a dozen denominations all professing "the doctrine of the True Metempsychosis as applied to the world and the New Era"; and saw, too, the respectable English newspapers shying, like frightened kine over the beautiful simplicity of the tale. The mind leaped forward a hundred—two hundred—a thousand years. I saw with sorrow that men would mutilate and garble the story; that rival creeds would turn it upside down till, at last, the western world which clings to the dread of death more closely than the hope of life, would set it aside as an interesting superstition and stampede after some faith so long forgotten that it seemed altogether new. Upon this I changed the terms of the bargain that I would make with the Lords of Life and Death. Only let me know, let me write, the story with sure knowledge that I wrote the truth, and I would burn the manuscript as a solemn sacrifice. Five minutes after the last line was written I would destroy it all. But I must be allowed to write it with absolute certainty.

There was no answer. The flaming colors of an Aquarium poster caught my eye, and I wondered whether it would be wise or prudent to lure Charlie into the hands of the professional mesmerist there, and whether, if he were under his power, he would speak of his past lives. If he did, and if people believed him . . . but Charlie would be frightened and fluttered, or made conceited by the interviews. In either case he would begin to lie, through fear or vanity. He was safest in my own hands.

"They are very funny fools, your English," said a voice at my elbow, and turning around I recognized a casual acquaintance, a young Bengali law student, called Grish Chunder, whose father had sent him to England to become civilized. The old man was a retired native official, and on an income of five pounds a month contrived to allow his son two hundred pounds a year, and the run of his teeth in a city where he could pretend to be the cadet of a royal house, and tell stories of the brutal Indian bureaucrats who ground the faces of the poor.

Grish Chunder was a young, fat, full-bodied Bengali, dressed with scrupulous care in frock coat, tall hat, light trousers, and tan gloves. But I had known him in the days when the brutal Indian Government paid for his university education, and he contributed cheap sedition to *Sachi Durpan*, and intrigued with the wives of his fourteen-year-old schoolmates.

"That is very funny and very foolish," he said nodding at the poster. "I am going down to the Northbrook Club. Will you come too?"

I walked with him for some time. "You are not well," he said. "What is there on your mind? You do not talk."

"Grish Chunder, you've been too well educated to believe in a God, haven't you?"

"Oah, yes, *here!* But when I go home I must conciliate popular superstition, and make ceremonies of purification, and my women will anoint idols."

"And hang up *tulsi* and feast the *purohit*, and take you back into caste again and make a good *khuttri* of you again, you advanced social Free-thinker. And you'll eat *desi* food, and like it all, from the smell in the courtyard to the mustard oil over you."

"I shall very much like it," said Grish Chunder unguardedly. "Once a Hindu—always a Hindu. But I like to know what the English think they know."

"I'll tell you something that one Englishman knows. It's an old tale to you."

I began to tell the story of Charlie in English, but Grish Chunder put a question in the vernacular, and the history went forward naturally in the tongue best suited for its telling. After all, it could never have been told in English. Grish Chunder heard me, nodding from time to time, and then came up to my rooms, where I finished the tale.

"Beshak," he said philosophically. *"Lekin darwaza band hai.* (Without doubt, but the door is shut.) I have heard of this remembering of previous existences among my people. It is of course an old tale with us, but, to happen to an Englishman—a cow-fed *Mlechh*—an outcast. By Jove, that is most peculiar!"

"Outcast yourself, Grish Chunder! You eat cow-beef every day. Let's think the thing over. The boy remembers his incarnations."

"Does he know that?" said Grish Chunder quietly, swinging his legs as he sat on my table. He was speaking in his English now.

"He does not know anything. Would I speak to you if he did? Go on!"

"There is no going on at all. If you tell that to your friends they will say you are mad and put it in the papers. Suppose, now, you prosecute for libel."

"Let's leave that out of the question entirely. Is there any chance of his being made to speak?"

"There is a chance. Oah, yess! But *if* he spoke it would mean that all this world would end now—*instanto*—fall down on your head. These things are not allowed, you know. As I said, the door is shut."

"Not a ghost of a chance?"

"How can there be? You are a Christi-án, and it is forbidden to eat, in your books, of the Tree of Life, or else you would never die. How shall you all fear death if you all know what your friend does not know that he knows? I am afraid to be kicked, but I am not afraid to die, because I know what I know. You are not afraid to be kicked, but you are afraid to die. If you were not, by God! you English would be all over the shop in an hour, upsetting the balances of power, and making commotions. It would not be good. But no fear. He will remember a little and a little less, and he will call it dreams. Then he will forget altogether. When I passed my First Arts Examination in Calcutta that was all in the cram-book on Wordsworth. 'Trailing clouds of glory,' you know."

"This seems to be an exception to the rule."

"There are no exceptions to rules. Some are not so hard-looking as others, but they are all the same when you touch. If this friend of yours said so-and-so and so-and-so, indicating that he remembered all his lost lives, or one piece of a lost life, he would not be in the bank another hour. He would be what you call sacked because he was mad, and they would send him to an asylum for lunatics. You can see that, my friend."

"Of course I can, but I wasn't thinking of him. His name need never appear in the story."

"Ah! I see. That story will never be written. You can try."

"I am going to."

"For your own credit and for the sake of money, *of* course?"

"No. For the sake of writing the story. On my honor that will be all."

"Even then there is no chance. You cannot play with the Gods. It is a very pretty story now. As they say, Let it go on that—I mean at that. Be quick; he will not last long."

"How do you mean?"

"What I say. He has never, so far, thought about a woman."

"Hasn't he, though!" I remembered some of Charlie's confidences.

"I mean no woman has thought about him. When that comes; *bus—hogya*—all up! I know. There are millions of women here. Housemaids, for instance. They kiss you behind doors."

I winced at the thought of my story being ruined by a housemaid. And yet nothing was more probable.

Grish Chunder grinned.

"Yes—also pretty girls—cousins of his house, and perhaps *not* of his house. One kiss that he gives back again and remembers will cure all this nonsense, or else——"

"Or else what? Remember he does not know that he knows."

"I know that. Or else, if nothing happens he will become immersed in the trade and the financial speculations like the rest. It must be so. You can see that it must be so. But the woman will come first, *I* think."

There was a rap at the door, and Charlie charged in impetuously. He had been released from office; and by the look in his eyes I could see that he had come over for a long talk; most probably with poems in his pockets. Charlie's poems were very wearying, but sometimes they led him to talk about the galley.

Grish Chunder looked at him keenly for a minute.

"I beg your pardon," Charlie said uneasily; "I didn't know you had anyone with you."

"I am going," said Grish Chunder.

He drew me into the lobby as he departed.

"That is your man," he said quickly. "I tell you he will never speak all you wish. That is rot—bosh! But he would be most good to make to see things. Suppose now we pretend that it was only play"—I had never seen Grish Chunder so excited—"and pour the ink-pool into his hand. Eh, what do you think? I tell you that he could see *anything* that a man could see. Let me get the ink and the camphor. He is a seer and he will tell us very many things."

"He may be all you say, but I'm not going to trust him to your gods and devils."

"They will not hurt him. He will only feel a little stupid and dull when he wakes up. You have seen boys look into the ink-pool before."

"That is the reason why I am not going to see it any more. You'd better go, Grish Chunder."

He went, insisting far down the staircase that it was throwing away my only chance of looking into the future.

This left me unmoved, for I was concerned for the past, and no peering of hypnotized boys into mirrors and ink-pools would help me to that. But I recognized Grish Chunder's point of view and sympathized with it.

"What a big black brute that was!" said Charlie, when I returned to him. "Well, look here, I've just done a poem; did it instead of playing dominoes after lunch. May I read it?"

"Let me read it to myself."

"Then you miss the proper expression. Besides, you always make my things sound as if the rhymes were all wrong."

"Read it aloud, then. You're like the rest of 'em."

Charlie mouthed me his poem, and it was not much worse than the average of his verses. He had been reading his books faithfully, but he was not pleased when I told him that I preferred my Longfellow undiluted with Charlie.

Then we began to go through the MS. line by line; Charlie parrying every objection and correction with:

"Yes, that may be better, but you don't catch what I'm driving at."

Charlie was, in one way at least, very like one kind of poet.

There was a pencil scrawl at the back of the paper and "What's that?" I said.

"Oh, that's not poetry at all. It's some rot I wrote last night before I went to bed, and it was too much bother to hunt for rhymes; so I made it a sort of blank verse instead."

Here is Charlie's "blank verse":—

"We pulled for you when the wind was against us and the sails were low.

Will you never let us go?

We ate bread and onions when you took towns or ran aboard quickly when you were beaten back by the foe,

The captains walked up and down the deck in fair weather singing songs, but we were below,

We fainted with our chins on the oars and you did not see that we were idle for we still swung to and fro.

Will you never let us go?

The salt made the oar-handles like sharkskin; our knees were cut to the bone with salt cracks; our hair was stuck to our foreheads; and our lips were cut to our gums and you whipped us because we could not row.

Will you never let us go?

But in a little time we shall run out of the portholes as the water runs along the oar-blade, and though you tell the others to row after us you will never catch us till you catch the oar-thresh and tie up the winds in the belly of the sail. Aho!

Will you never let us go?"

"H'm. What's oar-thresh, Charlie?"

"The water washed up by the oars. That's the sort of song they might sing in the galley y'know. Aren't you ever going to finish that story and give me some of the profits?"

"It depends on yourself. If you had only told me more about your hero in the first instance it might have been finished by now. You're so hazy in your notions."

"I only want to give you the general notion of it—the knocking about from place to place and the fighting and all that. Can't you fill in the rest yourself? Make the hero save a girl on a pirate-galley and marry her or do something."

"You're a really helpful collaborator. I suppose the hero went through some few adventures before he married."

"Well, then, make him a very artful card—a low sort of man—a sort of political man who went about making treaties and breaking them—a black-haired chap who hid behind the mast when the fighting began."

"But you said the other day that he was red-haired."

"I couldn't have. Make him black-haired of course. You've no imagination."

Seeing that I had just discovered the entire principles upon which our half-memory falsely called imagination is based, I felt entitled to laugh, but forbore, for the sake of the tale.

"You're right. *You're* the man with imagination. A black-haired chap in a decked ship," I said.

"No, an open ship—like a big boat."

This was maddening.

"Your ship has been built and designed, closed and decked in; you said so yourself," I protested.

"No, no, not that ship. That was open or half-decked because —— By jove you're right! You made me think of the hero as a red-haired chap. Of course if he were red, the ship would be an open one with painted sails."

Surely, I thought, he would remember now that he had served in two galleys at least—in a three-decked Greek one under the black-haired "political man," and again in a Viking's open sea serpent under the man "red as a red bear" who went to Markland. My devil prompted me to speak.

"Why, 'of course,' Charlie?" said I.

"I don't know. Are you making fun of me?"

The current was broken for the time being. I took up a note-book and pretended to make many entries in it.

"It's a pleasure to work with an imaginative chap like yourself," I said, after a pause. "The way that you've brought out the character of the hero is simply wonderful."

"Do you think so?" he answered with a pleased flush. "I often tell myself that there's more in me than my mo—— than people think."

"There's an enormous amount in you."

"Then, won't you let me send an essay on The Ways of Bank Clerks to *Tit-Bits,* and get the guinea prize?"

"That wasn't exactly what I meant, old fellow: perhaps it would be better to wait a little and go ahead with the galley-story."

"Ah, but I sha'n't get the credit of that. *Tit-Bits* would publish my name and address if I win. What are you grinning at? They *would.*"

"I know it. Suppose you go for a walk. I want to look through my notes about our story."

Now this reprehensible youth who left me, a little hurt and put back, might for aught he or I knew have been one of the crew of the Argo—had been certainly slave or comrade to Thorfin Karlsefne. Therefore he was deeply interested in guinea competitions. Remembering what Grish Chunder had said I laughed aloud. The Lords of Life and Death would never allow Charlie Mears to speak with full knowledge of his pasts; and I must even piece out what he had told me with my own poor inventions while Charlie wrote of the ways of bank clerks.

I got together and placed on one file all my notes; and the net result was not cheering. I read them a second time. There was nothing that might not have been compiled at secondhand from other people's books—except, perhaps, the story of the fight in the harbor. The adventures of a Viking had been written many times before; the history of a Greek galley slave was no new thing, and though I wrote both, who could challenge or confirm the accuracy of my details? I might as well tell a tale of two thousand years hence. The Lords of Life and Death were as cunning as Grish Chunder had hinted. They would allow nothing to escape that might trouble or make easy the minds of men. Though I was convinced of this, yet I could not leave the tale alone. Exaltation followed reaction, not once, but twenty times in the next few weeks. My moods varied with the March sunlight and flying clouds. By night or in the beauty of a spring morning I perceived that I could write that tale and shift continents thereby. In the wet windy afternoons, I saw that the tale might indeed be written, but would be nothing more than a faked, false-varnished, sham-rusted piece of Wardour Street work at the end. Then I blessed Charlie in many ways—though it was no fault of his. He seemed to be busy with prize competitions, and I saw less and less of him as the weeks went by and the earth cracked and grew ripe to spring, and the buds swelled in their sheaths. He did not care to read or talk of what he had read, and there was a new ring of self-assertion in his voice. I hardly cared to remind him of the galley when we met; but Charlie alluded to it on every occasion, always as a story from which money was to be made.

"I think I deserve twenty-five per cent, don't I, at least," he said, with beautiful frankness. "I supplied all the ideas, didn't I?"

This greediness for silver was a new side in his nature. I

assumed that it had been developed in the City, where Charlie was picking up the curious nasal drawl of the underbred City man.

"When the thing's done we'll talk about it. I can't make anything of it at present. Red-haired or black-haired hero are equally difficult."

He was sitting by the fire staring at the red coals. "I can't understand what you find so difficult. It's all as clear as mud to me," he replied. A jet of gas puffed out between the bars, took light, and whistled softly. "Suppose we take the red-haired hero's adventures first, from the time that he came south to my galley and captured it and sailed to the Beaches."

I knew better now than to interrupt Charlie. I was out of reach of pen and paper, and dared not move to get them lest I should break the current. The gas jet puffed and whinnied, Charlie's voice dropped almost to a whisper, and he told a tale of the sailing of an open galley to Furdurstrandi, of sunsets on the open sea, seen under the curve of the one sail evening after evening when the galley's beak was notched into the center of the sinking disc, and "we sailed by that for we had no other guide," quoth Charlie. He spoke of a landing on an island and explorations in its woods, where the crew killed three men whom they found asleep under the pines. Their ghosts, Charlie said, followed the galley, swimming and choking in the water, and the crew cast lots and threw one of their number overboard as a sacrifice to the strange gods whom they had offended. Then they ate seaweed when their provisions failed, and their legs swelled, and their leader, the red-haired man, killed two rowers who mutinied, and after a year spent among the woods they set sail for their own country, and a wind that never failed carried them back so safely that they all slept at night. This, and much more Charlie told. Sometimes the voice fell so low that I could not catch the words, though every nerve was on the strain. He spoke of their leader, the red-haired man, as a pagan speaks of his God; for it was he who cheered them and slew them impartially as he thought best for their needs; and it was he who steered them for three days among floating ice, each floe crowded with strange beasts that "tried to sail with us," said

Charlie, "and we beat them back with the handles of the oars."

The gas jet went out, a burnt coal gave way, and the fire settled with a tiny crash to the bottom of the grate. Charlie ceased speaking, and I said no word.

"By jove!" he said at last, shaking his head. "I've been staring at the fire till I'm dizzy. What was I going to say?"

"Something about the galley-book."

"I remember now. It's a quarter of the profits, isn't it?"

"It's anything you like when I've done the tale."

"I wanted to be sure of that. I must go now. I've—I've an appointment." And he left me.

Had not my eyes been held I might have known that that broken muttering over the fire was the swan song of Charlie Mears. But I thought it the prelude to fuller revelation. At last and at last I should cheat the Lords of Life and Death!

When next Charlie came to me I received him with rapture. He was nervous and embarrassed, but his eyes were very full of light, and his lips a little parted.

"I've done a poem," he said; and then, quickly: "it's the best I've ever done. Read it." He thrust it into my hand and retreated to the window.

I groaned inwardly. It would be the work of half an hour to criticize—that is to say praise—the poem sufficiently to please Charlie. Then I had good reason to groan, for Charlie, discarding his favorite centipede meters, had launched into shorter and choppier verse, and verse with a motive at the back of it. This is what I read:—

"The day is most fair, the cheery wind
  Halloos behind the hill
Where he bends the wood as seemeth good,
  And the sapling to his will!
Riot O wind; there is that in my blood
  That would not have thee still!

"She gave me herself, O Earth, O Sky;
  Gray sea, she is mine alone!
Let the sullen boulders hear my cry,
  And rejoice tho' they be but stone!

"Mine! I have won her, O good brown earth,
Make merry! 'Tis hard on Spring;
Make merry; my love is doubly worth
All worship your fields can bring!
Let the hind that tills you feel my mirth
At the early harrowing."

"Yes, it's the early harrowing, past a doubt," I said, with a dread at my heart. Charlie smiled, but did not answer.

"Red cloud of the sunset, tell it abroad;
I am victor. Greet me O Sun,
Dominant master and absolute lord
Over the soul of one!"

"Well?" said Charlie, looking over my shoulder.

I thought it far from well, and very evil indeed, when he silently laid a photograph on the paper—the photograph of a girl with a curly head, and a foolish slack mouth.

"Isn't it—isn't it wonderful?" he whispered, pink to the tips of his ears, wrapped in the rosy mystery of first love. "I didn't know; I didn't think—it came like a thunderclap."

"Yes. It comes like a thunderclap. Are you very happy, Charlie?"

"My God—she—she loves me!" He sat down repeating the last words to himself. I looked at the hairless face, the narrow shoulders already bowed by desk work, and wondered when, where, and how he had loved in his past lives.

"What will your mother say?" I asked cheerfully.

"I don't care a damn what she says."

At twenty the things for which one does not care a damn should, properly, be many, but one must not include mothers in the list. I told him this gently; and he described Her, even as Adam must have described to the newly-named beasts the glory and tenderness and beauty of Eve. Incidentally I learned that She was a tobacconist's assistant with a weakness for pretty dress, and had told him four or five times already that She had never been kissed by a man before.

Charlie spoke on and on, and on; while I, separated from him by thousands of years, was considering the beginnings of things. Now I understood why the Lords of Life and Death shut the doors so carefully behind us. It is that we may not remember our first and most beautiful wooings. Were it not so, our world would be without inhabitants in a hundred years.

"Now, about that galley-story," I said still more cheerfully, in a pause in the rush of the speech.

Charlie looked up as though he had been hit. "The galley —what galley? Good heavens, don't joke, man! This is serious! You don't know how serious it is!"

Grish Chunder was right. Charlie had tasted the love of woman that kills remembrance, and the finest story in the world would never be written.

THE STRANGE RIDE OF MORROWBIE JUKES

Alive or dead—there is no other way.
—NATIVE PROVERB

THERE is no invention about this tale. Jukes by accident stumbled upon a village that is well known to exist, though he is the only Englishman who has been there. A somewhat similar institution used to flourish on the outskirts of Calcutta, and there is a story that if you go into the heart of Bikanir, which is in the heart of the Great Indian Desert, you shall come across not a village but a town where the Dead who did not die but may not live have established their headquarters. And, since it is perfectly true that in the same Desert is a wonderful city where all the rich moneylenders retreat after they have made their fortunes (fortunes so vast that the owners cannot trust even the strong hand of the Government to protect them, but take refuge in the waterless sands), and drive sumptuous C-spring barouches, and buy beautiful girls and decorate their palaces with gold and ivory and Minton tiles and mother-o'-pearl, I do not see why Jukes's tale should not be true. He is a Civil Engineer, with a head for plans and distances and things of that kind, and he certainly would not take the trouble to invent imaginary traps. He could earn more by doing his legitimate work. He never varies the tale in the telling, and grows very hot and indignant when he thinks of the disrespectful treatment he received. He wrote this quite straightforwardly at first, but he has touched it up in places and introduced Moral Reflections: thus:—

In the beginning it all arose from a slight attack of fever. My work necessitated my being in camp for some months between Pakpattan and Mubarakpur—a desolate sandy stretch of country as everyone who has had the misfortune to go there may know. My coolies were neither more nor less exasperating than other gangs, and my work demanded sufficient attention to keep me from moping, had I been inclined to so unmanly a weakness.

On the 23rd December 1884, I felt a little feverish. There was a full moon at the time, and, in consequence, every dog near my tent was baying it. The brutes assembled in twos and threes and drove me frantic. A few days previously I had shot one loud-mouthed singer and suspended his carcass *in terrorem* about fifty yards from my tent door, but his friends fell upon, fought for, and ultimately devoured the body: and, as it seemed to me, sang their hymns of thanksgiving afterward with renewed energy.

The light-headedness which accompanies fever acts differently on different men. My irritation gave way, after a short time, to a fixed determination to slaughter one huge black and white beast who had been foremost in song and first in flight throughout the evening. Thanks to a shaking hand and a giddy head I had already missed him twice with both barrels of my shotgun, when it struck me that my best plan would be to ride him down in the open and finish him off with a hog-spear. This, of course, was merely the semi-delirious notion of a fever-patient; but I remember that it struck me at the time as being eminently practical and feasible.

I therefore ordered my groom to saddle Pornic and bring him around quietly to the rear of my tent. When the pony was ready, I stood at his head prepared to mount and dash out as soon as the dog should again lift up his voice. Pornic, by the way, had not been out of his pickets for a couple of days; the night air was crisp and chilly; and I was armed with a specially long and sharp pair of persuaders with which I had been rousing a sluggish cob that afternoon. You will easily believe, then, that when he was let go he went quickly. In one moment, for the brute bolted as straight as a die, the tent was left far behind, and we were flying over the smooth sandy soil at racing speed. In another we had passed the wretched dog, and I had almost forgotten why it was that I had taken horse and hog-spear.

The delirium of fever and the excitement of rapid motion through the air must have taken away the remnant of my senses. I have a faint recollection of standing upright in my stirrups, and of brandishing my hog-spear at the great white Moon that looked down so calmly on my mad gallop; and of shouting challenges to the camelthorn bushes as they whizzed past. Once or twice, I believe, I swayed forward on Pornic's neck, and literally hung on by my spurs—as the marks next morning showed.

The wretched beast went forward like a thing possessed, over what seemed to be a limitless expanse of moonlit sand. Next, I remember, the ground rose suddenly in front of us, and as we topped the ascent I saw the waters of the Sutlej shining like a silver bar below. Then Pornic blundered heavily on his nose, and we rolled together down some unseen slope.

I must have lost consciousness, for when I recovered I was lying on my stomach in a heap of soft white sand, and the dawn was beginning to break dimly over the edge of the slope down which I had fallen. As the light grew stronger I saw I was at the bottom of a horseshoe-shaped crater of sand, opening on one side directly onto the shoals of the Sutlej. My fever had altogether left me, and, with the exception of a slight dizziness in the head, I felt no bad effects from the fall over night.

Pornic, who was standing a few yards away, was naturally a good deal exhausted, but had not hurt himself in the least. His saddle, a favorite polo one, was much knocked about, and had been twisted under his belly. It took me some time to put him to rights, and in the meantime I had ample opportunities of observing the spot into which I had so foolishly dropped.

At the risk of being considered tedious, I must describe it at length; inasmuch as an accurate mental picture of its peculiarities will be of material assistance in enabling the reader to understand what follows.

Imagine then, as I have said before, a horseshoe-shaped crater of sand with steeply-graded sand walls about thirty-five feet high. (The slope, I fancy, must have been about 65°.) This crater enclosed a level piece of ground about fifty yards long by thirty at its broadest part, with a rude well in the center. Around the bottom of the crater, about three feet from the level of the ground proper, ran a series of eighty-three semicircular, ovoid, square, and multilateral holes, all about three feet at the mouth. Each hole on inspection showed that it was carefully shored internally with driftwood and bamboos, and over the mouth a wooden drip-board projected, like the peak of a jockey's cap, for two feet. No sign of life was visible in these tunnels, but a most sickening stench pervaded the entire amphitheater—a stench fouler than any which my wanderings in Indian villages have introduced me to.

Having remounted Pornic, who was as anxious as I to get back to camp, I rode around the base of the horseshoe to find some place whence an exit would be practicable. The inhabitants, whoever they might be, had not thought fit to put in an appearance, so I was left to my own devices. My first attempt to "rush" Pornic up the steep sandbanks showed me that I had fallen into a trap exactly on the same model as that which the ant-lion sets for its prey. At each step the shifting sand poured down from above in tons, and rattled on the drip-boards of the holes like small shot. A couple of ineffectual charges sent us both rolling down to the bottom, half choked with the torrents of sand; and I was constrained to turn my attention to the riverbank.

Here everything seemed easy enough. The sand hills ran down to the river edge, it is true, but there were plenty of shoals and shallows across which I could gallop Pornic, and find my way back to *terra firma* by turning sharply to the right or the left. As I led Pornic over the sands I was startled by the faint pop of a rifle across the river; and at the same moment a bullet dropped with a sharp *"whit"* close to Pornic's head.

There was no mistaking the nature of the missile—a regulation Martini-Henry "picket." About five hundred yards away a country-boat was anchored in midstream; and a jet of smoke drifting away from its bows in the still morning air showed me whence the delicate attention had come. Was ever a respectable gentleman in such an *impasse?* The treacherous sand slope allowed no escape from a spot which I had visited most involuntarily, and a promenade on the river frontage was the signal for a bombardment from some insane native in a boat. I'm afraid that I lost my temper very much indeed.

Another bullet reminded me that I had better save my breath to cool my porridge; and I retreated hastily up the sands and back to the horseshoe, where I saw that the noise of the rifle had drawn sixty-five human beings from the badger-holes which I had up till that point supposed to be untenanted. I found myself in the midst of a crowd of spectators—about forty men, twenty women, and one child who could not have been more than five years old. They were all scantily clothed in that salmon colored cloth which one associates with Hindu mendicants, and, at first sight, gave me the impression of a band of loathsome *fakirs*. The filth and repulsiveness of the assembly were beyond all description, and I shuddered to think what their life in the badger-holes must be.

Even in these days, when local self-government has destroyed the greater part of a native's respect for a Sahib, I have been accustomed to a certain amount of civility from my inferiors, and on approaching the crowd naturally expected that there would be some recognition of my presence. As a matter of fact there was; but it was by no means what I had looked for.

The ragged crew actually laughed at me—such laughter I hope I may never hear again. They cackled, yelled, whistled, and howled as I walked into their midst; some of them literally throwing themselves down on the ground in convulsions of unholy mirth. In a moment I had let go Pornic's head, and, irritated beyond expression at the morning's adventure, commenced cuffing those nearest to me with all the force I could. The wretches dropped under my blows like ninepins, and the laughter gave place to wails for mercy; while those yet untouched clasped me around the knees, imploring me in all sorts of uncouth tongues to spare them.

In the tumult, and just when I was feeling very much ashamed of myself for having thus easily given way to my temper, a thin, high voice murmured in English from behind my shoulder: "Sahib! Sahib! Do you not know me? Sahib, it is Gunga Dass, the telegraph-master."

I spun around quickly and faced the speaker.

Gunga Dass (I have, of course, no hesitation in mentioning the man's real name) I had known four years before as a Deccanee Brahmin lent by the Punjab Government to one of the Khalsia States. He was in charge of a branch telegraph office there, and when I had last met him was a jovial, full-stomached, portly Government servant with a marvelous capacity for making bad puns in English—a peculiarity which made me remember him long after I had forgotten his services to me in his official capacity. It is seldom that a Hindu makes English puns.

Now, however, the man was changed beyond all recognition. Caste mark, stomach, slate-colored continuations, and unctuous speech were all gone. I looked at a withered skeleton, turbanless and almost naked, with long matted hair and deep-set codfish-eyes. But for a crescent-shaped scar on the left cheek—the result of an accident for which I was responsible—I should never have known him. But it was indubitably Gunga Dass, and—for this I was thankful—an English-speaking native who might at least tell me the meaning of all that I had gone through that day.

The crowd retreated to some distance as I turned toward the miserable figure, and ordered him to show me some method of escaping from the crater. He held a freshly-plucked crow in his hand, and in reply to my question climbed slowly on a platform of sand which ran in front of the holes, and commenced lighting a fire there in silence. Dried bents, sand-poppies, and driftwood burn quickly; and I derived much consolation from the fact that he lit them with an ordinary sulphur match. When they were in a bright glow, and the crow was neatly spitted in front thereof, Gunga Dass began without a word of preamble:—

"There are only two kinds of men, Sar. The alive and the dead. When you are dead you are dead, but when you are alive you live." (Here the crow demanded his attention for an instant as it twirled before the fire in danger of being burnt to a cinder.) "If you die at home and do not die when you come to the ghât to be burned you come here."

The nature of the reeking village was made plain now, and all that I had known or read of the grostesque and the horrible paled before the fact just communicated by the ex-Brahmin. Sixteen years ago, when I first landed in Bombay, I had been told by a wandering Armenian of the existence, somewhere in India, of a place to which such Hindus as had the misfortune to recover from trance or catalepsy were conveyed and kept, and I recollect laughing heartily at what I was then pleased to consider a traveler's tale. Sitting at the bottom of the sand trap, the memory of Watson's Hotel, with its swinging punkahs, white-robed servants and the sallow-faced Armenian, rose up in my mind as vividly as a photograph, and I burst into a loud fit of laughter. The contrast was too absurd!

Gunga Dass, as he bent over the unclean bird, watched me curiously. Hindus seldom laugh, and his surroundings were not such as to move him that way. He removed the crow solemnly from the wooden spit and as solemnly devoured it. Then he continued his story, which I give in his own words:—

"In epidemics of the cholera you are carried to be burned almost before you are dead. When you come to the riverside the cold air, perhaps, makes you alive, and then, if you are only little alive, mud is put on your nose and mouth and you die conclusively. If you are rather more alive, more mud is put; but if you are too lively they let you go and take you away. I was too lively, and made protestation with anger against the indignities that they endeavored to press upon me. In those days I was Brahmin and proud man. Now I am dead man and eat"—here he eyed the well-gnawed breast bone with the first sign of emotion that I had seen in him since we met—"crows, and—other things. They took me from my sheets when they saw that I was too lively and gave me medicines for one week, and I survived successfully. Then they sent me by rail from my place to Okara Station, with a man to take care of me; and at Okara Station we met two other men, and they conducted us three on camels, in the night, from Okara Station to this place, and they propelled me from the top to the bottom, and the other two succeeded, and I have been here ever since two and a half years. Once I was Brahmin and proud man, and now I eat crows."

"There is no way of getting out?"

"None of what kind at all. When I first came I made experiments frequently and all the others also, but we have always succumbed to the sand which is precipitated upon our heads."

"But surely," I broke in at this point, "the river front is open, and it is worth while dodging the bullets; while at night——"

I had already matured a rough plan of escape which a natural instinct of selfishness forbade me sharing with Gunga Dass. He, however, divined my unspoken thought almost as soon as it was formed; and, to my intense astonishment, gave vent to a long low chuckle of derision—the laughter, be it understood, of a superior or at least of an equal.

"You will not"—he had dropped the Sir after his first sentence—"make any escape that way. But you can try. I have tried. Once only."

The sensation of nameless terror which I had in vain attempted to strive against, overmastered me completely. My long fast—it was now close upon ten o'clock, and I had eaten nothing since tiffin on the previous day—combined with the violent agitation of the ride had exhausted me, and I verily believe that, for a few minutes, I acted as one mad. I hurled myself against the sand-slope. I ran around the base of the crater, blaspheming and praying by turns. I crawled out among the sedges of the river front, only to be driven back each time in an agony of nervous dread by the rifle-bullets which cut up the sand around me—for I dared not face the death of a mad dog among that hideous crowd—and so fell, spent and raving, at the curb of the well. No one had taken the slightest notice of an exhibition which makes me blush hotly even when I think of it now.

Two or three men trod on my panting body as they drew water, but they were evidently used to this sort of thing, and had no time to waste upon me. Gunga Dass, indeed, when he had banked the embers of his fire with sand, was at some pains to throw half a cupful of fetid water over my head, an attention for which I could have fallen on my knees and thanked him, but he was laughing all the while in the same mirthless, wheezy key that greeted me on my first attempt to force the shoals. And so, in a half-fainting state, I lay till noon. Then, being only a man after all, I felt hungry, and said as much to Gunga Dass, whom I had begun to regard as my natural protector. Following the impulse of the outer world when dealing with natives, I put my hand into my pocket and drew out four annas. The absurdity of the gift struck me at once, and I was about to replace the money.

Gunga Dass, however, cried: "Give me the money, all you have, or I will get help, and we will kill you!"

A Briton's first impulse, I believe, is to guard the contents of his pockets; but a moment's thought showed me of the folly of differing with the one man who had it in his power to make me comfortable; and with whose help it was possible that I might eventually escape from the crater. I gave him all the money in my possession, Rs. 9-8-5—nine rupees, eight annas, and five pie—for I always keep small change as *bakshish* when I am in camp. Gunga Dass clutched the coins, and hid them at once in his ragged loincloth, looking around to assure himself that no one had observed us.

"*Now* I will give you something to eat," said he.

What pleasure my money could have given him I am unable to say; but inasmuch as it did please him I was not sorry that I had parted with it so readily, for I had no doubt that he would have had me killed if I had refused. One does not protest against the doings of a den of wild beasts; and my companions were lower than any beasts. While I ate what Gunga Dass had provided, a coarse *chapatti* and a cupful of the foul well-water, the people showed not the faintest sign of curiosity—that curiosity which is so rampant, as a rule, in an Indian village.

I could even fancy that they despised me. At all events they treated me with the most chilling indifference, and Gunga Dass was nearly as bad. I plied him with questions about the terrible village, and received extremely unsatisfactory answers. So far as I could gather, it had been in existence from time immemorial—whence I concluded that it was at least a century old—and during that time no one had ever been known to escape from it. [I had to control myself here with both hands, lest the blind terror should lay hold of me a second time and drive me raving round the crater.] Gunga Dass took a malicious pleasure in emphasizing this point and in watching me wince. Nothing that I could do would induce him to tell me who the mysterious "They" were.

"It is so ordered," he would reply, "and I do not yet know anyone who has disobeyed the orders."

"Only wait till my servant finds that I am missing," I retorted, "and I promise you that this place shall be cleared off the face of the earth, and I'll give you a lesson in civility, too, my friend."

"Your servants would be torn in pieces before they came near this place; and, besides, you are dead, my dear friend. It is not your fault, of course, but nonetheless you are dead *and* buried."

At irregular intervals supplies of food, I was told, were dropped down from the land side into the amphitheater, and the inhabitants fought for them like wild beasts. When a man felt his death coming on he retreated to his lair and died there. The body was sometimes dragged out of the hole and thrown onto the sand, or allowed to rot where it lay.

The phrase "thrown onto the sand" caught my attention, and I asked Gunga Dass whether this sort of thing was not likely to breed a pestilence.

"That," said he, with another of his wheezy chuckles, "you may see for yourself subsequently. You will have much time to make observations."

Whereat, to his great delight, I winced once more and hastily continued the conversation: "And how do you live here from day to day? What do you do?" The question elicited exactly the same answer as before—coupled with the information that "this place is like your European heaven; there is neither marrying nor giving in marriage."

Gunga Dass had been educated at a Mission School, and, as he himself admitted, had he only changed his religion "like a wise man," might have avoided the living grave which was now his portion. But as long as I was with him I fancy he was happy.

Here was a Sahib, a representative of the dominant race, helpless as a child and completely at the mercy of his native neighbors. In a deliberate lazy way he set himself to torture me as a schoolboy would devote a rapturous half-hour to watching the agonies of an impaled beetle, or as a ferret in a blind burrow might glue himself comfortably to the neck of a rabbit. The burden of his conversation was that there was no escape "of no kind whatever," and that I should stay here till I died and was "thrown onto the sand." If it were possible to forejudge the conversation of the Damned on the advent of a new soul in their abode, I should say that they would speak as Gunga Dass did to me throughout that long afternoon. I was powerless to protest or answer; all my energies being devoted to a struggle against the inexplicable terror that threatened to overwhelm me again and again. I can compare the feeling to nothing except the struggle of a man against the overpowering nausea of the Channel passage—only my agony was of the spirit and infinitely more terrible.

As the day wore on, the inhabitants began to appear in full strength to catch the rays of the afternoon sun, which were now sloping in at the mouth of the crater. They assembled by little knots, and talked among themselves without even throwing a glance in my direction. About four o'clock, so far as I could judge, Gunga Dass rose and dived into his lair for a moment, emerging with a live crow in his hands. The wretched bird was in a most draggled and deplorable condition, but seemed to be in no way afraid of its master. Advancing cautiously to the river front, Gunga Dass stepped from tussock to tussock until he had reached a smooth patch of sand directly in the line of the boat's fire. The occupants of the boat took no notice. Here he stopped, and, with a couple of dexterous turns of the wrist, pegged the bird on its back with outstretched wings. As was only natural, the crow began to shriek at once and beat the air with its claws. In a few seconds the clamor had attracted the attention of a bevy of wild crows on a shoal a few hundred yards away, where they were discussing something that looked like a corpse. Half a dozen crows flew over at once to see what was going on, and also, as it proved, to attack the pinioned bird. Gunga Dass, who had lain down on a tussock, motioned to me to be quiet, though I fancy this was a needless precaution. In a moment, and before I could see how it happened, a wild crow, who had grappled with the shrieking and helpless bird, was entangled in the latter's claws, swiftly disengaged by Gunga Dass, and pegged down beside its companion in adversity. Curiosity, it seemed, overpowered the rest of the flock, and almost before Gunga Dass and I had time to withdraw to the tussock, two more captives were struggling in the upturned claws of the decoys. So the chase—if I can give it so dignified a name—continued until Gunga Dass had captured seven crows. Five of them he throttled at once, reserving two for further operations another day. I was a good deal impressed by this, to me, novel method of securing food, and complimented Gunga Dass on his skill.

"It is nothing to do," said he. "Tomorrow you must do it for me. You are stronger than I am."

This calm assumption of superiority upset me not a little, and I answered peremptorily: "Indeed, you old ruffian? What do you think I have given you money for?"

"Very well," was the unmoved reply. "Perhaps not tomorrow, nor the day after, nor subsequently; but in the end, and for many years, you will catch crows and eat crows, and you will thank your European God that you have crows to catch and eat."

I could have cheerfully strangled him for this; but judged it best under the circumstances to smother my resentment. An hour later I was eating one of the crows; and, as Gunga Dass had said, thanking my God that I had a crow to eat. Never as long as I live shall I forget that evening meal. The whole population were squatting on the hard sand platform opposite their dens, huddled over tiny fires of refuse and dried rushes. Death, having once laid his hand upon these men and foreborne to strike, seemed to stand aloof from them now; for most of our company were old men, bent and worn and twisted with years, and women aged to all appearance as the Fates themselves. They sat together in knots and talked—God only knows what they found to discuss—in low equable tones, curiously in contrast to the strident babble with which natives are accustomed to make day hideous. Now and then an access of that sudden fury which had possessed me in the morning would lay hold on a man or woman; and with yells and imprecations the sufferer would attack the steep slope until, baffled and bleeding, he fell back on the platform incapable of moving a limb. The others would never even raise their eyes when this happened, as men too well aware of the futility of their fellows' attempts and wearied with their useless repetition. I saw four such outbursts in the course of that evening.

Gunga Dass took an eminently businesslike view of my situation, and while we were dining—I can afford to laugh at the recollection now, but it was painful enough at the time—propounded the terms of which he would consent to "do" for me. My nine rupees eight annas, he argued, at the rate of three annas a day, would provide me with food for fifty-one days, or about seven weeks; that is to say, he would be willing to cater for me for that length of time. At the end of it I was to look after myself. For a further consideration—*videlicet* my boots—he would be willing to allow me to occupy the den next to his own, and would supply me with as much dried grass for bedding as he could spare.

"Very well, Gunga Dass," I replied; "to the first terms I cheerfully agree, but, as there is nothing on earth to prevent my killing you as you sit here and taking everything that you have" (I thought of the two invaluable crows at the time), "I flatly refuse to give you my boots and shall take whichever den I please."

The stroke was a bold one, and I was glad when I saw that it had succeeded. Gunga Dass changed his tone immediately, and disavowed all intention of asking for my boots. At the time it did not strike me as at all strange that I, a Civil Engineer, a man of thirteen years' standing in the Service, and, I trust, an average Englishman, should thus calmly threaten murder and violence against the man who had, for a consideration it is true, taken me under his wing. I had left the world, it seemed, for centuries. I was as certain then as I am now of my own existence, that in the accursed settlement there was no law save that of the strongest; that the living dead men had thrown behind them every canon of the world which had cast them out; and that I had to depend for my own life on my strength and vigilance alone. The crew of the ill-fated *Mignonette* are the only men who would understand my frame of mind. "At present," I argued to myself, "I am strong and a match for six of these wretches. It is imperatively necessary that I should, for my own sake, keep both health and strength until the hour of my release comes—if it ever does."

Fortified with these resolutions, I ate and drank as much as I could, and made Gunga Dass understand that I intended to be his master, and that the least sign of insubordination on his part would be visited with the only punishment I had it in my power to inflict—sudden and violent death. Shortly after this I went to bed. That is to say, Gunga Dass gave me a double armful of dried bents which I thrust down the mouth of the lair to the right of his, and followed myself, feet foremost; the hole running about nine feet into the sand with a slight downward inclination, and being neatly shored with timbers. From my den, which faced the river front, I was able to watch the waters of the Sutlej flowing past under the light of a young moon and compose myself to sleep as best I might.

The horrors of that night I shall never forget. My den was nearly as narrow as a coffin, and the sides had been worn smooth and greasy by the contact of innumerable naked bodies, added to which it smelled abominably. Sleep was altogether out of the question to one in my excited frame of mind. As the night wore on, it seemed that the entire amphitheater was filled with legions of unclean devils that, trooping up from the shoals below, mocked the unfortunates in their lairs.

Personally I am not of an imaginative temperament—very few Engineers are—but on that occasion I was as completely prostrated with nervous terror as any woman. After half an hour or so, however, I was able once more to calmly review my chances of escape. Any exit by the steep sand walls was, of course, impracticable. I had been thoroughly convinced of this some time before. It was possible, just possible, that I might, in the uncertain moonlight, safely run the gauntlet of the rifle shots. The place was so full of terror for me that I was prepared to undergo any risk in leaving it. Imagine my delight, then, when after creeping stealthily to the river front I found that the infernal boat was not there. My freedom lay before me in the next few steps!

By walking out to the first shallow pool that lay at the foot of the projecting left horn of the horseshoe, I could wade across, turn the flank of the crater, and make my way inland. Without a moment's hesitation I marched briskly past the tussocks where Gunga Dass had snared the crows, and out in the direction of the smooth white sand beyond. My first step from the tufts of dried grass showed me how utterly futile was any hope of escape; for, as I put my foot down, I felt an indescribable drawing, sucking motion of the sand below. Another moment and my leg was swallowed up nearly to the knee. In the moonlight the whole surface of the sand seemed to be shaken with devilish delight at my disappointment. I struggled clear, sweating with terror and exertion, back to the tussocks behind me and fell on my face.

My only means of escape from the semicircle was protected with a quicksand!

How long I lay I have not the faintest idea; but I was roused at the last by the malevolent chuckle of Gunga Dass at my ear. "I would advise you, Protector of the Poor" (the ruffian was speaking English) "to return to your house. It is unhealthy to lie down here. Moreover, when the boat returns, you will most certainly be rifled at." He stood over me in the dim light of the dawn, chuckling and laughing to himself. Suppressing my first impulse to catch the man by the neck and throw him onto the quicksand, I rose sullenly and followed him to the platform below the burrows.

Suddenly, and futilely as I thought while I spoke, I asked: "Gunga Dass, what is the good of the boat if I can't get out *anyhow?*" I recollect that even in my deepest trouble I had been speculating vaguely on the waste of ammunition in guarding an already well protected foreshore.

Gunga Dass laughed again and made answer: "They have the boat only in daytime. It is for the reason that *there is a way*. I hope we shall have the pleasure of your company for much longer time. It is a pleasant spot when you have been here some years and eaten roast crow long enough."

I staggered, numbed and helpless, toward the fetid burrow allotted to me, and fell asleep. An hour or so later I was awakened by a piercing scream—the shrill, high-pitched scream of a horse in pain. Those who have once heard that will never forget the sound. I found some little difficulty in scrambling out of the burrow. When I was in the open, I saw Pornic, my poor old Pornic, lying dead on the sandy soil. How they had killed him I cannot guess. Gunga Dass explained that horse was better than crow, and "greatest good of greatest number is political maxim. We are now Republic, Mister Jukes, and you are entitled to a fair share of the beast. If you like, we will pass a vote of thanks. Shall I propose?"

Yes, we were a Republic indeed! A Republic of wild beasts penned at the bottom of a pit, to eat and fight and sleep till we died. I attempted no protest of any kind, but sat down and stared at the hideous sight in front of me. In less time almost than it takes me to write this, Pornic's body was divided, in some unclean way or other; the men and women had dragged the fragments onto the platform and were preparing their morning meal. Gunga Dass cooked mine. The almost irresistible impulse to fly at the sand walls until I was wearied laid hold of me afresh, and I had to struggle against it with all my might. Gunga Dass was offensively jocular till I told him that if he addressed another remark of any kind whatever to me I should strangle him where he sat. This silenced him till silence became insupportable, and I bade him say something.

"You will live here till you die like the other Feringhi," he said coolly, watching me over the fragment of gristle that he was gnawing.

"What other Sahib, you swine? Speak at once, and don't stop to tell me a lie."

"He is over there," answered Gunga Dass, pointing to a burrow-mouth about four doors to the left of my own. "You can see for yourself. He died in the burrow as you will die, and I will die, and as all these men and women and the one child will also die."

"For pity's sake tell me all you know about him. Who was he? When did he come, and when did he die?"

This appeal was a weak step on my part. Gunga Dass only leered and replied: "I will not—unless you give me something first."

Then I recollected where I was, and struck the man between the eyes, partially stunning him. He stepped down from the platform at once, and, cringing and fawning and weeping and attempting to embrace my feet, led me around to the burrow which he had indicated.

"I know nothing whatever about the gentleman. Your God be my witness that I do not. He was as anxious to escape as you were, and he was shot from the boat, though we all did all things to prevent him from attempting. He was shot here." Gunga Dass laid his hand on his lean stomach and bowed to the earth.

"Well, and what then? Go on!"

"And then—and then, Your Honor, we carried him into his

house and gave him water, and put wet cloths on the wound, and he laid down in his house and gave up the ghost."

"In how long? In how long?"

"About half an hour, after he received his wound. I call Vishn to witness," yelled the wretched man, "that I did everything for him. Everything which was possible, that I did!"

He threw himself down on the ground and clasped my ankles. But I had my doubts about Gunga Dass's benevolence, and kicked him off as he lay protesting.

"I believe you robbed him of everything he had. But I can find out in a minute or two. How long was the Sahib here?"

"Nearly a year and a half. I think he must have gone mad. But hear me swear, Protector of the Poor! Won't Your Honor hear me swear that I never touched an article that belonged to him? What is Your Worship going to do?"

I had taken Gunga Dass by the waist and had hauled him onto the platform opposite the deserted burrow. As I did so I thought of my wretched fellow-prisoner's unspeakable misery among all these horrors for eighteen months, and the final agony of dying like a rat in a hole, with a bullet wound in the stomach. Gunga Dass fancied I was going to kill him and howled pitifully. The rest of the population, in the plethora that follows a full flesh meal, watched us without stirring.

"Go inside, Gunga Dass," said I, "and fetch it out."

I was feeling sick and faint with horror now. Gunga Dass nearly rolled off the platform and howled aloud.

"But I am Brahmin, Sahib—a high-caste Brahmin. By your soul, by your father's soul, do not make me do this thing!"

"Brahmin or no Brahmin, by my soul and my father's soul, in you go!" I said, and, seizing him by the shoulders, I crammed his head into the mouth of the burrow, kicked the rest of him in, and, sitting down, covered my face with my hands.

At the end of a few minutes I heard a rustle and a creak; then Gunga Dass in a sobbing, choking whisper speaking to himself; then a soft thud—and I uncovered my eyes.

The dry sand had turned the corpse entrusted to its keeping into a yellow-brown mummy. I told Gunga Dass to stand off while I examined it. The body—clad in an olive-green hunting-suit much stained and worn, with leather pads on the shoulders

—was that of a man between thirty and forty, above middle height, with light, sandy hair, long mustache, and a rough unkempt beard. The left canine of the upper jaw was missing, and a portion of the lobe of the right ear was gone. On the second finger of the left hand was a ring—a shield-shaped bloodstone set in gold, with a monogram that might have been either "B.K." or "B.L." On the third finger of the right hand was a silver ring in the shape of a coiled cobra, much worn and tarnished. Gunga Dass deposited a handful of trifles he had picked out of the burrow at my feet, and, covering the face of the body with my handkerchief, I turned to examine these. I give the full list in the hope that it may lead to the identification of the unfortunate man:—

1. Bowl of a briarwood pipe, serrated at the edge; much worn and blackened; bound with string at the screw.
2. Two patent-lever keys; wards of both broken.
3. Tortoise-shell-handled penknife, silver or nickel, name-plate, marked with monogram "B.K."
4. Envelope, postmark undecipherable, bearing a Victorian stamp, addressed to "Miss Mon——" (rest illegible)—"ham" —"nt."
5. Imitation crocodile-skin notebook with pencil. First forty-five pages blank; four and a half illegible; fifteen others filled with private memoranda relating chiefly to three persons—a Mrs. L. Singleton, abbreviated several times to "Lot Single," "Mrs. S. May," and "Garmison," referred to in places as "Jerry" or "Jack."
6. Handle of small-sized hunting-knife. Blade snapped short. Buck's horn, diamond-cut, with swivel and ring on the butt; fragment of cotton cord attached.

It must not be supposed that I inventoried all these things on the spot as fully as I have here written them down. The notebook first attracted my attention, and I put it in my pocket with a view to studying it later on. The rest of the articles I conveyed to my burrow for safety's sake, and there, being a methodical man, I inventoried them. I then returned to the corpse and ordered Gunga Dass to help me to carry it out to the river front. While we were engaged in this, the exploded shell of an old brown cartridge dropped out of one of the pockets and rolled at my feet. Gunga Dass had not seen it; and I fell to thinking that a man does not carry exploded cartridge cases, especially "browns," which will not bear loading twice, about with him when shooting. In other words, that cartridge case had been fired inside the crater. Consequently there must be a gun somewhere. I was on the verge of asking Gunga Dass, but checked myself, knowing that he would lie. We laid the body down on the edge of the quicksand by the tussocks. It was my intention to push it out and let it be swallowed up—the only possible mode of burial that I could think of. I ordered Gunga Dass to go away.

Then I gingerly put the corpse out on the quicksand. In doing so, it was lying face downward, I tore the frail and rotten khaki shooting coat open, disclosing a hideous cavity in the back. I have already told you that the dry sand had, as it were, mummified the body. A moment's glance showed that the gaping hole had been caused by a gunshot wound; the gun must have been fired with the muzzle almost touching the back. The shooting coat, being intact, had been drawn over the body after death, which must have been instantaneous. The secret of the poor wretch's death was plain to me in a flash. Someone of the crater, presumably Gunga Dass, must have shot him with his own gun—the gun that fitted the brown cartridges. He had never attempted to escape in the face of the rifle-fire from the boat.

I pushed the corpse out hastily, and saw it sink from sight literally in a few seconds. I shuddered as I watched. In a dazed, half-conscious way I turned to peruse the notebook. A stained and discolored slip of paper had been inserted between the binding and the back, and dropped out as I opened the pages. This is what it contained: *"Four out from crow-clump; three left; nine out; two right; three back; two left; fourteen out; two left; seven out; one left; nine back; two right; six back; four right; seven back."* The paper had been burned and charred at the edges. What it meant I could not understand. I sat down on the dried bents turning it over and over between my fingers, until I was aware of Gunga Dass standing immediately behind me with glowing eyes and outstretched hands.

"Have you got it?" he panted. "Will you not let me look at it also? I swear that I will return it."

"Got what? Return what?" I asked.

"That which you have in your hands. It will help us both." He stretched out his long, birdlike talons, trembling with eagerness.

"I could never find it," he continued. "He had secreted it about his person. Therefore I shot him, but nevertheless I was unable to obtain it."

Gunga Dass had quite forgotten his little fiction about the rifle-bullet. I heard him calmly. Morality is blunted by consorting with the Dead who are alive.

"What on earth are you raving about? What is it you want me to give you?"

"The piece of paper in the notebook. It will help us both. Oh, you fool! You fool! Can you not see what it will do for us? We shall escape!"

His voice rose almost to a scream, and he danced with excitement before me. I own I was moved at the chance of getting away.

"Do you mean to say that this slip of paper will help us? What does it mean?"

"Read it aloud! Read it aloud! I beg and I pray to you to read it aloud."

I did so. Gunga Dass listened delightedly, and drew an irregular line in the sand with his fingers.

"See now! It was the length of his gun barrels without the stock. I have those barrels. Four gun barrels out from the place where I caught crows. Straight out do you mind me? Then three left. Ah! Now well I remember how that man worked it out night after night. Then nine out, and so on. Out is always straight before you across the quicksand to the North. He told me so before I killed him."

"But if you knew all this why didn't you get out before?"

"I did *not* know it. He told me that he was working it out a year and a half ago, and how he was working it out night after night when the boat had gone away, and he could get out near the quicksand safely. Then he said that we would get away together. But I was afraid that he would leave me behind one night when he had worked it all out, and so I shot him. Besides, it is not advisable that the men who once get in here should escape. Only I, and *I* am a Brahmin."

The hope of escape had brought Gunga Dass's caste back to him. He stood up, walked about and gesticulated violently. Eventually I managed to make him talk soberly, and he told me how this Englishman had spent six months night after night in exploring, inch by inch, the passage across the quicksand; how he had declared it to be simplicity itself up to within about twenty yards of the riverbank after turning the flank of the left horn of the horseshoe. This much he had evidently not completed when Gunga Dass shot him with his own gun.

In my frenzy of delight at the possibilities of escape I recollect shaking hands wildly with Gunga Dass, after we had decided that we were to make an attempt to get away that very night. It was weary work waiting throughout the afternoon.

About ten o'clock, as far as I could judge, when the Moon had just risen above the lip of the crater, Gunga Dass made a move for his burrow to bring out the gun barrels whereby to measure our path. All the other wretched inhabitants had retired to their lairs long ago. The guardian boat drifted downstream some hours before, and we were utterly alone by the crow-clump. Gunga Dass, while carrying the gun barrels, let slip the piece of paper which was to be our guide. I stooped down hastily to recover it, and, as I did so, I was aware that the creature was aiming a violent blow at the back of my head with the gun barrels. It was too late to turn around. I must have received the blow somewhere on the nape of my neck, for I fell senseless at the edge of the quicksand.

When I recovered consciousness, the Moon was going down, and I was sensible of intolerable pain in the back of my head. Gunga Dass had disappeared and my mouth was full of blood. I lay down again and prayed that I might die without more ado. Then the unreasoning fury which I have before mentioned laid hold upon me, and I staggered inland toward the walls of the crater. It seemed that someone was calling to me in a whisper— "Sahib! Sahib! Sahib!" exactly as my bearer used to call me in the mornings. I fancied that I was delirious until a handful of sand fell at my feet. Then I looked up and saw a head peering down into the amphitheater—the head of Dunnoo, my dog-boy, who attended to my collies. As soon as he had attracted my attention, he held up his hand and showed a rope. I motioned, staggering to and fro the while, that he should throw it down. It was a couple of leather punkah ropes knotted together, with a loop at one end. I slipped the loop over my head and under my arms; heard Dunnoo urge something forward; was conscious that I was being dragged, face downward, up the steep sand-slope, and the next instant found myself choked and half-fainting on the sand hills overlooking the crater. Dunnoo, with his face ashy gray in the moonlight, implored me not to stay but to get back to my tent at once.

It seems that he had tracked Pornic's footprints fourteen miles across the sands to the crater; had returned and told my servants, who flatly refused to meddle with anyone, white or black, once fallen into the hideous Village of the Dead; whereupon Dunnoo had taken one of my ponies and a couple of punkah ropes, returned to the crater, and hauled me out as I have described.

A MATTER OF FACT

And if ye doubt the tale I tell,
Steer through the South Pacific swell;
Go where the branching coral hives
Unending strife of endless lives,
Where, leagued about the 'wildered boat,
The rainbow jellies fill and float;
And, lilting where the laver lingers,
The starfish trips on all her fingers;
Where, 'neath his myriad spines ashock,
The sea-egg ripples down the rock;
An orange wonder dimly guessed,
From darkness where the cuttles rest,
Moored o'er the darker deeps that hide
The blind white Sea-snake and his bride;
Who, drowsing, nose the long-lost ships
Let down through darkness to their lips.

—THE PALMS

ONCE a priest always a priest; once a Mason always a Mason; but once a journalist always and forever a journalist.

There were three of us, all newspaper men, the only passengers on a little tramp-steamer that ran where her owners told her to go. She had once been in the Bilbao iron ore business, had been lent to the Spanish Government for service at Manilla; and was ending her days in the Cape Town coolie-trade, with occasional trips to Madagascar and even as far as England. We found her going to Southampton in ballast, and shipped in her because the fares were nominal. There was Keller, of an American paper, on his way back to the States from palace executions in Madagascar; there was a burly half Dutchman, called Zuyland, who owned and edited a paper up country near Johannesburg; and there was myself, who had solemnly put away all journalism, vowing to forget that I had ever known the difference between an imprint and a stereo advertisement.

Three minutes after Keller spoke to me, as the *Rathmines* cleared Cape Town, I had forgotten the aloofness I desired to

—"It was not human, and it certainly was not animal, for it did not belong to this earth as known to man."

feign, and was in heated discussion on the immorality of expanding telegrams beyond a certain fixed point. Then Zuyland came out of his stateroom, and we were all at home instantly, because we were men of the same profession needing no introduction. We annexed the boat formally, broke open the passengers' bath-room door—on the Manilla lines the Dons do not wash—cleaned out the orange peel and cigar-ends at the bottom of the bath, hired a Lascar to shave us throughout the voyage, and then asked each other's names.

Three ordinary men would have quarreled through sheer boredom before they reached Southampton. We, by virtue of our craft, were anything but ordinary men. A large percentage of the tales of the world, the thirty-nine that cannot be told to ladies and the one that can, are common property coming of a common stock. We told them all, as a matter of form, with all their local and specific variants which are surprising. Then came, in the intervals of steady card-play, more personal histories of adventure and things seen and reported; panics among white folk, when the blind terror ran from man to man on the Brooklyn Bridge, and the people crushed each other to death they knew not why; fires, and faces that opened and shut their mouths horribly at red-hot window frames; wrecks in frost and snow, reported from the sleet-sheathed rescue tug at the risk of frostbite; long rides after diamond thieves; skirmishes on the veldt and in municipal committees with the Boers; glimpses of lazy, tangled Cape politics and the mule-rule in the Transvaal; card-tales, horse-tales, woman-tales by the score and the half hundred; till the first mate, who had seen more than us all put together, but lacked words to clothe his tales with, sat open-mouthed far into the dawn.

When the tales were done we picked up cards till a curious hand or a chance remark made one or other of us say, "That reminds me of a man who—or a business which—" and the anecdotes would continue while the *Rathmines* kicked her way northward through the warm water.

In the morning of one specially warm night we three were sitting immediately in front of the wheel-house where an old Swedish boatswain whom we called "Frithiof the Dane" was at the wheel pretending that he could not hear our stories. Once or twice Frithiof spun the spokes curiously, and Keller lifted his head from a long chair to ask, "What is it? Can't you get any pull on her?"

"There is a feel in the water," said Frithiof, "that I cannot understand. I think that we run downhills or somethings. She steers bad this morning."

Nobody seems to know the laws that govern the pulse of the big waters. Sometimes even a landsman can tell that the solid ocean is atilt, and that the ship is working herself up a long unseen slope; and sometimes the captain says, when neither full steam nor fair wind justify the length of a day's run, that the ship is sagging downhill; but how these ups and downs come about has not yet been settled authoritatively.

"No, it is a following sea," said Frithiof; "and with a following sea you shall not get good steerage way."

The sea was as smooth as a duck pond, except for a regular oily swell. As I looked over the side to see where it might be following us from, the sun rose in a perfectly clear sky and struck the water with its light so sharply that it seemed as though the sea should clang like a burnished gong. The wake of the screw and the little white streak cut by the log-line hanging over the stern were the only marks on the water as far as eye could reach.

Keller rolled out of his chair and went aft to get a pineapple from the ripening stock that were hung inside the after awning.

"Frithiof, the log-line has got tired of swimming. It's coming home," he drawled.

"What?" said Frithiof, his voice jumping several octaves.

"Coming home," Keller repeated, leaning over the stern. I ran to his side and saw the log-line, which till then had been drawn tense over the stern railing, slacken, loop, and come up off the port quarter. Frithiof called up the speaking tube to the bridge, and the bridge answered, "Yes, nine knots." Then Frithiof spoke again, and the answer was, "What do you want of the skipper?" and Frithiof bellowed, "Call him up."

By this time Zuyland, Keller, and myself had caught something of Frithiof's excitement, for any emotion on shipboard is most contagious. The captain ran out of his cabin, spoke to

Frithiof, looked at the log-line, jumped on the bridge, and in a minute we felt the steamer swing around as Frithiof turned her.

"Going back to Cape Town?" said Keller.

Frithiof did not answer, but tore away at the wheel. Then he beckoned us three to help, and we held the wheel down till the *Rathmines* answered it, and we found ourselves looking into the white of our own wake, with the still oily sea tearing past our bows, though we were not going more than half steam ahead.

The captain stretched out his arm from the bridge and shouted. A minute later I would have given a great deal to have shouted too, for one-half of the sea seemed to shoulder itself above the other half, and came on in the shape of a hill. There was neither crest, comb, nor curl-over to it; nothing but black water with little waves chasing each other about the flanks. I saw it stream past and on a level with the *Rathmines*' bow-plates before the steamer made up her mind to rise, and I argued that this would be the last of all earthly voyages for me. Then we rose forever and ever and ever, till I heard Keller saying in my ear, "The bowels of the deep, good Lord!" and the *Rathmines* stood poised, her screw racing and drumming on the slope of a hollow that stretched downward for a good half-mile.

We went down that hollow, nose under for the most part, and the air smelled wet and muddy, like that of an emptied aquarium. There was a second hill to climb; I saw that much: but the water came aboard and carried me aft till it jammed me against the smoking-room door, and before I could catch breath or clear my eyes again we were rolling to and fro in torn water, with the scuppers pouring like eaves in a thunderstorm.

"There were three waves," said Keller; "and the stoke hold's flooded."

The firemen were on deck waiting, apparently, to be drowned. The engineer came and dragged them below, and the crew, gasping, began to work the clumsy Board of Trade pump. That showed nothing serious, and when I understood that the *Rathmines* was really on the water, and not beneath it, I asked what had happened.

"The captain says it was a blow up under the sea—a volcano," said Keller.

"It hasn't warmed anything," I said. I was feeling bitterly cold, and cold was almost unknown in those waters. I went below to change my clothes, and when I came up everything was wiped out by clinging white fog.

"Are there going to be any more surprises?" said Keller to the captain.

"I don't know. Be thankful you're alive, gentlemen. That's a tidal wave thrown up by a volcano. Probably the bottom of the sea has been lifted a few feet somewhere or other. I can't quite understand this cold spell. Our sea-thermometer says the surface water is 44°, and it should be 68°, at least."

"It's abominable," said Keller, shivering. "But hadn't you better attend to the foghorn? It seems to me that I heard something."

"Heard! Good heavens!" said the captain from the bridge, "I should think you did." He pulled the string of our foghorn, which was a weak one. It sputtered and choked, because the stoke-hold was full of water and the fires were half-drowned, and at last gave out a moan. It was answered from the fog by one of the most appalling steam-sirens I have ever heard. Keller turned as white as I did, for the fog, the cold fog, was upon us, and any man may be forgiven for fearing the death he cannot see.

"Give her steam there!" said the captain to the engine-room. "Steam for the whistle, if we have to go dead slow."

We bellowed again, and the damp dripped off the awnings to the deck as we listened for the reply. It seemed to be astern this time, but much nearer than before.

"The *Pembroke Castle,* by gum!" said Keller, and then, viciously, "Well, thank God, we shall sink her too."

"It's a side-wheel steamer," I whispered. "Can't you hear the paddles?"

This time we whistled and roared till the steam gave out, and the answer nearly deafened us. There was a sound of frantic threshing in the water, apparently about fifty yards away, and something shot past in the whiteness that looked as though it were gray and red.

"The *Pembroke Castle* bottom up," said Keller, who, being a journalist, always sought for explanations. "That's the colors of a Castle liner. We're in for a big thing."

"The sea is bewitched," said Frithiof from the wheelhouse. "There are two steamers."

Another siren sounded on our bow, and the little steamer rolled in the wash of something that had passed unseen.

"We're evidently in the middle of a fleet," said Keller quietly. "If one doesn't run us down, the other will. Phew! What in creation is that?"

I sniffed for there was a poisonous rank smell in the cold air—a smell that I had smelled before.

"If I was on land I should say that it was an alligator. It smells like musk," I answered.

"Not ten thousand alligators could make that smell," said Zuyland; "I have smelled them."

"Bewitched! Bewitched!" said Frithiof. "The sea she is turned upside down, and we are walking along the bottom."

Again the *Rathmines* rolled in the wash of some unseen ship, and a silver-gray wave broke over the bow, leaving on the deck a sheet of sediment—the gray broth that has its place in the fathomless deeps of the sea. A sprinkling of the wave fell on my face, and it was so cold that it stung as boiling water stings. The dead and most untouched deep water of the sea had been heaved to the top by the submarine volcano—the chill, still water that kills all life and smells of desolation and emptiness. We did not need either the blinding fog or that indescribable smell of musk to make us unhappy—we were shivering with cold and wretchedness where we stood.

"The hot air on the cold water makes this fog," said the captain. "It ought to clear in a little time."

"Whistle, oh! whistle, and let's get out of it," said Keller.

The captain whistled again, and far and far astern the invisible twin steam-sirens answered us. Their blasting shriek grew louder, till at last it seemed to tear out of the fog just above our quarter, and I cowered while the *Rathmines* plunged bows-under on a double swell that crossed.

"No more," said Frithiof, "it is not good any more. Let us get away, in the name of God."

"Now if a torpedo boat with a *City of Paris* siren went mad and broke her moorings and hired a friend to help her, it's just conceivable that we might be carried as we are now. Otherwise this thing is——"

The last words died on Keller's lips, his eyes began to start from his head, and his jaw fell. Some six or seven feet above the port bulwarks, framed in fog, and as utterly unsupported as the full moon, hung a Face. It was not human, and it certainly was not animal, for it did not belong to this earth as known to man. The mouth was open, revealing a ridiculously tiny tongue—as absurd as the tongue of an elephant; there were tense wrinkles of white skin at the angles of the drawn lips; white feelers like those of a barbel sprang from the lower jaw, and there was no sign of teeth within the mouth. But the horror of the face lay in the eyes, for those were sightless—white, in sockets as white as scraped bone, and blind. Yet for all this the face, wrinkled as the mask of a lion is drawn in Assyrian sculpture, was alive with rage and terror. One long white feeler touched our bulwarks. Then the face disappeared with the swiftness of a blind worm popping into its burrow, and the next thing that I remember is my own voice in my own ears, saying gravely to the mainmast, "But the air bladder ought to have been forced out of its mouth, you know."

Keller came up to me, ashy white. He put his hand into his pocket, took a cigar, bit it, dropped it, thrust his shaking thumb into his mouth and mumbled, "The giant gooseberry and the raining frogs! Gimme a light—gimme a light! I say, gimme a light." A little bead of blood dropped from his thumbnail.

I respected the motive, thought the manifestation was absurd. "Stop, you'll bite your thumb off," I said, and Keller laughed brokenly as he picked up his cigar. Only Zuyland, leaning over the port bulwarks, seemed self-possessed. He declared later that he was very sick.

"We've seen it," he said, turning around. "That is it."

"What?" said Keller, chewing the unlighted cigar.

As he spoke the fog was blown into shreds, and we saw the sea, gray with mud, rolling on every side of us and empty of all life. Then in one spot it bubbled and became like the pot of ointment that the Bible speaks of. From that wide-ringed trouble a Thing came up—a gray and red Thing with a neck—a Thing that bellowed and writhed in pain. Frithiof drew in his breath and held it till the red letters of the ship's name, woven across his jersey, straggled and opened out as though they had been type badly set. Then he said with a little cluck in his throat, "Ah, me! It is blind. *Hur illa!* That Thing is blind," and a murmur of pity went through us all, for we could see that the Thing on the water was blind and in pain. Something had gashed and cut the great sides cruelly and the blood was spurting out. The gray ooze of the undermost sea lay in the monstrous wrinkles of the back and poured away in sluices. The blind white head flung back and battered the wounds, and the body in its torment rose clear of the red and gray waves till we saw a pair of quivering shoulders streaked with weed and rough with shells, but as white in the clear spaces as the hairless, nameless, blind, toothless head. Afterward came a dot on the horizon and the sound of a shrill scream, and it was as though a shuttle shot all across the sea in one breath, and a second head and neck tore through the levels, driving a whispering wall of water to right and left. The two Things met—the one untouched and the other in its death throe—male and female, we said, the female coming to the male. She circled around him bellowing, and laid her neck across the curve of his great turtleback, and he disappeared underwater for an instant, but flung up again, grunting in agony while the blood ran. Once the entire head and neck shot clear of the water and stiffened, and I heard Keller saying, as though he was watching a street accident, "Give him air. For God's sake give him air!" Then the death struggle began, with crampings and twistings and jerkings of the white bulk to and fro, till our little steamer rolled again, and each gray wave coated her plates with the gray slime. The sun was clear, there was no wind, and we watched, the whole crew, stokers and all, in wonder and pity, but chiefly pity. The Thing was so helpless, and, save for his mate, so alone. No human eye should have beheld him; it was monstrous and indecent to exhibit him there in trade waters between atlas degrees of latitude. He had been spewed up, mangled and dying from his rest on the sea-floor, where he might have lived till the Judgment Day, and we saw the tides of his life go from him as an angry tide goes out across rocks in the teeth of a landward gale. The mate lay rocking on the water a little distance off, bellowing continually, and the smell of musk came down upon the ship making us cough.

At last the battle for life ended, in a batter of colored seas. We saw the writhing neck fall like a flail, the carcass turn sideways, showing the glint of a white belly and the inset of a gigantic hind-leg or flapper. Then all sank, and sea boiled over it, while the mate swam round and round, darting her blind head in every direction. Though we might have feared that she would attack the steamer, no power on earth could have drawn any one of us from our places that hour. We watched, holding our breaths. The mate paused in her search; we could hear the wash beating along her sides; reared her neck as high as she could reach, blind and lonely in all that loneliness of the sea, and sent one desperate bellow booming across the swells, as an oyster shell skips across a pond. Then she made off to the westward, the sun shining on the white head and the wake behind it, till nothing was left to see but a little pinpoint of silver on the horizon. We stood on our course again, and the *Rathmines,* coated with the sea-sediment, from bow to stern, looked like a ship made gray with terror.

"We must pool our notes," was the first coherent remark from Keller. "We're three trained journalists—we hold absolutely the biggest scoop on record. Start fair."

I objected to this. Nothing is gained by collaboration in journalism when all deal with the same facts, so we went to work each according to his own lights. Keller triple-headed his account, talked about our "gallant captain," and wound up with an allusion to American enterprise in that it was a citizen of Dayton, Ohio, that had seen the sea serpent. This sort of thing would have discredited the Creation, much more a mere sea tale, but as a specimen of the picture writing of a half-civilized people it was very interesting. Zuyland took a heavy column and a half, giving approximate lengths and breadths and the whole list of the crew whom he had sworn on oath to testify to his facts. There was nothing fantastic or flamboyant in Zuyland. I wrote three-quarters of a leaded bourgeois column, roughly speaking, and refrained from putting any journalese into it for reasons that had begun to appear to me.

Keller was insolent with joy. He was going to cable from Southampton to the New York *World,* mail his account to America on the same day, paralyze London with his three columns of loosely knitted headlines, and generally efface the earth. "You'll see how I work a big scoop when I get it," he said.

"Is this your first visit to England?" I asked.

"Yes," said he. "You don't seem to appreciate the beauty of our scoop. It's pyramidal—the death of the sea serpent! Good heavens alive man, it's the biggest thing ever vouchsafed to a paper!"

"Curious to think that it will never appear in any paper, isn't it?" I said.

Zuyland was near me, and he nodded quickly.

"What do you mean?" said Keller. "If you're enough of a Britisher to throw this thing away, I sha'n't. I thought you were a newspaper man."

"I am. That's why I know. Don't be an ass, Keller. Remember, I'm seven hundred years your senior, and what your grandchildren may learn five hundred years hence, I learned from my grandfathers about five hundred years ago. You won't do it, because you can't."

This conversation was held in open sea, where everything seems possible, some hundred miles from Southampton. We passed the Needles Light at dawn, and the lifting day showed the stucco villas on the green and the awful orderliness of England—line upon line, wall upon wall, solid stone dock and monolithic pier. We waited an hour in the Customs shed, and there was ample time for the effect to soak in.

"Now, Keller, you face the music. The *Havel* goes out today. Mail by her, and I'll take you to the telegraph office," I said.

I heard Keller gasp as the influence of the land closed about him, cowing him as they say Newmarket Heath cows a young horse unused to open country.

"I want to retouch my stuff. Suppose we wait till we get to London?" he said.

Zuyland, by the way, had torn up his account and thrown it overboard that morning early. His reasons were my reasons.

In the train Keller began to revise his copy, and every time that he looked at the trim little fields, the red villas, and the embankments of the line, the blue pencil plunged remorselessly through the slips. He appeared to have dredged the dictionary for adjectives. I could think of none that he had not used. Yet he was a perfectly sound poker player and never showed more cards than were sufficient to take the pool.

"Aren't you going to leave him a single bellow?" I asked sympathetically. "Remember, everything goes in the States, from a trouser-button to a double eagle."

"That's just the curse of it," said Keller below his breath. "We've played 'em for suckers so often that when it comes to the golden truth—I'd like to try this on a London paper. You have first call there, though."

"Not in the least. I'm not touching the thing in the papers. I shall be happy to leave 'em all to you; but surely you'll cable it home?"

"No. Not if I can make the scoop here and see the Britishers sit up."

"You won't do it with three columns of slushy headline, believe me. They don't sit up as quickly as some people."

"I'm beginning to think that too. Does *nothing* make any difference in this country?" he said, looking out of the window. "How old is that farmhouse?"

"New. It can't be more than two hundred years at the most."

"Um. Fields, too?"

"That hedge there must have been clipped for about eighty years."

"Labor cheap—eh?"

"Pretty much. Well, I suppose you'd like to try the *Times* wouldn't you?"

"No," said Keller, looking at Winchester Cathedral. "Might as well try to electrify a hay-rick. And to think that the *World* would take three columns and ask for more—with illustrations too! It's sickening."

"But the *Times* might," I began.

Keller flung his paper across the carriage, and it opened in its austere majesty of solid type—opened with the crackle of an encyclopedia.

"Might! You *might* work your way through the bow-plates of a cruiser. Look at that first page!"

"It strikes you that way, does it?" I said. "Then I'd recommend you to try a light and frivolous journal."

"With a thing like this of mine—of ours? It's sacred history!"

I showed him a paper which I conceived would be after his own heart, in that it was modeled on American lines.

"That's homey," he said, "but it's not the real thing. Now, I should like one of these fat old *Times*' columns. Probably there'd be a bishop in the office, though."

When we reached London Keller disappeared in the direction of the Strand. What his experiences may have been I cannot tell, but it seems that he invaded the office of an evening paper at 11:45 A.M. (I told him English editors were most idle at that hour), and mentioned my name as that of a witness to the truth of his story.

"I was nearly fired out," he said furiously at lunch. "As soon as I mentioned you, the old man said that I was to tell you that they didn't want any more of your practical jokes, and that you knew the hours to call if you had anything to sell, and that they'd see you condemned before they helped to puff one of your infernal yarns in advance. Say, what record do you hold for truth in this city, anyway?"

"A beauty. You ran up against it, that's all. Why don't you leave the English papers alone and cable to New York? Everything goes over there."

"Can't you see that's just why?" he repeated.

"I saw it a long time ago. You don't intend to cable, then?"

"Yes, I do," he answered, in the overemphatic voice of one who does not know his own mind.

That afternoon I walked him abroad and about, over the streets that run between the pavements like channels of grooved and tongued lava, over the bridges that are made of enduring stone, through subways floored and sided with yard-thick concrete, between houses that are never rebuilt, and by river steps hewn to the eye from the living rock. A black fog chased us into Westminster Abbey, and, standing there in the darkness, I could hear the wings of the dead centuries circling around the head of Litchfield A. Keller, journalist, of Dayton, Ohio, U.S.A., whose mission it was to make the Britishers sit up.

He stumbled gasping into the thick gloom, and the roar of the traffic came to his bewildered ears.

"Let's go to the telegraph office and cable," I said. "Can't you hear the New York *World* crying for news of the great sea serpent, blind, white, and smelling of musk, stricken to death by a submarine volcano, assisted by his loving wife to die in mid-ocean, as visualized by an independent American citizen, a breezy, newsy, brainy newspaper man of Dayton, Ohio? 'Rah for the Buckeye State. Step lively! Both gates! Szz! Boom—ah!" Keller was a Princeton man, and he seemed to need encouragement.

"You've got me on your own ground," said he, tugging at his overcoat pocket. He pulled out his copy, with the cable forms—for he had written out his telegram—and put them all into my hand, groaning, "I pass. If I hadn't come to your cursed country—if I'd sent it off at Southampton—if I ever get you west of the Alleghenies, if——"

"Never mind, Keller. It isn't your fault. It's the fault of your country. If you had been seven hundred years older you'd have done what I'm going to do."

"What are you going to do?"

"Tell it as a lie."

"Fiction?" This with the full-blooded disgust of a journalist for the illegitimate branch of the profession.

"You can call it that if you like. I shall call it a lie."

And a lie it has become, for Truth is a naked lady, and if by accident she is drawn up from the bottom of the sea, it behooves a gentleman either to give her a print petticoat or to turn his face to the wall, and vow that he did not see.

THE SENDING OF DANA DA

When the Devil rides on your chest remember the *chamar*.

—NATIVE PROVERB

ONCE upon a time, some people in India made a new Heaven and a new Earth out of broken teacups, a missing brooch or two, and a hairbrush. These were hidden under brushes, or stuffed into holes in the hillside, and an entire Civil Service of subordinate Gods used to find or mend them again; and every one said: "There are more things in Heaven and Earth than are dreamed of in our philosophy." Several other things happened also, but the Religion never seemed to get much beyond its first manifestations; though it added an air-line postal service, and orchestral effects in order to keep abreast of the times, and choke off competition.

This Religion was too elastic for ordinary use. It stretched itself and embraced pieces of everything that the medicine men of all ages have manufactured. It approved of and stole from Freemasonry; looted the Latter-day Rosicrucians of half their pet words; took any fragments of Egyptian philosophy that it found in the *Encyclopaedia Britannica;* annexed as many of the Vedas as had been translated into French or English, and talked of all the rest; built in the German versions of what is left of the Zend Avesta; encouraged White, Gray and Black Magic, including spiritualism, palmistry, fortune-telling by cards, hot chestnuts, double-kerneled nuts and tallow droppings; would have adopted Voodoo and Oboe had it known anything about them, and showed itself, in every way, one of the most accommodating arrangements that had ever been invented since the birth of the Sea.

When it was in thorough working order, with all the machinery, down to the subscriptions, complete, Dana Da came from nowhere, with nothing in his hands, and wrote a chapter in its history which has hitherto been unpublished. He said that his first name was Dana, and his second was Da. Now, setting aside Dana of the New York *Sun,* Dana is a Bhil name, and Da fits no native of India unless you except the Bengali Dé as the original spelling. Da is Lap or Finnish; and Dana Da was neither Finn, Chin, Bhil, Bengali, Lap, Nair, Gond, Romaney, Magh, Bokhariot, Kurd, Armenian, Levantine, Jew, Persian, Punjabi, Madrasi, Parsee, nor anything else known to ethnologists. He was simply Dana Da, and declined to give further information. For the sake of brevity and as roughly indicating his origin, he was called "The Native." He might have been the original Old Man of the Mountains, who is said to be the only authorized head of the Tea-cup Creed. Some people said that he was; but Dana Da used to smile and deny any connection with the cult; explaining that he was an "Independent Experimenter."

As I have said, he came from nowhere, with his hands behind his back, and studied the Creed for three weeks; sitting at the feet of those best competent to explain its mysteries. Then he laughed aloud and went away, but the laugh might have been either of devotion or derision.

When he returned he was without money, but his pride was unabated. He declared that he knew more about the Things in Heaven and Earth than those who taught him, and for this contumacy was abandoned altogether.

His next appearance in public life was at a big cantonment in Upper India, and he was then telling fortunes with the help of three leaden dice, a very dirty old cloth, and a little tin box of opium pills. He told better fortunes when he was allowed half a bottle of whiskey; but the things which he invented on the opium were quite worth the money. He was in reduced circumstances. Among other people's he told the fortune of an Englishman who had once been interested in the Simla Creed, but who, later on, had married and forgotten all his old knowledge in the study of babies and things. The Englishman allowed Dana Da to tell a fortune for charity's sake, and gave him five rupees, a dinner, and some old clothes. When he had eaten, Dana Da professed gratitude, and asked if there were anything he could do for his host—in the esoteric line.

"Is there anyone that you love?" said Dana Da. The Englishman loved his wife, but had no desire to drag her name into the conversation. He therefore shook his head.

"Is there anyone that you hate?" said Dana Da. The Englishman said that there were several men whom he hated deeply. "Very good," said Dana Da, upon whom the whiskey and the opium were beginning to tell. "Only give me their names, and I will dispatch a Sending to them and kill them."

Now a Sending is a horrible arrangement, first invented, they say, in Iceland. It is a Thing sent by a wizard, and may take any form, but, most generally, wanders about the land in the shape of a little purple cloud till it finds the Sendee, and him it kills by changing into the form of a horse, or a cat, or a man without a face. It is not strictly a native patent, though *chamars* of the skin and hide castes can, if irritated, dispatch a Sending which sits on the breast of their enemy by night and nearly kills him. Very few natives care to irritate *chamars* for this reason.

"Let me dispatch a Sending," said Dana Da; "I am nearly dead now with want, and drink, and opium; but I should like to kill a man before I die. I can send a Sending anywhere you choose, and in any form except in the shape of a man."

The Englishman had no friends that he wished to kill, but partly to soothe Dana Da, whose eyes were rolling, and partly to see what would be done, he asked whether a modified Sending could not be arranged for—such a Sending as should make a man's life a burden to him, and yet do him no harm. If this were possible, he notified his willingness to give Dana Da ten rupees for the job.

"I am not what I was once," said Dana Da, "and I must take the money because I am poor. To what Englishman shall I send it?"

"Send a Sending to Lone Sahib," said the Englishman, naming a man who had been most bitter in rebuking him for his apostasy from the Tea-cup Creed. Dana Da laughed and nodded.

"I could have chosen no better man myself," said he. "I will see that he finds the Sending about his path and about his bed."

He lay down on the hearth-rug, turned up the whites of his eyes, shivered all over and began to snort. This was Magic, or Opium, or the Sending, or all three. When he opened his eyes he vowed that the Sending had started upon the war-path, and was at that moment flying up to the town where Lone Sahib lives.

"Give me my ten rupees," said Dana Da, wearily, "and write a letter to Lone Sahib, telling him, and all who believe with him, that you and a friend are using a power greater than theirs. They will see that you are speaking the truth."

He departed unsteadily, with the promise of some more rupees if anything came of the Sending.

The Englishman sent a letter to Lone Sahib, couched in what he remembered of the terminology of the Creed. He wrote: "I also, in the days of what you held to be my backsliding, have obtained Enlightenment, and with Enlightenment has come Power." Then he grew so deeply mysterious that the recipient of the letter could make neither head nor tail of it, and was proportionately impressed; but he fancied that his friend had become a "fifth-rounder." When a man is a "fifth-rounder" he can do more than Slade and Houdin combined.

Lone Sahib read the letter in five different fashions, and was beginning a sixth interpretation when his bearer dashed in with the news that there was a cat on the bed. Now if there was one thing that Lone Sahib hated more than another, it was a cat. He scolded the bearer for not turning it out of the house. The bearer said that he was afraid. All the doors of the bedroom had been shut throughout the morning, and no *real* cat could possibly have entered the room. He would prefer not to meddle with the creature.

Lone Sahib entered the room gingerly, and there, on the pillow of his bed, sprawled and whimpered a wee white kitten; not a jumpsome, frisky little beast, but a slug-like crawler with its eyes barely opened and its paws lacking strength or direction—a kitten that ought to have been in a basket with its mamma. Lone Sahib caught it by the scruff of its neck, handed it over to the sweeper to be drowned, and fined the bearer four annas.

That evening, as he was reading in his room, he fancied that he saw something moving about on the hearth rug, outside the circle of light from his reading-lamp. When the thing began to miaow, he realized that it was a kitten—a wee white kitten, nearly blind and very miserable. He was seriously angry, and spoke bitterly to his bearer, who said that there was no kitten in the room when he brought in the lamp, and *real* kittens of tender age generally had mother-cats in attendance.

"If the Presence will go out into the veranda and listen," said the bearer, "he will hear no cats. How, therefore, can the kitten on the bed and the kitten on the hearth-rug be real kittens?"

Lone Sahib went out to listen, and the bearer followed him, but there was no sound of anyone mewing for her children. He returned to his room, having hurled the kitten down the hill-side, and wrote out the incidents of the day for the benefit of his co-religionists. Those people were so absolutely free from superstition that they ascribed anything a little out of the common to Agencies. As it was their business to know all about the Agencies, they were on terms of almost indecent familiarity with Manifestations of every kind. Their letters dropped from the ceiling—unstamped—and Spirits used to squatter up and down their staircases all night; but they had never come into contact with kittens. Lone Sahib wrote out the facts, noting the hour and the minute, as every Psychical Observer is bound to do, and appending the Englishman's letter because it was the most mysterious document and might have had a bearing upon anything in this world or the next. An outsider would have translated all the tangle thus: "Look out! You laughed at me once, and now I am going to make you sit up."

Lone Sahib's co-religionists found that meaning in it; but their translation was refined and full of four-syllable words. They held a sederunt, and were filled with tremulous joy, for, in spite of their familiarity with all the other worlds and cycles, they had a very human awe of things sent from Ghost-land. They met in Lone Sahib's room in shrouded and sepulchral gloom, and their conclave was broken up by clinking among the photo frames on the mantelpiece. A wee white kitten, nearly blind, was looping and writhing itself between the clock and the candlesticks. That stopped all investigations or doubtings. Here was the Manifestation in the flesh. It was, so far as could be seen, devoid of purpose, but it was a Manifestation of undoubted authenticity.

They drafted a Round Robin to the Englishman, the backslider of old days, adjuring him in the interests of the Creed to explain whether there was any connection between the embodiment of some Egyptian God or other (I have forgotten the name) and his communication. They called the kitten Ra, or Toth, or Tum, or something; and when Lone Sahib confessed that the first one had, at his most misguided instance, been drowned by the sweeper, they said consolingly that in his next life he would be a "bounder," and not even a "rounder" of the lowest grade. These words may not be quite correct, but they accurately express the sense of the house.

When the Englishman received the Round Robin—it came by post—he was startled and bewildered. He sent into the *bazar* for Dana Da, who read the letter and laughed. "That is my Sending," said he. "I told you I would work well. Now give me another ten rupees."

"But what in the world is this gibberish about Egyptian Gods?" asked the Englishman.

"Cats," said Dana Da, with a hiccough, for he had discovered the Englishman's whiskey bottle. "Cats, and cats, and cats! Never was such a Sending. A hundred of cats. Now give me ten more rupees and write as I dictate."

Dana Da's letter was a curiosity. It bore the Englishman's signature, and hinted at cats—at a Sending of Cats. The mere words on paper were creepy and uncanny to behold.

"What have you done, though?" said the Englishman; "I am as much in the dark as ever. Do you mean to say that you can actually send this absurd Sending you talk about?"

"Judge for yourself," said Dana Da. "What does that letter mean? In a little time they will all be at my feet and yours, and I—O Glory!—will be drugged or drunk all day long."

Dana Da knew his people.

When a man who hates cats wakes up in the morning and finds a little squirming kitten on his breast, or puts his hands into his ulster pocket and finds a little half-dead kitten where his gloves should be, or opens his trunk and finds a vile kitten among his dress shirts, or goes for a long ride with his mackintosh strapped on his saddlebow and shakes a little squalling kitten from its folds when he opens it, or goes out to dinner and finds a little blind kitten under his chair, or stays at home and finds a writhing kitten under the quilt, or wriggling among his boots, or hanging, head downward, in his tobacco jar, or being mangled by his terrier in the veranda—when such a man finds one kitten, neither more nor less, once a day in a place where no kitten rightly could or should be, he is naturally upset. When he dare not murder his daily trove because he believes it to be a Manifestation, an Emissary, an Embodiment, and half a dozen other things all out of the regular course of nature, he is more than upset. He is actually distressed. Some of Lone Sahib's co-religionists thought that he was a highly favored individual; but many said that if he had treated the first kitten with proper respect—as suited a Toth-Ra-Tum-Sennacherib Embodiment—all this trouble would have been averted. They compared him to the Ancient Mariner, but nonetheless they were proud of him and proud of the Englishman who had sent the Manifestation. They did not call it a Sending because Icelandic magic was not in their program.

After sixteen kittens, that is to say after one fortnight, for there were three kittens on the first day to impress the fact of the Sending, the whole camp was uplifted by a letter—it came flying through a window—from the Old Man of the Mountains—the Head of all the Creed—explaining the Manifestation in the most beautiful language and soaking up all the credit of it for himself. The Englishman, said the letter, was not there at all. He was a backslider without Power or Asceticism, who couldn't even raise a table by force of volition, much less project an army of kittens through space. The entire arrangement, said the letter, was strictly orthodox, worked and sanctioned by the highest Authorities within the pale of the Creed. There was great joy at this, for some of the weaker brethren seeing that an outsider who had been working on independent lines could create kittens, whereas their own rulers had never gone beyond crockery—and broken at best—were showing a desire to break line on their own trail. In fact, there was the promise of a schism. A second Round Robin was drafted to the Englishman, beginning: "O Scoffer," and ending with a selection of curses from the Rites of Mizraim and Memphis and the Commination of Jugana, who was a "fifth-rounder," upon whose name an upstart "third-rounder" once traded. A papal excommunication is a *billet-doux* compared to the Commination of Jugana. The Englishman had been proved, under the hand and seal of the

Old Man of the Mountains, to have appropriated Virtue and pretended to have Power which, in reality, belonged only to the Supreme Head. Naturally the Round Robin did not spare him.

He handed the letter to Dana Da to translate into decent English. The effect on Dana Da was curious. At first he was furiously angry, and then he laughed for five minutes.

"I had thought," he said, "that they would have come to me. In another week I would have shown that I sent the Sending, and they would have discrowned the Old Man of the Mountains who has sent this Sending of mine. Do you do nothing. The time has come for me to act. Write as I dictate, and I will put them to shame. But give me ten more rupees."

At Dana Da's dictation the Englishman wrote nothing less than a formal challenge to the Old Man of the Mountains. It wound up: "And if this Manifestation be from your hand, then let it go forward; but if it be from my hand, I will that the Sending shall cease in two days' time. On that day there shall be twelve kittens and thenceforward none at all. The people shall judge between us." This was signed by Dana Da, who added pentacles and pentagrams, and a *crux ansata,* and half a dozen *swastikas,* and a Triple Tau to his name, just to show that he was all he laid claim to be.

The challenge was read out to the gentlemen and ladies, and they remembered then that Dana Da had laughed at them some years ago. It was officially announced that the Old Man of the Mountains would treat the matter with contempt; Dana Da being an Independent Investigator without a single "round" at the back of him. But this did not soothe his people. They wanted to see a fight. They were very human for all their spirituality. Lone Sahib, who was really being worn out with kittens, submitted meekly to his fate. He felt that he was being "kittened to prove the power of Dana Da," as the poet says.

When the stated day dawned, the shower of kittens began. Some were white and some were tabby, and all were about the same loathsome age. Three were on his hearth-rug, three in his bathroom, and the other six turned up at intervals among the visitors who came to see the prophecy break down. Never was a more satisfactory Sending. On the next day there were no kittens, and the next and all the other days were kittenless and quiet. The people murmured and looked to the Old Man of the Mountains for an explanation. A letter, written on a palm-leaf, dropped from the ceiling, but everyone except Lone Sahib felt that letters were not what the occasion demanded. There should have been cats, there should have been cats—full-grown ones. The letter proved conclusively that there had been a hitch in the Psychic Current which, colliding with a Dual Identity, had interfered with the Percipient Activity all along the main line. The kittens were still going on, but owing to some failure in the Developing Fluid, they were not materialized. The air was thick with letters for a few days afterward. Unseen hands played Glück and Beethoven on fingerbowls and clock-shades; but all men felt that Psychic Life was a mockery without materialized Kittens. Even Lone Sahib shouted with the majority on this head. Dana Da's letters were very insulting, and if he had then offered to lead a new departure, there is no knowing what might not have happened.

But Dana Da was dying of whiskey and opium in the Englishman's godown, and had small heart for honors.

"They have been put to shame," said he. "Never was such a Sending. It has killed me."

"Nonsense," said the Englishman, "you are going to die, Dana Da, and that sort of stuff must be left behind. I'll admit that you have made some queer things come about. Tell me honestly, now, how was it done?"

"Give me ten more rupees," said Dana Da, faintly, "and if I die before I spend them, bury them with me." The silver was counted out while Dana Da was fighting with Death. His hand closed upon the money and he smiled a grim smile.

"Bend low," he whispered. The Englishman bent.

"*Bunnia*—Mission-school—expelled—*box-wallah* (peddler) —Ceylon pearl-merchant—all mine English education—outcasted, and made up name Dana Da—England with American thought-reading man and—and—you gave me ten rupees several times—I gave the Sahib's bearer two-eight a month for cats—little, little cats. I wrote, and he put them about—very clever man. Very few kittens now in the *bazar*. Ask Lone Sahib's sweeper's wife."

So saying, Dana Da gasped and passed away into a land where, if all be true, there are no materializations and the making of new creeds is discouraged.

But consider the gorgeous simplicity of it all!

THE PHANTOM 'RICKSHAW

May no ill dreams disturb my rest,
Nor Powers of Darkness me molest.
—EVENING HYMN

ONE of the few advantages that India has over England is a great Knowability. After five years' service a man is directly or indirectly acquainted with the two or three hundred Civilians in his Province, all the Messes of ten or twelve Regiments and Batteries, and some fifteen hundred other people of the non-official caste. In ten years his knowledge should be doubled, and at the end of twenty he knows, or knows something about, every Englishman in the Empire, and may travel anywhere and everywhere without paying hotel-bills.

Globe-trotters who expect entertainment as a right, have, even within my memory, blunted this openheartedness, but nonetheless today, if you belong to the Inner Circle and are neither a Bear nor a Black Sheep, all houses are open to you, and our small world is very, very kind and helpful.

Rickett of Kamartha stayed with Polder of Kumaon some fifteen years ago. He meant to stay two nights, but was knocked down by rheumatic fever, and for six weeks disorganized Polder's establishment, stopped Polder's work, and nearly died in Polder's bedroom. Polder behaves as though he had been placed under eternal obligation by Rickett, and yearly sends the little Ricketts a box of presents and toys. It is the same everywhere. The men who do not take the trouble to conceal from you their opinion that you are an incompetent ass, and the women who blacken your character and misunderstand your wife's amusements, will work themselves to the bone in your behalf if you fall sick or into serious trouble.

Heatherlegh, the Doctor, kept, in addition to his regular practice, a hospital on his private account—an arrangement of loose boxes for Incurables, his friend called it—but it was really a sort of fitting-up shed for craft that had been damaged by stress of weather. The weather in India is often sultry, and since the tale of bricks is always a fixed quantity, and the only liberty allowed is permission to work overtime and get no thanks, men occasionally break down and become as mixed as the metaphors in this sentence.

Heatherlegh is the dearest doctor that ever was, and his invariable prescription to all his patients is, "Lie low, go slow, and keep cool." He says that more men are killed by overwork than the importance of this world justifies. He maintains that overwork slew Pansay, who died under his hands about three years ago. He has, of course, the right to speak authoritatively, and he laughs at my theory that there was a crack in Pansay's head and a little bit of the Dark World came through and pressed him to death. "Pansay went off the handle," says Heatherlegh, "after the stimulus of long leave at Home. He may or he may not have behaved like a blackguard to Mrs. Keith-Wessington. My notion is that the work of the Katabundi Settlement ran him off his legs, and that he took to brooding and making much of an ordinary P. & O. flirtation. He certainly was engaged to Miss Mannering, and she certainly broke off the engagement. Then he took a feverish chill and all that nonsense about ghosts developed. Overwork started his illness, kept it alight, and killed him, poor devil. Write him off to the System that uses one man to do the work of two and a half men."

I do not believe this. I used to sit up with Pansay sometimes when Heatherlegh was called out to patients and I happened to be within claim. The man would make me most unhappy by describing in a low, even voice, the procession that was always passing at the bottom of his bed. He had a sick man's command of language. When he recovered I suggested that he should write out the whole affair from beginning to end, knowing that ink might assist him to ease his mind.

He was in a high fever while he was writing, and the blood-and-thunder Magazine diction he adopted did not calm him. Two months afterward he was reported fit for duty, but, in spite of the fact that he was urgently needed to help an undermanned Commission stagger through a deficit, he preferred to die; vowing at the last that he was hagridden. I got his manuscript before he died, and this is his version of the affair, dated 1885, exactly as he wrote it:—

My doctor tells me that I need rest and change of air. It is not improbable that I shall get both ere long—rest that neither the red-coated messenger nor the mid-day gun can break, and change of air far beyond that which any homeward-bound steamer can give me. In the meantime I am resolved to stay where I am; and, in flat defiance of my doctor's orders, to take all the world into my confidence. You shall learn for yourselves the precise nature of my malady, and shall, too, judge for yourselves whether any man born of woman on this weary earth was ever so tormented as I.

Speaking now as a condemned criminal might speak ere the drop-bolts are drawn, my story, wild and hideously improbable as it may appear, demands at least attention. That it will ever receive credence I utterly disbelieve. Two months ago I should have scouted as mad or drunk the man who had dared tell me the like. Two months ago I was the happiest man in India. To-day, from Peshawar to the sea, there is no one more wretched. My doctor and I are the only two who know this. His explanation is, that my brain, digestion, and eyesight are all slightly affected; giving rise to my frequent and persistent "delusions." Delusions, indeed I call him a fool; but he attends me still with the same unwearied smile, the same bland professional manner, the same neatly-trimmed red whiskers, till I begin to suspect that I am an ungrateful, evil-tempered invalid. But you shall judge for yourselves.

Three years ago it was my fortune—my great misfortune—to sail from Gravesend to Bombay, on return from long leave, with one Agnes Keith-Wessington, wife of an officer on the Bombay side. It does not in the least concern you to know what manner of woman she was. Be content with the knowledge that, ere the voyage had ended, both she and I were desperately and unreasoningly in love with one another. Heaven knows that I can make the admission now without one particle of vanity. In matters of this sort there is always one who gives and another who accepts. From the first day of our ill-omened attachment, I was conscious that Agnes' passion was a stronger, a more dominant, and—if I may use the expression—a purer sentiment than mine. Whether she recognized the fact then, I do not know. Afterward it was bitterly plain to both of us.

Arrived at Bombay in the spring of the year, we went our

respective ways, to meet no more for the next three or four months, when my leave and her love took us both to Simla. There we spent the season together; and there my fire of straw burned itself out to a pitiful end with the closing year. I attempt no excuse. I make no apology. Mrs. Wessington had given up much for my sake, and was prepared to give up all. From my own lips, in August 1882, she learned that I was sick of her presence, tired of her company, and weary of the sound of her voice. Ninety-nine women out of a hundred would have wearied of me as I wearied of them; seventy-five of that number would have promptly avenged themselves by active and obtrusive flirtation with other men. Mrs. Wessington was the hundredth. On her neither my openly-expressed aversion nor the cutting brutalities with which I garnished our interviews had the least effect.

"Jack, darling!" was her one eternal cuckoo cry: "I'm sure it's all a mistake—a hideous mistake; and we'll be good friends again some day. *Please* forgive me, Jack, dear."

I was the offender, and I knew it. That knowledge transformed my pity into passive endurance, and, eventually, into blind hate—the same instinct, I suppose, which prompts a man to savagely stamp on the spider he has but half killed. And with this hate in my bosom the season of 1882 came to an end.

Next year we met again at Simla—she with her monotonous face and timid attempts at reconciliation, and I with loathing of her in every fiber of my frame. Several times I could not avoid meeting her alone; and on each occasion her words were identically the same. Still the unreasoning wail that it was all a "mistake"; and still the hope of eventually "making friends." I might have seen, had I cared to look, that that hope only was keeping her alive. She grew more wan and thin month by month. You will agree with me, at least, that such conduct would have driven anyone to despair. It was uncalled for; childish, unwomanly. I maintain that she was much to blame. And again, sometimes, in the black, fever-stricken night-watches, I have begun to think that I might have been a little kinder to her. But that really *is* a "delusion." I could not have continued pretending to love her when I didn't; could I? It would have been unfair to us both.

Last year we met again—on the same terms as before. The same weary appeals, and the same curt answers from my lips. At least I would make her see how wholly wrong and hopeless were her attempts at resuming the old relationship. As the season wore on, we fell apart—that is to say, she found it difficult to meet me, for I had other and more absorbing interests to attend to. When I think it over quietly in my sickroom, the season of 1884 seems a confused nightmare wherein light and shade were fantastically intermingled—my courtship of little Kitty Mannering; my hopes, doubts, and fears; our long rides together; my trembling avowal of attachment; her reply; and now and again a vision of a white face flitting by in the 'rickshaw with the black and white liveries I once watched for so earnestly; the wave of Mrs. Wessington's gloved hand; and, when she met me alone, which was but seldom, the irksome monotony of her appeal. I loved Kitty Mannering; honestly, heartily loved her, and with my love for her grew my hatred for Agnes. In August Kitty and I were engaged. The next day I met those accursed "magpie" *jhampanies* at the back of Jakko, and, moved by some passing sentiment of pity, stopped to tell Mrs. Wessington everything. She knew it already.

"So I hear you're engaged, Jack dear." Then, without a moment's pause: "I'm sure it's all a mistake—a hideous mistake. We shall be as good friends someday, Jack, as we ever were."

My answer might have made even a man wince. It cut the dying woman before me like the blow of a whip. "Please forgive me, Jack; I didn't mean to make you angry; but it's true, it's true!"

And Mrs. Wessington broke down completely. I turned away and left her to finish her journey in peace, feeling, but only for a moment or two, that I had been an unutterably mean hound. I looked back, and saw that she had turned her 'rickshaw with the idea, I suppose, of overtaking me.

The scene and its surroundings were photographed on my memory. The rain-swept sky (we were at the end of the wet weather), the sodden, dingy pines, the muddy road, and the black powder-riven cliffs formed a gloomy background against which the black and white liveries of the *jhampanies,* the yellow-paneled 'rickshaw and Mrs. Wessington's down-bowed golden head stood out clearly. She was holding her handkerchief in her left hand and was leaning back exhausted against the 'rickshaw cushions. I turned my horse up a bypath near the Sanjowlie Reservoir and literally ran away. Once I fancied I heard a faint call of "Jack!" This may have been imagination. I never stopped to verify it. Ten minutes later I came across Kitty on horseback; and, in the delight of a long ride with her, forgot all about the interview.

A week later Mrs. Wessington died, and the inexpressible burden of her existence was removed from my life. I went Plainsward perfectly happy. Before three months were over I had forgotten all about her, except that at times the discovery of some of her old letters reminded me unpleasantly of our bygone relationship. By January I had disinterred what was left of our correspondence from among my scattered belongings and had burned it. At the beginning of April of this year, 1885, I was at Simla—semi-deserted Simla—once more, and was deep in lover's talks and walks with Kitty. It was decided that we should be married at the end of June. You will understand, therefore, that, loving Kitty as I did, I am not saying too much when I pronounce myself to have been, at that time, the happiest man in India.

Fourteen delightful days passed almost before I noticed their flight. Then, aroused to the sense of what was proper among mortals circumstanced as we were, I pointed out to Kitty that an engagement ring was the outward and visible sign of her dignity as an engaged girl; and that she must forthwith come to Hamilton's to be measured for one. Up to that moment, I give you my word, we had completely forgotten so trivial a matter. To Hamilton's we accordingly went on the 15th of April 1885. Remember that—whatever my doctor may say to the contrary—I was then in perfect health, enjoying a well-balanced mind and an *absolutely* tranquil spirit. Kitty and I entered Hamilton's shop together, and there, regardless of the order of affairs, I measured Kitty for the ring in the presence of the amused assistant. The ring was a sapphire with two diamonds. We then rode out down the slope that leads to the Combermere Bridge and Peliti's shop.

While my Waler was cautiously feeling his way over the loose shale, and Kitty was laughing and chattering at my side—while all Simla, that is to say as much of it as had then come from the Plains, was grouped around the Reading-room and Peliti's veranda—I was aware that someone, apparently at a vast distance, was calling me by my Christian name. It struck me that I had heard the voice before, but when and where I could not at once determine. In the short space it took to cover the road between the path from Hamilton's shop and the first plank of the Combermere Bridge I had thought over half a dozen people who might have committed such a solecism, and had eventually decided that it must have been some singing in my ears. Immediately opposite Peliti's shop my eye was arrested by the sight of four *jhampanies* in "mag-pie" livery, pulling a yellow-paneled, cheap, bazar 'rickshaw. In a moment my mind flew back to the previous season and Mrs. Wessington with a sense of irritation and disgust. Was it not enough that the woman was dead and done with, without her black and white servitors reappearing to spoil the day's happiness? Whoever employed them now I thought I would call upon, and ask as a personal favor to change her *jhampanies*' livery. I would hire the men myself, and, if necessary, buy their coats from off their backs. It is impossible to say here what a flood of undesirable memories their presence evoked.

"Kitty," I cried, "there are poor Mrs. Wessington's *jhampanies* turned up again! I wonder who has them now?"

Kitty had known Mrs. Wessington slightly last season, and had always been interested in the sickly woman.

"What? Where?" she asked. "I can't see them anywhere."

Even as she spoke, her horse, swerving from a laden mule, threw himself directly in front of the advancing 'rickshaw. I had scarcely time to utter a word of warning when to my unutterable horror, horse and rider passed *through* men and carriage as if they had been thin air.

"What's the matter?" cried Kitty; "what made you call out so foolishly, Jack? If I *am* engaged I don't want all creation to know about it. There was lots of space between the mule and the veranda; and, if you think I can't ride—— There!"

Whereupon willful Kitty set off, her dainty little head in the air, at a hand-gallop in the direction of the Bandstand; fully expecting, as she herself afterward told me, that I should follow her. What was the matter? Nothing indeed. Either that I was mad or drunk, or that Simla was haunted with devils. I reined in my impatient cob, and turned around. The 'rickshaw had turned too, and now stood immediately facing me, near the left railing of the Combermere Bridge.

"Jack! Jack, darling!" (There was no mistake about the words this time: they rang through my brain as if they had been shouted in my ear.) "It's some hideous mistake, I'm sure. *Please* forgive me, Jack, and let's be friends again."

The 'rickshaw-hood had fallen back, and inside, as I hope and pray daily for the death I dread by night, sat Mrs. Keith-Wessington, handkerchief in hand, and golden head bowed on her breast.

How long I stared motionless I do not know. Finally, I was aroused by my syce taking the Waler's bridle and asking whether I was ill. From the horrible to the commonplace is but a step. I tumbled off my horse and dashed, half-fainting, into Peliti's for a glass of cherry-brandy. There two or three couples were gathered around the coffee tables discussing the gossip of the day. Their trivialities were more comforting to me just then than the consolations of religion could have been. I plunged into the midst of the conversation at once; chatted, laughed, and jested with a face (when I caught a glimpse of it in a mirror) as white and drawn as that of a corpse. Three or four men noticed my condition; and, evidently setting it down to the results of over-many pegs, charitably endeavored to draw me apart from the rest of the loungers. But I refused to be led away. I wanted the company of my kind—as a child rushes into the midst of the dinner party after a fright in the dark. I must have talked for about ten minutes or so, though it seemed an eternity to me, when I heard Kitty's clear voice outside inquiring for me. In another minute she had entered the shop, prepared to upbraid me for failing so signally in my duties. Something in my face stopped her.

"Why, Jack," she cried, "what *have* you been doing? What *has* happened? Are you ill?" Thus driven into a direct lie, I said that the sun had been a little too much for me. It was close upon five o'clock of a cloudy April afternoon, and the sun had been hidden all day. I saw my mistake as soon as the words were out of my mouth: attempted to recover it; blundered hopelessly and followed Kitty, in a regal rage, out of doors, amid the smiles of my acquaintances. I made some excuse (I have forgotten what) on the score of my feeling faint; and cantered away to my hotel, leaving Kitty to finish the ride by herself.

In my room I sat down and tried calmly to reason out the matter. Here was I, Theobald Jack Pansay, a well-educated Bengal Civilian in the year of grace 1885, presumably sane, certainly healthy, driven in terror from my sweetheart's side by the apparition of a woman who had been dead and buried eight months ago. These were facts that I could not blink. Nothing was further from my thought than any memory of Mrs. Wessington when Kitty and I left Hamilton's shop. Nothing was more utterly commonplace than the stretch of wall opposite Peliti's. It was broad daylight. The road was full of people; and yet here, look you, in defiance of every law of probability, in direct outrage of Nature's ordinance, there had appeared to me a face from the grave.

Kitty's Arab had gone *through* the 'rickshaw: so that my first hope that some woman marvelously like Mrs. Wessington had hired the carriage and the coolies with their old livery was lost. Again and again I went around this treadmill of thought; and again and again gave up baffled and in despair. The voice was as inexplicable as the apparition. I had originally some wild notion of confiding it all to Kitty; of begging her to marry me at once; and in her arms defying the ghostly occupant of the 'rickshaw. "After all," I argued, "the presence of the 'rickshaw is in itself enough to prove the existence of a spectral illusion. One may see ghosts of men and women, but surely never coolies and carriages. The whole thing is absurd. Fancy the ghost of a hillman!"

Next morning I sent a penitent note to Kitty, imploring her to overlook my strange conduct of the previous afternoon. My Divinity was still very wroth, and a personal apology was necessary. I explained, with a fluency born of night-long pondering over a falsehood, that I had been attacked with a sudden palpitation of the heart—the result of indigestion. This eminently practical solution had its effect: and Kitty and I rode out that afternoon with the shadow of my first lie dividing us.

Nothing would please her save a canter around Jakko. With my nerves still unstrung from the previous night I feebly protested against the notion, suggesting Observatory Hill, Jutogh, the Boileaugunge road—anything rather than the Jakko round. Kitty was angry and a little hurt; so I yielded from fear of provoking further misunderstanding, and we set out together toward Chota Simla. We walked a greater part of the way, and, according to our custom, cantered from a mile or so below the Convent to the stretch of level road by the Sanjowlie Reservoir. The wretched horses appeared to fly, and my heart beat quicker and quicker as we neared the crest of the ascent. My mind had been full of Mrs. Wessington all the afternoon; and every inch of the Jakko road bore witness to our old-time walks and talks. The boulders were full of it; the pines sang it aloud overhead; the rain-fed torrents giggled and chuckled unseen over the shameful story; and the wind in my ears chanted the iniquity aloud.

As a fitting climax, in the middle of the level men call the Ladies' Mile the Horror was awaiting me. No other 'rickshaw was in sight—only the four black and white *jhampanies,* the yellow-paneled carriage, and the golden head of the women within—all apparently just as I had left them eight months and one fortnight ago! For an instant I fancied that Kitty *must* see what I saw—we were so marvelously sympathetic in all things. Her next words undeceived me—"Not a soul in sight! Come along, Jack, and I'll race you to the Reservoir buildings!" Her wiry little Arab was off like a bird, my Waler following close behind, and in this order we dashed under the cliffs. Half a minute brought us within fifty yards of the 'rickshaw. I pulled my Waler and fell back a little. The 'rickshaw was directly in the middle of the road; and once more the Arab passed through it, my horse following. "Jack! Jack dear! *Please* forgive me," rang with a wail in my ears, and, after an interval: "It's all a mistake, a hideous mistake!"

I spurred my horse like a man possessed. When I turned my head at the Reservoir works, the black and white liveries were still waiting—patiently waiting—under the gray hillside, and the wind brought me a mocking echo of the words I had just heard. Kitty bantered me a good deal on my silence throughout the remainder of the ride. I had been talking up till then wildly and at random. To save my life I could not speak afterward naturally, and from Sanjowlie to the Church wisely held my tongue.

I was to dine with the Mannerings that night, and had barely time to canter home to dress. On the road to Elysium Hill I overheard two men talking together in the dusk.—"It's a curious thing," said one, "how completely all trace of it disappeared. You know my wife was insanely fond of the woman (never could see anything in her myself), and wanted me to pick up her old 'rickshaw and coolies if they were to be got for love or money. Morbid sort of fancy I call it; but I've got to do what the *Memsahib* tells me. Would you believe that the man she hired it from tells me that all four of the men—they were brothers—died of cholera on the way to Hardwar, poor devils; and the 'rickshaw has been broken up by the man himself. 'Told me he never used a dead *Memsahib's* 'rickshaw. 'Spoilt his luck. Queer notion, wasn't it? Fancy poor little Mrs. Wessington spoiling anyone's luck except her own!" I laughed aloud at this point; and my laugh jarred on me as I uttered it. So there *were* ghosts of 'rickshaws after all, and ghostly employments in the other world! How much did Mrs. Wessington give her men? What were their hours? Where did they go?

And for visible answer to my last question I saw the infernal Thing blocking my path in the twilight. The dead travel fast, and by short cuts unknown to ordinary coolies. I laughed aloud a second time and checked my laughter suddenly, for I was afraid I was going mad. Mad to a certain extent I must have been, for I recollect that I reined in my horse at the head of the 'rickshaw, and politely wished Mrs. Wessington "Good-evening." Her answer was one I knew only too well. I listened to the end; and replied that I had heard it all before, but should be delighted if she had anything further to say. Some malignant devil stronger than I must have entered into me that evening, for I have a dim recollection of talking the commonplaces of the day for five minutes to the Thing in front of me.

"Mad as a hatter, poor devil—or drunk. Max, try and get him to come home."

Surely *that* was not Mrs. Wessington's voice! The two men had overheard me speaking to the empty air, and had returned to look after me. They were very kind and considerate, and from their words evidently gathered that I was extremely drunk. I thanked them confusedly and cantered away to my hotel, there changed, and arrived at the Mannerings' ten minutes late. I pleaded the darkness of the night as an excuse; was rebuked by Kitty for my unlover-like tardiness; and sat down.

The conversation had already become general; and under cover of it, I was addressing some tender small talk to my sweetheart when I was aware that at the further end of the table a short red-whiskered man was describing, with much broidery, his encounter with a mad unknown that evening.

A few sentences convinced me that he was repeating the incident of half an hour ago. In the middle of the story he looked around for applause, as professional storytellers do, caught my eye, and straightway collapsed. There was a moment's awkward silence, and the red-whiskered man muttered something to the effect that he had "forgotten the rest," thereby sacrificing a reputation as a good storyteller which he had built up for six seasons past. I blessed him from the bottom of my heart, and—went on with my fish.

In the fullness of time that dinner came to an end; and with genuine regret I tore myself away from Kitty—as certain as I was of my own existence that It would be waiting for me outside the door. The red-whiskered man, who had been introduced to me as Dr. Heatherlegh of Simla, volunteered to bear me company as far as our roads lay together. I accepted his offer with gratitude.

My instinct had not deceived me. It lay in readiness in the Mall, and, in what seemed devilish mockery of our ways, with a lighted head lamp. The red-whiskered man went to the point at once, in a manner that showed he had been thinking over it all dinnertime.

"I say, Pansay, what the deuce was the matter with you this evening on the Elysium Road?" The suddenness of the question wrenched an answer from me before I was aware.

"That!" said I, pointing to It.

"*That* may be either D. T. or Eyes for aught I know. Now you don't liquor. I saw as much at dinner, so it can't be D. T. There's nothing whatever where you're pointing, though you're sweating and trembling with fright, like a scared pony. Therefore, I conclude that it's Eyes. And I ought to understand all about them. Come along home with me. I'm on the Blessington lower road."

To my intense delight the 'rickshaw instead of waiting for us kept about twenty yards ahead—and this, too, whether we walked, trotted, or cantered. In the course of that long night ride I had told my companion almost as much as I have told you here.

"Well, you've spoiled one of the best tales I've ever laid tongue to," said he, "but I'll forgive you for the sake of what you've gone through. Now come home and do what I tell you; and when I've cured you, young man, let this be a lesson to you to steer clear of women and indigestible food until the day of your death."

The 'rickshaw kept steady in front; and my red-whiskered friend seemed to derive great pleasure from my account of its exact whereabouts.

"Eyes, Pansay—all Eyes, Brain, and Stomach. And the greatest of these three is Stomach. You've too much conceited Brain, too little Stomach, and thoroughly unhealthy Eyes. Get your Stomach straight and the rest follows. And all that's French for a liver pill. I'll take sole medical charge of you from this hour! for you're too interesting a phenomenon to be passed over."

By this time we were deep in the shadow of the Blessington lower road and the 'rickshaw came to a dead stop under a pine-clad, overhanging shale cliff. Instinctively I halted too, giving my reason. Heatherlegh rapped out an oath.

"Now, if you think I'm going to spend a cold night on the hillside for the sake of a Stomach-*cum*-Brain-*cum*-Eye illusion—— Lord, ha' mercy! What's that?"

There was a muffled report, a blinding smother of dust just in front of us, a crack, the noise of rent boughs, and about ten yards of the cliffside—pines, undergrowth, and all—slid down into the road below, completely blocking it up. The uprooted trees swayed and tottered for a moment like drunken giants in the gloom, and then fell prone among their fellows with a thunderous crash. Our two horses stood motionless and sweating with fear. As soon as the rattle of falling earth and stone had subsided, my companion muttered: "Man, if we'd gone forward we should have been ten feet deep in our graves by now. 'There are more things in heaven and earth' . . . Come home, Pansay, and thank God. I want a peg badly."

We retraced our way over the Church Ridge, and I arrived at Dr. Heatherlegh's house shortly after midnight.

His attempts toward my cure commenced almost immediately, and for a week I never left his sight. Many a time in the course of that week did I bless the good fortune which had thrown me in contact with Simla's best and kindest doctor. Day by day my spirits grew lighter and more equable. Day by day, too, I became more and more inclined to fall in with Heatherlegh's "spectral illusion" theory, implicating eyes, brain, and stomach. I wrote to Kitty, telling her that a slight sprain caused by a fall from my horse kept me indoors for a few days; and that I should be recovered before she had time to regret my absence.

Heatherlegh's treatment was simple to a degree. It consisted of liver pills, cold-water baths, and strong exercise, taken in the dusk or at early dawn—for, as he sagely observed: "A man with a sprained ankle doesn't walk a dozen miles a day, and your young woman might be wondering if she saw you."

At the end of the week, after much examination of pupil and pulse, and strict injunctions as to diet and pedestrianism, Heatherlegh dismissed me as brusquely as he had taken charge of me. Here is his parting benediction: "Man, I certify to your mental cure, and that's as much as to say I've cured most of your bodily ailments. Now, get your traps out of this as soon as you can; and be off to make love to Miss Kitty."

I was endeavoring to express my thanks for his kindness. He cut me short.

"Don't think I did this because I like you. I gather that you've behaved like a blackguard all through. But, all the same, you're a phenomenon, and as queer a phenomenon as you are a blackguard. No!"—checking me a second time—"not a rupee, please. Go out and see if you can find the eyes-brain-and-stomach business again. I'll give you a lakh for each time you see it."

Half an hour later I was in the Mannerings' drawing room with Kitty—drunk with the intoxication of present happiness and the foreknowledge that I should never more be troubled with Its hideous presence. Strong in the sense of my new-found security, I proposed a ride at once; and, by preference, a canter around Jakko.

Never had I felt so well, so overladen with vitality and mere animal spirits, as I did on the afternoon of the 30th of April. Kitty was delighted at the change in my appearance, and complimented me on it in her delightfully frank and outspoken manner. We left the Mannerings' house together, laughing and talking, and cantered along the Chota Simla road as of old.

I was in haste to reach the Sanjowlie Reservoir and there make my assurance doubly sure. The horses did their best, but seemed all too slow to my impatient mind. Kitty was astonished at my boisterousness. "Why, Jack!" she cried at last, "you are behaving like a child. What are you doing?"

We were just below the Convent, and from sheer wantonness I was making my Waler plunge and curvet across the road as I tickled it with the loop of my riding whip.

"Doing?" I answered; "nothing, dear. That's just it. If you'd been doing nothing for a week except lie up, you'd be as riotous as I."

> "Singing and murmuring in your feastful mirth,
> Joying to feel yourself alive;
> Lord over Nature, Lord of the visible Earth,
> Lord of the senses five."

My quotation was hardly out of my lips before we had rounded the corner above the Convent; and a few yards farther on could see across to Sanjowlie. In the center of the level road stood the black and white liveries, the yellow-paneled 'rickshaw, and Mrs. Keith-Wessington. I pulled up, looked, rubbed my eyes, and, I believe, must have said something. The next thing I knew was that I was lying face downward on the road, with Kitty kneeling above me in tears.

"Has it gone, child?" I gasped. Kitty only wept more bitterly.

"Has what gone, Jack dear? what does it all mean? There must be a mistake somewhere, Jack. A hideous mistake." Her last words brought me to my feet—mad—raving for the time being.

"Yes, there *is* a mistake somewhere," I repeated, "a hideous mistake. Come and look at It."

I have an indistinct idea that I dragged Kitty by the wrist along the road up to where It stood, and implored her for pity's sake to speak to It; to tell It that we were betrothed; that neither Death nor Hell could break the tie between us: and Kitty only knows how much more to the same effect. Now and again I appealed passionately to the Terror in the 'rickshaw to bear witness to all I had said, and to release me from a torture that was killing me. As I talked I suppose I must have told Kitty of my old relations with Mrs. Wessington, for I saw her listen intently with white face and blazing eyes.

"Thank you, Mr. Pansay," she said, "that's *quite* enough. *Syce ghora láo.*"

The syces, impassive as Orientals always are, had come up with the recaptured horses; and as Kitty sprang into her saddle I caught hold of her bridle, entreating her to hear me out and forgive. My answer was the cut of her riding whip across my face from mouth to eye, and a word or two of farewell that even now I cannot write down. So I judged and judged rightly, that Kitty knew all; and I staggered back to the side of the 'rickshaw. My face was cut and bleeding, and the blow of the riding whip had raised a livid blue wheal on it. I had no self-respect. Just then, Heatherlegh, who must have been following Kitty and me at a distance, cantered up.

"Doctor," I said, pointing to my face, "here's Miss Mannering's signature to my order of dismissal and—— I'll thank you for that lakh as soon as convenient."

Heatherlegh's face, even in my abject misery, moved me to laughter.

"I'll stake my professional reputation——" he began.

"Don't be a fool," I whispered. "I've lost my life's happiness and you'd better take me home."

As I spoke the 'rickshaw was gone. Then I lost all knowledge

—"My answer was the cut of her riding whip across my face from mouth to eye, and a word or two of farewell that even now I cannot write down."

of what was passing. The crest of Jakko seemed to heave and roll like the crest of a cloud and fall in upon me.

Seven days later (on the 7th of May, that is to say) I was aware that I was lying in Heatherlegh's room as weak as a little child. Heatherlegh was watching me intently from behind the papers on his writing table. His first words were not encouraging; but I was too far spent to be much moved by them.

"Here's Miss Kitty has sent back your letters. You corresponded a good deal, you young people. Here's a packet that looks like a ring and a cheerful sort of a note from Mannering Papa, which I've taken the liberty of reading and burning. The old gentleman's not pleased with you."

"And Kitty?" I asked dully.

"Rather more drawn than her father from what she says. By the same token you must have been letting out any number of queer reminiscences just before I met you. 'Says that a man who would have behaved to a woman as you did to Mrs. Wessington ought to kill himself out of sheer pity for his kind. She's a hot-headed little virago, your mash. 'Will have it too that you were suffering from *D. T.* when that row on the Jakko road turned up. 'Says she'll die before she ever speaks to you again."

I groaned and turned over on the other side.

"Now you've got your choice, my friend. This engagement has to be broken off; and the Mannerings don't want to be too hard on you. Was it broken through *D. T.* or epileptic fits? Sorry I can't offer you a better exchange unless you'd prefer hereditary insanity. Say the word and I'll tell 'em it's fits. All Simla knows about that scene on the Ladies' Mile. Come! I'll give you five minutes to think over it."

During those five minutes I believe that I explored thoroughly the lowest circles of the Inferno which it is permitted man to tread on earth. And at the same time I myself was watching myself faltering through the dark labyrinths of doubt, misery, and utter despair. I wondered, as Heatherlegh in his chair might have wondered, which dreadful alternative I should adopt. Presently I heard myself answering in a voice that I hardly recognized—

"They're confoundedly particular about morality in these parts. Give 'em fits, Heatherlegh, and my love. Now let me sleep a bit longer."

Then my two selves joined, and it was only I (half crazed, devil-driven I) that tossed in my bed tracing step by step the history of the past month.

"But I am in Simla," I kept repeating to myself. "I, Jack Pansay, am in Simla, and there are no ghosts here. It's unreasonable of that woman to pretend there are. Why couldn't Agnes have left me alone? I never did her any harm. It might just as well have been me as Agnes. Only I'd never have come back on purpose to kill *her*. Why can't I be left alone—left alone and happy?"

It was high noon when I first awoke: and the sun was low in the sky before I slept—slept as the tortured criminal sleeps on his rack, too worn to feel further pain.

Next day I could not leave my bed. Heatherlegh told me in

the morning that he had received an answer from Mr. Mannering, and that, thanks to his (Heatherlegh's) friendly offices, the story of my affliction had traveled through the length and breadth of Simla, where I was on all sides much pitied.

"And that's rather more than you deserve," he concluded pleasantly, "though the Lord knows you've been going through a pretty severe mill. Never mind; we'll cure you yet, you perverse phenomenon."

I declined firmly to be cured. "You've been much too good to me already, old man," said I; "but I don't think I need trouble you further."

In my heart I knew that nothing Heatherlegh could do would lighten the burden that had been laid upon me.

With that knowledge came also a sense of hopeless, impotent rebellion against the unreasonableness of it all. There were scores of men no better than I whose punishments had at least been reserved for another world; and I felt that it was bitterly, cruelly unfair that I alone should have been singled out for so hideous a fate. This mood would in time give place to another where it seemed that the 'rickshaw and I were the only realities in a world of shadows; that Kitty was a ghost; that Mannering, Heatherlegh, and all the other men and women I knew were all ghosts; and the great, gray hills themselves but vain shadows devised to torture me. From mood to mood I tossed backward and forward for seven weary days; my body growing daily stronger and stronger, until the bedroom looking glass told me that I had returned to everyday life, and was as other men once more. Curiously enough my face showed no signs of the struggle I had gone through. It was pale indeed, but as expressionless and commonplace as ever. I had expected some permanent alteration—visible evidence of the disease that was eating me away. I found nothing.

On the 15th of May I left Heatherlegh's house at eleven o'clock in the morning; and the instinct of the bachelor drove me to the Club. There I found that every man knew my story as told by Heatherlegh, and was, in clumsy fashion, abnormally kind and attentive. Nevertheless I recognized that for the rest of my natural life I should be among but not of my fellows; and I envied very bitterly indeed the laughing coolies on the

Mall below. I lunched at the Club, and at four o'clock wandered aimlessly down the Mall in the vague hope of meeting Kitty. Close to the Bandstand the black and white liveries joined me; and I heard Mrs. Wessington's old appeal at my side. I had been expecting this ever since I came out; and was only surprised at her delay. The phantom 'rickshaw and I went side by side along the Chota Simla road in silence. Close to the bazar, Kitty and a man on horseback overtook and passed us. For any sign she gave I might have been a dog in the road. She did not even pay me the compliment of quickening her pace; though the rainy afternoon had served for an excuse.

So Kitty and her companion, and I and my ghostly Light-o'-Love, crept around Jakko in couples. The road was streaming with water; the pines dripped like roof-pipes on the rocks below, and the air was full of fine, driving rain. Two or three times I found myself saying to myself almost aloud: "I'm Jack Pansay on leave at Simla—*at Simla!* Everyday, ordinary Simla. I mustn't forget that—I mustn't forget that." Then I would try to recollect some of the gossip I had heard at the Club: the prices of So-and-So's horses—anything, in fact, that related to the work-a-day Anglo-Indian world I knew so well. I even repeated the multiplication table rapidly to myself, to make quite sure that I was not taking leave of my senses. It gave me much comfort; and must have prevented my hearing Mrs. Wessington for a time.

Once more I wearily climbed the Convent slope and entered the level road. Here Kitty and the man started off at a canter, and I was left alone with Mrs. Wessington. "Agnes," said I, "will you put back your hood and tell me what it all means?" The hood dropped noiselessly, and I was face to face with my dead and buried mistress. She was wearing the dress in which I had last seen her alive; carried the same tiny handkerchief in her right hand; and the same card-case in her left. (A woman eight months dead with a card-case!) I had to pin myself down to the multiplication table, and to set both hands on the stone parapet of the road, to assure myself that that at least was real.

"Agnes," I repeated, "for pity's sake tell me what it all means." Mrs. Wessington leaned forward, with that odd, quick turn of the head I used to know so well, and spoke.

If my story had not already so madly overleaped the bounds of all human belief I should apologize to you now. As I know that no one—no, not even Kitty, for whom it is written as some sort of justification of my conduct—will believe me, I will go on. Mrs. Wessington spoke and I walked with her from the Sanjowlie road to the turning below the Commander-in-Chief's house as I might walk by the side of any living woman's 'rickshaw, deep in conversation. The second and most tormenting of my moods of sickness had suddenly laid hold upon me, and like the Prince in Tennyson's poem, "I seemed to move amid a world of ghosts." There had been a garden party at the Commander-in-Chief's, and we two joined the crowd of homeward-bound folk. As I saw them it seemed that *they* were the shadows—impalpable fantastic shadows—that divided for Mrs. Wessington's 'rickshaw to pass through. What we said during the course of that weird interview I cannot—indeed, I dare not—tell. Heatherlegh's comment would have been a short laugh and a remark that I had been "mashing a brain-eye-and-stomach chimera." It was a ghastly and yet in some indefinable way a marvelously dear experience. Could it be possible, I wondered, that I was in this life to woo a second time the woman I had killed by my own neglect and cruelty?

I met Kitty on the homeward road—a shadow among shadows.

If I were to describe all the incidents of the next fortnight in their order, my story would never come to an end; and your patience would be exhausted. Morning after morning and evening after evening the ghostly 'rickshaw and I used to wander through Simla together. Wherever I went there the four black and white liveries followed me and bore me company to and from my hotel. At the Theater I found them amid the crowd of yelling *jhampanies;* outside the Club veranda, after a long evening of whist; at the Birthday Ball, waiting patiently for my reappearance; and in broad daylight when I went calling. Save that it cast no shadow, the 'rickshaw was in every respect as real to look upon as one of wood and iron. More than once, indeed, I have had to check myself from warning some hard-riding friend against cantering over it. More than once I have walked down the Mall deep in conversation with Mrs. Wessington to the unspeakable amazement of the passersby.

Before I had been out and about a week I learned that the "fit" theory had been discarded in favor of insanity. However, I made no change in my mode of life. I called, rode, and dined out as freely as ever. I had a passion for the society of my kind which I had never felt before; I hungered to be among the realities of life; and at the same time I felt vaguely unhappy when I had been separated too long from my ghostly companion. It would be almost impossible to describe my varying moods from the 15th of May up to today.

The presence of the 'rickshaw filled me by turns with horror, blind fear, a dim sort of pleasure, and utter despair. I dared not leave Simla; and I knew that my stay there was killing me. I knew, moreover, that it was my destiny to die slowly and a little every day. My only anxiety was to get the penance over as quietly as might be. Alternately I hungered for a sight of Kitty and watched her outrageous flirtations with my successor—to speak more accurately, my successors—with amused interest. She was as much out of my life as I was out of hers. By day I wandered with Mrs. Wessington almost content. By night I implored Heaven to let me return to the world as I used to know it. Above all these varying moods lay the sensation of dull, numbing wonder that the seen and the Unseen should mingle so strangely on this earth to hound one poor soul to its grave.

August 27.—Heatherlegh has been indefatigable in his attendance on me; and only yesterday told me that I ought to send in an application for sick leave. An application to escape the company of a phantom! A request that the Government would graciously permit me to get rid of five ghosts and an airy 'rickshaw by going to England! Heatherlegh's proposition moved me to almost hysterical laughter. I told him that I should await the end quietly at Simla; and I am sure that the end is not far off. Believe me that I dread its advent more than any word can say; and I torture myself nightly with a thousand speculations as to the manner of my death.

Shall I die in my bed decently and as an English gentleman

should die; or, in one last walk on the Mall, will my soul be wrenched from me to take its place forever and ever by the side of that ghastly phantasm? Shall I return to my old lost allegiance in the next world, or shall I meet Agnes loathing her and bound to her side through all eternity? Shall we two hover over the scene of our lives till the end of Time? As the day of my death draws nearer, the intense horror that all living flesh feels toward escaped spirits from beyond the grave grows more and more powerful. It is an awful thing to go down quick among the dead with scarcely one-half of your life completed. It is a thousand times more awful to wait as I do in your midst, for I know not what unimaginable terror. Pity me, at least on the score of my "delusion," for I know you will never believe what I have written here. Yet as surely as ever a man was done to death by the Powers of Darkness, I am that man.

In justice, too, pity her. For as surely as ever woman was killed by man, I killed Mrs. Wessington. And the last portion of my punishment is even now upon me.

THE BULL THAT THOUGHT

Westward from a town by the mouths of the Rhône, runs a road so mathematically straight, so barometrically level, that it ranks among the world's measured miles and motorists use it for records.

I had attacked the distance several times, but always with a Mistral blowing, or the unchancy cattle of those parts on the move. But once, running from the East, into a high-piled, almost Egyptian, sunset, there came a night which it would have been sin to have wasted. It was warm with the breath of summer in advance; moonlit till the shadow of every rounded pebble and pointed cypress windbreak lay solid on that vast flat-floored waste; and my Mr. Leggatt, who had slipped out to make sure, reported that the road surface was unblemished.

"Now," he suggested, "we might see what she'll do under strict road conditions. She's been pullin' like the Blue de Luxe all day. Unless I'm all off, it's her night out."

We arranged the trial for after dinner—thirty kilometers as near as might be; and twenty-two of them without even a level crossing.

There sat beside me at table d'hôte an elderly, bearded Frenchman wearing the rosette of by no means the lowest grade of the Legion of Honor, who had arrived in a talkative Citroën. I gathered that he had spent much of his life in the French Colonial Service in Annam and Tonquin. When the War came, his years barring him from the front line, he had supervised Chinese woodcutters who, with axe and dynamite, deforested the center of France for trench-props. He said my chauffeur had told him that I contemplated an experiment. He was interested in cars—had admired mine—would, in short, be greatly indebted to me if I permitted him to assist as an observer. One could not well refuse; and, knowing my Mr. Leggatt, it occurred to me there might also be a bet in the background.

While he went to get his coat, I asked the proprietor his name. "Voiron—Monsieur André Voiron," was the reply. "And his business?" "Mon Dieu! He is Voiron! He is all those things, there!" The proprietor waved his hands at brilliant advertisements on the dining-room walls, which declared that Voiron Frères dealt in wines, agricultural implements, chemical manures, provisions and produce throughout that part of the globe.

He said little for the first five minutes of our trip, and nothing at all for the next ten—it being, as Leggatt had guessed, Esmeralda's night out. But, when her indicator climbed to a certain figure and held there for three blinding kilometers, he expressed himself satisfied, and proposed to me that we should celebrate the event at the hotel. "I keep yonder," said he, "a wine on which I should value your opinion."

On our return, he disappeared for a few minutes, and I heard him rumbling in a cellar. The proprietor presently invited me to the dining room, where, beneath one frugal light, a table had been set with local dishes of renown. There was, too, a bottle beyond most known sizes, marked black on red, with a date. Monsieur Voiron opened it, and we drank to the health of my car. The velvety, perfumed liquor, between fawn and topaz, neither too sweet nor too dry, creamed in its generous glass. But I knew no wine composed of the whispers of angels' wings, the breath of Eden and the foam and pulse of Youth renewed. So I asked what it might be.

"It is champagne," he said gravely.

"Then what have I been drinking all my life?"

"If you were lucky, before the War, and paid thirty shillings a bottle, it is possible you may have drunk one of our better-class *tisanes*."

"And where does one get this?"

"Here, I am happy to say. Elsewhere, perhaps, it is not so easy. We growers exchange these real wines among ourselves."

I bowed my head in admiration, surrender, and joy. There stood the most ample bottle, and it was not yet eleven o'clock. Doors locked and shutters banged throughout the establishment. Some last servant yawned on his way to bed. Monsieur Voiron opened a window and the moonlight flooded in from a small pebbled court outside. One could almost hear the town of Chambres breathing in its first sleep. Presently, there was a thick noise in the air, the passing of feet and hooves, lowings, and a stifled bark or two. Dust rose over the courtyard wall, followed by the strong smell of cattle.

"They are moving some beasts," said Monsieur Voiron, cocking an ear. "Mine, I think. Yes, I hear Christophe. Our beasts do not like automobiles—so we move at night. You do not know our country—the Crau, here, or the Camargue? I was—I am now, again—of it. All France is good; but this is the best." He spoke, as only a Frenchman can, of his own loved part of his own lovely land.

"For myself, if I were not so involved in all these affairs," he pointed to the advertisements—"I would live on our farm with my cattle, and worship them like a Hindu. You know our cattle of the Camargue, Monsieur. No? It is not an acquaintance to rush upon lightly. There are no beasts like them. They have a mentality superior to that of others. They graze and they ruminate, by choice, facing our Mistral, which is more than some automobiles will do. Also they have in them the potentiality of thought—and when cattle think—I have seen what arrives."

"Are they so clever as all that?" I asked idly.

"Monsieur, when your sportif chauffeur camouflaged your limousine so that she resembled one of your Army lorries, I would not believe her capacities. I bet him—ah—two to one—she would not touch ninety kilometers. It was proved that she could. I can give you no proof, but will you believe me if I tell you what a beast who thinks can achieve?"

"After the War," said I spaciously, "everything is credible."

"That is true! Everything inconceivable has happened; but still we learn nothing and we believe nothing. When I was a child in my father's house—before I became a Colonial Administrator—my interest and my affection were among our cattle. We of the old rock live here—have you seen?—in big farms like castles. Indeed, some of them may have been Saracenic. The barns group around them—great white-walled barns, and yards solid as our houses. One gate shuts all. It is a world apart; an administration of all that concerns beasts. It was there I learned something about cattle. You see, they are our playthings in the Camargue and the Crau. The boy measures his strength against the calf that butts him in play among the manure heaps. He moves in and out among the cows, who are—not so amiable. He rides with the herdsmen in the open to shift the herds. Sooner or later, he meets as bulls the little calves that knocked him over. So it was with me—till it became necessary that I should go to our Colonies." He laughed. "Very necessary. That is a good time in youth, Monsieur, when one does these things which shock our parents. Why is it always Papa who is so shocked and has never heard of such things—and Mamma who supplies the excuses? . . . And when my brother—my elder who stayed and created the business—begged me to return and help him, I resigned my Colonial career gladly enough. I returned to our own lands, and my well-loved, wicked white and yellow cattle of the Camargue and the Crau. My Faith, I could talk of them all night, for this stuff unlocks the heart, without making repentance in the morning. . . . Yes! It was after the War that this happened. There was a calf, among Heaven knows how many of ours—a bull-calf—an infant indistinguishable from his companions. He was sick, and he had been taken up with his mother into the big farmyard at home with us. Naturally the children of our herdsmen practiced on him from the first. It is in their blood. The Spaniards make a cult of bullfighting. Our little devils down here bait bulls as automatically as the English child kicks or throws balls. This calf would chase them with his eyes open, like a cow when she hunts a man. They would take refuge behind our tractors and wine-carts in the center of the yard: he would chase them in and out as a dog hunts rats. More than that, he would study their psychology, his eyes in their eyes. Yes, he watched their faces to divine which way they would run. He himself, also, would pretend sometimes to charge directly at a boy. Then he would wheel right or left—one could never tell—and knock over some child pressed against a wall who thought himself safe. After this, he would stand over him, knowing that his companions must come to his aid; and when they were all together, waving their jackets across his eyes and pulling his tail, he would scatter them—how he would scatter them! He could kick too, sideways like a cow. He knew his ranges as well as our gunners, and he was as quick on his feet as our Carpentier. I observed him often. Christophe—the man who passed just now—our chief herdsman, who had taught me to ride with our beasts when I was ten—Christophe told me that he was descended from a yellow cow of those days that had chased us once into the marshes. 'He kicks just like her,' said Christophe. 'He can side-kick as he jumps. Have you seen, too, that he is not deceived by the jacket when a boy waves it? He uses it to find the boy. They think they are feeling him. He is feeling them always. He thinks, that one.' I had come to the same conclusion. Yes—the creature was a thinker along the lines necessary to his sport; and he was a humorist also, like so many natural murderers. One knows the type among beasts as well as among men. It possesses a curious truculent mirth—almost indecent but infallibly significant——"

Monsieur Voiron replenished our glasses with the great wine that went better at each descent.

"They kept him for some time in the yards to practice upon. Naturally he became a little brutal; so Christophe turned him out to learn manners among his equals in the grazing lands, where the Camargue joins the Crau. How old was he then? About eight or nine months, I think. We met again a few months later—he and I. I was riding one of our little half-wild horses, along a road of the Crau, when I found myself almost unseated. It was he! He had hidden himself behind a windbreak till we passed, and had then charged my horse from behind. Yes, he had deceived even my little horse! But I recognized him. I gave him the whip across the nose, and I said: 'Apis, for this thou goest to Arles! It was unworthy of thee, between us two.' But that creature had no shame. He went away laughing, like an Apache. If he had dismounted me, I do not think it is I who would have laughed—yearling as he was."

"Why did you want to send him to Arles?" I asked.

"For the bullring. When your charming tourists leave us, we institute our little amusements there. Not a real bullfight, you understand, but young bulls with padded horns, and our boys from hereabouts and in the city, go to play with them. Naturally, before we send them we try them in our yards at home. So we brought up Apis from his pastures. He knew at once that he was among the friends of his youth—he almost shook hands with them—and he submitted like an angel to padding his horns.

He investigated the carts and tractors in the yards, to choose his lines of defense and attack. And then—he attacked with an *élan,* and he defended with a tenacity and forethought that delighted us. In truth, we were so pleased that I fear we trespassed upon his patience. We desired him to repeat himself, which no true artist will tolerate. But he gave us fair warning. He went out to the center of the yard, where there was some dry earth; he kneeled down and—you have seen a calf whose horns fret him thrusting and rooting into a bank? He did just that, very deliberately, till he had rubbed the pads off his horns. Then he rose, dancing on those wonderful feet that twinkled, and he said: 'Now, my friends, the buttons are off the foils. Who begins?' We understood. We finished at once. He was turned out again on the pastures until it should be time to amuse them at our little metropolis. But, some time before he went to Arles—yes, I think I have it correctly—Christophe, who had been out on the Crau, informed me that Apis had assassinated a young bull who had given signs of developing into a rival. That happens, of course, and our herdsmen should prevent it. But Apis had killed in his own style—at dusk, from the ambush of a windbreak—by an oblique charge from behind which knocked the other over. He had then disemboweled him. All very possible, *but*—the murder accomplished—Apis went to the bank of a windbreak, knelt, and carefully, as he had in our yard, cleaned his horns in the earth. Christophe, who had never seen such a thing, at once borrowed (do you know, it is most efficacious when taken that way?) some Holy Water from our little chapel in those pastures, sprinkled Apis (whom it did not affect), and rode in to tell me. It was obvious that a thinker of that bull's type would also be meticulous in his toilette; so, when he was sent to Arles, I warned our consignees to exercise caution with him. Happily, the change of scene, the music, the general attention, and the meeting again with old friends—all our bad boys attended—agreeably distracted him. He became for the time a pure *farceur* again; but his wheelings, his rushes, his rat-huntings were more superb than ever. There was in them now, you understand, a breadth of technique that comes of reasoned art, and, above all, the passion that arrives after experience. Oh, he had learned, out there on the Crau! At the end of his little turn, he was, according to local rules, to be handled in all respects except for the sword, which was a stick, as a professional bull who must die. He was maneuvered into, or he posed himself in, the proper attitude; made his rush; received the point on his shoulder and then—turned about and cantered toward the door by which he had entered the arena. He said to the world: 'My friends, the representation is ended. I thank you for your applause. I go to repose myself.' But our Arlesians, who are—not so clever as some, demanded an encore, and Apis was headed back again. We others from his country, we knew what would happen. He went to the center of the ring, kneeled, and, slowly, with full parade, plunged his horns alternately in the dirt till the pads came off. Christophe shouts: 'Leave him alone, you straight-nosed imbeciles! Leave him before you must.' But they required emotion; for Rome has always debauched her loved Provincia with bread and circuses. It was given. Have you, Monsieur, ever seen a servant, with pan and broom, sweeping around the baseboard of a room? In a half-minute Apis has them all swept out and over the barrier. Then he demands once more that the door shall be opened to him. It is opened and he retires as though—which truly, is the case—loaded with laurels."

Monsieur Voiron refilled the glasses, and allowed himself a cigarette, which he puffed for some time.

"And afterward?" I said.

"I am arranging it in my mind. It is difficult to do it justice. Afterward—yes, afterward—Apis returned to his pastures and his mistresses and I to my business. I am no longer a scandalous old 'sportif' in shirtsleeves howling encouragement to the yellow son of a cow. I revert to Voiron Frères—wines, chemical manures, *et cetera.* And next year, through some chicane which I have not the leisure to unravel, and also, thanks to our patriarchal system of paying our older men out of the increase of the herds, old Christophe possesses himself of Apis. Oh, yes, he proves it through descent from a certain cow that my father had given his father before the Republic. Beware, Monsieur, of the memory of the illiterate man! An ancestor of Christophe had been a soldier under our Soult against your Beresford, near Bayonne. He fell into the hands of Spanish guerrillas. Christophe and his wife used to tell me the details on certain Saints' Days when I was a child. Now, as compared with our recent war, Soult's campaign and retreat across the Bidassoa——"

"But did you allow Christophe just to annex the bull?" I demanded.

"You do not know Christophe. He had sold him to the Spaniards before he informed me. The Spaniards pay in coin—douros of very pure silver. Our peasants mistrust our paper. You know the saying: 'A thousand francs paper; eight hundred metal, and the cow is yours.' Yes, Christophe sold Apis, who was then two and a half years old, and to Christophe's knowledge thrice at least an assassin."

"How was that?" I said.

"Oh, his own kind only; and always, Christophe told me, by the same oblique rush from behind, the same sideways overthrow, and the same swift disembowelment, followed by this levitical cleaning of the horns. In human life he would have kept a manicurist—this Minotaur. And so, Apis disappears from our country. That does not trouble me. I know in due time I shall be advised. Why? Because, in this land, Monsieur, not a hoof moves between Berre and the Saintes Maries without the knowledge of specialists such as Christophe. The beasts are the substance, and the drama of their lives to them. So when Christophe tells me, a little before Easter Sunday, that Apis makes his début in the bullring of a small Catalan town on the road to Barcelona, it is only to pack my car and trundle there across the frontier with him. The place lacked importance and manufactures, but it had produced a matador of some reputation, who was condescending to show his art in his native town. They were even running one special train to the place. Now our French railway system is only execrable, but the Spanish——"

"You went down by road, didn't you?" said I.

"Naturally. It was not too good. Villamarti was the matador's name. He proposed to kill two bulls for the honor of his birthplace. Apis, Christophe told me, would be his second. It was an interesting trip, and that little city by the sea was ravishing. Their bullring dates from the middle of the seventeenth century. It is full of feeling. The ceremonial too—when the horsemen enter and ask the Mayor in his box to throw down the keys of the bullring—that was exquisitely conceived. You know, if the keys are caught in the horseman's hat, it is considered a good omen. They were perfectly caught. Our seats were in the front row beside the gates where the bulls enter, so we saw everything.

"Villamarti's first bull was not too badly killed. The second matador, whose name escapes me, killed his without distinction—a foil to Villamarti. And the third, Chisto, a laborious, middle-aged professional who had never risen beyond a certain dull competence, was equally of the background. Oh, they are as jealous as the girls of the Comédie Française, these matadors! Villamarti's troupe stood ready for his second bull. The gates opened, and we saw Apis, beautifully balanced on his feet, peer coquettishly around the corner, as though he were at home. A picador—a mounted man with the long lance-goad—stood near the barrier on his right. He had not even troubled to turn his horse, for the capeadors—the men with the cloaks—were advancing to play Apis—to feel his psychology and intentions, according to the rules that are made for bulls who do not think. . . . I did not realize the murder before it was accomplished! The wheel, the rush, the oblique charge from behind, the fall of horse and man were simultaneous. Apis leaped the horse, with whom he had no quarrel, and alighted, all four feet together (it was enough), between the man's shoulders, changed his beautiful feet on the carcass, and was away, pretending to fall nearly on his nose. Do you follow me? In that instant, by that stumble, he produced the impression that his adorable assassination was a mere bestial blunder. Then, Monsieur, I began to comprehend that it was an artist we had to deal with. He did not stand over the body to draw the rest of the troupe. He chose to reserve that trick. He let the attendants bear out the dead, and went on to amuse himself among the capeadors. Now to Apis, trained among our children in the yards, the cloak was simply a guide to the boy behind it. He pursued, you understand, the person, not the propaganda—the proprietor, not the journal. If a third of our electors of France were as wise, my friend! . . . But it was done leisurely, with humor and a touch of truculence. He romped after one man's cloak as a clumsy dog might do, but I observed that he kept the man on his terrible left side. Christophe whispered to me: 'Wait for his mother's kick. When he has made the fellow confident it will arrive.' It arrived in the middle of a gambol. My God! He lashed out in the air as he frisked. The man dropped like a sack, lifted one hand a little toward his head, and—that was all. So you see, a body was again at his disposition; a second time the cloaks ran up to draw him off, but a second time, Apis refused his grand scene. A second time he acted that his murder was accident and—he convinced his audience! It was as though he had knocked over a bridge-gate in the marshes by mistake. Unbelievable? I saw it."

The memory sent Monsieur Voiron again to the champagne, and I accompanied him.

"But Apis was not the sole artist present. They say Villamarti comes of a family of actors. I saw him regard Apis with a new eye. He, too, began to understand. He took his cloak and moved out to play him before they should bring on another picador. He had his reputation. Perhaps Apis knew it. Perhaps Villamarti reminded him of some boy with whom he had practiced at home. At any rate Apis permitted it—up to a certain point; but he did not allow Villamarti the stage. He cramped him throughout. He dived and plunged clumsily and slowly, but always with menace and always closing in. We could see that the man was conforming to the bull—not the bull to the man; for Apis was playing him toward the center of the ring, and, in a little while—I watched his face—Villamarti knew it. But I could not fathom the creature's motive. 'Wait,' said old Christophe. 'He wants that picador on the white horse yonder. When he reaches his proper distance he will get him. Villamarti is his cover. He used me once that way.' And so it was, my friend! With the clang of one of our own Seventy-fives, Apis dismissed Villamarti with his chest—breasted him over—and had arrived at his objective near the barrier. The same oblique charge; the head carried low for the sweep of the horns; the immense sideways fall of the horse, broken-legged and half-paralyzed; the senseless man on the ground and—behold Apis between them, backed against the barrier—his right covered by the horse; his left by the body of the man at his feet. The simplicity of it! Lacking the carts and tractors of his early parade grounds he, being a genius, had extemporized with the materials at hand, and dug himself in. The troupe closed up again, their left wing broken by the kicking horse, their right immobilized by the man's body which Apis bestrode with significance. Villamarti almost threw himself between the horns, but—it was more an appeal than an attack. Apis refused him. He held his base. A picador was sent at him—necessarily from the front, which alone was open. Apis charged—he who, till then, you realize, had not used the horn! The horse went over backward, the man half beneath him. Apis halted, hooked him under the heart, and threw him to the barrier. He heard his head crack, but he was dead before he hit the wood. There was no demonstration from the audience. They, also, had begun to realize this Foch among bulls! The arena occupied itself again with the dead. Two of the troupe irresolutely tried to play him—God knows in what hope!—but he moved out to the center of the ring. 'Look!' said Christophe. 'Now he goes to clean himself. That always frightened me.' He knelt down; he began to clean his horns. The earth was hard. He worried at it in an ecstasy of absorption. As he laid his head along and rattled his ears, it was as though he were interrogating the Devils themselves upon their secrets, and always saying impatiently: 'Yes, I know that—and *that*—and *that!* Tell me more—*more!*' In the silence that covered us, a woman cried: 'He digs a grave! Oh, Saints, he digs a grave!' Some others echoed this—not loudly—as a wave echoes in a grotto of the sea.

"And when his horns were cleaned, he rose up and studied poor Villamarti's troupe, eyes in eyes, one by one, with the gravity of an equal in intellect and the remote and merciless resolution of a master in his art. This was more terrifying than his toilette."

"And they—Villamarti's men?" I asked.

"Like the audience, were dominated. They had ceased to posture, or stamp, or address insults to him. They conformed to him. The two other matadors stared. Only Chisto, the oldest, broke silence with some call or other, and Apis turned his head toward him. Otherwise he was isolated, immobile—somber—meditating on those at his mercy. Ah!

"For some reason the trumpet sounded for the *banderillas*—those gay hooked darts that are planted in the shoulders of bulls who do not think, after their neck muscles are tired by lifting horses. When such bulls feel the pain, they check for an instant, and, in that instant, the men step gracefully aside. Villamarti's banderillero answered the trumpet mechanically—like one condemned. He stood out, poised the darts and stammered the usual patter of invitation. . . . And after? I do not assert that Apis shrugged his shoulders, but he reduced the episode to its lowest elements, as could only a bull of Gaul. With his truculence was mingled always—owing to the shortness of his tail—a certain Rabelaisian abandon, especially when viewed from the rear. Christophe had often commented upon it. Now, Apis brought that quality into play. He circulated around that boy, forcing him to break up his beautiful poses. He studied him from various angles, like an incompetent photographer. He presented to him every portion of his anatomy except his shoulders. At intervals he feigned to run in upon him. My God, he was cruel! But his motive was obvious. He was playing for a laugh from the spectators which should synchronize with the fracture of the human morale. It was achieved. The boy turned and ran toward the barrier. Apis was on him before the laugh ceased; passed him; headed him—what do I say?—herded him off to the left, his horns beside and a little in front of his chest: he did not intend him to escape into a refuge. Some of the troupe would have closed in, but Villamarti cried: 'If he wants him he will take him. Stand!' They stood. Whether the boy slipped or Apis nosed him over I could not see. But he dropped, sobbing. Apis halted like a car with four brakes, struck a pose, smelled him very completely and turned away. It was dismissal more ignominious than degradation at the head of one's battalion. The representation was finished. Remained only for Apis to clear his stage of the subordinate characters.

"Ah! His gesture then! He gave a dramatic start—this Cyrano of the Camargue—as though he was aware of them for the first time. He moved. All their beautiful breeches twinkled for an instant along the top of the barrier. He held the stage alone! But Christophe and I, we trembled! For, observe, he had now involved himself in a stupendous drama of which he only could supply the third act. And, except for an audience on the razoredge of emotion, he had exhausted his material. Molière himself—we have forgotten, my friend, to drink to the health of that great soul—might have been at a loss. And Tragedy is but a step behind Failure. We could see the four or five Civil Guards, who are sent always to keep order, fingering the breeches of their rifles. They were but waiting a word from the Mayor to fire on him, as they do sometimes at a bull who leaps the barrier among the spectators. They would, of course, have killed or wounded several people—but that would not have saved Apis."

Monsieur Voiron drowned the thought at once, and wiped his beard.

"At that moment Fate—the Genius of France, if you will—sent to assist in the incomparable finale, none other than Chisto, the eldest, and, I should have said (but never again will I judge!) the least inspired of all; mediocrity itself but, at heart—and it is the heart that conquers always, my friend—at heart an artist. He descended stiffly into the arena, alone and assured. Apis regarded him, his eyes in his eyes. The man took stance, with his cloak, and called to the bull as to an equal: 'Now, Señor, we will show these honorable caballeros something together.' He advanced thus against this thinker who at a plunge—a kick—a thrust—could, we all knew, have extinguished him. My dear friend, I wish I could convey to you something of the unaffected bonhomie, the humor, the delicacy, the consideration bordering on respect even, with which Apis, the supreme artist, responded to this invitation. It was the Master, wearied after a strenuous hour in the atelier, unbuttoned and at ease with some not inexpert but limited disciple. The telepathy was instantaneous between them. And for good reason! Christophe said to me: 'All's well. That Chisto began among the bulls. I was sure of it when I heard him call just now. He has been a herdsman. He'll pull it off.' There was a little feeling and adjustment, at first, for mutual distances and allowances.

"Oh, yes! And here occurred a gross impertinence of Villamarti. He had, after an interval, followed Chisto—to retrieve his reputation. My Faith! I can conceive the elder Dumas slamming his door on an intruder precisely as Apis did. He raced

Villamarti into the nearest refuge at once. He stamped his feet outside it, and he snorted: 'Go! I am engaged with an artist!' Villamarti went—his reputation left behind forever.

"Apis returned to Chisto saying: 'Forgive the interruption. I am not always master of my time, but you were about to observe, my dear confrère . . . ?' Then the play began. Out of compliment to Chisto, Apis chose as his objective (every bull varies in this respect) the inner edge of the cloak—that nearest to the man's body. This allows but a few millimeters clearance in charging. But Apis trusted himself as Chisto trusted him, and, this time, he conformed to the man, with inimitable judgment and temper. He allowed himself to be played into the shadow or the sun, as the delighted audience demanded. He raged enormously; he feigned defeat; he despaired in statuesque abandon, and thence flashed into fresh paroxysms of wrath—but always with the detachment of the true artist who knows he is but the vessel of an emotion whence others, not he, must drink. And never once did he forget that honest Chisto's cloak was to him the gauge by which to spare even a hair on the skin. He inspired Chisto too. My God! His youth returned to that meritorious beef-sticker—the desire, the grace, and the beauty of his early dreams. One could almost see that girl of the past for whom he was rising, rising to these present heights of skill and daring. It was his hour too—a miraculous hour of dawn returned to gild the sunset. All he knew was at Apis' disposition. Apis acknowledged it with all that he had learned at home, at Arles and in his lonely murders on our grazing-grounds. He flowed around Chisto like a river of death—around his knees, leaping at his shoulders, kicking just clear of one side or the other of his head; behind his back hissing as he shaved by; and once or twice—inimitable!—he reared wholly up before him while Chisto slipped back from beneath the avalanche of that instructed body. Those two, my dear friend, held five thousand people dumb with no sound but of their breathings—regular as pumps. It was unbearable. Beast and man realized together that we needed a change of note—a *détente*. They relaxed to pure buffoonery. Chisto fell back and talked to him outrageously. Apis pretended he had never heard such language. The audience howled with delight. Chisto slapped him; he took liberties with his short tail, to the end of which he clung while Apis pirouetted; he played about him in all postures; he had become the herdsman again—gross, careless, brutal, but comprehending. Yet Apis was always the more consummate clown. All that time (Christophe and I saw it) Apis drew off toward the gates of the *toril* where so many bulls enter but—have you ever heard of one that returned? *We* knew that Apis knew that as he had saved Chisto, so Chisto would save him. Life is sweet to us all; to the artist who lives many lives in one, sweetest. Chisto did not fail him. At the last, when none could laugh any longer, the man threw his cape across the bull's back, his arm around his neck. He flung up a hand at the gate, as Villamarti, young and commanding but *not* a herdsman, might have raised it, and he cried: 'Gentlemen, open to me and my honorable little donkey.' They opened—I have misjudged Spaniards in my time! —those gates opened to the man and the bull together, and closed behind them. And then? From the Mayor to the Guarda Civile they went mad for five minutes, till the trumpets blew and the fifth bull rushed out—an unthinking black Andalusian. I suppose someone killed him. My friend, my very dear friend, to whom I have opened my heart, I confess that I did not watch. Christophe and I we were weeping together like children of the same Mother. Shall we drink to Her?"

THE MARK OF THE BEAST

Your Gods and my Gods—do you or I know which are the stronger?

—NATIVE PROVERB

EAST of Suez, some hold, the direct control of Providence ceases; Man being there handed over to the power of the Gods and Devils of Asia, and the Church of England Providence only exercising an occasional and modified supervision in the case of Englishmen.

This theory accounts for some of the more unnecessary horrors of life in India: it may be stretched to explain my story.

My friend Strickland of the Police, who knows as much of the natives as is good for any man, can bear witness to the facts of the case. Dumoise, our doctor, also saw what Strickland and I saw. The inference which he drew from the evidence was entirely incorrect. He is dead now; he died, in a rather curious manner, which has been elsewhere described.

When Fleete came to India he owned a little money and some land in the Himalayas, near a place called Dharmsala. Both properties had been left him by an uncle, and he came out to finance them. He was a big, heavy, genial, and inoffensive man. His knowledge of natives was, of course, limited, and he complained of the difficulties of the language.

He rode in from his place in the hills to spend New Year in the station, and he stayed with Strickland. On New Year's Eve there was a big dinner at the club, and the night was excusably wet. When men foregather from the uttermost ends of the Empire, they have a right to be riotous. The Frontier had sent down a contingent o' Catch-'em-Alive-O's who had not seen twenty white faces a year, and were used to ride fifteen miles to dinner at the next Fort at the risk of a Khyberee bullet where there drinks should lie. They profited by their new security, for they tried to play pool with a curled-up hedgehog found in the garden, and one of them carried the marker around the room in his teeth. Half a dozen planters had come in from the south and were talking "horse" to the Biggest Liar in Asia, who was trying to cap all their stories at once. Everybody was there, and there was a general closing up of ranks and taking stock of our losses in dead or disabled that had fallen during the past year. It was a very wet night, and I remember that we sang "Auld Lang Syne" with our feet in the Polo Championship Cup, and our heads among the stars, and swore that we were all dear friends. Then some of us went away and annexed Burma, and some tried to open up the Soudan and were opened up by Fuzzies in that cruel scrub outside Suakim, and some found stars and medals, and some were married, which was bad, and some did other things which were worse, and the others of us stayed in our chains and strove to make money on insufficient experiences.

Fleete began the night with sherry and bitters, drank champagne steadily up to the dessert, then raw, rasping Capri with all the strength of whiskey, took Benedictine with his coffee, four or five whiskies and sodas to improve his pool strokes, beer and bones at half-past two, winding up with old brandy. Consequently, when he came out, at half-past three in the morning, into fourteen degrees of frost, he was very angry with his horse for coughing, and tried to leapfrog into the saddle. The horse broke away and went to his stables; so Strickland and I formed a Guard of Dishonor to take Fleete home.

Our road lay through the bazaar, close to a little temple of Hanuman, the Monkey-god, who is a leading divinity worthy of respect. All gods have good points, just as have all priests. Personally, I attach much importance to Hanuman, and am kind to his people—the great gray apes of the hills. One never knows when one may want a friend.

There was a light in the temple, and as we passed, we could hear voices of men chanting hymns. In a native temple, the priests rise at all hours of the night to do honor to their god. Before we could stop him, Fleete dashed up the steps, patted two priests on the back, and was gravely grinding the ashes of his cigar-butt into the forehead of the red stone image of Hanuman. Strickland tried to drag him out, but he sat down and said solemnly:

"Shee that? Mark of the B—beasht! *I* made it, Ishn't it fine?"

In half a minute the temple was alive and noisy, and Strickland, who knew what came of polluting gods, said that things might occur. He, by virtue of his official position, long residence in the country, and weakness for going among the natives, was known to the priests and he felt unhappy. Fleete sat on the ground and refused to move. He said that "good old Hanuman" made a very soft pillow.

Then, without any warning, a Silver Man came out of a recess behind the image of the god. He was perfectly naked in that bitter, bitter cold, and his body shone like frosted silver, for he was what the Bible calls "a leper as white as snow." Also he had no face, because he was a leper of some years' standing and his disease was heavy upon him. We two stooped to haul Fleete up, and the temple was filling and filling with folk who seemed to spring from the earth, when the Silver Man ran in under our arms, making a noise exactly like the mewing of an otter, caught Fleete around the body and dropped his head on Fleete's breast before we could wrench him away. Then he retired to a corner and sat mewing while the crowd blocked all the doors.

The priests were very angry until the Silver Man touched Fleete. That nuzzling seemed to sober them.

At the end of a few minutes' silence one of the priests came to Strickland and said, in perfect English, "Take your friend away. He has done with Hanuman, but Hanuman has not done with him." The crowd gave room and we carried Fleete into the road.

Strickland was very angry. He said that we might all three have been knifed, and that Fleete should thank his stars that he had escaped without injury.

Fleete thanked no one. He said that he wanted to go to bed. He was gorgeously drunk.

We moved on, Strickland silent and wrathful, until Fleete was taken with violent shivering fits and sweating. He said that the smells of the bazaar were overpowering, and he wondered what slaughterhouses were permitted so near English residences. "Can't you smell the blood?" said Fleete.

We put him to bed at last, just as the dawn was breaking, and Strickland invited me to have another whiskey and soda. While we were drinking he talked of the trouble in the temple, and admitted that it baffled him completely. Strickland hates being mystified by natives, because his business in life is to overmatch them with their own weapons. He has not yet succeeded in doing this, but in fifteen or twenty years he will have made some small progress.

"They should have mauled us," he said, "instead of mewing at us. I wonder what they meant. I don't like it one little bit."

I said that the Managing Committee of the temple would in all probability bring a criminal action against us for insulting their religion. There was a section of the Indian Penal Code which exactly met Fleete's offense. Strickland said he only hoped and prayed that they would do this. Before I left I looked into Fleete's room, and saw him lying on his right side, scratching his left breast. Then I went to bed cold, depressed, and unhappy, at seven o'clock in the morning.

At one o'clock I rode over to Strickland's house to inquire after Fleete's head. I imagined that it would be a sore one. Fleete was breakfasting and seemed unwell. His temper was gone, for he was abusing the cook for not supplying him with an underdone chop. A man who can eat raw meat after a wet night is a curiosity. I told Fleete this and he laughed.

"You breed queer mosquitoes in these parts," he said. "I've been bitten to pieces, but only in one place."

"Let's have a look at the bite," said Strickland. "It may have gone down since this morning."

While the chops were being cooked, Fleete opened his shirt and showed us, just over his left breast, a mark, the perfect double of the black rosettes—the five or six irregular blotches arranged in a circle—on a leopard's hide. Strickland looked and said, "It was only pink this morning. It's grown black now."

Fleete ran to a glass.

"By jove!" he said, "this is nasty. What is it?"

We could not answer. Here the chops came in, all red and juicy, and Fleete bolted three in a most offensive manner. He ate on his right grinders only, and threw his head over his right shoulder as he snapped the meat. When he had finished, it struck him that he had been behaving strangely, for he said apologetically, "I don't think I ever felt so hungry in my life. I've bolted like an ostrich."

After breakfast Strickland said to me, "Don't go. Stay here, and stay for the night."

Seeing that my house was not three miles from Strickland's, this request was absurd. But Strickland insisted, and was going to say something when Fleete interrupted by declaring in a shamefaced way that he felt hungry again. Strickland sent a man to my house to fetch over my bedding and a horse, and we three went down to Strickland's stables to pass the hours until it was time to go out for a ride. The man who has a weakness for horses never wearies of inspecting them; and when two men are killing time in this way they gather knowledge and lies the one from the other.

There were five horses in the stables, and I shall never forget the scene as we tried to look them over. They seemed to have gone mad. They reared and screamed and nearly tore up their pickets; they sweated and shivered and lathered and were distraught with fear. Strickland's horses used to know him as well as his dogs; which made the matter more curious. We left the stable for fear of the brutes throwing themselves in their panic. Then Strickland turned back and called me. The horses were still frightened, but they let us "gentle" and make much of them, and put their heads in our bosoms.

"They aren't afraid of *us,*" said Strickland. "D'you know, I'd give three months' pay if *Outrage* here could talk."

But *Outrage* was dumb and could only cuddle up to his master and blow out his nostrils, as is the custom of horses when they wish to explain things but can't. Fleete came up when we were in the stalls, and as soon as the horses saw him, their fright broke out afresh. It was all that we could do to escape from the place unkicked. Strickland said, "They don't seem to love you, Fleete."

"Nonsense," said Fleete; "my mare will follow me like a dog." He went to her; she was in a loose-box; but as he slipped the bars she plunged, knocked him down, and broke away into the garden. I laughed, but Strickland was not amused. He took his mustache in both fists and pulled at it till it nearly came out. Fleete, instead of going off to chase his property, yawned, saying that he felt sleepy. He went to house to lie down, which was a foolish way of spending New Year's Day.

Strickland sat with me in the stables and asked if I had noticed anything peculiar in Fleete's manner. I said that he ate his food like a beast; but that this might have been the result of living alone in the hills out of the reach of society as refined and elevating as ours for instance. Strickland was not amused. I do not think that he listened to me, for his next sentence referred to the mark on Fleete's breast, and I said that it might have been caused by blister-flies, or that it was possibly a birthmark newly born and now visible for the first time. We both agreed that it was unpleasant to look at, and Strickland found occasion to say that I was a fool.

"I can't tell you what I think now," said he, "because you would call me a madman; but you must stay with me for the next few days, if you can. I want you to watch Fleete, but don't tell me what you think till I have made up my mind."

"But I am dining out tonight," I said.

"So am I," said Strickland, "and so is Fleete. At least if he doesn't change his mind."

We walked about the garden smoking, but saying nothing—because we were friends, and talking spoils good tobacco—until our pipes were out. Then we went to wake up Fleete. He was wide awake and fidgeting about his room.

"I say, I want some more chops," he said. "Can I get them?"

We laughed and said, "Go and change. The ponies will be around in a minute."

"All right," said Fleete. "I'll go when I get the chops—underdone ones, mind."

He seemed to be quite in earnest. It was four o'clock, and we had had breakfast at one; still, for a long time, he demanded those underdone chops. Then he changed into riding clothes and went out into the veranda. His pony—the mare had not been caught—would not let him come near. All three horses were unmanageable—mad with fear—and finally Fleete said that he would stay at home and get something to eat. Strickland and I rode out wondering. As we passed the temple of Hanuman, the Silver Man came out and mewed at us.

"He is not one of the regular priests of the temple," said Strickland. "I think I should peculiarly like to lay my hands on him."

There was no spring in our gallop on the racecourse that evening. The horses were stale, and moved as though they had been ridden out.

"The fright after breakfast has been too much for them," said Strickland.

That was the only remark he made through the remainder of the ride. Once or twice I think he swore to himself; but that did not count.

We came back in the dark at seven o'clock, and saw that there were no lights in the bungalow. "Careless ruffians my servants are!" said Strickland.

My horse reared at something on the carriage drive, and Fleete stood up under its nose.

"What are you doing, groveling about the garden?" said Strickland.

But both horses bolted and nearly threw us. We dismounted by the stables and returned to Fleete, who was on his hands and knees under the orange-bushes.

"What the devil's wrong with you?" said Strickland.

"Nothing, nothing in the world," said Fleete, speaking very quickly and thickly. "I've been gardening—botanizing you know. The smell of the earth is delightful. I think I'm going for a walk—a long walk—all night."

Then I saw that there was something excessively out of order somewhere, and I said to Strickland, "I am not dining out."

"Bless you!" said Strickland. "Here, Fleete, get up. You'll catch fever there. Come in to dinner and let's have the lamps lit. We'll all dine at home."

Fleete stood up unwillingly, and said, "No lamps—no lamps. It's much nicer here. Let's dine outside and have some more chops—lots of 'em and underdone—bloody ones with gristle."

Now a December evening in Northern India is bitterly cold, and Fleete's suggestion was that of a maniac.

"Come in," said Strickland sternly. "Come in at once."

Fleete came, and when the lamps were brought, we saw that he was literally plastered with dirt from head to foot. He must have been rolling in the garden. He shrank from the light and went to his room. His eyes were horrible to look at. There was a green light behind them, not in them, if you understand, and the man's lower lip hung down.

Strickland said, "There is going to be trouble—big trouble—tonight. Don't you change your riding-things."

We waited and waited for Fleete's reappearance, and ordered dinner in the meantime. We could hear him moving about his own room, but there was no light there. Presently from the room came the long-drawn howl of a wolf.

People write and talk lightly of blood running cold and hair standing up and things of that kind. Both sensations are too horrible to be trifled with. My heart stopped as though a knife had been driven through it, and Strickland turned as white as the tablecloth.

The howl was repeated, and was answered by another howl far across the fields.

That set the gilded roof on the horror. Strickland dashed into Fleete's room. I followed, and we saw Fleete getting out of the window. He made beast-noises in the back of his throat. He could not answer us when we shouted at him. He spat.

I don't quite remember what followed, but I think that Strickland must have stunned him with the long boot-jack or else I should never have been able to sit on his chest. Fleete could not speak, he could only snarl, and his snarls were those of a wolf, not of a man. The human spirit must have been giving way all day and have died out with the twilight. We were dealing with a beast that had once been Fleete.

The affair was beyond any human and rational experience. I tried to say "Hydrophobia," but the word wouldn't come, because I knew that I was lying.

We bound this beast with leather thongs of the punkah-rope, and tied its thumbs and big toes together, and gagged it with a shoehorn, which makes a very efficient gag if you know how to arrange it. Then we carried it into the dining room, and sent a man to Dumoise, the doctor, telling him to come over at once. After we had dispatched the messenger and were drawing breath, Strickland said, "It's no good. This isn't any doctor's work." I, also, knew that he spoke the truth.

The beast's head was free, and it threw it about from side to side. Anyone entering the room would have believed that we

—"I don't quite remember what followed, but I think that Strickland must have stunned him with the long boot-jack or else I should never have been able to sit on his chest."

were curing a wolf's pelt. That was the most loathsome accessory of all.

Strickland sat with his chin in the heel of his fist, watching the beast as it wriggled on the ground, but saying nothing. The shirt had been torn open in the scuffle and showed the black rosette mark on the left breast. It stood out like a blister.

In the silence of the watching we heard something without mewing like a she-otter. We both rose to our feet, and, I answer for myself, not Strickland, felt sick—actually and physically sick. We told each other, as did the men in *Pinafore,* that it was the cat.

Dumoise arrived, and I never saw a little man so unprofessionally shocked. He said that it was a heart-rending case of hydrophobia, and that nothing could be done. At least any palliative measures would only prolong the agony. The beast was foaming at the mouth. Fleete, as we told Dumoise, had been bitten by dogs once or twice. Any man who keeps half a dozen terriers must expect a nip now and again. Dumoise could offer no help. He could only certify that Fleete was dying of hydrophobia. The beast was then howling, for it had managed to spit out the shoehorn. Dumoise said that he would be ready to certify to the cause of death, and that the end was certain. He was a good little man, and he offered to remain with us; but Strickland refused the kindness. He did not wish to poison Dumoise's New Year. He would only ask him not to give the real cause of Fleete's death to the public.

So Dumoise left, deeply agitated; and as soon as the noise of the cartwheels had died away, Strickland told me, in a whisper, his suspicions. They were so wildly improbable that he dared not say them out aloud; and I, who entertained all Strickland's beliefs, was so ashamed of owning to them that I pretended to disbelieve.

"Even if the Silver Man had bewitched Fleete for polluting the image of Hanuman, the punishment could not have fallen so quickly."

As I was whispering this the cry outside the house rose again, and the beast fell into a fresh paroxysm of struggling till we were afraid that the thongs that held it would give way.

"Watch!" said Strickland. "If this happens six times I shall take the law into my own hands. I order you to help me."

He went into his room and came out in a few minutes with the barrels of an old shotgun, a piece of fishing line, some thick cord, and his heavy wooden bedstead. I reported that the convulsions had followed the cry by two seconds in each case, and the beast seemed perceptibly weaker.

Strickland muttered, "But he can't take away the life! He can't take away the life!"

I said, though I knew that I was arguing against myself, "It may be a cat. It must be a cat. If the Silver Man is responsible, why does he dare to come here?"

Strickland arranged the wood on the hearth, put the gun barrels into the glow of the fire, spread the twine on the table and broke a walking stick in two. There was one yard of fishing line, gut, lapped with wire, such as is used for *mahseer*-fishing, and he tied the two ends together in a loop.

Then he said, "How can we catch him? He must be taken alive and unhurt."

I said that we must trust in Providence, and go out softly with polo sticks into the shrubbery at the front of the house. The man or animal that made the cry was evidently moving around the house as regularly as a night watchman. We could wait in the bushes till he came by and knock him over.

Strickland accepted this suggestion, and we slipped out from a bath-room window into the front veranda and then across the carriage drive into the bushes.

In the moonlight we could see the leper coming around the corner of the house. He was perfectly naked, and from time to time he mewed and stopped to dance with his shadow. It was an unattractive sight, and thinking of poor Fleete, brought to such degradation by so foul a creature, I put away all my doubts and resolved to help Strickland from the heated gun barrels to the loop of twine—from the loins to the head and back again—with all tortures that might be needful.

The leper halted in the front porch for a moment and we jumped out on him with the sticks. He was wonderfully strong, and we were afraid that he might escape or be fatally injured before we caught him. We had an idea that lepers were frail creatures, but this proved to be incorrect. Strickland knocked his legs from under him and I put my foot on his neck. He mewed hideously, and even through my riding boots I could feel that his flesh was not the flesh of a clean man.

He struck at us with his hand and feet-stumps. We looped the last of a dog-whip around him, under the armpits, and dragged him backward into the hall and so into the dining room where the beast lay. There we tied him with trunk straps. He made no attempt to escape, but mewed.

When we confronted him with the beast the scene was beyond description. The beast doubled backward into a bow as though he had been poisoned with strychnine, and moaned in the most pitiable fashion. Several other things happened also, but they cannot be put down here.

"I think I was right," said Strickland. "Now we will ask him to cure this case."

But the leper only mewed. Strickland wrapped a towel around his hand and took the gun barrels out of the fire. I put the half of the broken walking stick through the loop of fishing line and buckled the leper comfortably to Strickland's bedstead. I understood then how men and women and little children can endure to see a witch burned alive; for the beast was moaning on the floor, and though the Silver Man had no face, you could see horrible feelings passing through the slab that took its place, exactly as waves of heat play across red-hot iron—gun barrels for instance.

Strickland shaded his eyes with his hands for a moment and we got to work. This part is not to be printed.

The dawn was beginning to break when the leper spoke. His mewings had not been satisfactory up to that point. The beast had fainted from exhaustion and the house was very still. We unstrapped the leper and told him to take away the evil spirit. He crawled to the beast and laid his hand upon the left breast. That was all. Then he fell face down and whined, drawing in his breath as he did so.

We watched the face of the beast, and saw the soul of Fleete coming back into the eyes. Then a sweat broke out on the forehead and the eyes—they were human eyes—closed. We waited for an hour but Fleete still slept. We carried him to his room and bade the leper go, giving him the bedstead, and the sheet on the bedstead to cover his nakedness, the gloves and the towels with which we had touched him, and the whip that had been hooked around his body. He put the sheet about him and went out into the early morning without speaking or mewing.

Strickland wiped his face and sat down. A night-gong, far away in the city, made seven o'clock.

"Exactly four-and-twenty hours!" said Strickland. "And I've done enough to insure my dismissal from the service, besides permanent quarters in a lunatic asylum. Do you believe that we are awake?"

The red-hot gun barrel had fallen on the floor and was singeing the carpet. The smell was entirely real.

That morning at eleven we two together went to wake up Fleete. We looked and saw that the black leopard-rosette on his chest had disappeared. He was very drowsy and tired, but as soon as he saw us, he said, "Oh! Confound you fellows. Happy New Year to you. Never mix your liquors. I'm nearly dead."

"Thanks for your kindness, but you're overtime," said Strickland. "Today is the morning of the second. You've slept the clock around with a vengeance."

The door opened, and little Dumoise put his head in. He had come on foot, and fancied that we were laying out Fleete.

"I've brought a nurse," said Dumoise. "I suppose that she can come in for . . . what is necessary."

"By all means," said Fleete cheerily, sitting up in bed. "Bring on your nurses."

Dumoise was dumb. Strickland led him out and explained that there must have been a mistake in the diagnosis. Dumoise remained dumb and left the house hastily. He considered that his professional reputation had been injured, and was inclined to make a personal matter of the recovery. Strickland went out too. When he came back, he said that he had been to call on the Temple of Hanuman to offer redress for the pollution of the god, and had been solemnly assured that no white man had ever touched the idol and that he was an incarnation of all the virtues laboring under a delusion. "What do you think?" said Strickland.

I said, "'There are more things . . .'"

But Strickland hates that quotation. He says that I have worn it threadbare.

One other curious thing happened which frightened me as much as anything in all the night's work. When Fleete was dressed he came into the dining room and sniffed. He had a quaint trick of moving his nose when he sniffed. "Horrid doggy smell, here," said he. "You should really keep those terriers of yours in better order. Try sulphur, Strick."

But Strickland did not answer. He caught hold of the back of a chair, and, without warning, went into an amazing fit of hysterics. It is terrible to see a strong man overtaken with hysteria. Then it struck me that we had fought for Fleete's soul with the Silver Man in that room, and had disgraced ourselves as Englishmen forever, and I laughed and gasped and gurgled just as shamefully as Strickland, while Fleete thought that we had both gone mad. We never told him what we had done.

Some years later, when Strickland had married and was a church-going member of society for his wife's sake, we reviewed the incident dispassionately, and Strickland suggested that I should put it before the public.

I cannot myself see that this step is likely to clear up the mystery; because, in the first place, no one will believe a rather unpleasant story, and, in the second, it is well known to every right-minded man that the gods of the heathen are stone and brass, and any attempt to deal with them otherwise is justly condemned.

THE MAN WHO WOULD BE KING

Brother to a Prince and fellow to a beggar if he be found worthy.

THE LAW, as quoted, lays down a fair conduct of life, and one not easy to follow. I have been fellow to a beggar again and again under circumstances which prevented either of us finding out whether the other was worthy. I have still to be brother to a Prince, though I once came near to kinship with what might have been a veritable King and was promised the reversion of a Kingdom—army, law courts, revenue and policy all complete. But, today, I greatly fear that my King is dead, and if I want a crown I must go hunt it for myself.

The beginning of everything was in a railway train upon the road to Mhow from Ajmir. There had been a Deficit in the Budget, which necessitated traveling, not Second-class, which is only half as dear as First-class, but by Intermediate, which is very awful indeed. There are no cushions in the Intermediate class, and the population are either Intermediate, which is Eurasian, or native, which for a long night journey is nasty, or Loafer, which is amusing though intoxicated. Intermediates do not buy from refreshment rooms. They carry their food in bundles and pots, and buy sweets from the native sweetmeat-sellers, and drink the roadside water. That is why in hot weather Intermediates are taken out of the carriages dead, and in all weathers are most properly looked down upon.

My particular Intermediate happened to be empty until I reached Nasirabad, when a big black-browed gentleman in shirtsleeves entered, and, following the custom of Intermediates, passed the time of day. He was a wanderer and a vagabond like myself, but with an educated taste for whiskey. He told tales of things he had seen and done, of out-of-the-way corners of the Empire into which he had penetrated, and of adventures in which he risked his life for a few days' food.

"If India was filled with men like you and me, not knowing more than the crows where they'd get their next day's rations, it isn't seventy millions of revenue the land would be paying—

it's seven hundred millions," said he; and as I looked at his mouth and chin I was disposed to agree with him.

We talked politics—the politics of Loaferdom that sees things from the underside where the lath and plaster is not smoothed off—and we talked postal arrangements because my friend wanted to send a telegram back from the next station to Ajmir, the turning-off place from the Bombay to the Mhow line as you travel westward. My friend had no money beyond eight annas which he wanted for dinner, and I had no money at all, owing to the hitch in the Budget before mentioned. Further, I was going into a wilderness where, though I should resume touch with the Treasury, there were no telegraph offices. I was, therefore, unable to help him in any way.

"We might threaten a Stationmaster, and make him send a wire on tick," said my friend, "but that'd mean inquiries for you and for me, and *I've* got my hands full these days. Did you say you were traveling back along this line within any days?"

"Within ten," I said.

"Can't you make it eight?" said he. "Mine is rather urgent business."

"I can send your telegram within ten days if that will serve you," I said.

"I couldn't trust the wire to fetch him now I think of it. It's this way. He leaves Delhi on the 23rd for Bombay. That means he'll be running through Ajmir about the night of the 23rd."

"But I'm going into the Indian Desert," I explained.

"Well *and* good," said he. "You'll be changing at Marwar Junction to get into Jodhpore territory—you must do that—and he'll be coming through Marwar Junction in the early morning of the 24th by the Bombay Mail. Can you be at Marwar Junction on that time? 'Twon't be inconveniencing you because I know that there's precious few pickings to be got out of these Central India States—even though you pretend to be correspondent of the *Backwoodsman*."

"Have you ever tried that trick?" I asked.

"Again and again, but the Residents find you out, and then you get escorted to the Border before you've time to get your knife into them. But about my friend here. I *must* give him a word o' mouth to tell him what's come to me or else he won't know where to go. I would take it more than kind of you if you was to come out of Central India in time to catch him at Marwar Junction, and say to him: 'He has gone South for the week.' He'll know what that means. He's a big man with a red beard, and a great swell he is. You'll find him sleeping like a gentleman with all his luggage around him in a Second-class apartment. But don't you be afraid. Slip down the window and say: 'He has gone South for the week,' and he'll tumble. It's only cutting your time of stay in those parts by two days. I ask you as a stranger—going to the West," he said with emphasis.

"Where have *you* come from?" said I.

"From the East," said he, "and I am hoping that you will give him the message on the Square—for the sake of my Mother as well as your own."

Englishmen are not usually softened by appeals to the memory of their mothers; but for certain reasons, which will be fully apparent, I saw fit to agree.

"It's more than a little matter," said he, "and that's why I asked you to do it—and now I know that I can depend on you doing it. A Second-class carriage at Marwar Junction, and a red-haired man asleep in it. You'll be sure to remember. I get out at the next station, and I must hold on there till he comes or sends me what I want."

"I'll give the message if I catch him," I said, "and for the sake of your Mother as well as mine I'll give you a word of advice. Don't try to run the Central India States just now as the correspondent of the *Backwoodsman*. There's a real one knocking about here, and it might lead to trouble."

"Thank you," said he simply, "and when will the swine be gone? I can't starve because he's ruining my work. I wanted to get hold of the Degumber Rajah down here about his father's widow, and give him a jump."

"What did he do to his father's widow, then?"

"Filled her up with red pepper and slippered her to death as she hung from a beam. I found that out myself and I'm the only man that would dare going into the State to get hush-money for it. They'll try to poison me, same as they did in

Chortumna when I went on the loot there. But you'll give the man at Marwar Junction my message?"

He got out at a little roadside station, and I reflected. I had heard, more than once, of men personating correspondents of newspapers and bleeding small Native States with threats of exposure, but I had never met any of the caste before. They lead a hard life, and generally die with great suddenness. The Native States have a wholesome horror of English newspapers, which may throw light on their peculiar methods of government, and do their best to choke correspondents with champagne, or drive them out of their mind with four-in-hand barouches. They do not understand that nobody cares a straw for the internal administration of Native States so long as oppression and crime are kept within decent limits, and the ruler is not drugged, drunk, or diseased from one end of the year to the other. They are the dark places of the earth, full of unimaginable cruelty, touching the Railway and the Telegraph on one side, and, on the other, the days of Harun-al-Raschid. When I left the train I did business with divers Kings, and in eight days passed through many changes of life. Sometimes I wore dress clothes and consorted with Princes and Politicals, drinking from crystal and eating from silver. Sometimes I lay out upon the ground and devoured what I could get, from a plate of leaves, and drank the running water, and slept under the same rug as my servant. It was all in the day's work.

Then I headed for the Great Indian Desert upon the proper date, as I had promised, and the night Mail set me down at Marwar Junction, where a funny little, happy-go-lucky, native-managed railway runs to Jodhpore. The Bombay Mail from Delhi makes a short halt at Marwar. She arrived as I got in, and I had just time to hurry to her platform and go down the carriages. There was only one Second-class on the train. I slipped the window and looked down upon a flaming red beard, half covered by a railway rug. That was my man, fast asleep, and I dug him gently in the ribs. He woke with a grunt and I saw his face in the light of the lamps. It was a great and shining face.

"Tickets again?" said he.

"No," said I. "I am to tell you that he is gone South for the week. He has gone South for the week!"

The train had begun to move out. The red man rubbed his eyes. "He has gone South for the week," he repeated. "Now that's just like his impidence. Did he say that I was to give you anything? 'Cause I won't."

"He didn't," I said and dropped away, and watched the red lights die out in the dark. It was horribly cold because the wind was blowing off the sands. I climbed into my own train—not an Intermediate carriage this time—and went to sleep.

If the man with the beard had given me a rupee I should have kept it as a memento of a rather curious affair. But the consciousness of having done my duty was my only reward.

Later on I reflected that two gentlemen like my friends could not do any good if they foregathered and personated correspondents of newspapers, and might, if they blackmailed one of the little rattrap states of Central India or Southern Rajputana, get themselves into serious difficulties. I therefore took some trouble to describe them as accurately as I could remember to people who would be interested in deporting them: and succeeded, so I was later informed, in having them headed back from the Degumber borders.

Then I became respectable, and returned to an Office where there were no Kings and no incidents outside the daily manufacture of a newspaper. A newspaper office seems to attract every conceivable sort of person, to the prejudice of discipline. Zenana-mission ladies arrive, and beg that the Editor will instantly abandon all his duties to describe a Christian prize-giving in a back-slum of a perfectly inaccessible village; Colonels who have been overpassed for command sit down and sketch the outline of a series of ten, twelve, or twenty-four leading articles on Seniority *versus* Selection; missionaries wish to know why they have not been permitted to escape from their regular vehicles of abuse and swear at a brother-missionary under special patronage of the editorial We; stranded theatrical companies troop up to explain that they cannot pay for their advertisements, but on their return from New Zealand or Tahiti will do so with interest; inventors of patent punkah-pulling machines, carriage couplings and unbreakable swords and axletrees call with specifications in their pockets and hours at their disposal; tea-companies enter and elaborate their prospectuses with the office pens; secretaries of ball-committees clamor to have the glories of their last dance more fully described; strange ladies rustle in and say: "I want a hundred lady's cards printed *at once,* please," which is manifestly part of an Editor's duty; and every dissolute ruffian that ever tramped the Grand Trunk Road makes it his business to ask for employment as a proof-reader. And, all the time, the telephone bell is ringing madly, and Kings are being killed on the Continent, and Empires are saying—"You're another," and Mister Gladstone is calling down brimstone upon the British Dominions, and the little black copyboys are whining, *"kaa-pi chay-ha-yeh"* (copy wanted) like tired bees, and most of the paper is as blank as Modred's shield.

But that is the amusing part of the year. There are six other months when none ever come to call, and the thermometer walks inch by inch up to the top of the glass, and the office is darkened to just above reading light, and the press machines are red-hot of touch, and nobody writes anything but accounts of amusements in the Hill-stations or obituary notices. Then the telephone becomes a tinkling terror, because it tells you of the sudden deaths of men and women that you knew intimately, and the prickly heat covers you with a garment, and you sit down and write: "A slight increase of sickness is reported from the Khuda Janta Khan District. The outbreak is purely sporadic in its nature, and, thanks to the energetic efforts of the District authorities, is now almost at an end. It is, however, with deep regret we record the death," etc.

Then the sickness really breaks out, and the less recording and reporting the better for the peace of the subscribers. But the Empires and the Kings continue to divert themselves as selfishly as before, and the Foreman thinks that a daily paper really ought to come out once in twenty-four hours, and all the people at the Hill-stations in the middle of their amusements say: "Good gracious! Why can't the paper be sparkling? I'm sure there's plenty going on up here."

That is the dark half of the moon, and, as the advertisements say, "must be experienced to be appreciated."

It was in that season, and a remarkably evil season, that the paper began running the last issue of the week on Saturday night, which is to say Sunday morning, after the custom of a London paper. This was a great convenience, for immediately after the paper was put to bed, the dawn would lower the thermometer from 96° to almost 84° for half an hour, and in that chill—you have no idea how cold is 84° on the grass until you begin to pray for it—a very tired man could get off to sleep ere the heat roused him.

One Saturday night it was my pleasant duty to put the paper to bed alone. A King or courtier or a courtesan or a Community was going to die or get a new Constitution, or do something that was important on the other side of the world, and the paper was to be held open till the latest possible minute in order to catch the telegram.

It was a pitchy black night, as stifling as a June night can be, and the *loo*, the red-hot wind from the westward, was booming among the tinder-dry trees and pretending that the rain was on its heels. Now and again a spot of almost boiling water would fall on the dust with the flop of a frog, but all our weary world knew that was only pretense. It was a shade cooler in the pressroom than the office, so I sat there, while the type ticked and clicked, and the nightjars hooted at the windows, and the all but naked compositors wiped the sweat from their foreheads, and called for water. The thing that was keeping us back, whatever it was, would not come off, though the *loo* dropped and the last type was set, and the whole round earth stood still in the choking heat, with its finger on its lip, to wait the event. I drowsed, and wondered whether the telegraph was a blessing, and whether this dying man, or struggling people, might be aware of the inconvenience the delay was causing. There was no special reason beyond the heat and worry to make tension, but, as the clock hands crept up to three o'clock and the machines spun their flywheels two and three times to see that all was in order, before I said the word that would set them off, I could have shrieked aloud.

Then the roar and rattle of the wheels shivered the quiet into little bits. I rose to go away, but two men in white clothes stood in front of me. The first one said: "It's him!" The second said: "So it is!" And they both laughed almost as loudly as the machinery roared, and mopped their foreheads. "We seed there was a light burning across the road and we were sleeping in that ditch there for coolness, and I said to my friend here, 'The office is open. Let's come along and speak to him as turned us back from the Degumber State,'" said the smaller of the two. He was the man I had met in the Mhow train, and his fellow was the red-bearded man of Marwar Junction. There was no mistaking the eyebrows of the one or the beard of the other.

I was not pleased, because I wished to go to sleep, not to squabble with loafers. "What do you want?" I asked.

"Half an hour's talk with you, cool and comfortable in the office," said the red-bearded man. "We'd *like* some drink—the Contrack doesn't begin yet, Peachey, so you needn't look—but what we really want is advice. We don't want money. We ask you as a favor, because we found out you did us a bad turn about Degumber State."

I led from the press room to the stifling office with the maps on the walls, and the red-haired man rubbed his hands. "That's something like," said he. "This was the proper shop to come to. Now, Sir, let me introduce to you Brother Peachey Carnehan, that's him, and Brother Daniel Dravot, that is *me,* and the less said about our professions the better, for we have been most things in our time. Soldier, sailor, compositor, photographer, proofreader, street-preacher, and correspondents of the *Backwoodsman* when we thought the paper wanted one. Carnehan is sober, and so am I. Look at us first, and see that's sure. It will save you cutting into my talk. We'll take one of your cigars apiece, and you shall see us light up."

I watched the test. The men were absolutely sober, so I gave them each a tepid whiskey and soda.

"Well *and* good," said Carnehan of the eyebrows, wiping the froth from his mustache. "Let me talk now, Dan. We have been all over India, mostly on foot. We have been boilerfitters, engine drivers, petty contractors, and all that, and we have decided that India isn't big enough for such as us."

They certainly were too big for the office. Dravot's beard seemed to fill half the room and Carnehan's shoulders the other half, as they sat on the big table. Carnehan continued: "The country isn't half worked out because they that governs it won't let you touch it. They spend all their blessed time in governing it, and you can't lift a spade, nor chip a rock, nor look for oil, nor anything like that without all the Government saying—'Leave it alone, and let us govern.' Therefore, such *as* it is, we will let it alone, and go away to some other place where a man isn't crowded and can come to his own. We are not little men, and there is nothing we are afraid of except Drink, and we have signed a Contrack on that. *Therefore,* we are going away to be Kings."

"Kings in our own right," muttered Dravot.

"Yes, of course," I said. "You've been tramping in the sun, and it's a very warm night, and hadn't you better sleep over the notion? Come tomorrow."

"Neither drunk nor sunstruck," said Dravot. "We have slept over the notion half a year, and require to see Books and Atlases, and we have decided that there is only one place now in the world that two strong men can Sar-a-*whack*. They call it Kafiristan. By my reckoning it's the top right-hand corner of Afghanistan, nor more than three hundred miles from Peshawar. They have two-and-thirty heathen idols there, and we'll be the thirty-third and fourth. It's a mountainous country, and the women of those parts are very beautiful."

"But that is provided against in the Contrack," said Carnehan. "Neither Woman nor Liqu-or, Daniel."

"And that's all we know, except that no one has gone there, and they fight, and in any place where they fight a man who knows how to drill men can always be a King. We shall go to those parts and say to any King we find—'D'you want to vanquish your foes?' and we will show him how to drill men; for that we know better than anything else. Then we will subvert that King and seize his Throne and establish a Dy-nasty."

"You'll be cut to pieces before you're fifty miles across the Border," I said. "You have to travel through Afghanistan to get to that country. It's one mass of mountains and peaks and glaciers, and no Englishman has been through it. The people are utter brutes, and even if you reached them you couldn't do anything."

"That's more like," said Carnehan. "If you could think us a

little more mad we would be more pleased. We have come to you to know about this country, to read a book about it, and to be shown maps. We want you to tell us that we are fools and to show us your books." He turned to the book cases.

"Are you at all in earnest?" I said.

"A little," said Dravot sweetly. "As big a map as you have got, even if it's all blank where Kafiristan is, and any books you've got. We can read, though we aren't very educated."

I uncased the big thirty-two-miles-to-the-inch map of India, and two smaller Frontier maps, hauled down volumn INF-KAN of the *Encyclopaedia Britannica,* and the men consulted them.

"See here!" said Dravot, his thumb on the map. "Up to Jagdallak, Peachey and me know the road. We was there with Roberts' Army. We'll have to turn off to the right at Jagdallak through Laghmann territory. Then we get among the hills—fourteen thousand feet—fifteen thousand—it will be cold work there, but it don't look very far on the map."

I handed him Wood on the *Sources of the Oxus.* Carnehan was deep in the *Encyclopaedia.*

"They're a mixed lot," said Dravot reflectively; "and it won't help us to know the names of their tribes. The more tribes the more they'll fight, and the better for us. From Jagdallak to Ashang. H'mm!"

"But all the information about the country is as sketchy and inaccurate as can be," I protested. "No one knows anything about it really. Here's the file of the *United Services' Institute.* Read what Bellew says."

"Blow Bellew!" said Carnehan. "Dan, they're a stinkin' lot of heathens, but this book here says they think they're related to us English."

I smoked while the men pored over *Raverty, Wood,* the maps, and the *Encyclopaedia.*

"There is no use your waiting," said Dravot politely. "It's about four o'clock now. We'll go before six o'clock if you want to sleep, and we won't steal any of the papers. Don't you sit up. We're two harmless lunatics, and if you come tomorrow evening down to the Serai we'll say good-bye to you."

"You *are* two fools," I answered. "You'll be turned back at the Frontier or cut up the minute you set foot in Afghanistan.

Do you want any money or a recommendation down-country? I can help you to the chance of work next week."

"Next week we shall be hard at work ourselves, thank you," said Dravot. "It isn't so easy being a King as it looks. When we've got our Kingdom in going order we'll let you know, and you can come up and help us to govern it."

"Would two lunatics make a Contrack like that?" said Carnehan, with subdued pride, showing me a greasy half-sheet of notepaper on which was written the following. I copied it, then and there, as a curiosity—

This Contract between me and you persuing witnesseth in the name of God—Amen and so forth.

(*One*) *That me and you will settle this matter together; i.e., to be Kings of Kafiristan.*

(*Two*) *That you and me will not, while this matter is being settled, look at any Liquor, nor any Woman black, white, or brown, so as to get mixed up with one or the other harmful.*

(*Three*) *That we conduct ourselves with Dignity and Discretion, and if one of us gets into trouble the other will stay by him.*

Signed by you and me this day.
Peachey Taliaferro Carnehan.
Daniel Dravot.
Both Gentlemen at Large.

"There was no need for the last article," said Carnehan, blushing modestly; "but it looks regular. Now you know the sort of men that loafers are—we *are* loafers, Dan, until we get out of India—and *do* you think that we would sign a Contrack like that unless we was in earnest? We have kept away from the two things that make life worth having."

"You won't enjoy your lives much longer if you are going to try this idiotic adventure. Don't set the office on fire," I said, "and go away before nine o'clock."

I left them still poring over the maps and making notes on the back of the "Contrack." "Be sure to come down to the Serai tomorrow," were their parting words.

The Kumharsen Serai is the great four-square sink of humanity where the strings of camels and horses from the North load and unload. All the nationalities of Central Asia may be found there, and most of the folk of India proper. Balkh and Bokhara there meet Bengal and Bombay, and try to draw eyeteeth. You can buy ponies, turquoises, Persian pussy-cats, saddlebags, fat-tailed sheep and musk in the Kumharsen Serai, and get many strange things for nothing. In the afternoon I went down to see whether my friends intended to keep their word or were lying there drunk.

A priest attired in fragments of ribbons and rags stalked up to me, gravely twisting a child's paper whirligig. Behind him was his servant bending under the load of a crate of mud toys. The two were loading up two camels, and the inhabitants of the Serai watched them with shrieks of laughter.

"The priest is mad," said a horse dealer to me. "He is going up to Kabul to sell toys to the Amir. He will either be raised to honor or have his head cut off. He came in here this morning and has been behaving madly ever since."

"The witless are under the protection of God," stammered a flat-cheeked Usbeg in broken Hindi. "They foretell future events."

"Would they could have foretold that my caravan would have been cut up by the Shinwaris almost within shadow of the Pass!" grunted the Eusufzai agent of a Rajputana trading house whose goods had been diverted into the hands of other robbers just across the Border, and whose misfortunes were the laughing-stock of the bazar. "Ohé, priest, whence come you and whither do you go?"

"From Roum have I come," shouted the priest, waving his whirligig; "from Roum, blown by the breath of a hundred devils across the sea! O thieves, robbers, liars, the blessing of Pir Khan on pigs, dogs, and perjurers! Who will take the protected of God to the North to sell charms that are never still to the Amir? The camels shall not gall, the sons shall not fall sick, and the wives shall remain faithful while they are away, of the men who give me place in their caravan. Who will assist me to slipper the King of the Roos with a golden slipper with a silver heel? The protection of Pir Khan be upon his labors!" He spread out the skirts of his gaberdine and pirouetted between the lines of tethered horses.

"There starts a caravan from Peshawar to Kabul in twenty days, *Huzrut,"* said the Eusufzai trader. "My camels go therewith. Do thou also go and bring us good luck."

"I will go even now!" shouted the priest. "I will depart upon my winged camels, and be at Peshawar in a day! Ho! Hazar Mir Khan," he yelled to his servant, "drive out the camels, but let me first mount my own."

He leaped on the back of his beast as it knelt, and, turning around to me, cried: "Come thou also, Sahib, a little along the road, and I will sell thee a charm—an amulet that shall make thee King of Kafiristan."

Then the light broke upon me, and I followed the two camels out of the Serai till we reached open road and the priest halted.

"What d'you think o' that?" said he in English. "Carnehan can't talk their patter, so I've made him my servant. He makes a handsome servant. 'Tisn't for nothing that I've been knocking about the country for fourteen years. Didn't I do that talk neat? We'll hitch onto a caravan at Peshawar till we get to Jagdallak, and then we'll see if we can get donkeys for our camels, and strike into Kafiristan. Whirligigs for the Amir, O Lor! Put your hand under the camel-bags and tell me what you feel."

I felt the butt of a Martini, and another and another.

"Twenty of 'em," said Dravot placidly. "Twenty of 'em and ammunition to correspond, under the whirligigs and the mud dolls."

"Heaven help you if you are caught with those things!" I said. "A Martini is worth her weight in silver among the Pathans."

"Fifteen hundred rupees of capital—every rupee we could beg, borrow, or steal—are invested on these two camels," said Dravot. "We won't get caught. We're going through the Khaiber with a regular caravan. Who'd touch a poor mad priest?"

"Have you got everything you want?" I asked, overcome with astonishment.

"Not yet, but we shall soon. Give us a memento of your kindness, *Brother*. You did me a service, yesterday, and that time in Marwar. Half my Kingdom shall you have, as the saying is." I slipped a small charm compass from my watch chain and handed it up to the priest.

"Good-bye," said Dravot, giving me his hand cautiously. "It's the last time we'll shake hands with an Englishman these many days. Shake hands with him, Carnehan," he cried, as the second camel passed me.

Carnehan leaned down and shook hands. Then the camels passed away along the dusty road, and I was left alone to wonder. My eye could detect no failure in the disguises. The scene in the Serai proved that they were complete to the native mind. There was just the chance, therefore, that Carnehan and Dravot would be able to wander through Afghanistan without detection. But, beyond, they would find death—certain and awful death.

Ten days later a native correspondent giving me the news of the day from Peshawar, wound up his letter with: "There has been much laughter here on account of a certain mad priest who is going in his estimation to sell petty gauds and insignificant trinkets which he ascribes as great charms to H.H. the Amir of Bokhara. He passed through Peshawar and associated himself to the Second Summer caravan that goes to Kabul. The merchants are pleased because through superstition they imagine that such mad fellows bring good-fortune."

The two, then, were beyond the Border. I would have prayed for them, but, that night, a real King died in Europe, and demanded an obituary notice.

The wheel of the world swings through the same phases again and again. Summer passed and winter thereafter, and came and passed again. The daily paper continued and I with it, and upon the third summer there fell a hot night, a night-issue, and a strained waiting for something to be telegraphed from the other side of the world, exactly as had happened before. A few great men had died in the past two years, the machines worked with more clatter, and some of the trees in the Office garden were a few feet taller. But that was all the difference.

I passed over to the pressroom, and went through just such a scene as I have already described. The nervous tension was stronger than it had been two years before, and I felt the heat more acutely. At three o'clock I cried, "Print off," and turned to go, when there crept to my chair what was left of a man. He was bent into a circle, his head was sunk between his shoulders, and he moved his feet one over the other like a bear. I could hardly see whether he walked or crawled—this rag-wrapped, whining cripple who addressed me by name, crying that he was come back. "Can you give me a drink?" he whimpered. "For the Lord's sake, give me a drink!"

I went back to the office, the man following with groans of pain, and I turned up the lamp.

"Don't you know me?" he gasped, dropping into a chair and he turned his drawn face, surmounted by a shock of gray hair, to the light.

I looked at him intently. Once before had I seen eyebrows that met over the nose in an inch-broad black band, but for the life of me I could not tell where.

"I don't know you," I said, handing him the whiskey. "What can I do for you?"

He took a gulp of the spirit raw, and shivered in spite of the suffocating heat.

"I've come back," he repeated; "and I was the King of Kafiristan—me and Dravot—crowned Kings we was! In this office we settled it—you setting there and giving us the books. I am Peachey—Peachey Taliaferro Carnehan, and you've been setting here ever since—O Lord!"

I was more than a little astonished, and expressed my feelings accordingly.

"It's true," said Carnehan, with a dry cackle, nursing his feet, which were wrapped in rags. "True as gospel. Kings we were, with crowns upon our heads—me and Dravot—poor Dan—oh, poor, poor Dan, that would never take advice, not though I begged of him!"

"Take the whiskey," I said, "and take your own time. Tell me all you can recollect of everything from beginning to end. You got across the border on your camels, Dravot dressed as a mad priest and you his servant. Do you remember that?"

"I ain't mad—yet, but I shall be that way soon. Of course I remember. Keep looking at me, or maybe my words will go all to pieces. Keep looking at me in my eyes and don't say anything."

I leaned forward and looked into his face as steadily as I could. He dropped one hand upon the table and I grasped it by the wrist. It was twisted like a bird's claw, and upon the back was a ragged, red, diamond-shaped scar.

"No, don't look there. Look at *me,*" said Carnehan. "That comes afterward, but for the Lord's sake don't distrack me. We left with that caravan, me and Dravot playing all sorts of antics to amuse the people we were with. Dravot used to make us laugh in the evenings when all the people was cooking their dinners—cooking their dinners, and . . . what did they do then? They lit little fires with sparks that went into Dravot's beard, and we all laughed—fit to die. Little red fires they was, going into Dravot's big red beard—so funny." His eyes left mine and he smiled foolishly.

"You went as far as Jagdallak with that caravan," I said at a venture, "after you had lit those fires. To Jagdallak, where you turned off to try to get into Kafiristan."

"No, we didn't, neither. What are you talking about? We turned off before Jagdallak, because we heard the roads was good. But they wasn't good enough for our two camels—mine and Dravot's. When we left the caravan, Dravot took off all his clothes and mine too, and said we would be heathen, because the Kafirs didn't allow Mohammedans to talk to them. So we dressed betwixt and between, and such a sight as Daniel Dravot I never saw yet nor expect to see again. He burned half his beard, and slung a sheep-skin over his shoulder, and shaved his head into patterns. He shaved mine, too, and made me wear outrageous things to look like a heathen. That was in a most mountainous country, and our camels couldn't go along any more because of the mountains. They were tall and black, and coming home I saw them fight like wild goats—there are lots of goats in Kafiristan. And these mountains, they never keep still, no more than the goats. Always fighting they are, and don't let you sleep at night."

"Take some more whiskey," I said very slowly. "What did you and Daniel Dravot do when the camels could go no farther because of the rough roads that led into Kafiristan?"

"What did which do? There was a party called Peachey Taliaferro Carnehan that was with Dravot. Shall I tell you about him? He died out there in the cold. Slap from the bridge fell old Peachey, turning and twisting in the air like a penny whirligig that you can sell to the Amir.—No; they was two for three ha'pence, those whirligigs, or I am much mistaken and woeful sore. . . . And then these camels were no use, and Peachey said to Dravot—'For the Lord's sake let's get out of this before our heads are chopped off,' and with that they killed the camels all among the mountains, not having anything in particular to eat, but first they took off the boxes with the guns and the ammunition, till two men came along driving four mules. Dravot up and dances in front of them, singing—'Sell me four mules.' Says the first man—'If you are rich enough to buy, you are rich enough to rob'; but before ever he could put his hand to his knife, Dravot breaks his neck over his knee, and the other party runs away. So Carnehan loaded the mules with the rifles that was taken off the camels, and together we starts forward into those bitter cold mountainous parts, and never a road broader than the back of your hand."

He paused for a moment, while I asked him if he could remember the nature of the country through which he had journeyed.

"I am telling you as straight as I can, but my head isn't as good as it might be. They drove nails through it to make me hear better how Dravot died. The country was mountainous and the mules were most contrary, and the inhabitants were dispersed and solitary. They went up and up, and down and down, and that other party, Carnehan, was imploring of Dravot not to sing and whistle so loud, for fear of bringing down the tremenjus avalanches. But Dravot says that if a King couldn't sing it wasn't worth being King, and whacked the mules over the rump, and never took no heed for ten cold days. We came to a big level valley all among the mountains, and the mules were near dead, so we killed them, not having anything in special for them or us to eat. We sat upon the boxes, and played odd and even with the cartridges that was jolted out.

"Then ten men with bows and arrows ran down that valley, chasing twenty men with bows and arrows, and the row was tremenjus. They was fair men—fairer than you or me—with yellow hair and remarkable well built. Says Dravot, unpacking the guns—'This is the beginning of the business. We'll fight for the ten men,' and with that he fires two rifles at the twenty men, and drops one of them at two hundred yards from the rock where he was sitting. The other men began to run, but Carnehan and Dravot sits on the boxes picking them off at all ranges, up and down the valley. Then we goes up to the ten men that had run across the snow too, and they fires a footy little arrow at us. Dravot he shoots above their heads and they all falls down flat. Then he walks over them and kicks them, and then he lifts them up and shakes hands all around to make them friendly like. He calls them and gives them the boxes to carry, and waves his hand for all the world as though he was King already. They takes the boxes and him across the valley and up the hill into a pinewood on the top, where there was half a dozen big stone idols. Dravot he goes to the biggest—a fellow they call Imbra—and lays a rifle and a cartridge at his feet, rubbing his nose respectful with his own nose, patting him on the head, and saluting in front of it. He turns around to the men and nods his head, and says—'That's all right. I'm in the know too, and all these old jim-jams are my friends.' Then he opens his mouth and points down it, and when the first man brings him food, he says—'No'; and when the second man brings him food he says—'No'; but when one of the old priests and the boss of the village brings him food, he says—'Yes'; very haughty, and eats it slow. That was how we came to our first village, without any trouble, just as though we had tumbled from the skies. But we tumbled from one of those damned rope-bridges, you see and—you couldn't expect a man to laugh much after that?"

"Take some more whiskey and go on," I said. "That was the first village you came into. How did you get to be King?"

"I wasn't King," said Carnehan. "Dravot he was the King, and a handsome man he looked with the gold crown on his head and all. Him and the other party stayed in that village, and every morning Dravot sat by the side of old Imbra, and the people came and worshiped. That was Dravot's order. Then a lot of men came into the valley, and Carnehan and Dravot picks them off with the rifles before they knew where they was, and runs down into the valley and up again the other side and finds another village, same as the first one, and the people all falls down flat on their faces, and Dravot says—'Now what is the trouble between you two villages?' and the people points to a woman, as fair as you or me, that was carried off, and Dravot takes her back to the first village and counts up the dead—eight there was. For each dead man Dravot pours a little milk on the ground and waves his arms like a whirligig and 'That's all right,' says he. Then he and Carnehan takes the big boss of each village by the arm and walks them down into the valley, and shows them how to scratch a line with a spear right down the valley, and gives each a sod of turf from both sides of the line. Then all the people comes down and shouts like the devil and all, and Dravot says—'Go and dig the land, and be fruitful and multiply,' which they did, though they didn't understand. Then we asks the names of things in their lingo—bread and water and fire and idols and such, and Dravot leads the priest of each village up to the idol, and says he must sit there and judge the people, and if anything goes wrong he is to be shot.

"Next week they was all turning up the land in the valley as quiet as bees and much prettier, and the priests heard all the complaints and told Dravot in dumb show what it was about. 'That's just the beginning,' says Dravot. 'They think we're Gods.' He and Carnehan picks out twenty good men and shows them how to click off a rifle, and form fours, and advance in line, and they was very pleased to do so, and clever to see the hang of it. Then he takes out his pipe and his baccy-pouch and leaves one at one village, and one at the other, and off we two goes to see what was to be done in the next valley. That was all rock, and there was a little village there, and Carnehan says—'Send 'em to the old valley to plant,' and takes 'em there and gives 'em some land that wasn't took before. They were a poor lot, and we blooded 'em with a kid before letting 'em into the new Kingdom. That was to impress the people, and then they settled down quiet, and Carnehan went back to Dravot who had got into another valley, all snow and ice and most mountainous. There was no people there and the Army got afraid, so Dravot shoots one of them, and goes on till he finds some people in a village, and the Army explains that unless the people wants to be killed they had better not shoot their little matchlocks; for they had matchlocks. We makes friends with the priest and I stays there alone with two of the Army, teaching the men how to drill, and a thundering big Chief comes across the snow with kettledrums and horns twanging, because he heard there was a new God kicking about. Carnehan sights for the brown of the men half a mile across the snow and wings one of them. Then he sends a message to the Chief that, unless he wished to be killed, he must come and shake hands with me and leave his arms behind. The Chief comes alone first, and Carnehan shakes hands with him and whirls his arms about, same as Dravot used, and very much surprised that Chief was, and strokes my eyebrows. Then Carnehan goes alone to the Chief, and asks him in dumb show if he had an enemy he hated. 'I have,' says the Chief. So Carnehan weeds out the pick of his men, and sets the two of the Army to show them drill and at the end of two weeks the men can maneuver about as well as Volunteers. So he marches with the Chief to a great big plain on the top of a mountain, and the Chief's men rushes into a village and takes it; we three Martinis firing into the brown of the enemy. So we took that village too, and I gives the Chief a rag from my coat and says, 'Occupy till I come'; which was scriptural. By way of a reminder, when me and the Army was eighteen hundred yards away, I drops a bullet near him standing on the snow, and all the people falls flat on their faces. Then I sends a letter to Dravot wherever he be by land or by sea."

At the risk of throwing the creature out of train I interrupted—"How could you write a letter up yonder?"

"The letter?—Oh!—The letter! Keep looking at me between the eyes, please. It was a string-talk letter, that we'd learned the way of it from a blind beggar in the Punjab."

I remember that there had once come to the office a blind man with a knotted twig and a piece of string which he wound around the twig according to some cipher of his own. He could, after the lapse of days or hours, repeat the sentence which he had reeled up. He had reduced the alphabet to eleven primitive sounds; and tried to teach me his method, but I could not understand.

"I sent that letter to Dravot," said Carnehan; "and told him to come back because this Kingdom was growing too big for me to handle, and then I struck for the first valley, to see how the priests were working. They called the village we took along with the Chief, Bashkai, and the first village we took, Er-Heb. The priests at Er-Heb was doing all right, but they had a lot of pending cases about land to show me, and some men from another village had been firing arrows at night. I went out and looked for that village, and fired four rounds at it from a thousand yards. That used all the cartridges I cared to spend, and I waited for Dravot, who had been away two or three months, and I kept my people quiet.

"One morning I heard the devil's own noise of drums and horns, and Dan Dravot marches down the hill with his Army and a tail of hundreds of men, and, which was the most amazing, a great gold crown on his head. 'My Gord, Carnehan,' says Daniel, 'this is a tremenjus business, and we've got the whole country as far as it's worth having. I am the son of Alexander by Queen Semiramis, and you're my younger brother and a God too! It's the biggest thing we've ever seen. I've been marching and fighting for six weeks with the Army, and every footy little village for fifty miles has come in rejoiceful; and more than that, I've got the key of the whole show, as you'll see, and I've got a crown for you! I told 'em to make two of 'em at a place called Shu, where the gold lies in the rock like suet in mutton. Gold I've seen, and turquoise I've kicked out of the cliffs, and there's garnets in the sands of the river, and here's a chunk of amber that a man brought me. Call up all the priests, and, here, take your crown.'

"One of the men opens a black hair bag, and I slips the crown on. It was too small and too heavy, but I wore it for the glory. Hammered gold it was—five pound weight, like a hoop of a barrel.

"'Peachey,' says Dravot, 'we don't want to fight no more. The Craft's the trick so help me!' and he brings forward that same Chief that I left at Bashkai—Billy Fish we called him afterward, because he was so like Billy Fish that drove the big tank-engine at Mach on the Bolan in the old days. 'Shake hands with him,' says Dravot, and I shook hands and nearly dropped, for Billy Fish gave me the Grip. I said nothing, but tried him with the Fellow Craft Grip. He answers, all right, and I tried the Master's Grip, but that was a slip. 'A Fellow Craft he is!' I says to Dan. 'Does he know the word?'—'He does,' says Dan, 'and all the priests know. It's a miracle! The Chiefs and the priests can work a Fellow Craft Lodge in a way that's very like ours, and they've cut the marks on the rocks, but they don't know the Third Degree, and they've come to find out. It's Gord's Truth. I've known these long years that the Afghans knew up to the Fellow Craft Degree, but this is a miracle. A God and a Grand Master of the Craft am I, and a Lodge in the Third Degree I will open, and we'll raise the head priests and the Chiefs of the villages.'

"'It's against all the law,' I says, 'holding a Lodge without warrant from anyone; and you know we never held office in any Lodge.'

"'It's a master-stroke o' policy,' says Dravot. 'It means running the country as easy as a four-wheeled bogie on a down grade. We can't stop to inquire now, or they'll turn against us. I've forty Chiefs at my heel, and passed and raised according to their merit they shall be. Billet these men on the villages, and see that we run up a Lodge of some kind. The temple of Imbra will do for the Lodge room. The women must make aprons as you show them. I'll hold a levee of Chiefs tonight and Lodge tomorrow.'

"I was fair run off my legs, but I wasn't such a fool as not to see what a pull this Craft business gave us. I showed the priests' families how to make aprons of the degrees, but for Dravot's apron the blue border and marks was made of turquoise lumps on white hide, not cloth. We took a great square stone in the temple for the Master's chair, and little stones for the officers' chairs, and painted the black pavement with white squares, and did what we could to make things regular.

"At the levee which was held that night on the hillside with big bonfires, Dravot gives out that him and me were Gods and sons of Alexander, and Past Grand Masters in the Craft, and was come to make Kafiristan a country where every man should eat in peace and drink in quiet, and specially obey us. Then the Chiefs come around to shake hands, and they were so hairy and white and fair it was just like shaking hands with old friends. We gave them names according as they was like men we had known in India—Billy Fish, Holly Dilworth, Pikky Kergan, that was Bazar-master when I was at Mhow, and so on, and so on.

"*The* most amazing miracles was at Lodge next night. One of the old priests was watching us continuous, and I felt uneasy, for I knew we'd have to fudge the Ritual, and I didn't know what the men knew. The old priest was a stranger come in from beyond the village of Bashkai. The minute Dravot puts on the Master's apron that the girls had made for him, the priest fetches a whoop and a howl, and tries to overturn the stone that Dravot was sitting on. 'It's all up now,' I says. 'That comes of meddling with the Craft without warrant!' Dravot never winked an eye, not when ten priests took and tilted over the Grand Master's chair—which was to say the stone of Imbra. The priest begins rubbing the bottom end of it to clear away the black dirt, and presently he shows all the other priests the Master's Mark, same as was on Dravot's apron, cut into the stone. Not even the priests of the temple of Imbra knew it was there. The old chap falls flat on his face at Dravot's feet and kisses 'em. 'Luck again,' said Dravot, across the Lodge to me, 'they say it's the missing Mark that no one could understand the why of. We're more than safe now.' Then he bangs the butt of his gun for a gavel and says: 'By virtue of the authority vested in me by my own right hand and the help of Peachey, I declare myself Grand Master of all Freemasonry in Kafiristan in this the Mother Lodge o' the country, and King of Kafiristan equally with Peachey!' At that he puts on his crown and I puts on mine—I was doing Senior Warden—and we opens the Lodge in most ample form. It was a amazing miracle! The priests moved in Lodge through the first two degrees almost without telling, as if the memory was coming back to them. After that, Peachey and Dravot raised such as was worthy—high priests and Chiefs of far-off villages. Billy Fish was the first, and I can tell you we scared the soul out of him. It was not in any way according to Ritual, but it served our turn. We didn't raise more than ten of the biggest men, because we didn't want to make the Degree common. And they was clamoring to be raised.

"'In another six months,' said Dravot, 'we'll hold another Communication, and see how you are working.' Then he asks them about their villages, and learns that they was fighting one against the other, and were sick and tired of it. And when they wasn't doing that they was fighting with the Mohammedans. 'You can fight those when they come into our country,' says Dravot. 'Tell off every tenth man of your tribes for a Frontier guard, and send two hundred at a time to this valley to be drilled. Nobody is going to be shot or speared any more so long as he does well, and I know that you won't cheat me, because you're white people—sons of Alexander—and not like common, black Mohammedans. You are *my* people, and by God,' says he, running off into English at the end—'I'll make a damned fine Nation of you, or I'll die in the making!'

"I can't tell all we did for the next six months, because Dravot did a lot I couldn't see the hang of, and he learned their lingo in a way I never could. My work was to help the people plow, and now and again go out with some of the Army and see what the other villages were doing, and make 'em throw rope-bridges across the ravines which cut up the country horrid. Dravot was very kind to me, but when he walked up and down in the pinewood pulling that bloody red beard of his with both fists I knew he was thinking plans I could not advise about, and I just waited for orders.

"But Dravot never showed me disrespect before the people. They were afraid of me and the Army, but they loved Dan. He was the best of friends with the priests and the Chiefs; but anyone could come across the hills with a complaint, and Dravot would hear him out fair, and call four priests together and say what was to be done. He used to call in Billy Fish from Bashkai, and Pikky Kergan from Shu, and an old Chief we called Kafuzelum—it was like enough to his real name—and hold councils with 'em when there was any fighting to be done in small villages. That was his Council of War, and the four priests of Bashkai, Shu, Khawak, and Madora was his Privy Council. Between the lot of 'em they sent me, with forty men and twenty rifles, and sixty men carrying turquoises, into the Ghorband country to buy those handmade Martini rifles, that come out of the Amir's workshops at Kabul, from one of the Amir's Herati regiments that would have sold the very teeth out of their mouths for turquoises.

"I stayed in Ghorband a month, and gave the Governor there the pick of my baskets for hush money, and bribed the Colonel of the regiment some more, and, between the two and the tribes-people, we got more than a hundred handmade Martinis, a hundred good Kohat Jezails that'll throw to six hundred yards, and forty man-loads of very bad ammunition for the rifles. I came back with what I had, and distributed 'em among the men that the Chiefs sent in to me to drill. Dravot was too busy to attend to those things, but the old Army that we first made helped me, and we turned out five hundred men that could drill, and two hundred that knew how to hold arms pretty straight. Even those corkscrewed, handmade guns was a miracle to them. Dravot talked big about powder shops and factories, walking up and down in the pinewood when the winter was coming on.

"'I won't make a Nation,' says he. 'I'll make an Empire! These men aren't niggers; they're English! Look at their eyes—look at their mouths. Look at the way they stand up. They sit on chairs in their own houses. They're the Lost Tribes, or something like it, and they've grown to be English. I'll take a census in the spring if the priests don't get frightened. There must be a fair two million of 'em in these hills. The villages are full o' little children. Two million people—two hundred and fifty thousand fighting men—and all English! They only want the rifles and a little drilling. Two hundred and fifty thousand men, ready to cut in on Russia's right flank when she tries for India! Peachey, man,' he says, chewing his beard in great hunks, 'we shall be Emperors—Emperors of the Earth! Rajah Brooke will be a suckling to us. I'll treat with the Viceroy on equal terms. I'll ask him to send me twelve picked English—twelve that I know of—to help us govern a bit. There's Mackray, Sergeant-pensioner at Segowli—many's the good dinner he's given me, and his wife a pair of trousers. There's Donkin, the Warder of Tounghoo Jail; there's hundreds that I could lay my hand on if I was in India. The Viceroy shall do it for me, I'll send a man through in the spring for those men, and I'll write for a dispensation from the Grand Lodge for what I've done as Grand Master. That—and all the Sniders that'll be thrown out when the native troops in India take up the Martini. They'll be worn smooth, but they'll do for fighting in these hills. Twelve English, a hundred thousands Sniders run through the Amir's country in driblets—I'd be content with twenty thousand in one year—and we'd be an Empire. When everything was shipshape, I'd hand over the crown—this crown I'm wearing now—to Queen Victoria on my knees, and she'd say: "Rise up, Sir Daniel Dravot." Oh, it's big! It's big, I tell you! But there's so much to be done in every place—Bashkai, Khawak, Shu, and everywhere else.'

"'What is it?' I says. 'There are no more men coming in to be drilled this autumn. Look at those, fat, black clouds. They're bringing the snow.'

"'It isn't that,' says Daniel, putting his hand very hard on my shoulder; 'and I don't wish to say anything that's against you, for no other living man would have followed me and made me what I am as you have done. You're a first-class Commander-in-Chief, and the people know you; but—it's a big country, and somehow you can't help me, Peachey, in the way I want to be helped.'

"'Go to your blasted priests, then!' I said, and I was sorry when I made that remark, but it did hurt me sore to find Daniel talking so superior when I'd drilled all the men, and done all he told me.

"'Don't let's quarrel, Peachey,' says Daniel without cursing. 'You're a King too, and the half of this Kingdom is yours; but can't you see, Peachey, we want cleverer men than us now—three or four of 'em, that we can scatter about for our Deputies. It's a hugeous great State, and I can't always tell the right thing to do, and I haven't time for all I want to do, and here's the winter coming on and all.' He put half his beard into his mouth, all red like the gold of his crown.

"'I'm sorry, Daniel,' says I. 'I've done all I could. I've drilled the men and shown the people how to stack their oats better; and I've brought in those tinware rifles from Ghorband—but I know what you're driving at. I take it Kings always feel oppressed that way.'

"'There's another thing too,' says Dravot, walking up and down. 'The winter's coming and these people won't be giving much trouble, and if they do we can't move about. I want a wife.'

"'For Gord's sake leave the women alone!' I says. 'We've both got all the work we can, though I *am* a fool. Remember the Contrack, and keep clear o' women.'

"'The Contrack only lasted till such time as we was Kings; and Kings we have been these months past,' says Dravot, weighing his crown in his hand. 'You go get a wife too, Peachey—a nice, strappin', plump girl that'll keep you warm in the winter. They're prettier than English girls, and we can take the pick of 'em. Boil 'em once or twice in hot water, and they'll come out like chicken and ham.'

"'Don't tempt me!' I says. 'I will not have any dealings with a woman not till we are a dam' sight more settled than we are now. I've been doing the work o' two men, and you've been doing the work o' three. Let's lie off a bit, and see if we can get some better tobacco from Afghan country and run in some good liquor; but no women.'

"'Who's talking o' *women?*' says Dravot. 'I said *wife*—a Queen to breed a King's son for the King. A Queen out of the strongest tribe, that'll make them your blood brothers, and that'll lie by your side and tell you all the people thinks about you and their own affairs. That's what I want.'

"'Do you remember that Bengali woman I kept at Mogul Serai when I was a plate-layer?' says I. 'A fat lot o' good she was to me. She taught me the lingo and one or two other things; but what happened? She ran away with the Stationmaster's servant and half my month's pay. Then she turned up at Dadur Junction in tow of a half-caste, and had the impidence to say I was her husband—all among the drivers in the running-shed too!'

"'We've done with that,' says Dravot, 'these women are whiter than you or me, and a Queen I will have for the winter months.'

"'For the last time o' asking, Dan, do *not,*' I says. 'It'll only bring us harm. The Bible says that Kings ain't to waste their strength on women, 'specially when they've got a new raw Kingdom to work over.'

"'For the last time of answering I will,' said Dravot, and he went away through the pine trees looking like a big red devil, the sun being on his crown and beard and all.

"But getting a wife was not as easy as Dan thought. He put it before the Council, and there was no answer till Billy Fish said that he'd better ask the girls. Dravot damned them all around. 'What's wrong with me?' he shouts, standing by the idol Imbra. 'Am I a dog or am I not enough of a man for your wenches? Haven't I put the shadow of my hand over this country? Who stopped the last Afghan raid?' It was me really, but Dravot was too angry to remember. 'Who bought your guns? Who repaired the bridges? Who's the Grand Master of the sign cut in the stone?' says he, and he thumped his hand on the block that he used to sit on in Lodge, and at Council, which opened like Lodge always. Billy Fish said nothing and no more did the others. 'Keep your hair on, Dan,' said I; 'and ask the girls. That's how it's done at Home, and these people are quite English.'

"'The marriage of the King is a matter of State,' says Dan, in a white-hot rage, for he could feel, I hope, that he was going against his better mind. He walked out of the Council room, and the others sat still, looking at the ground.

"'Billy Fish,' says I to the Chief of Bashkai, 'what's the difficulty here? A straight answer to a true friend.'

"'You know,' says Billy Fish. 'How should a man tell you who knows everything? How can daughters of men marry Gods or Devils? It's not proper.'

"I remembered something like that in the Bible; but if, after seeing us as long as they had, they still believed we were Gods, it wasn't for me to undeceive them.

"'A God can do anything,' says I. 'If the King is fond of a girl he'll not let her die.'—'She'll have to,' said Billy Fish. 'There are all sorts of Gods and Devils in these mountains, and now and again a girl marries one of them and isn't seen any more. Besides, you two know the Mark cut in the stone. Only the Gods know that. We thought you were men till you showed the sign of the Master.'

"I wished then that we had explained about the loss of the genuine secrets of a Master Mason at the first go-off; but I said nothing. All that night there was a blowing of horns in a little dark temple halfway down the hill, and I heard a girl crying fit to die. One of the priests told us that she was being prepared to marry the King.

"'I'll have no nonsense of that kind,' says Dan. 'I don't want to interfere with your customs, but I'll take my own wife.'—'The girl's a little bit afraid,' says the priest. 'She thinks she's going to die, and they are a-heartening of her up down in the temple.'

"'Hearten her very tender, then,' says Dravot, 'or I'll hearten you with the butt of a gun so you'll never want to be heartened again.' He licked his lips, did Dan, and stayed up walking about more than half the night, thinking of the wife that he was going to get in the morning. I wasn't any means comfortable, for I knew that dealings with a woman in foreign parts, though you was a crowned King twenty times over, could not but be risky. I got up very early in the morning while Dravot was asleep, and I saw the priests talking together in whispers, and the Chiefs talking together too, and they looked at me out of the corners of their eyes.

"'What is up, Fish?' I says to the Bashkai man, who was wrapped up in his furs and looking splendid to behold.

"'I can't rightly say,' says he; 'but if you can make the King drop all this nonsense about marriage, you'll be doing him and me and yourself a great service.'

"'That I do believe,' says I. 'But sure, you know, Billy, as well as me, having fought against and for us, that the King and me are nothing more than two of the finest men that God Almighty ever made. Nothing more, I do assure you.'

"'That may be,' says Billy Fish, 'and yet I should be sorry if it was.' He sinks his head upon his great fur cloak for a minute and thinks. 'King,' says he, 'be you man or God or Devil, I'll stick by you today. I have twenty of my men with me, and they will follow me. We'll go to Bashkai until the storm blows over.'

"A little snow had fallen in the night, and everything was

white except the greasy fat clouds that blew down and down from the north. Dravot came out with his crown on his head, swinging his arms and stamping his feet, and looking more pleased than Punch.

"'For the last time, drop it, Dan,' says I in a whisper, 'Billy Fish here says that there will be a row.'

"'A row among my people!' says Dravot. 'Not much. Peachey, you're a fool not to get a wife too. Where's the girl?' says he with a voice as loud as the braying of a jackass. 'Call up all the Chiefs and priests, and let the Emperor see if his wife suits him.'

"There was no need to call anyone. They were all there leaning on their guns and spears around the clearing in the center of the pinewood. A lot of priests went down to the little temple to bring up the girl, and the horns blew fit to wake the dead. Billy Fish saunters around and gets as close to Daniel as he could, and behind him stood his twenty men with matchlocks. Not a man of them under six feet. I was next to Dravot, and behind me was twenty men of the regular Army. Up comes the girl, and a strapping wench she was, covered with silver and turquoises but white as death, and looking back every minute at the priests.

"'She'll do,' said Dan, looking her over. 'What's to be afraid of, lass? Come and kiss me.' He puts his arm around her. She shuts her eyes, gives a bit of a squeak, and down goes her face in the side of Dan's flaming red beard.

"'The slut's bitten me!' says he, clapping his hand to his neck, and, sure enough, his hand was red with blood. Billy Fish and two of his matchlock-men catches hold of Dan by the shoulders and drags him into the Bashkai lot, while the priests howls in their lingo—'Neither God nor Devil but a man!' I was all taken aback, for a priest cut at me in front, and the Army behind began firing into the Bashkai men.

"'God A'mighty!' says Dan. 'What is the meaning o' this?'

"'Come back! Come away!' says Billy Fish. 'Ruin and Mutiny is the matter. We'll break for Bashkai if we can.'

"I tried to give some sort of orders to my men—the men o' the regular Army—but it was no use, so I fired into the brown of 'em with an English Martini and drilled three beggars in a line. The valley was full of shouting, howling creatures, and every soul was shrieking, 'Not a God nor a Devil but only a man!' The Bashkai troops stuck to Billy Fish all they were worth, but their matchlocks wasn't half as good as the Kabul breech-loaders, and four of them dropped. Dan was bellowing like a bull, for he was very wrathy; and Billy Fish had a hard job to prevent him running out at the crowd.

"'We can't stand,' says Billy Fish. 'Make a run for it down the valley! The whole place is against us.' The matchlock-men ran, and we went down the valley in spite of Dravot. He was swearing horrible and crying out he was a King. The priests rolled great stones on us, and the regular Army fired hard, and there wasn't more than six men, not counting Dan, Billy Fish, and Me, that came down to the bottom of the valley alive.

"Then they stopped firing and the horns in the temple blew again. 'Come away—for Gord's sake come away!' says Billy Fish. 'They'll send runners out to all the villages before ever we get to Bashkai. I can protect you there, but I can't do anything now.'

"My own notion is that Dan began to go mad in his head from that hour. He stared up and down like a stuck pig. Then he was all for walking back alone and killing the priests with his bare hands; which he could have done. 'An Emperor am I,' says Daniel, 'and next year I shall be a Knight of the Queen.'

"'All right, Dan,' says I; 'but come along now while there's time.'

"'It's your fault,' says he, 'for not looking after your Army better. There was mutiny in the midst, and you didn't know—you damned engine-driving, plate-laying, missionary's-pass-hunting hound!' He sat upon a rock and called me every foul name he could lay tongue to. I was too heartsick to care, though it was all his foolishness that brought the smash.

"'I'm sorry, Dan,' says I, 'but there's no accounting for natives. This business is our Fifty-Seven. Maybe we'll make something out of it yet, when we've got to Bashkai.'

"'Let's get to Bashkai, then,' says Dan, 'and, by God, when I come back here again I'll sweep the valley so there isn't a bug in a blanket left!'

"We walked all that day, and all that night Dan was stumping up and down on the snow, chewing his beard and muttering to himself.

"'There's no hope o' getting clear,' said Billy Fish. 'The priests will have sent runners to the villages to say that you are only men. Why didn't you stick on as Gods till things was more settled? I'm a dead man,' says Billy Fish, and he throws himself down on the snow and begins to pray to his Gods.

"Next morning we was in a cruel bad country—all up and down, no level ground at all, and no food either. The six Bashkai men looked at Billy Fish hungry-way as if they wanted to ask something, but they said never a word. At noon we came to the top of a flat mountain all covered with snow, and when we climbed up into it, behold, there was an Army in position waiting in the middle!

"'The runners have been very quick,' says Billy Fish, with a little bit of a laugh. 'They are waiting for us.'

"Three or four men began to fire from the enemy's side, and a chance shot took Daniel in the calf of the leg. That brought him to his senses. He looks across the snow at the Army, and sees the rifles that we had brought into the country.

"'We're done for,' says he. 'They are Englishmen, these people—and it's my blasted nonsense that has brought you to this. Get back, Billy Fish, and take your men away; you've done what you could, and now cut for it. Carnehan,' says he, 'shake hands with me and go along with Billy. Maybe they won't kill you. I'll go and meet 'em alone. It's me that did it. Me, the King!'

"'Go!' says I. 'Go to Hell, Dan. I'm with you here. Billy Fish, you clear out, and we two will meet those folk.'

"'I'm a Chief,' says Billy Fish, quite quiet. 'I stay with you. My men can go.'

"The Bashkai fellows didn't wait for a second word but ran off, and Dan and Me and Billy Fish walked across to where the drums were drumming and the horns were horning. It was cold—awful cold. I've got that cold in the back of my head now. There's a lump of it there."

The punkah-coolies had gone to sleep. Two kerosene lamps were blazing in the office, and the perspiration poured down my face and splashed on the blotter as I leaned forward.

Carnehan was shivering, and I feared that his mind might go. I wiped my face, took a fresh grip of the piteously mangled hands, and said: "What happened after that?"

The momentary shift of my eyes had broken the clear current.

"What was you pleased to say?" whined Carnehan. "They took them without any sound. Not a little whisper all along the snow, not though the King knocked down the first man that set hand on him—not though old Peachey fired his last cartridge into the brown of 'em. Not a single solitary sound did those swines make. They just closed up tight, and I tell you their furs stunk. There was a man called Billy Fish, a good friend of us all, and they cut his throat, Sir, then and there, like a pig; and the King kicks up the bloody snow and says: 'We've had a dashed fine run for our money. What's coming next?' But Peachey, Peachey Taliaferro, I tell you, Sir, in confidence as betwixt two friends, he lost his head, Sir. No, he didn't neither. The King lost his head, so he did, all along o' one of those cunning rope-bridges. Kindly let me have the paper cutter, Sir. It tilted this way. They marched him a mile across that snow to a rope-bridge over a ravine with a river at the bottom. You may have seen such. They prodded him behind like an ox. 'Damn your eyes!' says the King. 'D'you suppose I can't die like a gentleman?' He turns to Peachey—Peachey that was crying like a child. 'I've brought you to this, Peachey,' says he. 'Brought you out of your happy life to be killed in Kafiristan, where you was late Commander-in-Chief of the Emperor's forces. Say you forgive me, Peachey.'—'I do,' says Peachey. 'Fully and freely do I forgive you, Dan.'—'Shake hands, Peachey,' says he. 'I'm going now.' Out he goes, looking neither right nor left, and when he was plumb in the middle of those dizzy dancing ropes—'Cut, you beggars,' he shouts; and they cut, and old Dan fell, turning round and round and round, twenty thousand miles, for he took half an hour to fall till he struck the water, and I could see his body caught on a rock with the gold crown close beside.

"But do you know what they did to Peachey between two pine trees? They crucified him, Sir, as Peachey's hand will show. They used wooden pegs for his hands and his feet; and he didn't die. He hung there and screamed, and they took him down next day, and said it was a miracle that he wasn't dead. They took him down—poor old Peachey that hadn't done them any harm—that hadn't done them any——"

He rocked to and fro and wept bitterly, wiping his eyes with the back of his scarred hands and moaning like a child for some ten minutes.

"They was cruel enough to feed him up in the temple, because they said he was more of a God than old Daniel that was a man. Then they turned him out on the snow, and told him to go home, and Peachey came home in about a year, begging along the roads quite safe; for Daniel Dravot he walked before and said: 'Come along, Peachey. It's a big thing we're doing.' The mountains they danced at night, and the mountains they tried to fall on Peachey's head, but Dan he held up his hand, and Peachey came along bent double. He never let go of Dan's hand, and he never let go of Dan's head. They gave it to him as a present in the temple, to remind him not to come again, and though the crown was pure gold, and Peachey was starving, never would Peachey sell the same. You knew Dravot, Sir! You knew Right Worshipful Brother Dravot! Look at him now!"

He fumbled in the mass of rags around his bent waist; brought out a black horsehair bag embroidered with silver thread; and shook therefrom onto my table—the dried, withered head of Daniel Dravot! The morning sun that had long been paling the lamps struck the red beard and blind sunken eyes; struck, too, a heavy circlet of gold studded with raw turquoises, that Carnehan placed tenderly on the battered temples.

"You be'old now," said Carnehan, "the Emperor in his 'abit as he lived—the King of Kafiristan with his crown upon his head. Poor old Daniel that was a monarch once!"

I shuddered, for, in spite of defacements manifold, I recognized the head of the man of Marwar Junction. Carnehan rose to go. I attempted to stop him. He was not fit to walk abroad. "Let me take away the whiskey, and give me a little money," he gasped. "I was a King once. I'll go to the Deputy Commissioner and ask to set in the Poorhouse till I get my health.

No, thank you, I can't wait till you get a carriage for me. I've urgent private affairs—in the south—at Marwar."

He shambled out of the office and departed in the direction of the Deputy Commissioner's house. That day at noon I had occasion to go down the blinding hot Mall, and I saw a crooked man crawling along the white dust of the roadside, his hat in his hand, quavering dolorously after the fashion of street-singers at Home. There was not a soul in sight, and he was out of all possible earshot of the houses. And he sang through his nose, turning his head from right to left:—

"The Son of Man goes forth to war,
A golden crown to gain;
His blood-red banner streams afar—
Who follows in his train?"

I waited to hear no more, but put the poor wretch into my carriage and drove him off to the nearest missionary for eventual transfer to the Asylum. He repeated the hymn twice while he was with me whom he did not in the least recognize, and I left him singing it to the missionary.

Two days later I inquired after his welfare of the Superintendent of the Asylum.

"He was admitted suffering from sunstroke. He died early yesterday morning," said the Superintendent. "Is it true that he was half an hour bareheaded in the sun at midday?"

"Yes," said I, "but do you happen to know if he had anything upon him by any chance when he died?"

"Not to my knowledge," said the Superintendent.

And there the matter rests.

"THEY"

ONE view called me to another; one hilltop to its fellow, half across the county, and since I could answer at no more trouble than the snapping forward of a lever, I let the country flow under my wheels. The orchid-studded flats of the East gave way to the thyme, ilex, and gray grass of the Downs; these again to the rich cornland and fig-trees of the lower coast, where you carry the beat of the tide on your left hand for fifteen level miles; and when at last I turned inland through a huddle of rounded hills and woods I had run myself clean out of my known marks. Beyond that precise hamlet which stands godmother to the capital of the United States, I found hidden villages where bees, the only things awake, boomed in eighty-foot lindens that overhung gray Norman churches; miraculous brooks diving under stone bridges built for heavier traffic than would ever vex them again; tithe-barns larger than their churches, and an old smithy that cried out aloud how it had once been a hall of the Knights of the Temple. Gypsies I found on a common where the gorse, bracken, and heath fought it out together up a mile of Roman road; and a little farther on I disturbed a red fox rolling dog-fashion in the naked sunlight.

As the wooded hills closed about me I stood up in the car to take the bearings of that great Down whose ringed head is a landmark for fifty miles across the low countries. I judged that the lie of the country would bring me across some westward running road that went to his feet, but I did not allow for the confusing veils of the woods. A quick turn plunged me first into a green cutting brimful of liquid sunshine, next into a gloomy tunnel where last year's dead leaves whispered and scuffled about my tires. The strong hazel stuff meeting overhead had not been cut for a couple of generations at least, nor had any axe helped the moss-cankered oak and beech to spring above them. Here the road changed frankly into a carpeted ride on whose brown velvet spent primrose-clumps showed like jade, and a few sickly, white-stalked bluebells nodded together. As the slope favored I shut off the power and slid over the whirled leaves, expecting every moment to meet a keeper; but I only heard a jay, far off, arguing against the silence under the twilight of the trees.

Still the track descended. I was on the point of reversing and working my way back on the second speed ere I ended in some swamp, when I saw sunshine through the tangle ahead and lifted the brake.

It was down again at once. As the light beat across my face my forewheels took the turf of a great still lawn from which sprang horsemen ten feet high with leveled lances, monstrous peacocks, and sleek round-headed maids of honor—blue, black, and glistening—all of clipped yew. Across the lawn—the marshaled woods besieged it on three sides—stood an ancient house of lichened and weather-worn stone, with mullioned windows and roofs of rose-red tile. It was flanked by semi-circular walls, also rose-red, that closed the lawn on the fourth side, and at their feet a box hedge grew man-high. There were doves on the roof about the slim brick chimneys, and I caught a glimpse of an octagonal dove-house behind the screening wall.

Here, then, I stayed; a horseman's green spear laid at my breast; held by the exceeding beauty of that jewel in that setting.

"If I am not packed off for a trespasser, or if this knight does not ride a wallop at me," thought I, "Shakespeare and Queen Elizabeth at least must come out of that half-open garden door and ask me to tea."

A child appeared at an upper window, and I thought the little thing waved a friendly hand. But it was to call a companion, for presently another bright head showed. Then I heard a laugh among the yew-peacocks, and turning to make sure (till then I had been watching the house only) I saw the silver of a fountain behind a hedge thrown up against the sun. The doves on the roof cooed to the cooing water; but between the two notes I caught the utterly happy chuckle of a child absorbed in some light mischief.

The garden door—heavy oak sunk deep in the thickness of the wall—opened further: a woman in a big garden hat set her foot slowly on the time-hollowed stone step and as slowly walked across the turf. I was forming some apology when she lifted up her head and I saw that she was blind.

"I heard you," she said. "Isn't that a motor car?"

"I'm afraid I've made a mistake in my road. I should have turned off up above—I never dreamed"—I began.

"But I'm very glad. Fancy a motor car coming into the garden! It will be such a treat——" She turned and made as though looking about her. "You—you haven't seen anyone have you—perhaps?"

"No one to speak to, but the children seemed interested at a distance."

"Which?"

"I saw a couple up at the window just now, and I think I heard a little chap in the grounds."

"Oh, lucky you!" she cried, and her face brightened. "I hear them, of course, but that's all. You've seen them and heard them?"

"Yes," I answered. "And if I know anything of children one of them's having a beautiful time by the fountain yonder. Escaped, I should imagine."

"You're fond of children?"

I gave her one or two reasons why I did not altogether hate them.

"Of course, of course," she said. "Then you understand. Then you won't think it foolish if I ask you to take your car through the gardens, once or twice—quite slowly. I'm sure they'd like to see it. They see so little, poor things. One tries to make their life pleasant, but——" she threw out her hands toward the woods. "We're so out of the world here."

"That will be splendid," I said. "But I can't cut up your grass."

She faced to the right. "Wait a minute," she said. "We're at the South gate, aren't we? Behind those peacocks there's a flagged path. We call it the Peacock's Walk. You can't see it from here, they tell me, but if you squeeze along by the edge of the wood you can turn at the first peacock and get onto the flags."

It was a sacrilege to wake that dreaming house-front with the clatter of machinery, but I swung the car to clear the turf, brushed along the edge of the wood and turned in on the broad stone path where the fountain basin lay like one star sapphire.

"May I come too?" she cried. "No, please don't help me. They'll like it better if they see me."

She felt her way lightly to the front of the car, and with one foot on the step she called: "Children, oh, children! Look and see what's going to happen!"

The voice would have drawn lost souls from the Pit, for the yearning that underlay its sweetness, and I was not surprised to hear an answering shout behind the yews. It must have been the child by the fountain, but he fled at our approach, leaving a little toy boat in the water. I saw the glint of his blue blouse among the still horsemen.

Very disposedly we paraded the length of the walk and at her request backed again. This time the child had got the better of his panic, but stood far off and doubting.

"The little fellow's watching us," I said. "I wonder if he'd like a ride."

"They're very shy still. Very shy. But, oh, lucky you to be able to see them! Let's listen."

I stopped the machine at once, and the humid stillness, heavy with the scent of box, cloaked us deep. Shears I could hear where some gardener was clipping; a mumble of bees and broken voices that might have been the doves.

"Oh, unkind!" she said weariedly.

"Perhaps they're only shy of the motor. The little maid at the window looks tremendously interested."

"Yes?" She raised her head. "It was wrong of me to say that. They are really fond of me. It's the only thing that makes life worth living—when they're fond of you, isn't it? I daren't think what the place would be without them. By the way, is it beautiful?"

"I think it is the most beautiful place I have ever seen."

"So they all tell me. I can feel it, of course, but that isn't quite the same thing."

"Then have you never——?" I began, but stopped abashed.

"Not since I can remember. It happened when I was only a few months old, they tell me. And yet I must remember something, else how could I dream about colors. I see light in my dreams, and colors, but I never see *them*. I only hear them just as I do when I'm awake."

"It's difficult to see faces in dreams. Some people can, but most of us haven't the gift," I went on, looking up at the window where the child stood all but hidden.

"I've heard that too," she said. "And they tell me that one never sees a dead person's face in a dream. Is that true?"

"I believe it is—now I come to think of it."

"But how is it with yourself—yourself?" The blind eyes turned toward me.

"I have never seen the faces of my dead in any dream," I answered.

"Then it must be as bad as being blind."

The sun had dipped behind the woods and the long shades were possessing the insolent horsemen one by one. I saw the light die from off the top of a glossy-leaved lance and all the brave hard green turn to soft black. The house, accepting another day at end, as it had accepted an hundred thousand gone, seemed to settle deeper into its rest among the shadows.

"Have you ever wanted to?" she said after the silence.

"Very much sometimes," I replied. The child had left the window as the shadows closed upon it.

"Ah! So've I, but I don't suppose it's allowed. . . . Where d'you live?"

"Quite the other side of the county—sixty miles and more, and I must be going back. I've come without my big lamp."

"But it's not dark yet. I can feel it."

"I'm afraid it will be by the time I get home. Could you lend me someone to set me on my road at first? I've utterly lost myself."

"I'll send Madden with you to the crossroads. We are so out of the world, I don't wonder you were lost! I'll guide you around to the front of the house; but you will go slowly, won't you, till you're out of the grounds? It isn't foolish, do you think?"

"I promise you I'll go like this," I said, and let the car start herself down the flagged path.

We skirted the left wing of the house, whose elaborately cast lead guttering alone was worth a day's journey; passed under a great rose-grown gate in the red wall, and so around to the high front of the house which in beauty and stateliness as much excelled the back as that all others I had seen.

"Is it so very beautiful?" she said wistfully when she heard my raptures. "And you like the lead-figures too? There's the old azalea garden behind. They say that this place must have been made for children. Will you help me out, please? I should like to come with you as far as the crossroads, but I mustn't leave them. Is that you, Madden? I want you to show this gentleman the way to the crossroads. He has lost his way but—he has seen them."

A butler appeared noiselessly at the miracle of old oak that must be called the front door, and slipped aside to put on his hat. She stood looking at me with open blue eyes in which no sight lay, and I saw for the first time that she was beautiful.

"Remember," she said quietly, "if you are fond of them you will come again," and disappeared within the house.

The butler in the car said nothing until we were nearly at the lodge gates, where catching a glimpse of a blue blouse in a shrubbery I swerved amply lest the devil that leads little boys to play should drag me into child-murder.

"Excuse me," he asked of a sudden, "but why did you do that, Sir?"

"The child yonder."

"Our young gentleman in blue?"

"Of course."

"He runs about a good deal. Did you see him by the fountain, Sir?"

"Oh, yes, several times. Do we turn here?"

"Yes, Sir. And did you 'appen to see them upstairs too?"

"At the upper window? Yes."

"Was that before the mistress come out to speak to you, Sir?"

"A little before that. Why d'you want to know?"

He paused a little. "Only to make sure that—that they had seen the car, Sir, because the children running about, though I'm sure you're driving particularly careful, there might be an accident. That was all, Sir. Here are the crossroads. You can't miss your way from now on. Thank you, Sir, but that isn't *our* custom, not with——"

"I beg your pardon," I said, and thrust away the British silver.

"Oh, it's quite right with the rest of 'em as a rule. Good-bye, Sir."

He retired into the armor-plated conning tower of his caste and walked away. Evidently a butler solicitous for the honor of his house, and interested, probably through a maid, in the nursery.

Once beyond the signposts at the crossroads I looked back, but the crumpled hills interlaced so jealously that I could not see where the house had lain. When I asked its name at a cottage along the road, the fat woman who sold sweetmeats there gave me to understand that people with motor cars had small right to live—much less to "go about talking like carriage folk." They were not a pleasant-mannered community.

When I retraced my route on the map that evening I was little wiser. Hawkin's Old Farm appeared to be the survey title of the place, and the old County Gazeteer, generally so ample, did not allude to it. The big house of those parts was Hodnington Hall, Georgian with early Victorian embellishments, as an atrocious steel engraving attested. I carried my difficulty to a neighbor—a deep-rooted tree of that soil—and he gave me a name of a family which conveyed no meaning.

A month or so later—I went again, or it may have been that my car took the road of her own volition. She overran the fruitless Downs, threaded every turn of the maze of lanes below the hills, drew through the high-walled woods, impenetrable in their full leaf, came out at the crossroads where the butler had left me, and a little further on developed an internal trouble which forced me to turn her in on a grass way-waste that cut into a summer-silent hazel wood. So far as I could make sure by the sun and a six-inch Ordnance map, this should be the road flank of that wood which I had first explored from the heights above. I made a mighty serious business of my repairs and a glittering shop of my repair kit, spanners, pump, and the like, which I spread out orderly upon a rug. It was a trap to catch all childhood, for on such a day, I argued, the children would not be far off. When I paused in my work I listened, but the wood was so full of the noises of summer (though the birds had mated) that I could not at first distinguish these from the tread of small cautious feet stealing across the dead leaves. I rang my bell in an alluring manner, but the feet fled, and I repented, for to a child a sudden noise is very real terror. I must have been at work half an hour when I heard in the wood the voice of the blind woman crying: "Children, oh children, where are you?" and the stillness made slow to close on the perfection of that cry. She came toward me, half feeling her way between the tree boles, and though a child it seemed clung to her skirt, it swerved into the leafage like a rabbit as she drew nearer.

"Is that you?" she said, "from the other side of the county?"

"Yes, it's me from the other side of the county."

"Then why didn't you come through the upper woods? They were there just now."

"They were here a few minutes ago. I expect they knew my car had broken down, and came to see the fun."

"Nothing serious, I hope? How do cars break down?"

"In fifty different ways. Only mine has chosen the fifty-first."

She laughed merrily at the tiny joke, cooed with delicious laughter, and pushed her hat back.

"Let me hear," she said.

"Wait a moment," I cried, "and I'll get you a cushion."

She set her foot on the rug all covered with spare parts, and stooped above it eagerly. "What delightful things!" The hands through which she saw glanced in the checkered sunlight. "A box here—another box! Why you've arranged them like playing shop!"

"I confess now that I put it out to attract them. I don't need half those things really."

"How nice of you! I heard your bell in the upper wood. You say they were here before that?"

"I'm sure of it. Why are they so shy? That little fellow in blue who was with you just now ought to have got over his fright. He's been watching me like a Red Indian."

"It must have been your bell," she said. "I heard one of them go past me in trouble when I was coming down. They're shy—so shy even with me." She turned her face over her shoulder and cried again: "Children! Oh, children! Look and see!"

"They must have gone off together on their own affairs," I suggested, for there was a murmur behind us of lowered voices broken by the sudden squeaking giggles of childhood. I returned to my tinkerings and she leaned forward, her chin on her hand, listening interestedly.

"How many are they?" I said at last. The work was finished, but I saw no reason to go.

Her forehead puckered a little in thought. "I don't quite know," she said simply. "Sometimes more—sometimes less. They come and stay with me because I love them, you see."

"That must be very jolly," I said, replacing a drawer, and as I spoke I heard the inanity of my answer.

"You—you aren't laughing at me," she cried. "I—I haven't any of my own. I never married. People laugh at me sometimes about them because—because——"

"Because they're savages," I returned. "It's nothing to fret for. That sort laugh at everything that isn't in their own fat lives."

"I don't know. How should I? I only don't like being laughed at about *them*. It hurts; and when one can't see. . . . I don't want to seem silly," her chin quivered like a child's as she spoke, "but we blindies have only one skin, I think. Everything outside hits straight at our souls. It's different with you. You've such good defenses in your eyes—looking out—before anyone can really pain you in your soul. People forget that with us."

I was silent reviewing that inexhaustible matter—the more than inherited (since it is also carefully taught) brutality of the Christian peoples, beside which the mere heathendom of the West Coast nigger is clean and restrained. It led me a long distance into myself.

"Don't do that!" she said of a sudden, putting her hands before her eyes.

"What?"

She made a gesture with her hand.

"That! It's—it's all purple and black. Don't! That color hurts."

"But, how in the world do you know about colors?" I exclaimed, for here was a revelation indeed.

"Colors as colors?" she asked.

"No. *Those* Colors which you saw just now."

"You know as well as I do," she laughed, "else you wouldn't have asked that question. They aren't in the world at all. They're in *you*—when you went so angry."

"D'you mean a dull purplish patch, like port wine mixed with ink?" I said.

"I've never seen ink or port wine, but the colors aren't mixed. They are separate—all separate."

"Do you mean black streaks and jags across the purple?"

She nodded. "Yes—if they are like this," and zigzagged her finger again, "but it's more red than purple—that bad color."

"And what are the colors at the top of the—whatever you see?"

Slowly she leaned forward and traced on the rug the figure of the Egg itself.

"I see them so," she said, pointing with a grass stem, "white, green, yellow, red, purple, and when people are angry or bad, black across the red—as you were just now."

"Who told you anything about it—in the beginning?" I demanded.

"About the colors? No one. I used to ask what colors were when I was little—in table covers and curtains and carpets, you see—because some colors hurt me and some made me happy. People told me; and when I got older that was how I saw people." Again she traced the outline of the Egg which it is given to very few of us to see.

"All by yourself?" I repeated.

"All by myself. There wasn't anyone else. I only found out afterward that other people did not see the Colors."

She leaned against the tree-bole plaiting and unplaiting chance-plucked grass stems. The children in the wood had drawn nearer. I could see them with the tail of my eye frolicking like squirrels.

"Now I am sure you will never laugh at me," she went on after a long silence. "Nor at *them.*"

"Goodness! No!" I cried, jolted out of my train of thought. "A man who laughs at a child—unless the child is laughing too—is a heathen!"

"I didn't mean that of course. You'd never laugh *at* children, but I thought—I used to think—that perhaps you might laugh about *them.* So now I beg your pardon. . . . What are you going to laugh at?"

I had made no sound, but she knew.

"At the notion of your begging my pardon. If you had done your duty as a pillar of the state and a landed proprietress you ought to have summoned me for trespass when I barged through your woods the other day. It was disgraceful of me—inexcusable."

She looked at me, her head against the tree trunk—long and steadfastly—this woman who could see the naked soul.

"How curious," she half whispered. "How very curious."

"Why, what have I done?"

"You don't understand . . . and yet you understood about the Colors. Don't you understand?"

She spoke with a passion that nothing had justified, and I faced her bewilderedly as she rose. The children had gathered themselves in a roundel behind a bramble bush. One sleek head bent over something smaller, and the set of the little shoulders told me that fingers were on lips. They too, had some child's tremendous secret. I alone was hopelessly astray there in the broad sunlight.

"No," I said, and shook my head as though the dead eyes could note. "Whatever it is, I don't understand yet. Perhaps I shall later—if you'll let me come again."

"You will come again," she answered. "You will surely come again and walk in the wood."

"Perhaps the children will know me well enough by that time to let me play with them—as a favor. You know what children are like."

"It isn't a matter of favor but of right," she replied, and while I wondered what she meant, a disheveled woman plunged round the bend of the road, loose-haired, purple, almost lowing with agony as she ran. It was my rude, fat friend of the sweetmeat shop. The blind woman heard and stepped forward. "What is it, Mrs. Madehurst?" she asked.

The woman flung her apron over her head and literally groveled in the dust, crying that her grandchild was sick to death, that the local doctor was away fishing, that Jenny the mother was at her wit's end, and so forth, with repetitions and bellowings.

"Where's the next nearest doctor?" I asked between paroxysms.

"Madden will tell you. Go around to the house and take him with you. I'll attend to this. Be quick!" She half-supported the fat woman into the shade. In two minutes I was blowing all the horns of Jericho under the front of the House Beautiful, and Madden, in the pantry, rose to the crisis like a butler and a man.

A quarter of an hour at illegal speeds caught us a doctor five miles away. Within the half-hour we had decanted him, much interested in motors, at the door of the sweetmeat shop, and drew up the road to await the verdict.

"Useful things cars," said Madden, all man and no butler. "If I'd had one when mine took sick she wouldn't have died."

"How was it?" I asked.

"Croup. Mrs. Madden was away. No one knew what to do. I drove eight miles in a tax cart for the doctor. She was choked when we came back. This car 'd ha' saved her. She'd have been close on ten now."

"I'm sorry," I said. "I thought you were rather fond of children from what you told me going to the crossroads the other day."

"Have you seen 'em again, Sir—this mornin'?"

"Yes, but they're well broke to cars. I couldn't get any of them within twenty yards of it."

He looked at me carefully as a scout considers a stranger—not as a menial should lift his eyes to his divinely appointed superior.

"I wonder why," he said just above the breath that he drew.

We waited on. A light wind from the sea wandered up and down the long lines of the woods, and the wayside grasses, whitened already with summer dust, rose and bowed in sallow waves.

A woman, wiping the suds off her arms, came out of the cottage next the sweetmeat shop.

"I've be'n listenin' in de back-yard," she said cheerily. "He says Arthur's unaccountable bad. Did ye hear him shruck just now? Unaccountable bad. I reckon 'twill come Jenny's turn to walk in de wood nex' week along Mr. Madden."

"Excuse me, Sir, but your lap-robe is slipping," said Madden deferentially. The woman started, dropped a curtsy, and hurried away.

"What does she mean by 'walking in the wood'?" I asked.

"It must be some saying they use hereabouts. I'm from Norfolk myself," said Madden. "They're an independent lot in this county. She took you for a chauffeur, Sir."

I saw the Doctor come out of the cottage followed by a draggle-tailed wench who clung to his arm as though he could make treaty for her with Death. "Dat sort," she wailed—"dey're just as much to us dat has 'em as if dey was lawful born. Just as much—just as much! An' God he'd be just as pleased if you saved 'un, Doctor. Don't take it from me. Miss Florence will tell ye de very same. Don't leave 'im, Doctor!"

"I know. I know," said the man, "but he'll be quiet for a while now. We'll get the nurse and the medicine as fast as we can." He signaled me to come forward with the car, and I strove not to be privy to what followed; but I saw the girl's face, blotched and frozen with grief, and I felt the hand without a ring clutching at my knees when we moved away.

The Doctor was a man of some humor, for I remember he claimed my car under the Oath of Aesculapius, and used it and me without mercy. First we convoyed Mrs. Madehurst and the blind woman to wait by the sick bed till the nurse should come. Next we invaded a neat county town for prescriptions (the Doctor said the trouble was cerebro-spinal meningitis), and when the County Institute, banked and flanked with scared market cattle, reported itself out of nurses for the moment we literally flung ourselves loose upon the county. We conferred with the owners of great houses—magnates at the ends of overarching avenues whose big-boned womenfolk strode away from their tea tables to listen to the imperious Doctor. At last a whitehaired lady sitting under a cedar of Lebanon and surrounded by a court of magnificent Borzois—all hostile to motors—gave the Doctor, who received them as from a princess, written orders which we bore many miles at top speed, through a park, to a French nunnery, where we took over in exchange a pallid-faced and trembling Sister. She knelt at the bottom of the tonneau telling her beads without pause until, by short cuts of the Doctor's invention, we had her to the sweetmeat shop once more. It was a long afternoon crowded with mad episodes that rose and dissolved like the dust of our wheels; cross sections of remote and incomprehensible lives through which we raced at right angles; and I went home in the dusk, wearied out, to dream of the clashing horns of cattle; round-eyed nuns walking in a garden of graves; pleasant tea parties beneath shaded trees; the carbolic-scented, gray-painted corridors of the County Institute; the steps of shy children in the wood, and the hands that clung to my knees as the motor began to move.

I had intended to return in a day or two, but it pleased Fate to hold me from that side of the county, on many pretexts, till the elder and the wild rose had fruited. There came at last a brilliant day, swept clear from the southwest, that brought the hills within hand's reach—a day of unstable airs and high filmy clouds. Through no merit of my own I was free, and set the car for the third time on that known road. As I reached the crest of the Downs I felt the soft air change, saw it glaze under the sun; and, looking down at the sea, in that instant beheld the blue of the Channel turn through polished silver and dulled steel to dingy pewter. A laden collier hugging the coast steered outward for deeper water and, across copper-colored haze, I saw sails rise one by one on the anchored fishing fleet. In a deep dene behind me an eddy of sudden wind drummed through sheltered oaks, and spun aloft the first day sample of autumn leaves. When I reached the beach road the sea fog fumed over the brickfields, and the side was telling all the groins of the gale beyond Ushant. In less than an hour summer England vanished in chill gray. We were again the shut island of the North, all the ships of the world bellowing at our perilous gates; and between their outcries ran the piping of bewildered gulls. My cap dripped moisture, the folds of the rug held it in pools or sluiced it away in runnels, and the salt-rime stuck to my lips.

Inland the smell of autumn loaded the thickened fog among

the trees, and the drip became a continuous shower. Yet the late flowers—mallow of the wayside, scabious of the field, and dahlia of the garden—showed gay in the midst, and beyond the sea's breath there was little sign of decay in the leaf. Yet in the villages the house doors were all open, and bare-legged, bare-headed children sat at ease on the damp doorsteps to shout "pip-pip" at the stranger.

I made bold to call at the sweetmeat shop, where Mrs. Madehurst met me with a fat woman's hospitable tears. Jenny's child, she said, had died two days after the nun had come. It was, she felt, best out of the way, even though insurance offices, for reasons which she did not pretend to follow, would not willingly insure such stray lives. "Not but what Jenny didn't tend to Arthur as though he'd come all proper at de end of de first year—like Jenny herself." Thanks to Miss Florence, the child had been buried with a pomp which, in Mrs. Madehurst's opinion, more than covered the small irregularity of its birth. She described the coffin, within and without, the glass hearse, and the evergreen lining of the grave.

"But how's the mother?" I asked.

"Jenny? Oh, she'll get over it. I've felt dat way with one or two o' my own. She'll get over. She's walkin' in de wood now."

"In this weather?"

Mrs. Madehurst looked at me with narrowed eyes across the counter.

"I dunno but it opens de 'eart like. Yes, it opens de 'eart. Dat's where losin' and bearin' comes so alike in de long run, we do say."

Now the wisdom of the old wives is greater than that of all the Fathers, and this last oracle sent me thinking so extendedly as I went up the road, that I nearly ran over a woman and a child at the wooded corner by the lodge gates of the House Beautiful.

"Awful weather!" I cried, as I slowed dead for the turn.

"Not so bad," she answered placidly out of the fog. "Mine's used to 'un. You'll find yours indoors, I reckon."

Indoors, Madden received me with professional courtesy, and kind inquiries for the health of the motor, which he would put under cover.

I waited in a still, nut-brown hall, pleasant with late flowers and warmed with a delicious wood fire—a place of good influence and great peace. (Men and women may sometimes, after great effort, achieve a creditable lie; but the house, which is their temple, cannot say anything save the truth of those who have lived in it.) A child's cart and a doll lay on the black-and-white floor, where a rug had been kicked back. I felt that the children had only just hurried away—to hide themselves, most like—in the many turns of the great adzed staircase that climbed statelily out of the hall, or to crouch at gaze behind the lions and roses of the carven gallery above. Then I heard her voice above me, singing as the blind sing—from the soul:—

In the pleasant orchard-closes.

And all my early summer came back at the call.

In the pleasant orchard-closes,
God bless all our gains say we—
But may God bless all our losses,
Better suits with our degree.

She dropped the marring fifth line, and repeated—

Better suits with our degree!

I saw her lean over the gallery, her linked hands white as pearl against the oak.

"Is that you—from the other side of the county?" she called.

"Yes, me—from the other side of the county," I answered laughing.

"What a long time before you had to come here again." She ran down the stairs, one hand lightly touching the broad rail. "It's two months and four days. Summer's gone!"

"I meant to come before, but Fate prevented."

"I knew it. Please do something to that fire. They won't let me play with it, but I can feel it's behaving badly. Hit it!"

I looked on either side of the deep fireplace, and found but a half-charred hedge-stake with which I punched a black log into flame.

"It never goes out, day or night," she said, as though explaining. "In case anyone comes in with cold toes, you see."

"It's even lovelier inside than it was out," I murmured. The red light poured itself along the age-polished dusky panels until the Tudor roses and lions of the gallery took color and motion. An old eagle-topped convex mirror gathered the picture into its mysterious heart, distorting afresh the distorted shadows, and curving the gallery lines into the curves of a ship. The day was shutting down in half a gale as the fog turned to stringy scud. Through the uncurtained mullions of the broad window I could see valiant horsemen of the lawn rear and recover against the wind that taunted them with legions of dead leaves.

"Yes, it must be beautiful," she said. "Would you like to go over it? There's still light enough upstairs."

I followed her up the unflinching, wagon-wide staircase to the gallery whence opened the thin fluted Elizabethan doors.

"Feel how they put the latch low down for the sake of the children." She swung a light door inward.

"By the way, where are they?" I asked. "I haven't even heard them today."

She did not answer at once. Then, "I can only hear them," she replied softly. "This is one of their rooms—everything ready, you see."

She pointed into a heavily-timbered room. There were little low gate tables and children's chairs. A doll's house, its hooked front half open, faced a great dappled rocking horse, from whose padded saddle it was but a child's scramble to the broad window seat overlooking the lawn. A toy gun lay in a corner beside a gilt wooden cannon.

"Surely they've only just gone," I whispered. In the failing light a door creaked cautiously. I heard the rustle of a frock and the patter of feet—quick feet through a room beyond.

"I heard that," she cried triumphantly. "Did you? Children, O children, where are you?"

The voice filled the walls that held it lovingly to the last perfect note, but there came no answering shout such as I had heard in the garden. We hurried on from room to oak-floored room; up a step here, down three steps there; among a maze of passages; always mocked by our quarry. One might as well have tried to work an unstopped warren with a single ferret. There were bolt-holes innumerable—recesses in walls, embrasures of deep slitten windows now darkened, whence they could start up behind us; and abandoned fireplaces, six feet deep in the masonry, as well as the tangle of communicating doors. Above all, they had the twilight for their helper in our game. I had caught one or two joyous chuckles of evasion, and once or twice had seen the silhouette of a child's frock against some darkening window at the end of a passage; but we returned empty-handed to the gallery, just as a middle-aged woman was setting a lamp in its niche.

"No, I haven't seen her either this evening, Miss Florence," I heard her say, "but that Turpin he says he wants to see you about his shed."

"Oh, Mr. Turpin must want to see me very badly. Tell him to come to the hall, Mrs. Madden."

I looked down into the hall whose only light was the dulled fire, and deep in the shadow I saw them at last. They must have slipped down while we were in the passages, and now thought themselves perfectly hidden behind an old gilt leather screen. By child's law, my fruitless chase was as good as an introduction, but since I had taken so much trouble I resolved to force them to come forward later by the simple trick, which children detest, of pretending not to notice them. They lay close, in a little huddle, no more than shadows except when a quick flame betrayed an outline.

"And now we'll have some tea," she said. "I believe I ought to have offered it you at first, but one doesn't arrive at manners somehow when one lives alone and is considered—h'm—peculiar." Then with very pretty scorn, "would you like a lamp to see to eat by?"

"The firelight's much pleasanter, I think." We descended into that delicious gloom and Madden brought tea.

I took my chair in the direction of the screen ready to surprise or be surprised as the game should go, and at her permission, since a hearth is always sacred, bent forward to play with the fire.

"Where do you get these beautiful short faggots from?" I asked idly. "Why, they are tallies!"

"Of course," she said. "As I can't read or write I'm driven

back on the early English tally for my accounts. Give me one and I'll tell you what it meant."

I passed her an unburned hazel-tally, about a foot long, and she ran her thumb down the nicks.

"This is the milk-record for the home farm for the month of April last year, in gallons," said she. "I don't know what I should have done without tallies. An old forester of mine taught me the system. It's out of date now for everyone else; but my tenants respect it. One of them's coming now to see me. Oh, it doesn't matter. He has no business here out of office hours. He's a greedy, ignorant man—very greedy or—he wouldn't come here after dark."

"Have you much land then?"

"Only a couple of hundred acres in hand, thank goodness. The other six hundred are nearly all let to folk who knew my folk before me, but this Turpin is quite a new man—and a highway robber."

"But are you sure I sha'n't be——?"

"Certainly not. You have the right. He hasn't any children."

"Ah, the children!" I said, and slid my low chair back till it nearly touched the screen that hid them. "I wonder whether they'll come out for me."

There was a murmur of voices—Madden's and a deeper note—at the low, dark side door, and a ginger-headed, canvas-gaitered giant of the unmistakable tenant farmer type stumbled or was pushed in.

"Come to the fire, Mr. Turpin," she said.

"If—if you please, Miss, I'll—I'll be quite as well by the door." He clung to the latch as he spoke like a frightened child. Of a sudden I realized that he was in the grip of some almost overpowering fear.

"Well?"

"About that new shed for the young stock—that was all. These first autumn storms settin' in . . . but I'll come again, Miss." His teeth did not chatter much more than the door latch.

"I think not," she answered levelly. "The new shed—m'm. What did my agent write you on the 15th?"

"I—fancied p'raps that if I came to see you—ma—man to man like, Miss. But——"

His eyes rolled into every corner of the room wide with horror. He half opened the door through which he had entered, but I noticed it shut again—from without and firmly.

"He wrote what I told him," she went on. "You are overstocked already. Dunnett's Farm never carried more than fifty bullocks—even in Mr. Wright's time. And *he* used cake. You've sixty-seven and you don't cake. You've broken the lease in that respect. You're dragging the heart out of the farm."

"I'm—I'm getting some minerals—superphosphates—next week. I've as good as ordered a truckload already. I'll go down to the station tomorrow about 'em. Then I can come and see you man to man like, Miss, in the daylight. . . . That gentleman's not going away, is he?" He almost shrieked.

I had only slid the chair a little further back, reaching behind me to tap on the leather of the screen, but he jumped like a rat.

"No. Please attend to me, Mr. Turpin." She turned in her chair and faced him with his back to the door. It was an old and sordid little piece of scheming that she forced from him—his plea for the new cowshed at his landlady's expense, that he might with the covered manure pay his next year's rent out of the valuation after, as she made clear, he had bled the enriched pastures to the bone. I could not but admire the intensity of his greed, when I saw him outfacing for its sake whatever terror it was that ran wet on his forehead.

I ceased to tap the leather—was, indeed, calculating the cost of the shed—when I felt my relaxed hand taken and turned softly between the soft hands of a child. So at last I had triumphed. In a moment I would turn and acquaint myself with those quick-footed wanderers. . . .

The little brushing kiss fell in the center of my palm—as a gift on which the fingers were, once, expected to close: as the all faithful half-reproachful signal of a waiting child not used to neglect even when grown-ups were busiest—a fragment of the mute code devised very long ago.

Then I knew. And it was as though I had known from the first day when I looked across the lawn at the high window.

I heard the door shut. The woman turned to me in silence, and I felt that she knew.

What time passed after this I cannot say. I was roused by the fall of a log, and mechanically rose to put it back. Then I returned to my place in the chair very close to the screen.

"Now you understand," she whispered, across the packed shadows.

"Yes, I understand—now. Thank you."

"I—I only hear them." She bowed her head in her hands. "I have no right, you know—no other right. I have neither borne nor lost—neither borne nor lost!"

"Be very glad then," said I, for my soul was torn open within me.

"Forgive me!"

She was still, and I went back to my sorrow and my joy.

"It was because I loved them so," she said at last, brokenly. "*That* was why it was, even from the first—even before I knew that they—they were all I should ever have. And I loved them so!"

She stretched out her arms to the shadows and the shadows within the shadow.

"They came because I loved them—because I needed them. I—I must have made them come. Was that wrong, think you?"

"No—no."

"I—I grant you that the toys and—and all that sort of thing were nonsense, but—but I used to so hate empty rooms myself when I was little." She pointed to the gallery. "And the passages all empty. . . . And how could I ever bear the garden door shut? Suppose——"

"Don't! For pity's sake, don't!" I cried. The twilight had brought a cold rain with gusty squalls that plucked at the leaded windows.

"And the same thing with keeping the fire in all night. *I* don't think it so foolish—do you?"

I looked at the broad brick hearth, saw, through tears I believe, that there was no unpassable iron on or near it, and bowed my head.

"I did all that and lots of other things—just to make believe. Then they came. I heard them, but I didn't know that they were not mine by right till Mrs. Madden told me——"

"The butler's wife? What?"

"One of them—I heard—she saw. And knew. Hers! *Not* for me. I didn't know at first. Perhaps I was jealous. Afterward, I began to understand that it was only because I loved them, not because—— . . . Oh, you *must* bear or lose," she said piteously. "There is no other way—and yet they love me. They must! Don't they?"

There was no sound in the room except the lapping voices of the fire, but we two listened intently, and she at least took comfort from what she heard. She recovered herself and half rose. I sat still in my chair by the screen.

"Don't think me a wretch to whine about myself like this, but—but I'm all in the dark, you know, and *you* can see."

In truth I could see, and my vision confirmed me in my resolve, though that was like the very parting of spirit and flesh. Yet a little longer I would stay since it was the last time.

"You think it is wrong, then?" she cried sharply, though I had said nothing.

"Not for you. A thousand times no. For you it is right. . . . I am grateful to you beyond words. For me it would be wrong. For me only. . . ."

"Why?" she said, but passed her hand before her face as she had done at our second meeting in the wood. "Oh, I see," she went on simply as a child. "For you it would be wrong." Then with a little indrawn laugh, "and, d'you remember, I called you lucky—once—at first. You who must never come here again!"

She left me to sit a little longer by the screen, and I heard the sound of her feet die out along the gallery above.

MY OWN TRUE GHOST STORY

As I came through the Desert thus it was—
As I came through the Desert.
—THE CITY OF DREADFUL NIGHT

THIS story deals entirely with ghosts. There are, in India, ghosts who take the form of fat, cold, pobby corpses, and hide in trees near the roadside till a traveler passes. Then they drop upon his neck and remain. There are also terrible ghosts of women who have died in childbed. These wander along the pathways at dusk, or hide in the crops near a village, and call seductively. But to answer their call is death in this world and the next. Their feet are turned backward that all sober men may recognize them. There are ghosts of little children who have been thrown in wells. These haunt well-curbs and the fringes of jungles, and wail under the stars, or catch women by the wrist and beg to be taken up and carried. These and the corpse-ghosts, however, are only vernacular articles and do not attack Sahibs. No native ghost has yet been authentically reported to have frightened an Englishman; but many English ghosts have scared the life out of both white and black.

Nearly every other Station owns a ghost. There are said to be two at Simla, not counting the woman who blows the bellows at Syree dâk-bungalow on the Old Road; Mussoorie has a house haunted by a very lively Thing; a White Lady is supposed to do night watchman round a house in Lahore; Dalhousie says that one of her houses "repeats" on autumn evenings all the incidents of a horrible horse-and-precipice accident; Murree has a merry ghost, and, now that she has been swept by cholera, will have room for a sorrowful one; there are Officers' Quarters in Mian Mir whose doors open without reason, and whose furniture is guaranteed to creak, not with the heat of June but with the weight of Invisibles who come to lounge in the chairs; Peshawur possesses houses that none will willingly rent; and there is something—not fever—wrong with a big bungalow in Allahabad. The older Provinces simply bristle with haunted houses, and march phantom armies along their main thoroughfares.

Some of the dâk-bungalows on the Grand Trunk Road have handy little cemeteries in their compound—witnesses to the "changes and chances of this mortal life" in the days when men drove from Calcutta to the Northwest. These bungalows are objectionable places to put up in. They are generally very old, always dirty, while the *khansamah* is as ancient as the bungalow. He either chatters senilely, or falls into the long trances of age. In both moods he is useless. If you get angry with him, he refers to some Sahib dead and buried these thirty years, and says that when he was in that Sahib's service not a *khansamah* in the Province could touch him. Then he jabbers and mows and trembles and fidgets among the dishes, and you repent of your irritation.

Not long ago it was my business to live in dâk-bungalows. I never inhabited the same house for three nights running, and grew to be learned in the breed. I lived in Government-built ones with red brick walls and rail ceilings, an inventory of the furniture posted in every room, and an excited cobra on the threshold to give welcome. I lived in "converted" ones—old houses officiating as dâk-bungalows—where nothing was in its proper place and there was not even a fowl for dinner. I lived in secondhand palaces where the wind blew through openwork marble tracery just as uncomfortably as though a broken pane. I lived in dâk-bungalows where the last entry in the visitors' book was fifteen months old, and where they slashed off the curry-kid's head with a sword. It was my good luck to meet all sorts of men, from sober traveling missionaries and deserters flying from British Regiments, to drunken loafers who threw whiskey bottles at all who passed; and my still greater good-fortune just to escape a maternity case. Seeing that a fair proportion of the tragedy of our lives in India acted itself in dâk-bungalows, I wondered that I had met no ghosts. A ghost that would voluntarily hang about a dâk-bungalow would be mad of course; but so many men have died mad in dâk-bungalows that there must be a fair percentage of lunatic ghosts.

In due time I found my ghost, or ghosts rather, for there were two of them.

We will call the bungalow Katmal dâk-bungalow; but *that* was the smallest part of the horror. A man with a sensitive hide has no right to sleep in dâk-bungalows. He should marry. Katmal dâk-bungalow was old and rotten and unrepaired. The floor was of worn brick, the walls were filthy, and the windows were nearly black with grime. It stood on a bypath largely used by native Sub-Deputy Assistants of all kinds, from Finance to Forests; but real Sahibs were rare. The *khansamah,* who was nearly bent double with old age, said so.

When I arrived, there was a fitful, undecided rain on the face of the land, accompanied by a restless wind, and every gust made a noise like the rattling of dry bones in the stiff toddy-palms outside. The *khansamah* completely lost his head on my arrival. He had served a Sahib once. Did I know that Sahib? He gave me the name of a well-known man who has been buried for more than a quarter of a century, and showed me an ancient daguerreotype of that man in his prehistoric youth. I had seen a steel engraving of him at the head of a double volume of Memoirs a month before, and I felt ancient beyond telling.

The day shut in and the *khansamah* went to get me food. He did not go through the pretense of calling it *"khana,"*—man's victuals. He said *"ratub,"* and that means, among other things, "grub"—dog's rations. There was no insult in his choice of the term. He had forgotten the other word, I suppose.

While he was cutting up the dead bodies of animals, I settled myself down, after exploring the dâk-bungalow. There were three rooms, beside my own, which was a corner kennel, each giving into the other through dingy white doors fastened with long iron bars. The bungalow was a very solid one, but the partition-walls of the rooms were almost jerry-built in their flimsiness. Every step or bang of a trunk echoed from my room down the other three, and every footfall came back tremulously from the far walls. For this reason I shut the door. There were no lamps—only candles in long glass shades. An oil wick was set in the bathroom.

For bleak, unadulterated misery that dâk-bungalow was the worst of the many that I had ever set foot in. There was no fireplace, and the windows would not open; so a brazier of charcoal would have been useless. The rain and the wind splashed and gurgled and moaned around the house, and the toddy-palms rattled and roared. Half a dozen jackals went through the compound singing, and a hyena stood afar off and mocked them. A hyena would convince a Sadducee of the Resurrection of the Dead—the worst sort of Dead. Then came the *ratub*—a curious meal, half native and half English in composition—with the old *khansamah* babbling behind my chair about dead and gone English people, and the windblown candles playing shadow-bo-peep with the bed and the mosquito-curtains. It was just the sort of dinner and evening to make a man think of every single one of his past sins, and of all the others that he intended to commit if he lived.

Sleep, for several hundred reasons, was not easy. The lamp in the bathroom threw the most absurd shadows into the room, and the wind was beginning to talk nonsense.

Just when the reasons were drowsy with blood-sucking I heard the regular—"Let-us-take-and-heave-him-over" grunt of doolie-bearers in the compound. First one doolie came in, then a second, and then a third. I heard the doolies dumped on the ground, and the shutter in front of my door shook.

"That's someone trying to come in," I said. But no one spoke, and I persuaded myself that it was the gusty wind. The shutter of the room next to mine was attacked, flung back, and the inner door opened. "That's some Sub-Deputy Assistant," I said, "and he has brought his friends with him. Now they'll talk and spit and smoke for an hour."

But there were no voices and no footsteps. No one was putting his luggage into the next room. The door shut, and I thanked Providence that I was to be left in peace. But I was curious to know where the doolies had gone. I got out of bed and looked into the darkness. There was never a sign of a doolie. Just as I was getting into bed again, I heard, in the next room, the sound that no man in his senses can possibly mistake—the whir of a billiard ball down the length of the slate when the striker is stringing for break. No other sound is like it. A minute afterward there was another whir, and I got into bed. I was not frightened—indeed I was not. I was very curious to know what had become of the doolies. I jumped into bed for that reason.

Next minute I heard the double click of a cannon, and my hair sat up. It is a mistake to say that hair stands up. The skin of the head tightens and you can feel a faint, prickly bristling all over the scalp. That is the hair sitting up.

There was a whir and a click, and both sounds could only have been made by one thing—a billiard ball. I argued the matter out at great length with myself; and the more I argued the less probable it seemed that one bed, one table, and two chairs—all the furniture of the room next to mine—could so exactly duplicate the sounds of a game of billiards. After another cannon, a three-cushion one to judge by the whir, I argued no more. I had found my ghost and would have given worlds to have escaped from that dâk-bungalow. I listened, and with each listen the game grew clearer. There was whir on whir and click on click. Sometimes there was a double click and a whir and another click. Beyond any sort of doubt, people were playing billiards in the next room. And the next room was not big enough to hold a billiard table!

Between the pauses of the wind I heard the game go forward—stroke after stroke. I tried to believe that I could not hear voices; but that attempt was a failure.

Do you know what fear is? Not ordinary fear of insult, injury, or death, but abject, quivering dread of something that you cannot see—fear that dries the inside of the mouth and half of the throat—fear that makes you sweat on the palms of the hands, and gulp in order to keep the uvula at work? This is a fine Fear—a great cowardice, and must be felt to be appreciated. The very improbability of billiards in a dâk-bungalow proved the reality of the thing. No man—drunk or sober—could imagine a game at billiards, or invent the spitting crack of a "screw cannon."

A severe course of dâk-bungalows has this disadvantage—it breeds infinite credulity. If a man said to a confirmed dâk-bungalow-haunter: "There is a corpse in the next room, and there's a mad girl in the next one, and the woman and man on that camel have just eloped from a place sixty miles away," the hearer would not disbelieve because he would know that nothing is too wild, grotesque, or horrible to happen in a dâk-bungalow.

This credulity, unfortunately, extends to ghosts. A rational person fresh from his own house would have turned on his side and slept. I did not. So surely as I was given up for a dry carcass by the scores of things in the bed, because the bulk of my blood was in my heart, so surely did I hear every stroke of a long game at billiards played in the echoing room behind the iron-barred door. My dominant fear was that the players might want a marker. It was an absurd fear; because creatures who could play in the dark would be above such superfluities. I only know that that was my terror; and it was real.

After a long, long while, the game stopped, and the door banged. I slept because I was dead tired. Otherwise I should have preferred to have kept awake. Not for everything in Asia would I have dropped the door-bar and peered into the dark of the next room.

When the morning came, I considered that I had done well and wisely, and inquired for the means of departure.

"By the way, *khansamah,*" I said, "what were those three doolies doing in my compound in the night?"

"There were no doolies," said the *khansamah.*

I went into the next room, and the daylight streamed through the open door. I was immensely brave. I would, at that hour, have played Black Pool with the owner of the big Black Pool down below.

"Has this place always been a dâk-bungalow?" I asked.

"No," said the *khansamah.* "Ten or twenty years ago, I have forgotten how long, it was a billiard room."

"A what?"

"A billiard-room for the Sahibs who built the Railway. I was *khansamah* then in the big house where all the Railway-Sahibs lived, and I used to come across with brandy-*shrab.* These three rooms were all one, and they held a big table on which the Sahibs played every evening. But the Sahibs are all dead now, and the Railway runs, you say, nearly to Kabul."

"Do you remember anything about the Sahibs?"

"It is long ago, but I remember that one Sahib, a fat man, and always angry, was playing here one night, and he said to me: 'Mangal Khan, brandy-*pani do,*' and I filled the glass, and he bent over the table to strike, and his head fell lower and lower till it hit the table, and his spectacles came off, and when we—the Sahibs and I myself—ran to lift him he was dead. I helped to carry him out. Aha, he was a strong Sahib! But he is dead, and I, old Mangal Khan, am still living, by your favor."

That was more than enough! I had my ghost—a firsthand, authenticated article. I would write to the Society for Psychical Research—I would paralyze the Empire with the news! But I would, first of all, put eighty miles of assessed cropland between myself and that dâk-bungalow before nightfall. The Society might send their regular agent to investigate later on.

I went into my own room and prepared to pack, after noting down the facts of the case. As I smoked I heard the game begin again—with a miss in balk this time, for the whir was a short one.

The door was open, and I could see into the room. *Click—click!* That was a cannon. I entered the room without fear, for there was sunlight within and a fresh breeze without. The unseen game was going on at a tremendous rate. And well it might, when a restless little rat was running to and fro inside the dingy ceiling-cloth, and a piece of loose window sash was making fifty breaks off the window-bolt as it shook in the breeze!

Impossible to mistake the sound of billiard balls! Impossible to mistake the whir of a ball over the slate! But I was to be excused. Even when I shut my enlightened eyes the sound was marvelously like that of a fast game.

Entered angrily the faithful partner of my sorrows, Kadir Baksh.

"This bungalow is very bad and low-caste! No wonder the Presence was disturbed and is speckled. Three sets of doolie-bearers came to the bungalow late last night when I was sleeping outside, and said that it was their custom to rest in the rooms set apart for the English people! What honor has the *khansamah?* They tried to enter, but I told them to go. No wonder, if these *Oorias* have been here, that the Presence is sorely spotted. It is shame, and the work of a dirty man!"

Kadir Baksh did not say that he had taken from each gang two annas for rent in advance, and then, beyond my earshot, had beaten them with the big green umbrella whose use I could never before divine. But Kadir Baksh has no notions of morality.

There was an interview with the *khansamah,* but as he promptly lost his head, wrath gave place to pity, and pity led to a long conversation, in the course of which he put the fat Engineer-Sahib's tragic death in three separate stations—two of them fifty miles away. The third shift was to Calcutta, and there the Sahib died while driving a dogcart.

I did not go away as soon as I intended. I stayed for the night, while the wind and the rat and the sash and the window-bolt played a ding-dong "hundred and fifty up." Then the wind ran out and the billiards stopped, and I felt that I had ruined my one genuine ghost story.

Had I only ceased investigating at the proper time, I could have made *anything* out of it.

That was the bitterest thought of all!

BEYOND THE PALE

Love heeds not caste nor sleep a broken bed. I went in search of love and lost myself.

—HINDU PROVERB

A MAN should, whatever happens, keep to his own caste, race and breed. Let the White go to the White and the Black to the Black. Then, whatever trouble falls is in the ordinary course of things—neither sudden, alien nor unexpected.

This is the story of a man who willfully stepped beyond the safe limits of decent everyday society, and paid for it heavily.

He knew too much in the first instance; and he saw too much in the second. He took too deep an interest in native life; but he will never do so again.

Deep away in the heart of the City, behind Jitha Megji's *bustee,* lies Amir Nath's Gully, which ends in a dead wall pierced by one grated window. At the head of the Gully is a big cowbyre, and the walls on either side of the Gully are without windows. Neither Suchet Singh nor Gaur Chand approve of their womenfolk looking into the world. If Durga Charan had been of their opinion, he would have been a happier man today, and little Bisesa would have been able to knead her own bread. Her room looked out through the grated window into the narrow dark Gully where the sun never came and where the buffaloes wallowed in the blue slime. She was a widow, fifteen years old, and she prayed the Gods, day and night, to send her a lover; for she did not approve of living alone.

One day, the man—Trejago was his name—came into Amir Nath's Gully on a wandering; and, after he had passed the buffaloes, stumbled over a big heap of cattle food.

Then he saw that the Gully ended in a trap, and heard a little laugh from behind the grated window. It was a pretty little laugh, and Trejago, knowing that, for all practical purposes, the old *Arabian Nights* are good guides, went forward to the window, and whispered that verse of "The Love Song of Har Dyal" which begins:—

Can a man stand upright in the face of the naked Sun; or a Lover in the Presence of his Beloved?

If my feet fail me, O Heart of my Heart, am I to blame, being blinded by the glimpse of your beauty?

There came the faint *tchink* of a woman's bracelets from behind the grating, and a little voice went on with the song at the fifth verse:—

Alas! alas! Can the Moon tell the Lotus of her love when the Gate of Heaven is shut and the clouds gather for the rains?

They have taken my Beloved, and driven her with the pack-horses to the North.

There are iron chains on the feet that were set on my heart.

Call to the bowmen to make ready——

The voice stopped suddenly, and Trejago walked out of Amir Nath's Gully, wondering who in the world could have capped "The Love Song of Har Dyal" so neatly.

Next morning, as he was driving to office, an old woman threw a packet into his dogcart. In the packet was the half of a broken glass-bangle, one flower of the blood-red *dhak,* a pinch of *bhusa* or cattle food, and eleven cardamoms. That packet was a letter—not a clumsy compromising letter, but an innocent unintelligible lover's epistle.

Trejago knew far too much about these things, as I have said. No Englishman should be able to translate object-letters. But Trejago spread all the trifles on the lid of his office-box and began to puzzle them out.

A broken glass-bangle stands for a Hindu widow all India over; because, when her husband dies, a woman's bracelets are broken on her wrists. Trejago saw the meaning of the little bit of the glass. The flower of the *dhak* means diversely "desire," "come," "write," or "danger," according to the other things with it. One cardamom means "jealousy"; but when any article is duplicated in an object-letter, it loses its symbolic meaning and stands merely for one of a number indicating time, or, if incense, curds, or saffron be sent also, place. The message ran then—"A widow—*dhak* flower and *bhusa*—at eleven o'clock." The pinch of *bhusa* enlightened Trejago. He saw—this kind of letter leaves much to instinctive knowledge—that the *bhusa* referred to the big heap of cattle food over which he had fallen in Amir Nath's Gully, and that the message must come from the person behind the grating; she being a widow. So the message ran then—"A widow, in the Gully in which is the heap of *bhusa,* desires you to come at eleven o'clock."

Trejago threw all the rubbish into the fireplace and laughed. He knew that men in the East do not make love under windows at eleven in the forenoon, nor do women fix appointments a week in advance. So he went, that very night at eleven, into Amir Nath's Gully, clad in a *boorka,* which cloaks a man as well as a woman. Directly the gongs of the City made the hour, the little voice behind the grating took up "The Love Song of Har Dyal" at the verse where the Panthan girl calls upon Har Dyal to return. The song is really pretty in the Vernacular. In English you miss the wail of it. It runs something like this—

Alone upon the housetops, to the North
  I turn and watch the lightning in the sky,—
The glamour of thy footsteps in the North,
  Come back to me, Beloved or I die!

Below my feet the still bazar is laid,
  Far, far, below the weary camels lie,—
The camels and the captives of thy raid.
  Come back to me, Beloved or I die!

My father's wife is old and harsh with years,
  And drudge of all my father's house am I.—
My bread is sorrow and my drink is tears,
  Come back to me, Beloved or I die!

As the song stopped, Trejago stepped up under the grating and whispered—"I am here."

Bisesa was good to look upon.

That night was the beginning of many strange things, and of a double life so wild that Trejago today sometimes wonders if it were not all a dream. Bisesa, or her old handmaiden who had thrown the object-letter, had detached the heavy grating from the brickwork of the wall; so that the window slid inside, leaving only a square of raw masonry into which an active man might climb.

In the daytime, Trejago drove through his routine of office-work, or put on his calling-clothes and called on the ladies of the Station; wondering how long they would know him if they knew of poor little Bisesa. At night, when all the City was still, came the walk under the evil-smelling *boorka,* the patrol through Jitha Megji's *bustee,* the quick turn into Amir Nath's Gully between the sleeping cattle and the dead walls, and then, last of all, Bisesa, and the deep, even breathing of the old woman who slept outside the door of the bare little room that Durga Charan allotted to his sister's daughter. Who or what Durga Charan was, Trejago never inquired; and why in the world he was not discovered and knifed never occurred to him till his madness was over, and Bisesa . . . But this comes later.

Bisesa was an endless delight to Trejago. She was as ignorant as a bird; and her distorted versions of the rumors from the outside world that had reached her in her room, amused Trejago almost as much as her lisping attempts to pronounce his name—"Christopher." The first syllable was always more than she could manage, and she made funny little gestures with her roseleaf hands, as one throwing the name away, and then, kneeling before Trejago asked him, exactly as an Englishwoman would do, if he were sure he loved her. Trejago swore that he loved her more than anyone else in the world. Which was true.

After a month of this folly, the exigencies of his other life compelled Trejago to be especially attentive to a lady of his acquaintance. You may take it for a fact that anything of this kind is not only noticed and discussed by a man's own race but by some hundred and fifty natives as well. Trejago had to walk with this lady and talk to her at the Bandstand, and once or twice to drive with her; never for an instant dreaming that this would affect his dearer, out-of-the-way life. But the news flew, in the usual mysterious fashion, from mouth to mouth, till Bisesa's duenna heard of it and told Bisesa. The child was so troubled that she did the household work evilly, and was beaten by Durga Charan's wife in consequence.

A week later, Bisesa taxed Trejago with the flirtation. She understood no gradations and spoke openly. Trejago laughed and Bisesa stamped her little feet—little feet, light as marigold flowers, that could lie in the palm of a man's one hand.

Much that is written about Oriental passion and impulsiveness is exaggerated and compiled at secondhand, but a little of it is true; and when an Englishman finds that little, it is quite as startling as any passion in his own proper life. Bisesa raged and stormed, and finally threatened to kill herself if Trejago did not at once drop the alien *Memsahib* who had come between them. Trejago tried to explain, and to show her that she did not understand these things from a Western standpoint. Bisesa drew herself up, and said simply—

"I do not. I know only this—it is not good that I should have made you dearer than my own heart to me, *Sahib*. You are an Englishman. I am only a black girl"—she was fairer than bar-gold in the Mint—"and the widow of a black man."

Then she sobbed and said—"But on my soul and my Mother's soul, I love you. There shall no harm come to you, whatever happens to me."

Trejago argued with the child, and tried to soothe her, but she seemed quite unreasonably disturbed. Nothing would satisfy her save that all relations between them should end. He was to go away at once. And he went. As he dropped out of the window, she kissed his forehead twice, and he walked home wondering.

A week, and then three weeks, passed without a sign from Bisesa. Trejago, thinking that the rupture had lasted quite long enough, went down to Amir Nath's Gully for the fifth time in the three weeks, hoping that his rap at the sill of the shifting grating would be answered. He was not disappointed.

There was a young moon, and one stream of light fell down into Amir Nath's Gully, and struck the grating which was drawn away as he knocked. From the black dark, Bisesa held out her arms into the moonlight. Both hands had been cut off at the wrists, and the stumps were nearly healed.

Then, as Bisesa bowed her head between her arms and sobbed, some one in the room grunted like a wild beast, and something sharp—knife, sword, or spear—thrust at Trejago in

—"The stroke missed his body, but cut into one of the muscles of the groin . . ."

sleigh is going at full speed. If you call one dog's name for "visiting," and accidentally lash another, the two will fight it out at once, and stop all the others. Again, if you travel with a companion and begin to talk, or by yourself and sing, the dogs will halt, turn around, and sit down to hear what you have to say. Kotuko was run away from once or twice through forgetting to block the sleigh when he stopped; and he broke many lashings, and ruined a few thongs before he could be trusted with a full team of eight and the light sleigh. Then he felt himself a person of consequence, and on smooth, black ice, with a bold heart and a quick elbow, he smoked along over the levels as fast as a pack in full cry. He would go ten miles to the seal holes, and when he was on the hunting grounds he would twitch a trace loose from the *pitu,* and free the big black leader, who was the cleverest dog in the team. As soon as the dog had scented a breathing-hole, Kotuko would reverse the sleigh, driving a couple of sawed-off antlers, that stuck up like perambulator-handles from the backrest, deep into the snow, so that the team could not get away. Then he would crawl forward inch by inch, and wait till the seal came up to breathe. Then he would stab down swiftly with his spear and running-line, and presently would haul his seal up to the lip of the ice, while the black leader came up and helped to pull the carcass across the ice to the sleigh. That was the time when the harnessed dogs yelled and foamed with excitement, and Kotuko laid the long lash like a red-hot bar across all their faces, till the carcass froze stiff. Going home was the heavy work. The loaded sleigh had to be humored among the rough ice, and the dogs sat down and looked hungrily at the seal instead of pulling. At last they would strike the well-worn sleigh-road to the village, and toodle-kiyi along the ringing ice, heads down and tails up, while Kotuko struck up the "Angutivaun tai-na tau-na-ne taina" (The Song of the Returning Hunter), and voices hailed him from house to house under all that dim, star-litten sky.

When Kotuko the dog came to his full growth he enjoyed himself too. He fought his way up the team steadily, fight after fight, till one fine evening, over their food, he tackled the big, black leader (Kotuko the boy saw fair play), and made second dog of him, as they say. So he was promoted to the long thong of the leading dog, running five feet in advance of all the others: it was his bounden duty to stop all fighting, in harness or out of it, and he wore a collar of copper wire, very thick and heavy. On special occasions he was fed with cooked food inside the house, and sometimes was allowed to sleep on the bench with Kotuko. He was a good seal-dog, and would keep a musk-ox at bay by running around him and snapping at his heels. He would even—and this for a sleigh-dog is the last proof of bravery—he would even stand up to the gaunt Arctic wolf, whom all dogs of the North, as a rule, fear beyond anything that walks the snow. He and his master—they did not count the team of ordinary dogs as company—hunted together, day after day and night after night, fur-wrapped boy and savage, long-haired, narrow-eyed, white-fanged, yellow brute. All an Inuit has to do is to get food and skins for himself and his family. The womenfolk make the skins into clothing, and occasionally help in trapping small game; but the bulk of the food—and they eat enormously—must be found by the men. If the supply fails there is no one up there to buy or beg or borrow from. The people must die.

An Inuit does not think of these chances till he is forced to. Kadlu, Kotuko, Amoraq, and the boy-baby who kicked about in Amoraq's fur hood and chewed pieces of blubber all day, were as happy together as any family in the world. They came of a very gentle race—an Inuit seldom loses his temper, and almost never strikes a child—who did not know exactly what telling a real lie meant, still less how to steal. They were content to spear their living out of the heart of the bitter, hopeless cold; to smile oily smiles, and tell queer ghost and fairy tales of evenings, and eat till they could eat no more, and sing the endless woman's song: "Amna aya, aya amna, ah! ah!" through the long lamplighted days as they mended their clothes and their hunting-gear.

But one terrible winter everything betrayed them. The Tununirmiut returned from the yearly salmon fishing, and made their houses on the early ice to the north of Bylot's Island, ready to go after the seal as soon as the sea froze. But it was an early and savage autumn. All through September there were continuous gales that broke up the smooth seal-ice when it was only four or five feet thick, and forced it inland, and piled a great barrier, some twenty miles broad, of lumped and ragged and needly ice, over which it was impossible to draw the dog-sleighs. The edge of the floe off which the seal were used to fish in winter lay perhaps twenty miles beyond this barrier, and out of reach of the Tununirmiut. Even so, they might have managed to scrape through the winter on their stock of frozen salmon and stored blubber, and what the traps gave them, but in December one of their hunters came across a *tupik* (a skin-tent) of three women and a girl nearly dead, whose men had come down from the far North and been crushed in their little skin hunting-boats while they were out after the long-horned narwhal. Kadlu, of course, could only distribute the women among the huts of the winter village, for no Inuit dare refuse a meal to a stranger. He never knows when his own turn may come to beg. Amoraq took the girl, who was about fourteen, into her own house as a sort of servant. From the cut of her sharp-pointed hood, and the long diamond pattern of her white deer-skin leggings, they supposed she came from Ellesmere Land. She had never seen tin cooking-pots or wooden-shod sleighs before; but Kotuko the boy and Kotuko the dog were rather fond of her.

Then all the foxes went south, and even the wolverine, that growling, blunt-headed little thief of the snow, did not take the trouble to follow the line of empty traps that Kotuko set. The tribe lost a couple of their best hunters, who were badly crippled in a fight with a musk-ox, and this threw more work on the others. Kotuko went out, day after day, with a light hunting-sleigh and six or seven of the strongest dogs, looking till his eyes ached for some patch of clear ice where a seal might perhaps have scratched a breathing-hole. Kotuko the dog ranged far and wide, and in the dead stillness of the ice fields Kotuko the boy could near his half-choked whine of excitement, above a seal hole three miles away, as plainly as though he were at his elbow. When the dog found a hole the boy would build himself a little, low snow wall to keep off the worst of the bitter wind, and there he would wait ten, twelve, twenty hours for the seal to come up to breathe, his eyes glued to the tiny mark he had made above the hole to guide the downward thrust of his harpoon, a little seal-skin mat under his feet, and his legs tied together in the *tutareang* (the buckle that the old hunters had talked about). This helps to keep a man's legs from twitching as he waits and waits and waits for the quick-eared seal to rise. Though there is no excitement in it, you can easily believe that the sitting still in the buckle with the thermometer perhaps forty degrees below zero is the hardest work an Inuit knows. When a seal was caught, Kotuko the dog would bound forward, his trace trailing behind him, and help to pull the body to the sleigh, where the tired and hungry dogs lay sullenly under the lee of the broken ice.

A seal did not go very far, for each mouth in the little village had a right to be filled, and neither bone, hide, nor sinew was wasted. The dogs' meat was taken for human use, and Amoraq fed the team with pieces of old summer skin-tents raked out from under the sleeping-bench, and they howled and howled again, and waked to howl hungrily. One could tell by the soap-stone lamps in the huts that famine was near. In good seasons, when blubber was plentiful, the light in the boat-shaped lamps would be two feet high—cheerful, oily, and yellow. Now it was a bare six inches: Amoraq carefully pricked down the moss wick, when an unwatched flame brightened for a moment, and the eyes of all the family followed her hand. The horror of famine up there in the great cold is not so much dying, as dying in the dark. All the Inuit dread the dark that presses on them without a break for six months in each year; and when the lamps are low in the houses the minds of people begin to be shaken and confused.

But worse was to come.

The underfed dogs snapped and growled in the passages, glaring at the cold stars, and snuffing into the bitter wind, night after night. When they stopped howling the silence fell down again as solid and as heavy as a snowdrift against a door, and men could hear the beating of their blood in the thin passages of the ear, and the thumping of their own hearts, that sounded as loud as the noise of sorcerers' drums beaten across the snow. One night Kotuko the dog, who had been unusually sullen in harness, leaped up and pushed his head against Kotuko's knee.

Kotuko patted him, but the dog still pushed blindly forward, fawning. Then Kadlu waked, and gripped the heavy wolf-like head, and stared into the glassy eyes. The dog whimpered and shivered between Kadlu's knees. The hair rose about his neck, and he growled as though a stranger were at the door; then he barked joyously, and rolled on the ground, and bit at Kotuko's boot like a puppy.

"What is it?" said Kotuko; for he was beginning to be afraid.

"The sickness," Kadlu answered. "It is the dog-sickness." Kotuko the dog lifted his nose and howled and howled again.

"I have not seen this before. What will he do?" said Kotuko.

Kadlu shrugged one shoulder a little, and crossed the hut for his short stabbing-harpoon. The big dog looked at him, howled again, and slunk away down the passage, while the other dogs drew aside right and left to give him ample room. When he was out on the snow he barked furiously, as though on the trail of a musk-ox, and, barking and leaping and frisking, passed out of sight. His trouble was not hydrophobia, but simple, plain madness. The cold and the hunger, and, above all, the dark, had turned his head; and when the terrible dog-sickness once shows itself in a team, it spreads like wildfire. Next hunting-day another dog sickened, and was killed then and there by Kotuko as he bit and struggled among the traces. Then the black second dog, who had been the leader in the old days, suddenly gave tongue on an imaginary reindeer-track, and when they slipped him from the *pitu* he flew at the throat of an ice-cliff, and ran away as his leader had done, his harness on his back. After that no one would take the dogs out again. They needed them for something else, and the dogs knew it; and though they were tied down and fed by hand, their eyes were full of despair and fear. To make things worse, the old women began to tell ghost-tales, and to say that they had met the spirits of the dead hunters lost that autumn, who prophesied all sorts of horrible things.

Kotuko grieved more for the loss of his dog than anything else; for though an Inuit eats enormously he also knows how to starve. But the hunger, the darkness, the cold, and the exposure told on his strength, and he began to hear voices inside his head, and to see people who were not there, out of the tail of his eye. One night—he had unbuckled himself after ten hours' waiting above a "blind" seal hole, and was staggering back to the village faint and dizzy—he halted to lean his back against a boulder which happened to be supported like a rocking-stone on a single jutting point of ice. His weight disturbed the balance of the thing, it rolled over ponderously, and as Kotuko sprang aside to avoid it, slid after him, squeaking and hissing on the ice-slope.

That was enough for Kotuko. He had been brought up to believe that every rock and boulder had its owner (its *inua*), who was generally a one-eyed kind of a Woman-Thing called a *tornaq,* and that when a *tornaq* meant to help a man she rolled after him inside her stone house, and asked him whether he would take her for a guardian spirit. (In summer thaws the ice-propped rocks and boulders roll and slip all over the face of the land, so you can easily see how the idea of live stones arose.) Kotuko heard the blood beating in his ears as he had heard it all day, and he thought that was the *tornaq* of the stone speaking to him. Before he reached home he was quite certain that he had held a long conversation with her, and as all his people believed that this was quite possible, no one contradicted him.

"She said to me, 'I jump down, I jump down from my place on the snow,'" cried Kotuko, with hollow eyes, leaning forward in the half-lighted hut. "She said, 'I will be a guide.' She says, 'I will guide you to the good seal holes.' Tomorrow I go out, and the *tornaq* will guide me."

Then the *angekok,* the village sorcerer, came in, and Kotuko told him the tale a second time. It lost nothing in the telling.

"Follow the *tornait* [the spirits of the stones], and they will bring us food again," said the *angekok.*

Now the girl from the North had been lying near the lamp, eating very little and saying less for days past; but when Amoraq and Kadlu next morning packed and lashed a little hand-sleigh for Kotuko, and loaded it with his hunting gear and as much blubber and frozen seal-meat as they could spare, she took the pulling-rope, and stepped out boldly at the boy's side.

"Your house is my house," she said, as the little bone-shod

sleigh squeaked and bumped behind them in the awful Arctic night.

"My house is your house," said Kotuko; "but *I* think that we shall both go to Sedna together."

Now Sedna is the Mistress of the Underworld, and the Inuit believe that every one who dies must spend a year in her horrible country before going to Quadliparmiut, the Happy Place, where it never freezes and the fat reindeer trot up when you call.

Through the village people were shouting: "The *tornait* have spoken to Kotuko. They will show him open ice. He will bring us the seal again!" Their voices were soon swallowed up by the cold, empty dark, and Kotuko and the girl shouldered close together as they strained on the pulling-rope or humored the sleigh through the ice in the direction of the Polar Sea. Kotuko insisted that the *tornaq* of the stone had told him to go north, and north they went under Tuktuqdjung the Reindeer—those stars that we call the Great Bear.

No European could have made five miles a day over the ice-rubbish and the sharp-edged drifts; but those two knew exactly the turn of the wrist that coaxes a sleigh around a hummock, the jerk that nearly lifts it out of an ice-crack, and the exact strength that goes to the few quiet strokes of the spearhead that make a path possible when everything looks hopeless.

The girl said nothing, but bowed her head, and the long wolverine-fur fringe of her ermine hood blew across her broad, dark face. The sky above them was an intense velvety black, changing to bands of Indian red on the horizon, where the great stars burned like street-lamps. From time to time a greenish wave of the Northern Lights would roll across the hollow of the high heavens, flick like a flag, and disappear; or a meteor would crackle from darkness to darkness, trailing a shower of sparks behind. Then they could see the ridged and furrowed surface of the floe tipped and laced with strange colors—red, copper, and bluish; but in the ordinary starlight everything turned to one frost-bitten gray. The floe, as you will remember, had been battered and tormented by the autumn gales till it was one frozen earthquake. There were gullies and ravines, and holes like gravel-pits, cut in ice; lumps and scattered pieces frozen down to the original floor of the floe; blotches of old black ice that had been thrust under the floe in some gale and heaved up again; roundish boulders of ice; saw-like edges of ice carved by the snow that flies before the wind; and sunken pits where thirty or forty acres lay below the level of the rest of the field. From a little distance you might have taken the lumps for seal or walrus, overturned sleighs or men on a hunting expedition, or even the great Ten-legged White Spirit-Bear himself; but in spite of these fantastic shapes, all on the very edge of starting into life, there was neither sound nor the least faint echo of sound. And through this silence and through this waste, where the sudden lights flapped and went out again, the sleigh and the two that pulled it crawled like things in a nightmare—a nightmare of the end of the world at the end of the world.

When they were tired Kotuko would make what the hunters call a "half-house," a very small snow hut, into which they would huddle with the traveling-lamp, and try to thaw out the frozen seal-meat. When they had slept, the march began again—thirty miles a day to get ten miles northward. The girl was always very silent, but Kotuko muttered to himself and broke out into songs he had learned in the Singing-House—summer songs, and reindeer and salmon songs—all horribly out of place at that season. He would declare that he heard the *tornaq* growling to him, and would run wildly up a hummock, tossing his arms and speaking in loud, threatening tones. To tell the truth, Kotuko was very nearly crazy for the time being; but the girl was sure that he was being guided by his guardian spirit, and that everything would come right. She was not surprised, therefore, when at the end of the fourth march Kotuko, whose eyes were burning like fireballs in his head, told her that his *tornaq* was following them across the snow in the shape of a two-headed dog. The girl looked where Kotuko pointed, and something seemed to slip into a ravine. It was certainly not human, but everybody knew that the *tornait* preferred to appear in the shape of bear and seal, and such like.

It might have been the Ten-legged White Spirit-Bear himself, or it might have been anything, for Kotuko and the girl were so starved that their eyes were untrustworthy. They had trapped nothing, and seen no trace of game since they had left the village; their food would not hold out for another week, and there was a gale coming. A Polar storm can blow for ten days without a break, and all that while it is certain death to be abroad. Kotuko laid up a snowhouse large enough to take in the hand-sleigh (never be separated from your meat), and while he was shaping the last irregular block of ice that makes the keystone of the roof, he saw a Thing looking at him from a little cliff of ice half a mile away. The air was hazy, and the Thing seemed to be forty feet long and ten feet high, with twenty feet of tail and a shape that quivered all along the outlines. The girl saw it too, but instead of crying aloud with terror, said quietly, "That is Quiquern. What comes after?"

"He will speak to me," said Kotuko; but the snow knife trembled in his hand as he spoke, because however much a man may believe that he is a friend of strange and ugly spirits, he seldom likes to be taken quite at his word. Quiquern, too, is the phantom of a gigantic toothless dog without any hair, who is supposed to live in the far North, and to wander about the country just before things are going to happen. They may be pleasant or unpleasant things, but not even the sorcerers care to speak about Quiquern. He makes the dogs go mad. Like the Spirit-Bear, he has several extra pairs of legs—six or eight—and this Thing jumping up and down in the haze had more legs than any real dog needed. Kotuko and the girl huddled into their hut quickly. Of course if Quiquern had wanted them, he could have torn it to pieces above their heads, but the sense of a foot-thick snow-wall between themselves and the wicked dark was great comfort. The gale broke with the shriek of wind like the shriek of a train, and for three days and three nights it held, never varying one point, and never lulling even for a minute. They fed the stone lamp between their knees, and nibbled at the half-warm seal-meat, and watched the black soot gather on the roof for seventy-two long hours. The girl counted up the food in the sleigh; there was not more than two days' supply, and Kotuko looked over the iron heads and the deer-sinew fastenings of his harpoon and his seal-lance and his bird-dart. There was nothing else to do.

"We shall go to Sedna soon—very soon," the girl whispered.

"In three days we shall lie down and go. Will your *tornaq* do nothing? Sing her an *angekok's* song to make her come here."

He began to sing in the high-pitched howl of the magic songs, and the gale went down slowly. In the middle of his song the girl started, laid her mittened hand and then her head to the ice floor of the hut. Kotuko followed her example, and the two kneeled, staring into each other's eyes, and listening with every nerve. He ripped a thin sliver of whalebone from the rim of a bird-snare that lay on the sleigh, and, after straightening, set it upright in a little hole in the ice, firming it down with his mitten. It was almost as delicately adjusted as a compass-needle, and now instead of listening they watched. The thin rod quivered a little—the least little jar in the world; then it vibrated steadily for a few seconds, came to rest, and vibrated again, this time nodding to another point of the compass.

"Too soon!" said Kotuko. "Some big floe has broken far away outside."

The girl pointed at the rod, and shook her head. "It is the big breaking," she said. "Listen to the ground-ice. It knocks."

When they kneeled this time they heard the most curious muffled grunts and knockings, apparently under their feet. Sometimes it sounded as though a blind puppy were squeaking above the lamp; then as if a stone were being ground on hard ice; and again, like muffled blows on a drum; but all dragged out and made small, as though they traveled through a little horn a weary distance away.

"We shall not go to Sedna lying down," said Kotuko. "It is the breaking. The *tornaq* has cheated us. We shall die."

All this may sound absurd enough, but the two were face to face with a very real danger. The three days' gale had driven the deep water of Baffin's Bay southerly, and piled it onto the edge of the far-reaching land-ice that stretches from Bylot's Island to the west. Also, the strong current which sets east out of Lancaster Sound carried with it mile upon mile of what they call pack ice—rough ice that has not frozen into fields; and this pack was bombarding the floe at the same time that the swell and heave of the storm-worked sea was weakening and undermining it. What Kotuko and the girl had been listening to were the faint echoes of that fight thirty or forty miles away, and the little tell-tale rod quivered to the shock of it.

Now, as the Inuit say, when the ice once wakes after its long winter sleep, there is no knowing what may happen, for solid floe-ice changes shape almost as quickly as a cloud. The gale was evidently a spring gale sent out of time, and anything was possible.

Yet the two were happier in their minds than before. If the floe broke up there would be no more waiting and suffering. Spirits, goblins, and witch-people were moving about on the racking ice, and they might find themselves stepping into Sedna's country side by side with all sorts of wild Things, the flush of excitement still on them. When they left the hut after the gale, the noise on the horizon was steadily growing, and the tough ice moaned and buzzed all around them.

"It is still waiting," said Kotuko.

On the top of a hummock sat or crouched the eight-legged Thing that they had seen three days before—and it howled horribly.

"Let us follow," said the girl. "It may know some way that does not lead to Sedna"; but she reeled from weakness as she took the pulling-rope. The Thing moved off slowly and clumsily across the ridges, heading always toward the westward and the land, and they followed, while the growling thunder at the edge of the floe rolled nearer and nearer. The floe's lip was split and cracked in every direction for three or four miles inland, and great pans of ten-foot-thick ice, from a few yards to twenty acres square, were jolting and ducking and surging into one another, and into the yet unbroken floe, as the heavy swell took and shook and spouted between them. This battering-ram ice was, so to speak, the first army that the sea was flinging against the floe. The incessant crash and jar of these cakes almost drowned the ripping sound of sheets of pack ice driven bodily under the floe as cards are hastily pushed under a tablecloth. Where the water was shallow these sheets would be piled one atop of the other till the bottommost touched mud fifty feet down, and the discolored sea banked behind the muddy ice till the increasing pressure drove all forward again. In addition to the floe and the pack ice, the gale and the currents were bringing down true bergs, sailing mountains of ice, snapped off from the Greenland side of the water or the north shore of Melville Bay. They pounded in solemnly, the waves breaking white around them, and advanced on the floe like an old-time fleet under full sail. A berg that seemed ready to carry the world before it would ground helplessly in deep water, reel over, and wallow in a lather of foam and mud and flying frozen spray, while a much smaller and lower one would rip and ride into the flat floe, flinging tons of ice on either side, and cutting a track half a mile long before it was stopped. Some fell like swords, sheering a raw-edged canal; and others splintered into a shower of blocks, weighing scores of tons apiece, that whirled and skirled among the hummocks. Others, again, rose up bodily out of the water when they shoaled, twisted as though in pain, and fell solidly on their sides, while the sea threshed over their shoulders. This trampling and crowding and bending and buckling and arching of the ice into every possible shape was going on as far as the eye could reach all along the north line of the floe. From where Kotuko and the girl were, the confusion looked no more than an uneasy, rippling, crawling movement under the horizon; but it came toward them each moment, and they could hear, far away to landward, a heavy booming, as it might have been the boom of artillery through a fog. That showed that the floe was being jammed home against the iron cliffs of Bylot's Island, the land to the southward behind them.

"This has never been before," said Kotuko, staring stupidly. "This is not the time. How can the floe break *now?*"

"Follow *that!*" the girl cried, pointing to the Thing half limping, half running distractedly before them. They followed, tugging at the hand-sleigh, while nearer and nearer came the roaring march of the ice. At last the fields around them cracked and starred in every direction, and the cracks opened and snapped like the teeth of wolves. But where the Thing rested, on a mound of old and scattered ice-blocks some fifty feet high, there was no motion. Kotuko leaped forward wildly, dragging the girl after him, and crawled to the bottom of the mound. The talking of the ice grew louder and louder around them, but the mound stayed fast, and, as the girl looked at him, he threw his right elbow upward and outward, making the Inuit sign for land in the shape of an island. And land it was that the eight-legged, limping Thing had led them to—some granite-tipped, sand-beached islet off the coast, shod and sheathed and masked with ice so that no man could have told it from the floe, but at the bottom solid earth, and not shifting ice! The smashing and rebound of the floes as they grounded and splintered marked the borders of it, and a friendly shoal ran out to the northward, and turned aside the rush of the heaviest ice, exactly as a plowshare turns over loam. There was danger, of course, that some heavily squeezed ice field might shoot up the beach, and plane off the top of the islet bodily; but that did not trouble Kotuko and the girl when they made their snowhouse and began to eat, and heard the ice hammer and skid along the beach. The Thing had disappeared, and Kotuko was talking excitedly about his power over spirits as he crouched around the lamp. In the middle of his wild sayings the girl began to laugh, and rock herself backward and forward.

Behind her shoulder, crawling into the hut crawl by crawl, there were two heads, one yellow and one black, that belonged to two of the most sorrowful and ashamed dogs that ever you saw. Kotuko the dog was one, and the black leader was the other. Both were now fat, well-looking, and quite restored to their proper minds, but coupled to each other in an extraordinary fashion. When the black leader ran off, you remember, his harness was still on him. He must have met Kotuko the dog, and played or fought with him, for his shoulder loop had caught in the plaited copper wire of Kotuko's collar, and had drawn tight, so that neither could get at the trace to gnaw it apart, but each was fastened sidelong to his neighbor's neck. That, with the freedom of hunting on their own account, must have helped to cure their madness. They were very sober.

The girl pushed the two shamefaced creatures toward Kotuko, and, sobbing with laughter, cried, "That is Quiquern, who led us to safe ground. Look at his eight legs and double head!"

Kotuko cut them free, and they fell into his arms, yellow and black together, trying to explain how they had got their senses back again. Kotuko ran a hand down their ribs, which were round and well clothed. "They have found food," he said, with a grin. "I do not think we shall go to Sedna so soon. My *tornaq* sent these. The sickness has left them."

As soon as they had greeted Kotuko, these two, who had been forced to sleep and eat and hunt together for the past few weeks, flew at each other's throat, and there was a beautiful battle in the snowhouse. "Empty dogs do not fight," Kotuko said. "They have found the seal. Let us sleep. We shall find food."

When they waked there was open water on the north beach of the island, and all the loosened ice had been driven landward. The first sound of the surf is one of the most delightful that the Inuit can hear, for it means that spring is on the road. Kotuko and the girl took hold of hands and smiled, for the clear, full roar of the surge among the ice reminded them of salmon and reindeer time and the smell of blossoming ground-willows. Even as they looked, the sea began to skim over between the floating cakes of ice, so intense was the cold; but on the horizon there was a vast red glare, and that was the light of the sunken sun. It was more like hearing him yawn in his sleep than seeing him rise, and the glare lasted for only a few minutes, but it marked the turn of the year. Nothing, they felt, could alter that.

Kotuko found the dogs fighting over a fresh-killed seal who was following the fish that a gale always disturbs. He was the first of some twenty or thirty seal that landed on the island in the course of the day, and until the sea froze hard there were hundreds of keen black heads rejoicing in the shallow free water and floating about with the floating ice.

It was good to eat seal-liver again; to fill the lamps recklessly with blubber, and watch the flame blaze three feet in the air; but as soon as the new sea ice bore, Kotuko and the girl loaded the hand-sleigh, and made the two dogs pull as they had never pulled in their lives, for they feared what might have happened in their village. The weather was as pitiless as usual; but it is easier to draw a sleigh loaded with good food than to hunt starving. They left five-and-twenty seal carcasses buried in the ice of the beach, all ready for use, and hurried back to their people. The dogs showed them the way as soon as Kotuko told them what was expected, and though there was no sign of a landmark, in two days they were giving tongue outside Kadlu's house. Only three dogs answered them; the others had been eaten, and the houses were all dark. But when Kotuko shouted, "Ojo!" (boiled meat), weak voices replied, and when he called the muster of the village name by name, very distinctly, there were no gaps in it.

An hour later the lamps blazed in Kadlu's house; snow water was heating; the pots were beginning to simmer, and the snow was dripping from the roof, as Amoraq made ready a meal for all the village, and the boy-baby in the hood chewed at a strip of rich nutty blubber, and the hunters slowly and methodically filled themselves to the very brim with seal-meat. Kotuko and the girl told their tale. The two dogs sat between them, and whenever their names came in, they cocked an ear apiece and looked most thoroughly ashamed of themselves. A dog who has once gone mad and recovered, the Inuit say, is safe against all further attacks.

"So the *tornaq* did not forget us," said Kotuko. "The storm blew, the ice broke, and the seal swam in behind the fish that were frightened by the storm. Now the new seal holes are not two days distant. Let the good hunters go tomorrow and bring back the seal I have speared—twenty-five seal buried in the ice. When we have eaten those we will all follow the seal on the floe."

"What do *you* do?" said the sorcerer in the same sort of voice as he used to Kadlu, richest of the Tununirmiut.

Kadlu looked at the girl from the North, and said quietly, "*We* build a house." He pointed to the northwest side of Kadlu's house, for that is the side on which the married son or daughter always lives.

The girl turned her hands palm upward, with a little despairing shake of her head. She was a foreigner, picked up starving, and could bring nothing to the housekeeping.

Amoraq jumped from the bench where she sat, and began to sweep things into the girl's lap—stone lamps, iron skin-scrapers, tin kettles, deerskins embroidered with musk-ox teeth, and real canvas-needles such as sailors use—the finest dowry that has ever been given on the far edge of the Arctic Circle, and the girl from the North bowed her head down to the very floor.

"Also these!" said Kotuko, laughing and signing to the dogs, who thrust their cold muzzles into the girl's face.

"Ah," said the *angekok,* with an important cough, as though he had been thinking it all over. "As soon as Kotuko left the village I went to the Singing-House and sang magic. I sang all the long nights, and called upon the Spirit of the Reindeer. *My* singing made the gale blow that broke the ice and drew the two dogs toward Kotuko when the ice would have crushed his bones. *My* song drew the seal in behind the broken ice. My body lay still in the *quaggi,* but my spirit ran about on the ice, and guided Kotuko and the dogs in all the things they did. I did it."

Everybody was full and sleepy, so no one contradicted; and the *angekok,* by virtue of his office, helped himself to yet another lump of boiled meat, and lay down to sleep with the others in the warm, well-lighted, oil-smelling home.

Now Kotuko, who drew very well in the Inuit fashion, scratched pictures of all these adventures on a long, flat piece of ivory with a hole at one end. When he and the girl went north to Ellesmere Land in the year of the Wonderful Open Winter, he left the picture-story with Kadlu, who lost it in the shingle when his dog-sleigh broke down one summer on the beach of Lake Netilling at Nikosiring, and there a Lake Inuit found it next spring and sold it to a man at Imigen who was interpreter on a Cumberland Sound whaler, and he sold it to Hans Olsen, who was afterward a quartermaster on board a big steamer that took tourists to the North Cape in Norway. When the tourist season was over, the steamer ran between London and Australia, stopping at Ceylon, and there Olsen sold the ivory to a Cingalese jeweler for two imitation sapphires. I found it under some rubbish in a house at Colombo, and have translated it from one end to the other.

THE BISARA OF POOREE

Little Blind Fish, thou art marvellous wise,
Little Blind Fish, who put out thy eyes?
Open thy ears while I whisper my wish—
Bring me a lover, thou little Blind Fish.
—THE CHARM OF THE BISARA

SOME natives say that it came from the other side of Kulu, where the eleven-inch Temple Sapphire is. Others, that it was made at the Devil-Shrine of Ao-Chung in Thibet, was stolen by a Kafir, from him by a Gurkha, from him again by a Lahouli, from him by a khitmatgar, and by this latter sold to an Englishman, so all its virtue was lost; because, to work properly, the Bisara of Pooree must be stolen—with bloodshed if possible, but, at any rate, stolen.

These stories of the coming into India are all false. It was made at Pooree ages since—the manner of its making would fill a small book—was stolen by one of the Temple dancing-girls there, for her own purposes, and then passed on from hand to hand, steadily northward, till it reached Hanle: always bearing the same name—the Bisara of Pooree. In shape it is a tiny square box of silver, studded outside with eight small balas-rubies. Inside the box, which opens with a spring, is a little eyeless fish, carved from some sort of dark, shiny nut and wrapped in a shred of faded gold cloth. That is the Bisara of Pooree, and it were better for a man to take a king cobra in his hand than to touch the Bisara of Pooree.

All kinds of magic are out of date and done away with except in India, where nothing changes in spite of the shiny, top-scum stuff that people call "civilization." Any man who knows about the Bisara of Pooree will tell you what its powers are—always supposing that it has been honestly stolen. It is the only regularly working, trustworthy love charm in the country, with one exception. [The other charm is in the hands of a trooper of the Nizam's Horse, at a place called Tuprani, due north of Hyderabad.] This can be depended upon for a fact. Someone else may explain it.

If the Bisara be not stolen, but given or bought or found, it turns against its owner in three years, and leads to ruin or death. This is another fact which you may explain when you have time. Meanwhile, you can laugh at it. At present the Bisara is safe on a hack-pony's neck, inside the blue bead-necklace that keeps off the Evil Eye. If the pony-driver ever finds it, and wears it, or gives it to his wife, I am sorry for him.

A very dirty Hill-coolie woman, with goiter, owned it at Theog in 1884. It came into Simla from the north before Churton's *khitmatgar* bought it, and sold it, for three times its silver-value, to Churton, who collected curiosities. The servant knew no more what he had bought than the master; but a man looking over Churton's collection of curiosities—Churton was an Assistant Commissioner by the way—saw and held his tongue. He was an Englishman, but knew how to believe. Which shows that he was different from most Englishmen. He knew that it was dangerous to have any share in the little box when working or dormant; for Love unsought is a terrible gift.

Pack—"Grubby" Pack, as we used to call him—was, in every way, a nasty little man who must have crawled into the Army by mistake. He was three inches taller than his sword, but not half so strong. And the sword was a fifty-shilling, tailor-made one. Nobody liked him, and, I suppose, it was his wizenedness and worthlessness that made him fall so hopelessly in love with Miss Hollis, who was good and sweet, and five-feet-seven in her tennis shoes. He was not content with falling in love quietly, but brought all the strength of his miserable little nature into the business. If he had not been so objectionable, one might have pitied him. He vapored, and fretted, and fumed, and trotted up and down, and tried to make himself pleasing in Miss Hollis' big, quiet, gray eyes, and failed. It was one of the cases that you sometimes meet, even in our country, where we marry by Code, of a really blind attachment all on one side, without the faintest possibility of return. Miss Hollis looked on Pack as some sort of vermin running about the road. He had no prospects beyond Captain's pay, and no wits to help that out by one penny. In a large-sized man love like his would have been touching. In a good man it would have been grand. He being what he was, it was only a nuisance.

You will believe this much. What you will not believe is what follows: Churton, and The Man who Knew what the Bisara was, were lunching at the Simla Club together. Churton was complaining of life in general. His best mare had rolled out of stable down the cliff and had broken her back; his decisions were being reversed by the upper Courts more than an Assistant Commissioner of eight years' standing has a right to expect; he knew liver and fever, and for weeks past had felt out of sorts. Altogether, he was disgusted and disheartened.

Simla Club dining room is built, as all the world knows, in two sections, with an arch-arrangement dividing them. Come in, turn to your own left, take the table under the window, and you cannot see anyone who has come in, turned to the right, and taken a table on the right side of the arch. Curiously enough, every word that you say can be heard, not only by the other diner, but by the servants beyond the screen through which they bring dinner. This is worth knowing; an echoing-room is a trap to be forewarned against.

Half in fun, and half hoping to be believed, The Man who Knew told Churton the story of the Bisara of Pooree at rather greater length than I have told it to you in this place; winding up with a suggestion that Churton might as well throw the little box down the hill and see whether all his troubles would go with it. In ordinary ears, English ears, the tale was only an interesting bit of folklore. Churton laughed, said that he felt better for his tiffin, and went out. Pack had been tiffining by himself to the right of the arch, and had heard everything. He was nearly mad with his absurd infatuation for Miss Hollis, that all Simla had been laughing about.

It is a curious thing that, when a man hates or loves beyond reason, he is ready to go beyond reason to gratify his feelings; which he would not do for money or power merely. Depend upon it, Solomon would never have built altars to Ashtaroth and all those ladies with queer names, if there had not been trouble of some kind in his *zenana,* and nowhere else. But this is beside the story. The facts of the case are these: Pack called on Churton next day when Churton was out, left his card, and stole the Bisara of Pooree from its place under the clock on the mantelpiece. Stole it like the thief he was by nature! Three days later all Simla was electrified by the news that Miss Hollis had accepted Pack—the shriveled rat, Pack! Do you desire clearer evidence than this? The Bisara of Pooree had been stolen, and it worked as it had always done when won by foul means.

There are three or four times in a man's life when he is justified in meddling with other people's affairs to play Providence.

The Man who Knew felt that he was justified; but believing and acting on a belief are quite different things. The insolent satisfaction of Pack as he ambled by the side of Miss Hollis, and Churton's striking release from liver, as soon as the Bisara of Pooree had gone, decided The Man. He explained to Churton, and Churton laughed, because he was not brought up to believe that men on the Government House List steal—at least little things. But the miraculous acceptance by Miss Hollis of that tailor, Pack, decided him to take steps on suspicion. He vowed that he only wanted to find out where his ruby-studded silver box had vanished to. You cannot accuse a man on the Government House List of stealing; and if you rifle his room, you are a thief yourself. Churton, prompted by The Man who Knew, decided on burglary. If he found nothing in Pack's room . . . but it is not nice to think of what would have happened in that case.

Pack went to a dance at Benmore—Benmore was Benmore in those days, and not an office—and danced fifteen waltzes out of twenty-two with Miss Hollis. Churton and The Man took all the keys that they could lay hands on, and went to Pack's room in the hotel, certain that his servants would be away. Pack was a cheap soul. He had not purchased a decent cashbox to keep his papers in, but one of those native imitations that you buy for ten rupees. It opened to any sort of key, and there at the bottom, under Pack's Insurance Policy, lay the Bisara of Pooree!

Churton called Pack names, put the Bisara of Pooree in his pocket, and went to the dance with The Man. At least, he came in time for supper, and saw the beginning of the end in Miss Hollis' eyes. She was hysterical after supper, and was taken away by her Mamma.

At the dance, with the abominable Bisara in his pocket, Churton twisted his foot on one of the steps leading down to the old Rink, and had to be sent home in a 'rickshaw, grumbling.

—"Pack went to a dance at Benmore—Benmore was Benmore in those days, and not an office—and danced fifteen waltzes out of twenty-two with Miss Hollis."

He did not believe in the Bisara of Pooree any the more for this manifestation, but he sought out Pack and called him some ugly names; and "thief" was the mildest of them. Pack took the names with the nervous smile of a little man who wants both soul and body to resent an insult, and went his way. There was no public scandal.

A week later Pack got his definite dismissal from Miss Hollis. There had been a mistake in the placing of her affections, she said. So he went away to Madras, where he can do no great harm even if he lives to be a Colonel.

Churton insisted upon The Man who Knew taking the Bisara of Pooree as a gift. The Man took it, went down to the Cart-Road at once, found a cart-pony with a blue bead-necklace, fastened the Bisara of Pooree inside the necklace with a piece of shoestring, and thanked Heaven that he was rid of a danger. Remember, in case you ever find it, that you must not destroy the Bisara of Pooree. I have not time to explain why just now, but the power lies in the little wooden fish. Mr. Gubernatis or Max Muller could tell you more about it than I.

You will say that all this story is made up. Very well. If ever you come across a little silver, ruby-studded box, seven-eighths of an inch long by three-quarters wide, with a dark brown wooden fish, wrapped in gold cloth, inside it, keep it. Keep it for three years, and then you will discover for yourself whether my story is true or false.

Better still, steal it as Pack did, and you will be sorry that you had not killed yourself in the beginning.

THE RETURN OF IMRAY

The doors were wide, the story saith,
Out of the night came the patient wraith,
He might not speak, and he could not stir
A hair of the Baron's minniver—
Speechless and strengthless, a shadow thin,
He roved the castle to seek his kin.
And oh, 'twas a piteous thing to see
The dumb ghost follow his enemy!

—THE BARON

IMRAY achieved the impossible. Without warning, for no conceivable motive, in his youth, at the threshold of his career he chose to disappear from the world—which is to say, the little Indian station where he lived.

Upon a day he was alive, well, happy, and in great evidence among the billiard tables at his Club. Upon a morning, he was not, and no manner of search could make sure where he might be. He had stepped out of his place; he had not appeared at his office at the proper time, and his dogcart was not upon the public roads. For these reasons, and because he was hampering, in a microscopical degree, the administration of the Indian Empire, that Empire paused for one microscopical moment to make inquiry into the fate of Imray. Ponds were dragged, wells were plumbed, telegrams were dispatched down the lines of railways and to the nearest seaport town—twelve hundred miles away; but Imray was not at the end of the dragropes nor the telegraph wires. He was gone, and his place knew him no more. Then the work of the great Indian Empire swept forward, because it could not be delayed, and Imray from being a man became a mystery—such a thing as men talk over at their tables in the Club for a month, and then forget utterly. His guns, horses, and carts were sold to the highest bidder. His superior officer wrote an altogether absurd letter to his mother, saying that Imray had unaccountably disappeared, and his bungalow stood empty.

After three or four months of the scorching hot weather had

gone by, my friend Strickland, of the Police, saw fit to rent the bungalow from the native landlord. This was before he was engaged to Miss Youghal—an affair which has been described in another place—and while he was pursuing his investigations into native life. His own life was sufficiently peculiar, and men complained of his manners and customs. There was always food in his house, but there were no regular times for meals. He ate, standing up and walking about, whatever he might find at the sideboard, and this is not good for human beings. His domestic equipment was limited to six rifles, three shotguns, five saddles, and a collection of stiff-jointed mahseer rods, bigger and stronger than the largest salmon rods. These occupied one-half of his bungalow, and the other half was given up to Strickland and his dog Tietjens—an enormous Rampur slut who devoured daily the rations of two men. She spoke to Strickland in a language of her own; and whenever, walking abroad, she saw things calculated to destroy the peace of Her Majesty the Queen-Empress, she returned to her master and laid information. Strickland would take steps at once, and the end of his labors was trouble and fine and imprisonment for other people. The natives believed that Tietjens was a familiar spirit, and treated her with the great reverence that is born of hate and fear. One room in the bungalow was set apart for her special use. She owned a bedstead, a blanket, and a drinking trough, and if anyone came into Strickland's room at night her custom was to knock down the invader and give tongue till some one came with a light. Strickland owed his life to her, when he was on the Frontier, in search of a local murderer, who came in the gray dawn to send Strickland much farther than the Andaman Islands. Tietjens caught the man as he was crawling into Strickland's tent with a dagger between his teeth; and after his record of iniquity was established in the eyes of the law he was hanged. From that date Tietjens wore a collar of rough silver, and employed a monogram on her night-blanket; and the blanket was of double woven Kashmir cloth, for she was a delicate dog.

Under no circumsatnces would she be separated from Strickland; and once, when he was ill with fever, made great trouble for the doctors, because she did not know how to help her master and would not allow another creature to attempt aid.

Macarnaght, of the Indian Medical Service, beat her over her head with a gun-butt before she could understand that she must give room for those who could give quinine.

A short time after Strickland had taken Imray's bungalow, my business took me through that Station, and naturally, the Club quarters being full, I quartered myself upon Strickland. It was a desirable bungalow, eight-roomed and heavily thatched against any chance of leakage from rain. Under the pitch of the roof ran a ceiling-cloth which looked just as neat as a white-washed ceiling. The landlord had repainted it when Strickland took the bungalow. Unless you knew how Indian bungalows were built you would never have suspected that above the cloth lay the dark three-cornered cavern of the roof, where the beams and the underside of the thatch harbored all manner of rats, bats, ants, and foul things.

Tietjens met me in the veranda with a bay like the boom of the bell of St. Paul's, putting her paws on my shoulder to show she was glad to see me. Strickland had contrived to claw together a sort of meal which he called lunch, and immediately after it was finished went out about his business. I was left alone with Tietjens and my own affairs. The heat of the summer had broken up and turned to the warm damp of the rains. There was no motion in the heated air, but the rain fell like ramrods on the earth, and flung up a blue mist when it splashed back. The bamboos, and the custard apples, the poinsettias, and the mango trees in the garden stood still while the warm water lashed through them, and the frogs began to sing among the aloe hedges. A little before the light failed, and when the rain was at its worst, I sat in the back veranda and heard the water roar from the eaves, and scratched myself because I was covered with the thing called prickly heat. Tietjens came out with me and put her head in my lap and was very sorrowful; so I gave her biscuits when tea was ready, and I took tea in the back veranda on account of the little coolness found there. The rooms of the house were dark behind me. I could smell Strickland's saddlery and the oil on his guns, and I had no desire to sit among these things. My own servant came to me in the twilight, the muslin of his clothes clinging tightly to his drenched body, and told me that a gentleman had called and wished to see someone. Very much against my will, but only because of the darkness of the rooms, I went into the naked drawing room, telling my man to bring the lights. There might or might not have been a caller waiting—it seemed to me that I saw a figure by one of the windows—but when the lights came there was nothing save the spikes of the rain without, and the smell of the drinking earth in my nostrils. I explained to my servant that he was no wiser than he ought to be, and went back to the veranda to talk to Tietjens. She had gone out into the wet, and I could hardly coax her back to me; even with biscuits with sugar tops. Strickland came home, dripping wet, just before dinner, and the first thing he said was.

"Has anyone called?"

I explained, with apologies, that my servant had summoned me into the drawing room on a false alarm; or that some loafer had tried to call on Strickland, and thinking better of it had fled after giving his name. Strickland ordered dinner, without comment, and since it was a real dinner with a white tablecloth attached, we sat down.

At nine o'clock Strickland wanted to go to bed, and I was tired too. Tietjens, who had been lying underneath the table, rose up, and swung into the least exposed veranda as soon as her master moved to his own room, which was next to the stately chamber set apart for Tietjens. If a mere wife had wished to sleep out of doors in that pelting rain it would not have mattered; but Tietjens was a dog, and therefore the better animal. I looked at Strickland, expecting to see him flay her with a whip. He smiled queerly, as a man would smile after telling some unpleasant domestic tragedy. "She has done this ever since I moved in here," said he. "Let her go."

The dog was Strickland's dog, so I said nothing, but I felt all that Strickland felt in being thus made light of. Tietjens encamped outside my bedroom window, and storm after storm came up, thundered on the thatch, and died away. The lightning spattered the sky as a thrown egg spatters a barn door, but the light was pale blue, not yellow; and, looking through my split bamboo blinds, I could see the great dog standing, not sleeping, in the veranda, the hackles alift on her back and her feet anchored as tensely as the drawn wire rope of a suspension bridge. In the very short pauses of the thunder I tried to sleep, but it seemed that someone wanted me very urgently. He, whoever he was, was trying to call me by name, but his voice was no more than a husky whisper. The thunder ceased, and Tietjens went into the garden and howled at the low moon. Somebody tried to open my door, walked about and about through the house and stood breathing heavily in the verandas, and just when I was falling asleep I fancied that I heard a wild hammering and clamoring above my head or on the door.

I ran into Strickland's room and asked him whether he was ill, and had been calling for me. He was lying on his bed half dressed, a pipe in his mouth. "I thought you'd come," he said. "Have I been walking around the house recently?"

I explained that he had been tramping in the dining room and the smoking room and two or three other places, and he laughed and told me to go back to bed. I went back to bed and slept until the morning, but through all my mixed dreams I was sure I was doing someone an injustice in not attending to his wants. What those wants were I could not tell; but a fluttering, whispering, bolt-fumbling, lurking, loitering Someone was reproaching me for my slackness, and, half awake, I heard the howling of Tietjens in the garden and the threshing of the rain.

I lived in that house for two days. Strickland went to his office daily, leaving me alone for eight or ten hours with Tietjens for my only companion. As long as the full light lasted I was comfortable, and so was Tietjens; but in the twilight she and I moved into the back veranda and cuddled each other for company. We were alone in the house, but nonetheless it was much too fully occupied by a tenant with whom I did not wish to interfere. I never saw him, but I could see the curtains between the rooms quivering where he had just passed through; I could hear the chairs creaking as the bamboos sprung under a weight that had just quitted them; and I could feel when I went to get a book from the dining room that somebody was waiting in the shadows of the front veranda till I should have gone away. Tietjens made the twilight more interesting by glaring into the darkened rooms with every hair erect, and following the motions of something that I could not see. She never entered the rooms, but her eyes moved interestedly: that was quite sufficient. Only when my servant came to trim the lamps and make all light and habitable she would come in with me and spend her time sitting on her haunches, watching an invisible extra man as he moved about behind my shoulder. Dogs are cheerful companions.

I explained to Strickland, gently as might be, that I would go over to the Club and find for myself quarters there. I admired his hospitality, was pleased with his guns and rods, but I did not much care for his house and its atmosphere. He heard me out to the end, and then smiled very wearily, but without contempt, for he is a man who understands things. "Stay on," he said, "and see what this thing means. All you have talked about I have known since I took the bungalow. Stay on and wait. Tietjens has left me. Are you going too?"

I had seen him through one little affair, connected with a heathen idol, that had brought me to the doors of a lunatic asylum, and I had no desire to help him through further experiences. He was a man to whom unpleasantnesses arrived as do dinners to ordinary people.

Therefore I explained more clearly than ever that I liked him immensely, and would be happy to see him in the daytime; but that I did not care to sleep under his roof. This was after dinner, when Tietjens had gone out to lie in the veranda.

" 'Pon my soul, I don't wonder," said Strickland, with his eyes on the ceiling-cloth. "Look at that!"

The tails of two brown snakes were hanging between the cloth and the cornice of the wall. They threw long shadows in the lamplight.

"If you are afraid of snakes of course——" said Strickland.

I hate and fear snakes, because if you look into the eyes of any snake you will see that it knows all and more of the mystery of man's fall, and that it feels all the contempt that the Devil felt when Adam was evicted from Eden. Besides which its bite is generally fatal, and it twists up trouser legs.

"You ought to get your thatch overhauled," I said. "Give me a mahseer rod, and we'll poke 'em down."

"They'll hide among the roofbeams," said Strickland. "I can't stand snakes overhead. I'm going up into the roof. If I shake 'em down, stand by with a cleaning-rod and break their backs."

I was not anxious to assist Strickland in his work, but I took the cleaning-rod and waited in the dining room while Strickland brought a gardener's ladder from the veranda, and set it against the side of the room. The snaketails drew themselves up and disappeared. We could hear the dry rushing scuttle of long bodies running over the baggy ceiling-cloth. Strickland took a lamp with him, while I tried to make clear to him the danger of hunting roof-snakes between a ceiling-cloth and a thatch, apart from the deterioration of property caused by ripping out ceiling-cloths.

"Nonsense!" said Strickland. "They're sure to hide near the walls by the cloth. The bricks are too cold for 'em, and the heat of the room is just what they like." He put his hand to the corner of the stuff and ripped it from the cornice. It gave with a great sound of tearing, and Strickland put his head through the opening into the dark of the angle of the roof beams. I set my teeth and lifted the rod, for I had not the least knowledge of what might descend.

"H'm!" said Strickland, and his voice rolled and rumbled in the roof. "There's room for another set of rooms up here, and, by Jove, some one is occupying 'em!"

"Snakes?" I said from below.

"No. It's a buffalo. Hand me up the two last joints of a mahseer rod, and I'll prod it. It's lying on the main roof beam."

I handed up the rod.

"What a nest for owls and serpents! No wonder the snakes live here," said Strickland, climbing farther into the roof. I could see his elbow thrusting with the rod. "Come out of that, whoever you are! Heads below there! It's falling."

I saw the ceiling-cloth nearly in the center of the room bag with a shape that was pressing it downward and downward toward the lighted lamp on the table. I snatched the lamp out of danger and stood back. Then the cloth ripped out from the walls, tore, split, swayed, and shot down upon the table something that I dared not look at, till Strickland had slid down the ladder and was standing by my side.

He did not say much, being a man of few words; but he

picked up the loose end of the tablecloth and threw it over the remnants on the table.

"It strikes me," said he, putting down the lamp, "our friend Imray has come back. Oh! you would, would you?"

There was a movement under the cloth, and a little snake wriggled out, to be back-broken by the butt of the mahseer rod. I was sufficiently sick to make no remarks worth recording.

Strickland meditated, and helped himself to drinks. The arrangement under the cloth made no more signs of life.

"Is it Imray?" I said.

Strickland turned back the cloth for a moment, and looked.

"It is Imray," he said; "and his throat is cut from ear to ear."

Then we spoke, both together and to ourselves: "That's why he whispered about the house."

Tietjens, in the garden, began to bay furiously. A little later her great nose heaved open the dining-room door.

She sniffed and was still. The tattered ceiling-cloth hung down almost to the level of the table, and there was hardly room to move away from the discovery.

Tietjens came in and sat down; her teeth bared under her lip and her forepaws planted. She looked at Strickland.

"It's a bad business, old lady," said he. "Men don't climb up into the roofs of their bungalows to die, and they don't fasten up the ceiling cloth behind 'em. Let's think it out."

"Let's think it out somewhere else," I said.

"Excellent idea! Turn the lamps out. We'll get into my room."

I did not turn the lamps out. I went into Strickland's room first, and allowed him to make the darkness. Then he followed me, and we lit tobacco and thought. Strickland thought. I smoked furiously, because I was afraid.

"Imray is back," said Strickland. "The question is—who killed Imray? Don't talk, I've a notion of my own. When I took this bungalow I took over most of Imray's servants. Imray was guileless and inoffensive, wasn't he?"

I agreed; though the heap under the cloth had looked neither one thing nor the other.

"If I call in all the servants they will stand fast in a crowd and lie like Aryans. What do you suggest?"

"Call 'em in one by one," I said.

"They'll run away and give the news to all their fellows," said Strickland. "We must segregate 'em. Do you suppose your servant knows anything about it?"

"He may, for aught I know; but I don't think it's likely. He has only been here two or three days," I answered. "What's your notion?"

"I can't quite tell. How the dickens did the man get the wrong side of the ceiling-cloth?"

There was a heavy coughing outside Strickland's bedroom door. This showed that Bahadur Khan, his body servant, had waked from sleep and wished to put Strickland to bed.

"Come in," said Strickland. "It's a very warm night, isn't it?"

Bahadur Khan, a great, green-turbaned, six-foot Mahomedan, said that it was a very warm night; but that there was more rain pending, which, by his Honor's favor, would bring relief to the country.

"It will be so, if God pleases," said Strickland, tugging off his boots. "It is in my mind, Bahadur Khan, that I have worked thee remorselessly for many days—ever since that time when thou first camest into my service. What time was that?"

"Has the Heaven-born forgotten? It was when Imray Sahib went secretly to Europe without warning given; and I—even I—came into the honored service of the protector of the poor."

"And Imray Sahib went to Europe?"

"It is so said among those who were his servants."

"And thou wilt take service with him when he returns?"

"Assuredly, Sahib. He was a good master, and cherished his dependents."

"That is true. I am very tired, but I go buck-shooting to-morrow. Give me the little sharp rifle that I use for black-buck; it is in the case yonder."

The man stooped over the case; handed barrels, stock, and fore-end to Strickland, who fitted all together, yawning dolefully. Then he reached down to the gun-case, took a solid-drawn cartridge, and slipped it into the breech of the .360 Express.

"And Imray Sahib has gone to Europe secretly! That is very strange, Bahadur Khan, is it not?"

"What do I know of the ways of the white man, Heaven-born?"

"Very little, truly. But thou shalt know more anon. It has reached me that Imray Sahib has returned from his so long journeys, and that even now he lies in the next room, waiting his servant."

"Sahib!"

The lamplight slid along the barrels of the rifle as they leveled themselves at Bahadur Khan's broad breast.

"Go and look!" said Strickland. "Take a lamp. Thy master is tired, and he waits thee. Go!"

The man picked up a lamp, and went into the dining room, Strickland following, and almost pushing him with the muzzle of the rifle. He looked for a moment at the black depths behind the ceiling-cloth; at the writhing snake under foot; and last, a gray glaze settling on his face, at the thing under the tablecloth.

"Hast thou seen?" said Strickland after a pause.

"I have seen. I am clay in the white man's hands. What does the Presence do?"

"Hang thee within the month. What else?"

"For killing him? Nay, Sahib, consider. Walking among us, his servants, he cast his eyes upon my child, who was four years old. Him he bewitched, and in ten days he died of the fever—my child!"

"What said Imray Sahib?"

"He said he was a handsome child, and patted him on the head; wherefore my child died. Wherefore I killed Imray Sahib in the twilight, when he had come back from office, and was sleeping. Wherefore I dragged him up into the roof beams and made all fast behind him. The Heaven-born knows all things. I am the servant of the Heaven-born."

Strickland looked at me above the rifle, and said, in the vernacular, "Thou art witness to this saying? He has killed."

Bahadur Khan stood ashen gray in the light of the one lamp. The need for justification came upon him very swiftly. "I am trapped," he said, "but the offense was that man's. He cast an evil eye upon my child, and I killed and hid him. Only such as are served by devils," he glared at Tietjens, couched stolidly before him, "only such could know what I did."

"It was clever. But thou shouldst have lashed him to the beam with a rope. Now, thou thyself wilt hang by a rope. Orderly!"

A drowsy policeman answered Strickland's call. He was followed by another, and Tietjens sat wondrous still.

"Take him to the police station," said Strickland. "There is a case toward."

"Do I hang, then?" said Bahadur Khan, making no attempt to escape, and keeping his eyes on the ground.

"If the sun shines or the water runs—yes!" said Strickland.

Bahadur Khan stepped back one long pace, quivered, and stood still. The two policemen awaited further orders.

"Go!" said Strickland.

"Nay; but I go very swiftly," said Bahadur Khan. "Look! I am even now a dead man."

He lifted his foot, and to the little toe there clung the head of the half-killed snake, firm fixed in the agony of death.

"I come of land-holding stock," said Bahadur Khan, rocking where he stood. "It were a disgrace to me to go to the public scaffold: therefore I take this way. Be it remembered that the Sahib's shirts are correctly enumerated, and that there is an extra piece of soap in his washbasin. My child was bewitched, and I slew the wizard. Why should you seek to slay me with the rope? My honor is saved, and—and—I die."

At the end of an hour he died, as they die who are bitten by the little brown *karait,* and the policemen bore him and the thing under the tablecloth to their appointed places. All were needed to make clear the disappearance of Imray.

"This," said Strickland, very calmly, as he climbed into bed, "is called the nineteenth century. Did you hear what that man said?"

"I heard," I answered. "Imray made a mistake."

"Simply and solely through not knowing the nature of the Oriental, and the coincidence of a little seasonal fever. Bahadur Khan had been with him for four years."

I shuddered. My own servant had been with me for exactly that length of time. When I went over to my own room I found my man waiting, impassive as the copper head on a penny, to pull off my boots.

"What has befallen Bahadur Khan?" said I.

"He was bitten by a snake and died. The rest the Sahib knows," was the answer.

"And how much of this matter hast thou known?"

"As much as might be gathered from One coming in in the twilight to seek satisfaction. Gently, Sahib. Let me pull off those boots."

I had just settled to the sleep of exhaustion when I heard Strickland shouting from his side of the house—

"Tietjens has come back to her place!"

And so she had. The great deerhound was couched statelily on her own bedstead on her own blanket, while, in the next room, the idle, empty, ceiling-cloth waggled as it trailed on the table.

BY WORD OF MOUTH

Not though you die to-night, O Sweet, and wail,
A spectre at my door,
Shall mortal Fear make Love immortal fail—
I shall but love you more,
Who, from Death's house returning, give me still
One moment's comfort in my matchless ill.

—SHADOW HOUSES

THIS tale may be explained by those who know how souls are made, and where the bounds of the Possible are put down. I have lived long enough in this India to know that it is best to know nothing, and can only write the story as it happened.

Dumoise was our Civil Surgeon at Meridki, and we called him "Dormouse," because he was a round little, sleepy little man. He was a good Doctor and never quarreled with anyone, not even with our Deputy Commissioner who had the manners of a bargee and the tact of a horse. He married a girl as round and as sleepy-looking as himself. She was a Miss Hillardyce, daughter of "Squash" Hillardyce of the Berars, who married his Chief's daughter by mistake. But that is another story.

A honeymoon in India is seldom more than a week long; but there is nothing to hinder a couple from extending it over two or three years. India is a delightful country for married folk who are wrapped up in one another. They can live absolutely alone and without interruption—just as the Dormice did. Those two little people retired from the world after their marriage, and were very happy. They were forced, of course, to give occasional dinners, but they made no friends thereby, and the Station went its own way and forgot them; only saying, occasionally, that Dormouse was the best of good fellows though dull. A Civil Surgeon who never quarrels is a rarity, appreciated as such.

Few people can afford to play Robinson Crusoe anywhere—least of all in India, where we are few in the land and very much dependent on each other's kind offices. Dumoise was wrong in shutting himself from the world for a year, and he discovered his mistake when an epidemic of typhoid broke out in the Station in the heart of the cold weather, and his wife went down. He was a shy little man, and five days were wasted before he realized that Mrs. Dumoise was burning with something worse than simple fever, and three days more passed before he ventured to call on Mrs. Shute, the Engineer's wife, and timidly speak about his trouble. Nearly every household in India knows that Doctors are very helpless in typhoid. The battle must be fought out between Death and the Nurses minute by minute and degree by degree. Mrs. Shute almost boxed Dumoise's ears for what she called his "criminal delay," and went off at once to look after the poor girl. We had seven cases of typhoid in the Station that winter and, as the average of death is about one in every five cases, we felt certain that we should have to lose somebody. But all did their best. The women sat up nursing the women, and the men turned to and tended the bachelors who were down, and we wrestled with those typhoid cases for fifty-six days, and brought them through the Valley of the Shadow in triumph. But, just when we thought all was over, and were going to give a dance to celebrate the victory, little Mrs. Dumoise got a relapse and died in a week and the Station went to the funeral. Dumoise broke down utterly at the brink of the grave, and had to be taken away.

After the death, Dumoise crept into his own house and refused to be comforted. He did his duties perfectly, but we all felt that he should go on leave, and the other men of his own Service told him so. Dumoise was very thankful for the suggestion—he was thankful for anything in those days—and went to Chini on a walking-tour. Chini is some twenty marches from Simla, in the heart of the Hills, and the scenery is good if you are in trouble. You pass through big, still deodar-forests, and under big, still cliffs, and over big, still grass-downs swelling like a woman's breasts; and the wind across the grass, and the rain among the deodars says—"Hush—hush—hush." So little Dumoise was packed off to Chini, to wear down his grief with a full-plate camera and a rifle. He took also a useless bearer, because the man had been his wife's favorite servant. He was idle and a thief, but Dumoise trusted everything to him.

On his way back from Chini, Dumoise turned aside to Bagi,

through the Forest Reserve which is on the spur of Mount Huttoo. Some men who have traveled more than a little say that the march from Kotegarh to Bagi is one of the finest in creation. It runs through dark wet forest, and ends suddenly in bleak, nipped hillside and black rocks. Bagi dâk-bungalow is open to all the winds and is bitterly cold. Few people go to Bagi. Perhaps that was the reason why Dumoise went there. He halted at seven in the evening, and his bearer went down the hillside to the village to engage coolies for the next day's march. The sun had set, and the night-winds were beginning to croon among the rocks. Dumoise leaned on the railing of the veranda, waiting for his bearer to return. The man came back almost immediately after he had disappeared, and at such a rate that Dumoise fancied he must have crossed a bear. He was running as hard as he could up the face of the hill.

But there was no bear to account for his terror. He raced to the veranda and fell down, the blood spurting from his nose and his face irony-gray. Then he gurgled—"I have seen the *Memsahib!* I have seen the *Memsahib!*"

"Where?" asked Dumoise.

"Down there, walking on the road to the village. She was in a blue dress, and she lifted the veil of her bonnet and said—'Ram Dass, give my *salaams* to the *Sahib,* and tell him that I shall meet him next month at Nuddea.' Then I ran away, because I was afraid."

What Dumoise said or did I do not know. Ram Dass declares that he said nothing, but walked up and down the veranda all the cold night, waiting for the *Memsahib* to come up the hill and stretching out his arms into the dark like a madman. But no *Memsahib* came, and, next day, he went on to Simla cross-questioning the bearer every hour.

Ram Dass could only say that he had met Mrs. Dumoise and that she had lifted up her veil and given him the message which he had faithfully repeated to Dumoise. To this statement Ram Dass adhered. He did not know where Nuddea was, had no friends at Nuddea, and would most certainly never go to Nuddea; even though his pay were doubled.

Nuddea is in Bengal and has nothing whatever to do with a

Doctor serving in the Punjab. It must be more than twelve hundred miles south of Meridki.

Dumoise went through Simla without halting, and returned to Meridki, there to take over charge from the man who had been officiating for him during his tour. There were some Dispensary accounts to be explained, and some recent orders of the Surgeon-General to be noted, and, altogether, the taking-over was a full day's work. In the evening, Dumoise told his *locum tenens,* who was an old friend of his bachelor days, what had happened at Bagi; and the man said that Ram Dass might as well have chosen Tuticorin while he was about it.

At that moment, a telegraph-peon came in with a telegram from Simla, ordering Dumoise not to take over charge at Meridki, but to go at once to Nuddea on special duty. There was a nasty outbreak of cholera at Nuddea, and the Bengal Government, being shorthanded, as usual, had borrowed a Surgeon from the Punjab.

Dumoise threw the telegram across the table and said—"Well?"

The other Doctor said nothing. It was all that he could say.

Then he remembered that Dumoise had passed through Simla on his way from Bagi; and thus might, possibly, have heard first news of the impending transfer.

He tried to put the question, and the implied suspicion into words, but Dumoise stopped him with—"If I had desired *that,* I should never have come back from Chini. I was shooting there. I wish to live, for I have things to do . . . but I shall not be sorry."

The other man bowed his head, and helped, in the twilight, to pack up Dumoise's just opened trunks. Ram Dass entered with the lamps.

"Where is the *Sahib* going?" he asked.

"To Nuddea," said Dumoise, softly.

Ram Dass clawed Dumoise's knees and boots and begged him not to go. Ram Dass wept and howled till he was turned out of the room. Then he wrapped up all his belongings and came back to ask for a character. He was not going to Nuddea to see his *Sahib* die and, perhaps, to die himself.

So Dumoise gave the man his wages and went down to Nuddea alone; the other Doctor bidding him good-bye as one under sentence of death.

Eleven days later he had joined his *Memsahib;* and the Bengal Government had to borrow a fresh Doctor to cope with that epidemic at Nuddea. The first importation lay dead in Chooadanga Dâk-Bungalow.

THE MIRACLE OF PURUN BHAGAT

The night we felt the Earth would move
  We stole and plucked him by the hand,
Because we loved him with the love
  That knows but cannot understand.

And when the roaring hillside broke
  And all our world fell down in rain,
We saved him, we the Little Folk;
  But lo! he will not come again!

Mourn now, we saved him for the sake
  Of such poor love as wild ones may.
Mourn ye! Our brother does not wake
  And his own kind drive us away!

—DIRGE OF THE LANGURS

THERE was once a man in India who was Prime Minister of one of the semi-independent native States in the northwestern part of the country. He was a Brahmin, so high-caste that caste ceased to have any particular meaning for him; and his father had been an important official in the gay-colored tag-rag and bob-tail of an old-fashioned Hindu Court. But as Purun Dass grew up he realized that the ancient order of things was changing, and that if anyone wished to get on he must stand well with the English, and imitate all the English believed to be good. At the same time a native official must keep his own master's favor. This was a difficult game, but the quiet, close-mouthed young Brahmin, helped by a good English education at a Bombay University, played it coolly, and rose, step by step, to be Prime Minister of the kingdom. That is to say, he held more real power than his master, the Maharajah.

When the old king—who was suspicious of the English, their railways and telegraphs—died, Purun Dass stood high with his young successor, who had been tutored by an Englishman; and between them, though he always took care that his master should have the credit, they established schools for little girls, made roads, and started State dispensaries and shows of agricultural implements, and published a yearly blue book on the "Moral and Material Progress of the State," and the Foreign Office and the Government of India were delighted. Very few native States take up English progress without reservations, for they will not believe, as Purun Dass showed he did, that what is good for the Englishman must be twice as good for the Asiatic. The Prime Minister became the honored friend of Viceroys and Governors, and Lieutenant-Governors, and medical missionaries, and common missionaries, and hard-riding English officers who came to shoot in the State preserves, as well as of whole hosts of tourists who traveled up and down India in the cold weather, showing how things ought to be managed. In his spare time he would endow scholarships for the study of medicine and manufactures on strictly English lines, and write letters to the *Pioneer,* the greatest Indian daily paper, explaining his master's aims and objects.

At last he went to England on a visit, and had to pay enormous sums to the priests when he came back; for even so high-caste a Brahmin as Purun Dass lost caste by crossing the black sea. In London he met and talked with every one worth knowing—men whose names go all over the world—and saw a great deal more than he said. He was given honorary degrees by learned universities, and he made speeches and talked of Hindu social reform to English ladies in evening dress, till all London cried, "This is the most fascinating man we have ever met at dinner since cloths were first laid!"

When he returned to India there was a blaze of glory, for the Viceroy himself made a special visit to confer upon the Maharajah the Grand Cross of the Star of India—all diamonds and ribbons and enamel; and at the same ceremony, while the cannon boomed, Purun Dass was made a Knight Commander of the Order of the Indian Empire; so that his name stood Sir Purun Dass, K.C.I.E.

That evening at dinner in the big Viceregal tent he stood up with the badge and the collar of the Order on his breast, and replying to the toast of his master's health, made a speech that few Englishmen could have surpassed.

Next month, when the city had returned to its sun-baked quiet, he did a thing no Englishman would have dreamed of doing, for, so far as the world's affairs went, he died. The jeweled order of his knighthood returned to the Indian Government, and a new Prime Minister was appointed to the charge of affairs, and a great game of General Post began in all the subordinate appointments. The priests knew what had happened and the people guessed; but India is the one place in the world where a man can do as he pleases and nobody asks why; and the fact that Dewan Sir Purun Dass, K.C.I.E., had resigned position, palace, and power, and taken up the begging-bowl and ocher-colored dress of a Sunnyasi or holy man, was considered nothing extraordinary. He had been, as the Old Law recommends, twenty years a youth, twenty years a fighter—though he had never carried a weapon in his life—and twenty years head of a household. He had used his wealth and his power for what he knew both to be worth; he had taken honor when it came his way; he had seen men and cities far and near, and men and cities had stood up and honored him. Now he would let these things go, as a man drops the cloak he needs no longer.

Behind him, as he walked through the city gates, an antelope skin and brass-handled crutch under his arm, and a begging-bowl of polished brown *coco-de-mer* in his hand, barefoot, alone, with eyes cast on the ground—behind him they were firing salutes from the bastions in honor of his happy successor. Purun Dass nodded. All that life was ended; and he bore it no more ill will or good will than a man bears to a colorless dream of the night. He was a Sunnyasi—a houseless, wandering mendicant, depending on his neighbors for his daily bread; and so long as there is a morsel to divide in India neither priest nor beggar starves. He had never in his life tasted meat, and very seldom eaten even fish. A five-pound note would have covered his personal expenses for food through any one of the many years in which he had been absolute master of millions of money. Even when he was being lionized in London he had held before him his dream of peace and quiet—the long, white, dusty Indian road, printed all over with bare feet, the incessant, slow-moving traffic, and the sharp-smelling wood-smoke curling up under the fig trees in the twilight, where the wayfarers sat at their evening meal.

When the time came to make that dream true the Prime

Minister took the proper steps, and in three days you might more easily have found a bubble in the trough of the long Atlantic seas than Purun Dass among the roving, gathering, separating millions of India.

At night his antelope skin was spread where the darkness overtook him—sometimes in a Sunnyasi monastery by the roadside; sometimes by a mud pillar shrine of Kala Pir, where the Jogis, who are another misty division of holy men, would receive him as they do those who know what castes and divisions are worth; sometimes on the outskirts of a little Hindu village, where the children would steal up with the food their parents had prepared; and sometimes on the pitch of the bare grazing-grounds where the flame of his stick fire waked the drowsy camels. It was all one to Purun Dass—or Purun Bhagat, as he called himself now. Earth, people, and food were all one. But, unconsciously, his feet drew him northward and eastward; from the south to Rohtak; from Rohtak to Kurnool; from Kurnool to ruined Samanah, and then upstream along the dried bed of the Gugger River that fills only when the rain falls in the hills, until, one day, he saw the far line of the great Himalayas.

Then Purun Bhagat smiled, for he remembered that his mother was of Rajput Brahmin birth, from Kulu way—a Hill-woman, always homesick for the snows—and that the least touch of Hill blood draws a man in the end back to where he belongs.

"Yonder," said Purun Bhagat, breasting the lower slopes of the Sewaliks, where the cacti stand up like seven-branched candlesticks, "yonder I shall sit down and get knowledge"; and the cool wind of the Himalayas whistled about his ears as he trod the road that led to Simla.

The last time he had come that way it had been in state, with a clattering cavalry escort, to visit the gentlest and most affable of Viceroys; and the two had talked for an hour together about mutual friends in London, and what the Indian common folk really thought of things. This time Purun Bhagat paid no calls, but leaned on the rail of the Mall, watching the glorious view of the Plains spread out forty miles below, till a native Mohammedan policeman told him he was obstructing traffic; and Purun Bhagat salaamed reverently to the Law, because he knew the value of it, and was seeking for a Law of his own. Then he moved on, and slept that night in an empty hut at Chota Simla, which looks like the very last end of the earth, but it was only the beginning of his journey. He followed the Himalaya-Thibet road, the little ten-foot track that is blasted out of solid rock, or strutted out on timbers over gulfs a thousand feet deep; that dips into warm, wet, shut-in valleys, and climbs across bare, grassy hill-shoulders where the sun strikes like a burning glass; or turns through dripping, dark forests where the tree ferns dress the trunks from head to heel, and the pheasant calls to his mate. And he met Thibetan herdsmen with their dogs and flocks of sheep, each sheep with a little bag of borax on his back, and wandering woodcutters, and cloaked and blanketed Lamas from Thibet, coming into India on pilgrimage, and envoys of little solitary Hill-states, posting furiously on ring-streaked and piebald ponies, or the cavalcade of a Rajah paying a visit, or else for a long, clear day he would see nothing more than a black bear grunting and rooting down below in the valley. When he first started, the roar of the world he had left still rang in his ears, as the roar of a tunnel rings a little after the train has passed through; but when he had put the Mutteeanee Pass behind him that was all done, and Purun Bhagat was alone with himself, walking, wondering, and thinking, his eyes on the ground, and his thoughts with the clouds.

One evening he crossed the highest pass he had met till then—it had been a two days' climb—and came out on a line of snow peaks that belted all the horizon—mountains from fifteen to twenty thousand feet high, looking almost near enough to hit with a stone, though they were fifty or sixty miles away. The pass was crowned with dense, dark forest—deodar, walnut, wild cherry, wild olive, and wild pear but mostly deodar, which is the Himalayan cedar; and under the shadow of the deodars stood a deserted shrine to Kali—who is Durga, who is Sitala, who is sometimes worshiped against the smallpox.

Purun Dass swept the stone floor clean, smiled at the grinning statue, made himself a little mud fireplace at the back of the shrine, spread his antelope skin on a bed of fresh pine needles, tucked his *bairagi*—his brass-handled crutch—under his armpit, and sat down to rest.

Immediately below him the hillside fell away, clean and cleared for fifteen hundred feet, to where a little village of stone-walled houses, with roofs of beaten earth, clung to the steep tilt. All around it tiny terraced fields lay out like aprons of patchwork on the knees of the mountain, and cows no bigger than beetles grazed between the smooth stone circles of the threshing floors. Looking across the valley the eye was deceived by the size of things, and could not at first realize that what seemed to be low scrub, on the opposite mountain-flank, was in truth a forest of hundred-foot pines. Purun Bhagat saw an eagle swoop across the enormous hollow, but the great bird dwindled to a dot ere it was half-way over. A few bands of scattered clouds strung up and down the valley, catching on a shoulder of the hills, or rising up and dying out when they were level with the head of the pass. And "Here shall I find peace," said Purun Bhagat.

Now, a Hill-man makes nothing of a few hundred feet up or down, and as soon as the villagers saw the smoke in the deserted shrine, the village priest climbed up the terraced hillside to welcome the stranger.

When he met Purun Bhagat's eyes—the eyes of a man used to control thousands—he bowed to the earth, took the begging-bowl without a word, and returned to the village, saying, "We have at last a holy man. Never have I seen such a man. He is of the plains—but pale colored—a Brahmin of the Brahmins." Then all the housewives of the village said, "Think you he will stay with us?" and each did her best to cook the most savory meal for the Bhagat. Hill-food is very simple, but with buckwheat and Indian corn, and rice and red pepper, and little fish out of the stream in the little valley, and honey from the flue-like hives built in the stone walls, and dried apricots, and turmeric, and wild ginger, and bannocks of flour, a devout woman can make good things; and it was a full bowl that the priest carried to the Bhagat. Was he going to stay? asked the priest. Would he need a *chela*—a disciple—to beg for him? Had he a blanket against the cold weather? Was the food good?

Purun Bhagat ate, and thanked the giver. It was in his mind

to stay. That was sufficient, said the priest. Let the begging-bowl be placed outside the shrine, in the hollow made by those two twisted roots, and daily should the Bhagat be fed; for the village felt honored that such a man—he looked timidly into the Bhagat's face—should tarry among them.

That day saw the end of Purun Bhagat's wanderings. He had come to the place appointed for him—the silence and the space. After this, time stopped, and he, sitting at the mouth of the shrine, could not tell whether he were alive or dead; a man with control of his limbs, or a part of the hills, and the clouds, and the shifting rain, and sunlight. He would repeat a Name softly to himself a hundred hundred times, till, at each repetition, he seemed to move more and more out of his body, sweeping up to the doors of some tremendous discovery; but, just as the door was opening, his body would drag him back, and, with grief, he felt he was locked up again in the flesh and bones of Purun Bhagat.

Every morning the filled begging-bowl was laid silently in the crotch of the roots outside the shrine. Sometimes the priest brought it; sometimes a Ladakhi trader, lodging in the village, and anxious to get merit, trudged up the path; but, more often, it was the woman who had cooked the meal overnight; and she would murmur, hardly above her breath: "Speak for me before the gods, Bhagat. Speak for such a one, the wife of so-and-so!" Now and then some bold child would be allowed the honor, and Purun Bhagat would hear him drop the bowl and run as fast as his little legs could carry him, but the Bhagat never came down to the village. It was laid out like a map at his feet. He could see the evening gatherings held on the circle of the threshing floors, because that was the only level ground; could see the wonderful unnamed green of the young rice, the indigo blues of the Indian corn; the dock-like patches of buckwheat, and, in its season, the red bloom of the amaranth, whose tiny seeds, being neither grain nor pulse, make a food that can be lawfully eaten by Hindus in time of fasts.

When the year turned, the roofs of the huts were all little squares of purest gold, for it was on the roofs that they laid out their cobs of the corn to dry. Hiving and harvest, rice-sowing and husking, passed before his eyes, all embroidered down there on the many-sided fields, and he thought of them all, and wondered what they all led to at the long last.

Even in populated India a man cannot a day sit still before the wild things run over him as though he were a rock; and in that wilderness very soon the wild things, who knew Kali's Shrine well, came back to look at the intruder. The *langurs,* the big gray-whiskered monkeys of the Himalayas, were, naturally, the first, for they are alive with curiosity; and when they had upset the begging-bowl, and rolled it around the floor, and tried their teeth on the brass-handled crutch, and made faces at the antelope skin, they decided that the human being who sat so still was harmless. At evening, they would leap down from the pines, and beg with their hands for things to eat, and then swing off in graceful curves. They liked the warmth of the fire, too, and huddled around it until Purun Bhagat had to push them aside to throw on more fuel; and in the morning, as often as not, he would find a furry ape sharing his blanket. All day long, one or other of the tribe would sit by his side, staring out at the snows, crooning and looking unspeakably wise and sorrowful.

After the monkeys came the *barasingh,* that big deer which is like our red deer, but stronger. He wished to rub off the velvet of his horns against the cold stones of Kali's statue, and stamped his feet when he saw the man at the shrine. But Purun Bhagat never moved, and, little by little, the royal stag edged up and nuzzled his shoulder. Purun Bhagat slid one cool hand along the hot antlers, and the touch soothed the fretted beast, who bowed his head, and Purun Bhagat very softly rubbed and raveled off the velvet. Afterward, the *barasingh* brought his doe and fawn—gentle things that mumbled on the holy man's blanket—or would come alone at night, his eyes green in the fire-flicker, to take his share of fresh walnuts. At last, the musk-deer, the shyest and almost the smallest of the deerlets, came, too, her big, rabbity ears erect; even brindled, silent *mushick-nabha* must needs find out what the light in the shrine meant, and drop her moose-like nose into Purun Bhagat's lap, coming and going with the shadows of the fire. Purun Bhagat called them all "my brothers," and his low call of "*Bhai! Bhai!*" would draw them from the forest at noon if they were within earshot. The Himalayan black bear, moody and suspicious—Sona, who has the V-shaped white mark under his chin—passed that way more than once; and since the Bhagat showed no fear, Sona showed no anger, but watched him, and came closer, and begged a share of the caresses, and a dole of bread or wild berries. Often, in the still dawns, when the Bhagat would climb to the very crest of the notched pass to watch the red day walking along the peaks of the snows, he would find Sona shuffling and grunting at his heels, thrusting a curious forepaw under fallen trunks, and bringing it away with a *whoof* of impatience; or his early steps would wake Sona where he lay curled up, and the great brute, rising erect, would think to fight, till he heard the Bhagat's voice and knew his best friend.

Nearly all hermits and holy men who live apart from the big cities have the reputation of being able to work miracles with the wild things, but all the miracle lies in keeping still, in never making a hasty movement, and, for a long time, at least, in never looking directly at a visitor. The villagers saw the outlines of the *barasingh* stalking like a shadow through the dark forest behind the shrine; saw the *minaul,* the Himalayan pheasant, blazing in her best colors before Kali's statue; and the *langurs* on their haunches, inside, playing with the walnut shells. Some of the children, too, had heard Sona singing to himself, bear-fashion, behind the fallen rocks, and the Bhagat's reputation as miracle-worker stood firm.

Yet nothing was further from his mind than miracles. He believed that all things were one big Miracle, and when a man knows that much he knows something to go upon. He knew for a certainty that there was nothing great and nothing little in this world; and day and night he strove to think out his way into the heart of things, back to the place whence his soul had come.

So thinking, his untrimmed hair fell down about his shoulders, the stone slab at the side of the antelope-skin was dented into a little hole by the foot of his brass-handled crutch, and the place between the tree trunks, where the begging-bowl rested day after day, sunk and wore into a hollow almost as smooth as the brown shell itself; and each beast knew his exact place at the fire. The fields changed their colors with the seasons; the threshing floors filled and emptied, and filled again and again; and again and again, when winter came, the *langurs* frisked among the branches feathered with light snow, till the mother-monkeys brought their sad-eyed little babies up from the warmer valleys with the spring. There were few changes in the village. The priest was older, and many of the little children who used to come with the begging-dish sent their own children now; and when you asked of the villagers how long their holy man had lived in Kali's Shrine at the head of the pass, they answered, "Always."

Then came such summer rains as had not been known in the Hills for many seasons. Through three good months the valley was wrapped in cloud and soaking mist—steady, unrelenting downfall, breaking off into thundershower after thundershower. Kali's Shrine stood above the clouds, for the most part, and there was a whole month in which the Bhagat never caught a glimpse of his village. It was packed away under a white floor of cloud that swayed and shifted and rolled on itself and bulged upward, but never broke from its piers—the streaming flanks of the valley.

All that time he heard nothing but the sound of a million little waters, overhead from the trees, and underfoot along the ground, soaking through the pine needles, dripping from the tongues of draggled fern, and spouting in newly-torn muddy channels down the slopes. Then the sun came out, and drew forth the good incense of the deodars and the rhododendrons, and that far-off, clean smell the Hill People call "the smell of the snows." The hot sunshine lasted for a week, and then the rains gathered together for their last downpour, and the water fell in sheets that flayed off the skin of the ground and leaped back in mud. Purun Bhagat heaped his fire high that night, for he was sure his brothers would need warmth; but never a beast came to the shrine, though he called and called till he dropped asleep, wondering what had happened in the woods.

It was in the black heart of the night, the rain drumming like a thousand drums, that he was roused by a plucking at his blanket, and, stretching out, felt the little hand of a *langur*. "It is better here than in the trees," he said sleepily, loosening

—"It was in the black heart of the night, the rain drumming like a thousand drums, that he was roused by a plucking at his blanket, and, stretching out, felt the little hand of a *langur*."

a fold of blanket; "take it and be warm." The monkey caught his hand and pulled hard. "Is it food, then?" said Purun Bhagat. "Wait awhile, and I will prepare some." As he kneeled to throw fuel on the fire the *langur* ran to the door of the shrine, crooned, and ran back again, plucking at the man's knee.

"What is it? What is thy trouble, Brother?" said Purun Bhagat, for the *langur's* eyes were full of things that he could not tell. "Unless one of thy caste be in a trap—and none set traps here—I will not go into that weather. Look, Brother, even the *barasingh* comes for shelter."

The deer's antlers clashed as he strode into the shrine, clashed against the grinning statue of Kali. He lowered them in Purun Bhagat's direction and stamped uneasily, hissing through his half-shut nostrils.

"Hai! Hai! Hai!" said the Bhagat, snapping his fingers. "Is *this* payment for a night's lodging?" But the deer pushed him toward the door, and as he did so Purun Bhagat heard the sound of something opening with a sigh, and saw two slabs of the floor draw away from each other, while the sticky earth below smacked its lips.

"Now I see," said Purun Bhagat. "No blame to my brothers that they did not sit by the fire tonight. The mountain is falling. And yet—why should I go?" His eye fell on the empty begging-bowl, and his face changed. "They have given me good food daily since—since I came, and, if I am not swift, tomorrow there will not be one mouth in the valley. Indeed, I must go and warn them below. Back there, Brother! Let me get to the fire."

The *barasingh* backed unwillingly as Purun Bhagat drove a torch deep into the flame, twirling it till it was well lit. "Ah! ye came to warn me," he said, rising. "Better than that we shall do, better than that. Out, now, and lend me thy neck, Brother, for I have but two feet."

He clutched the bristling withers of the *barasingh* with his right hand, held the torch away with his left, and stepped out of the shrine into the desperate night. There was no breath of wind, but the rain nearly drowned the torch as the great deer hurried down the slope, sliding on his haunches. As soon as they were clear of the forest more of the Bhagat's brothers joined them. He heard, though he could not see, the *langurs* pressing about him, and behind them the *uhh! uhh!* of Sona. The rain matted his long white hair into ropes; the water splashed beneath his bare feet, and his yellow robe clung to his frail old body, but he stepped down steadily, leaning against the *barasingh*. He was no longer a holy man, but Sir Purun Dass, K.C.I.E., Prime Minister of no small State, a man accustomed to command, going out to save life. Down the steep plashy path they poured all together, the Bhagat and his brothers, down and down till the deer clicked and stumbled on the wall of a threshing floor, and snorted because he smelt Man. Now they were at the head of the one crooked village street, and the Bhagat beat with his crutch at the barred windows of the blacksmith's house as his torch blazed up in the shelter of the eaves. "Up and out!" cried Purun Bhagat; and he did not know his own voice, for it was years since he had spoken aloud to a man. "The hill falls! The hill is falling! Up and out, oh, you within!"

"It is our Bhagat," said the blacksmith's wife. "He stands among the beasts. Gather the little ones and give the call."

It ran from house to house, while the beasts, cramped in the narrow way, surged and huddled around the Bhagat, and Sona puffed impatiently.

The people hurried into the street—they were no more than seventy souls all told—and in the glare of their torches they saw their Bhagat holding back the terrified *barasingh*, while the monkeys plucked piteously at his skirts, and Sona sat on his haunches and roared.

"Across the valley and up the hill!" shouted Purun Bhagat. "Leave none behind! We follow!"

Then the people ran as only Hill-folk can run, for they knew that in a landslip you must climb for the highest ground across the valley. They fled, splashing through the little river at the bottom, and panted up the terraced fields on the far side, while the Bhagat and his brethren followed. Up and up the opposite mountain they climbed, calling to each other by name—the roll call of the village—and at their heels toiled the big *barasingh*, weighted by the failing strength of Purun Bhagat. At last the deer stopped in the shadow of a deep pinewood, five hundred feet up the hillside. His instinct, that had warned him of the coming slide, told him he would be safe here.

Purun Bhagat dropped fainting by his side, for the chill of the rain and that fierce climb was killing him; but first he called to the scattered torches ahead, "Stay and count your numbers"; then, whispering to the deer as he saw the lights gather in a cluster: "Stay with me, Brother. Stay—till—I—go!"

There was a sigh in the air that grew to a mutter, and a mutter that grew to a roar, and a roar that passed all sense of hearing, and the hillside on which the villagers stood was hit in the darkness, and rocked to the blow. Then a note as steady, deep, and true as the deep C of the organ drowned everything for perhaps five minutes, while the very roots of the pines quivered to it. It died away, and the sound of the rain falling on miles of hard ground and grass changed to the muffled drums of water on soft earth. That told its own tale.

Never a villager—not even the priest—was bold enough to speak to the Bhagat who had saved their lives. They crouched under the pines and waited until the day. When it came they looked across the valley, and saw that what had been forest, and terraced field, and track-threaded grazing ground was one raw, red, fan-shaped smear, with a few trees flung head down on the scarp. That red ran high up the hill of their refuge, damming back the little river, which had begun to spread into a brick-colored lake. Of the village, of the road to the shrine, of the shrine itself, and the forest behind, there was no trace. For one mile in width and two thousand feet in sheer depth the mountainside had come away bodily, planed clean from head to heel.

And the villagers, one by one, crept through the wood to pray before their Bhagat. They saw the *barasingh* standing over him, who fled when they came near, and they heard the *langurs* wailing in the branches, and Sona moaning up the hill; but their Bhagat was dead, sitting cross-legged, his back against a tree, his crutch under his armpit, and his face turned to the northeast.

The priest said: "Behold a miracle after a miracle, for in this